THE SUBTLE KNIFE

HIS DARK MATERIALS

"Once in a lifetime a new children's author
emerges who is so extraordinary that the
imagination of generations is altered.
Lewis Carroll, E. Nesbit, C. S. Lewis and Tolkien
were all of this cast. So, too, is Philip Pullman"

New Statesman

"Two nights ago I was up until after 1 a.m., fascinated and moved by *The Subtle Knife*. This is as uncompromising and passionate as writing gets. A friend gave me volume one with the endorsement that it was extraordinary. It is, but the second might be even better"

New Statesman

"Exquisite, lyrical writing and a carefully planned and highly involving plot combine to produce a must-read fantasy"

Irish Independent

"I can't stand fantasy novels. Show me a talking bear, and I'm first out of the door. But this book gave me a good slap, and told me not to be so stupid. Pullman doesn't just create a fantasy world, he takes hold of huge concepts – life and death, Heaven and Hell – rips them up and builds something new. And somehow, he makes all that epic stuff intimate. I had to read one of the closing chapters on a train; I was crying so much, the ticket inspector asked me if I needed help"

Russell T. Davies, *Guardian*

"My hands shook, turning the pages"

The Times

Also by Philip Pullman

His Dark Materials
Northern Lights
The Amber Spyglass

Lyra's Oxford
Once Upon a Time in the North

The Sally Lockhart Quartet
The Ruby in the Smoke
The Shadow in the North
The Tiger in the Well
The Tin Princess

The New Cut Gang
Thunderbolt's Waxwork
The Gas-Fitters' Ball

Contemporary Novels
The Broken Bridge
The Butterfly Tattoo
The Good Man Jesus and the Scoundrel Christ

Books with Pictures and Fairy Tales
The Scarecrow and his Servant
Spring-Heeled Jack
Count Karlstein
The Firework-Maker's Daughter
I Was A Rat!
Puss in Boots
Mossycoat
Aladdin
Clockwork

Plays
Frankenstein *(adaptation)*
Sherlock Holmes and the Limehouse Horror

About the Author

Born in Norwich in 1946, Philip Pullman is a world-renowned writer. His novels have won every major award for children's fiction, and are now also established as adult best-sellers. The HIS DARK MATERIALS trilogy came third in the BBC's 2003 "Big Read" competition to find the nation's favourite book. In 2005 he was awarded the Astrid Lindgren Memorial Award, the world's biggest prize for children's literature. Philip is married with two grown-up children, and lives in Oxford.

"Stories are the most important thing in the world.
Without stories, we wouldn't be human beings at all"

PHILIP PULLMAN

www.philip-pullman.com

THE SUBTLE KNIFE

KNIFE

HIS DARK MATERIALS

PHILIP PULLMAN

SCHOLASTIC

Scholastic Children's Books
An imprint of Scholastic Ltd
Euston House, 24 Eversholt Street
London, NW1 1DB, UK
Registered office: Westfield Road, Southam, Warwickshire, CV47 0RA
SCHOLASTIC and associated logos are trademarks and/or
registered trademarks of Scholastic Inc.

First published by Scholastic UK Ltd, 1997
This edition published by Scholastic UK Ltd, 2013

ISBN 978 1 407 13976 0

A CIP catalogue record for this book is available
from the British Library.

Printed and bound by CPI Group (UK) Ltd, Croydon, CR0 4YY
Papers used by Scholastic Children's Books are made from
wood grown in sustainable forests.

1 3 5 7 9 10 8 6 4 2

www.scholastic.co.uk/zone

THE SUBTLE KNIFE is the second part of a story in three volumes, which was begun by NORTHERN LIGHTS. This volume moves between three universes: the universe of NORTHERN LIGHTS, which is like ours but different in many ways; the universe we know; and a third universe, which differs from ours in other ways again.

Contents

1

The Cat and the Hornbeam Trees

W ill tugged at his mother's hand and said, "Come *on*, come *on*..."

But his mother hung back. She was still afraid. Will looked up and down the narrow street in the evening light, along the little terrace of houses, each behind its tiny garden and its box hedge, with the sun glaring off the windows of one side and leaving the other in shadow. There wasn't much time. People would be having their meal about now, and soon there would be other children around, to stare and comment and notice. It was dangerous to wait, but all he could do was persuade her, as usual.

"Mum, let's go in and see Mrs Cooper," he said. "Look, we're nearly there."

"Mrs Cooper?" she said doubtfully.

But he was already ringing the bell. He had to put down the bag to do it, because his other hand still held his mother's. It might have bothered him at twelve years of age to be seen holding his mother's hand, but he knew what would happen to her if he didn't.

The door opened, and there was the stooped elderly figure of the piano teacher, with the scent of lavender water about her as he remembered.

"Who's that? Is that William?" the old lady said. "I haven't seen you for over a year. What do you want, dear?"

"I want to come in, please, and bring my mother," he said firmly.

Mrs Cooper looked at the woman with the untidy hair and the distracted half-smile, and at the boy with the fierce unhappy glare in his eyes, the tight-set lips, the jutting jaw. And then she saw that Mrs Parry, Will's mother, had put make-up on one eye but not on the other. And she hadn't noticed. And neither had Will. Something was wrong.

"Well…" she said, and stepped aside to make room in the narrow hall.

Will looked up and down the road before closing the door, and Mrs Cooper saw how tightly Mrs Parry was clinging to her son's hand, and how tenderly he guided her into the sitting room where the piano was (of course, that was the only room he knew); and she noticed that Mrs Parry's clothes smelt slightly musty, as if they'd been too long in the washing machine before drying; and how similar the two of them looked as they sat on the sofa with the evening sun full on their faces, their broad cheekbones, their wide eyes, their straight black brows.

"What is it, William?" the old lady said. "What's the matter?"

"My mother needs somewhere to stay for a few days," he said. "It's too difficult to look after her at home just now. I don't mean she's ill. She's just kind of confused and muddled and she gets a bit worried. She won't be hard to look after. She just needs someone to be kind to her and I think you could do that quite easily, probably."

The woman was looking at her son without seeming to understand, and Mrs Cooper saw a bruise on her cheek. Will hadn't taken his eyes off Mrs Cooper, and his expression was desperate.

"She won't be expensive," he went on. "I've brought some

packets of food, enough to last, I should think. You could have some of it too. She won't mind sharing."

"But… I don't know if I should… Doesn't she need a doctor?"

"No! She's not ill."

"But there must be someone who can… I mean, isn't there a neighbour or someone in the family –"

"We haven't got any family. Only us. And the neighbours are too busy."

"What about the social services? I don't mean to put you off, dear, but –"

"No! No. She just needs a bit of help. I can't do it any more for a little while but I won't be long. I'm going to… I've got things to do. But I'll be back soon and I'll take her home again, I promise. You won't have to do it for long."

The mother was looking at her son with such trust, and he turned and smiled at her with such love and reassurance that Mrs Cooper couldn't say no.

"Well," she said, turning to Mrs Parry, "I'm sure it won't matter for a day or so. You can have my daughter's room, dear; she's in Australia; she won't be needing it again."

"Thank you," said Will, and stood up as if he were in a hurry to leave.

"But where are you going to be?" said Mrs Cooper.

"I'm going to be staying with a friend," he said. "I'll phone up as often as I can. I've got your number. It'll be all right."

His mother was looking at him, bewildered. He bent over and kissed her clumsily.

"Don't worry," he said. "Mrs Cooper will look after you better than me, honest. And I'll phone up and talk to you tomorrow."

They hugged tightly, and then Will kissed her again and gently unfastened her arms from his neck before going to the front door. Mrs Cooper could see he was upset, because his eyes were glistening, but he turned, remembering his manners, and held out his hand.

"Goodbye," he said, "and thank you very much."

"William," she said, "I wish you'd tell me what the matter is –"

"It's a bit complicated," he said, "but she won't be any trouble, honestly."

That wasn't what she meant, and they both knew it; but somehow Will was in charge of this business, whatever it was. The old lady thought she'd never seen a child so implacable.

He turned away, already thinking about the empty house.

The close where Will and his mother lived was a loop of road in a modern estate, with a dozen identical houses of which theirs was by far the shabbiest. The front garden was just a patch of weedy grass; his mother had planted some shrubs earlier in the year, but they'd shrivelled and died for lack of watering. As Will came round the corner, his cat Moxie rose up from her favourite spot under the still-living hydrangea and stretched before greeting him with a soft miaow and butting her head against his leg.

He picked her up and whispered, "Have they come back, Moxie? Have you seen them?"

The house was silent. In the last of the evening light the man across the road was washing his car, but he took no notice of Will, and Will didn't look at him. The less notice people took, the better.

Holding Moxie against his chest, he unlocked the door and went in quickly. Then he listened very carefully before putting her down. There was nothing to hear; the house was empty.

He opened a tin for her and left her to eat in the kitchen. How long before the man came back? There was no way of telling, so he'd better move quickly. He went upstairs and began to search.

He was looking for a battered green leather writing-case. There are a surprising number of places to hide something that size even in any ordinary modern house; you don't need secret panels and extensive cellars in order to make something hard to find. Will searched his mother's bedroom first, ashamed to be looking through the drawers where she kept her underclothes, and then he worked systematically through the rest of the rooms upstairs, even his own. Moxie came to see what he was doing and sat and cleaned herself nearby, for company.

But he didn't find it.

By that time it was dark, and he was hungry. He made himself baked beans on toast and sat at the kitchen table wondering about the best order to look through the downstairs rooms.

As he was finishing his meal, the phone rang.

He sat absolutely still, his heart thumping. He counted: twenty-six rings, and then it stopped. He put his plate in the sink and started to search again.

Four hours later he still hadn't found the green leather case. It was half-past one, and he was exhausted. He lay on his bed fully clothed and fell asleep at once, his dreams tense and crowded, his mother's unhappy frightened face always there just out of reach.

And almost at once, it seemed (though he'd been asleep for nearly three hours) he woke up knowing two things simultaneously.

First, he knew where the case was. And second, he knew that the men were downstairs, opening the kitchen door.

He lifted Moxie out of the way and softly hushed her sleepy protest. Then he swung his legs over the side of the bed and put on his shoes, straining every nerve to hear the sounds from downstairs: very quiet sounds: a chair being lifted and replaced, a short whisper, the creak of a floorboard.

Moving more silently than they were, he left his bedroom and tiptoed to the spare room at the top of the stairs. It wasn't quite pitch dark, and in the ghostly grey pre-dawn light he could see the old treadle sewing machine. He'd been through the room thoroughly only hours before, but he'd forgotten the compartment at the side of the sewing machine, where all the patterns and bobbins were kept.

He felt for it delicately, listening all the while. The men were moving about downstairs, and Will could see a dim flicker of light at the edge of the door that might have been a torch.

Then he found the catch of the compartment and clicked it open, and there, just as he'd known it would be, was the leather writing-case.

And now what could he do?

Nothing, for the moment. He crouched in the dimness, heart pounding, listening hard.

The two men were in the hall. He heard one of them say quietly, "Come on. I can hear the milkman down the road."

"It's not here, though," said the other voice. "We'll have to look upstairs."

"Go on, then. Don't hang about."

Will braced himself as he heard the quiet creak of the top step. The man was making no noise at all, but he couldn't help the creakif he wasn't expecting it. Then there was a pause. A very thin beam of torchlight swept along the floor outside: Will saw it through the crack.

Then the door began to move. Will waited till the man was framed in the open doorway, and then exploded up out of the dark and crashed into the intruder's belly.

But neither of them saw the cat.

As the man had reached the top step, Moxie had come silently out of the bedroom and stood with raised tail just behind the man's legs, ready to rub herself against them. The man could have dealt with Will, because he was trained and fit and hard, but the cat was in the way, and as he tried to move back he tripped over her. With a sharp gasp he fell backwards down the stairs, crashing his head brutally against the hall table.

Will heard a hideous crack, and didn't stop to wonder about it: he swung himself down the banisters, leaping over the man's body that lay twitching and crumpled at the foot of the flight, seized the tattered shopping bag from the table, and was out of the front door and away before the other man could do more than come out of the living room and stare.

Even in his fear and haste Will wondered why the other man didn't shout after him, or chase him. They'd be after him soon, though, with their cars and their cellphones. The only thing to do was run.

He saw the milkman turning into the close, the lights of his electric cart pallid in the dawn glimmer that was already filling the sky. Will jumped over the fence into next-door's garden, down the passage beside the house, over the next garden wall, across a dew-wet lawn, through the hedge, into the tangle of shrubs and trees between the housing estate and the main road, and there he crawled under a bush and lay panting and trembling. It was too early to be out on the road: wait till later, when the rush hour started.

He couldn't get out of his mind the crack as the man's head had struck the table, and the way his neck was bent so far and in such a wrong way, and the dreadful twitching of his limbs. The man was dead. He'd killed him.

He couldn't get it out of his mind, but he had to. There was quite enough to think about. His mother: would she really be safe where she was? Mrs Cooper wouldn't tell, would she? Even if Will didn't turn up as he'd said he would? Because he couldn't, now he'd killed someone.

And Moxie. Who'd feed Moxie? Would Moxie worry about where they both were? Would she try to follow them?

It was getting lighter by the minute. It was light enough already to check through the things in the shopping bag: his mother's purse, the latest letter from the lawyer, the road map of southern England, chocolate bars, toothpaste, spare socks and pants. And the green leather writing-case.

Everything was there. Everything was going to plan, really.

Except that he'd killed someone.

Will had first realized his mother was different from other people, and that he had to look after her, when he was seven. They were in a supermarket, and they were playing a game: they were only allowed to put an item in the cart when no one was looking. It was Will's job to look all around and whisper "Now," and she would snatch a tin or a packet from the shelf and put it silently in the cart. When things were in there they were safe, because they became invisible.

It was a good game, and it went on for a long time, because this was a Saturday morning and the shop was full, but they were good at it and worked well together. They trusted each other. Will loved his mother very much and often told her so, and she told him the same.

So when they reached the checkout Will was excited and happy because they'd nearly won. And when his mother couldn't find her purse, that was part of the game too, even when she said the enemies must have stolen it; but Will was getting tired by this time, and hungry too, and Mummy wasn't so happy any more; she was really frightened, and they went round and round putting things back on the shelves, but this time they had to be extra careful because the enemies were tracking them down by means of her credit card numbers, which they knew because they had her purse…

And Will got more and more frightened himself. He realized how clever his mother had been to make this real danger into a game so that he wouldn't be alarmed, and how, now that he knew the truth, he had to pretend not to be frightened, so as to reassure her.

So the little boy pretended it was a game still, so she didn't have to worry that he was frightened, and they went home without any shopping, but safe from the enemies; and then Will found the purse on the hall table anyway. On Monday they went to the bank and closed her account, and opened another somewhere else, just to be sure. Thus the danger passed.

But some time during the next few months, Will realized slowly and unwillingly that those enemies of his mother's were not in the world out there, but in her mind. That made them no less real, no less frightening and dangerous; it just meant he had to protect her even more carefully. And from the moment in the supermarket when he realized he had to pretend in order not to worry his mother, part of Will's mind was always alert to her anxieties. He loved her so much he would have died to protect her.

As for Will's father, he had vanished long before Will was able to remember him. Will was passionately curious about his father, and he used to plague his mother with questions, most of which she couldn't answer.

"Was he a rich man?"

"Where did he go?"

"Why did he go?"

"Is he dead?"

9

"Will he come back?"

"What was he like?"

The last question was the only one she could help him with. John Parry had been a handsome man, a brave and clever officer in the Royal Marines, who had left the army to become an explorer and lead expeditions to remote parts of the world. Will thrilled to hear about this. No father could be more exciting than an explorer. From then on, in all his games he had an invisible companion: he and his father were together hacking through the jungle, shading their eyes to gaze out across stormy seas from the deck of their schooner, holding up a torch to decipher mysterious inscriptions in a bat-infested cave... They were the best of friends, they saved each other's life countless times, they laughed and talked together over campfires long into the night.

But the older he got the more Will began to wonder. Why were there no pictures of his father in this part of the world or that, with frost-bearded men on Arctic sledges or examining creeper-covered ruins in the jungle? Had nothing survived of the trophies and curiosities he must have brought home? Was nothing written about him in a book?

His mother didn't know. But one thing she said stuck in his mind.

She said, "One day, you'll follow in your father's footsteps. You're going to be a great man too. You'll take up his mantle..."

And though Will didn't know what that meant, he understood the sense of it, and felt uplifted with pride and purpose. All his games were going to come true. His father was alive, lost somewhere in the wild, and he was going to rescue him and take up his mantle... It was worth living a difficult life, if you had a great aim like that.

So he kept his mother's trouble secret. There were times when she was calmer and clearer than others, and he took care to learn from her then how to shop and cook and keep the house clean, so that he could do it when she was confused and frightened. And he learned how to conceal himself too, how to remain unnoticed at school, how not to attract attention from the neighbours, even when his mother was in such a state of fear and madness that she could barely speak. What Will himself feared more than anything was that the authorities would find out about her, and take her away, and put him in a home among strangers. Any difficulty was better than that. Because there came times when the darkness cleared from her mind, and she was happy again, and she laughed at her fears and blessed him for looking after her so well; and she was so full of love and sweetness then that he could think of no better companion, and wanted nothing more than to live with her alone for ever.

But then the men came.

They weren't police, and they weren't social services, and they weren't criminals – at least, as far as Will could judge. They wouldn't tell him what they wanted, in spite of his efforts to keep them away; they'd only speak to his mother. And her state was fragile just then.

But he listened outside the door, and heard them ask about his father, and felt his breath come more quickly.

The men wanted to know where John Parry had gone, and whether he'd sent anything back to her, and when she'd last heard from him, and whether he'd had contact with any foreign embassies. Will heard his mother getting more and more distressed, and finally he ran into the room and told them to go.

He looked so fierce that neither of the men laughed, though he was so young. They could easily have knocked him down, or held him off the floor with one hand, but he was fearless, and his anger was hot and deadly.

So they left. Naturally, this episode strengthened Will's

11

conviction: his father was in trouble somewhere, and only he could help. His games weren't childish any more, and he didn't play so openly. It was coming true, and he had to be worthy of it.

And not long afterwards the men came back, insisting that Will's mother had something to tell them. They came when Will was at school, and one of them kept her talking downstairs while the other searched the bedrooms. She didn't realize what they were doing. But Will came home early and found them, and once again he blazed at them, and once again they left.

They seemed to know that he wouldn't go to the police, for fear of losing his mother to the authorities, and they got more and more persistent. Finally they broke into the house when Will had gone to fetch his mother home from the park: it was getting worse for her now, and she believed that she had to touch every separate slat in every separate bench beside the pond. Will would help her, to get it done quicker. When they got home they saw the back of the men's car disappearing out of the close, and he got inside to find that they'd been through the house and searched most of the drawers and cupboards.

He knew what they were after. The green leather case was his mother's most precious possession; he would never dream of looking through it, and he didn't even know where she kept it. But he knew it contained letters, and he knew she read them sometimes, and cried, and it was then that she talked about his father. So Will supposed that this was what the men were after, and knew he had to do something about it.

He decided first to find somewhere safe for his mother to stay. He thought and thought, but he had no friends to ask, and the neighbours were already suspicious, and the only person he thought he could trust was Mrs Cooper. Once his mother was safely there, he was going to find the green leather case, and look at what was in it, and then he was going to go to Oxford, where he'd find the answer to some of his questions. But the men came too soon.

And now he'd killed one of them.

So the police would be after him too.

Well, he was good at not being noticed. He'd have to *not be noticed* harder than he'd ever done in his life before, and keep it up as long as he could, till either he found his father or they found him. And if they found him first, he didn't care how many more of them he killed.

Later that day, towards midnight in fact, Will was walking out of the city of Oxford, forty miles away. He was tired to his very bones. He had hitch-hiked, and ridden on two buses, and walked, and reached Oxford at six in the evening, too late to do what he needed to do; and he'd eaten at a Burger King and gone to a cinema to hide (though what the film was, he forgot even as he was watching it) and now he was walking along an endless road through the suburbs, heading north.

No one had noticed him so far. But he was aware that he'd better find somewhere to sleep before long, because the later it got, the more noticeable he'd be. The trouble was that there was nowhere to hide in the gardens of the comfortable houses along this road, and there was still no sign of open country.

He came to a large roundabout where the road going north crossed the Oxford ring road going east and west. At this time of night there was very little traffic, and the road where he stood was quiet, with comfortable houses set back behind a wide expanse of grass on either side. Planted along the grass at the road's edge were two lines of hornbeam trees, odd-looking things with perfectly symmetrical close-leafed crowns, more like children's drawings than like real trees, and the street lights made the scene look artificial, like a stage set. Will was stupefied with exhaustion, and he might have gone on to the north, or he might have laid his head on the grass under one of those trees and slept; but as he stood trying to clear his head, he saw a cat.

She was a tabby, like Moxie. She padded out of a garden on the Oxford side of the road, where Will was standing. Will put down his shopping bag and held out his hand, and the cat came up to rub her head against his knuckles, just as Moxie did. Of course, every cat behaved like that, but all the same Will felt such a longing to turn for home that tears scalded his eyes.

Eventually this cat turned away. This was night, and there was a territory to patrol, there were mice to hunt. She padded across the road and towards the bushes just beyond the hornbeam trees, and there she stopped.

Will, still watching, saw the cat behave curiously.

She reached out a paw to pat something in the air in front of her, something quite invisible to Will. Then she leapt backwards, back arched and fur on end, tail held out stiffly. Will knew cat-behaviour. He watched more alertly as the cat approached the spot again, just an empty patch of grass between the hornbeams and the bushes of a garden hedge, and patted the air once more.

Again she leapt back, but less far and with less alarm this time. After another few seconds of sniffing, touching, whisker-twitching, curiosity overcame wariness.

The cat stepped forward, and vanished.

Will blinked. Then he stood still, close to the trunk of the nearest tree, as a truck came round the circle and swept its lights over him. When it had gone past he crossed the road, keeping his eyes on the spot where the cat had been investigating. It wasn't easy, because there was nothing to fix on, but when he came to the place and cast about to look closely, he saw it.

At least, he saw it from some angles. It looked as if someone had cut a patch out of the air, about two metres from the edge of the road, a patch roughly square in shape and less than a metre across. If you were level with the patch so that it was edge-on, it was nearly invisible, and it was completely invisible from behind. You could only see it from the side nearest the road, and you couldn't see it easily even from there, because all you could see through it was exactly the same kind of thing that lay in front of it on this side: a patch of grass lit by a street light.

But Will knew without the slightest doubt that that patch of grass on the other side was in a different world.

He couldn't possibly have said why. He knew it at once, as strongly as he knew that fire burned and kindness was good. He was looking at something profoundly alien.

And for that reason alone, it enticed him to stoop and look further. What he saw made his head swim and his heart thump harder, but he didn't hesitate: he pushed his shopping bag through, and then scrambled through himself, through the hole in the fabric of this world and into another.

He found himself standing under a row of trees. But not hornbeam trees: these were tall palms, and they were growing, like the trees in Oxford, in a line along the grass. But this was the centre of a broad boulevard, and at the side of the boulevard was a line of cafés and small shops, all brightly lit, all open, and all utterly silent and empty beneath a sky thick with stars. The hot night was laden with the scent of flowers and with the salt smell of the sea.

Will looked around carefully. Behind him the full moon shone down over a distant prospect of great green hills, and on the slopes at the foot of the hills there were houses with rich gardens and an open parkland with groves of trees and the white gleam of a classical temple.

Just beside him was that bare patch in the air, as hard to see from this side as from the other, but definitely there. He bent to look through and saw the road in Oxford, his own world. He turned away with a shudder: whatever this new world was, it had to be better than what he'd just left. With a dawning light-headedness, the feeling that he was dreaming but awake at the same time, he stood up and looked around for the cat, his guide.

She was nowhere in sight. No doubt she was already exploring those narrow streets and gardens beyond the cafés whose lights were so inviting. Will lifted up his tattered shopping bag and walked slowly across the road towards them, moving very carefully in case it all disappeared.

The air of the place had something Mediterranean or maybe Caribbean about it. Will had never been out of England, so he couldn't compare it with anywhere he knew, but it was the kind of place where people came out late at night to eat and drink, to dance and enjoy music. Except that there was no one here, and the silence was immense.

On the first corner he reached there stood a café, with little green tables on the pavement and a zinc-topped bar and an espresso machine. On some of the tables glasses stood half-empty; in one ashtray a cigarette had burned down to the butt; a plate of risotto stood next to a basket of stale rolls as hard as cardboard.

He took a bottle of lemonade from the cooler behind the bar and then thought for a moment before dropping a pound coin in the till. As soon as he'd shut it, he opened it again, realizing that the money in there might say what this place was called. The currency was called the corona, but he couldn't tell any more than that.

He put the money back and opened the bottle on the opener fixed to the counter before leaving the café and wandering down the street going away from the boulevard. Little grocers' shops and bakeries stood between jewellers and florists and bead-curtained doors opening into private houses, where wrought iron balconies thick with flowers overhung the narrow pavement, and where the silence, being enclosed, was even more profound.

The streets were leading downwards, and before very long they opened out on to a broad avenue where more palm trees reached high into the air, the underside of their leaves glowing in the street lights.

On the other side of the avenue was the sea.

Will found himself facing a harbour enclosed from the left by a stone breakwater and from the right by a headland on which a large building with stone columns and wide steps and ornate balconies stood floodlit among flowering trees and bushes. In the harbour one or two rowing boats lay still at anchor, and beyond the breakwater the starlight glittered on a calm sea.

By now, Will's exhaustion had been wiped out. He was wide awake and possessed by wonder. From time to time, on his way through the narrow streets, he'd put out a hand to touch a wall or a doorway or the flowers in a window-box, and found them solid and convincing. Now he wanted to touch the whole landscape in front of him, because it was too wide to take in through his eyes alone. He stood still, breathing deeply, almost afraid.

He discovered that he was still holding the bottle he'd taken from the café. He drank from it, and it tasted like what it was, ice-cold lemonade; and welcome too, because the night air was hot.

He wandered along to the right, past hotels with awnings over brightly-lit entrances and bougainvillea flowering beside them, until he came to the gardens on the little headland. The building in the trees with its ornate façade lit by floodlights might have been a casino, or even an opera house. There were paths leading here and there among the lamp-hung oleander trees, but not a sound of life could be heard: no night-birds singing, no insects, nothing but the sound of Will's own footsteps.

The only sound he could hear came from the regular quiet breaking of delicate waves from the beach beyond the palm trees at the edge of the garden. Will made his way there. The tide was half-way in, or half-way out, and a row of pedal-boats was drawn up on the soft white sand above the high-water line. Every few seconds a tiny wave folded itself over at the sea's edge before sliding back neatly under the next. Fifty metres or so out on the calm water was a diving platform.

Will sat on the side of one of the pedal-boats and kicked off his shoes, his cheap trainers that were coming apart and cramping his hot feet. He dropped his socks beside them and pushed his toes deep into the sand. A few seconds later he had thrown off the rest of his clothes and was walking into the sea.

The water was deliciously between cool and warm. He splashed out to the diving platform and pulled himself out to sit on its weather-softened planking and look back at the city.

To his right the harbour lay enclosed by its breakwater. Beyond it a mile or so away stood a red and white striped lighthouse. And beyond the lighthouse, distant cliffs rose dimly, and beyond them, those great wide rolling hills he'd seen from the place he'd first come through.

Closer at hand were the light-bearing trees of the casino gardens, and the streets of the city, and the waterfront with its hotels and cafés and warm-lit shops, all silent, all empty.

And all safe. No one could follow him here; the man who'd searched the house would never know; the police would never find him. He had a whole world to hide in.

For the first time since he'd run out of his front door that morning, Will began to feel secure.

He was thirsty again, and hungry too, because he'd last eaten in another world, after all. He slipped back into the water and swam back more slowly to the beach, where he put on his underpants and carried the rest of his clothes and the shopping bag. He dropped the empty bottle into the first rubbish bin he found and walked barefoot along the pavement towards the harbour.

When his skin had dried a little he pulled on his jeans and looked for somewhere he'd be likely to find food. The hotels were too grand. He looked inside the first hotel, but it was so large that he felt uncomfortable, and he kept moving down the waterfront until he found a little café that looked like the right place. He couldn't have said why; it was very similar to a dozen others, with its first-floor balcony laden with flower-pots and its tables and chairs on the pavement outside, but it welcomed him.

There was a bar with photographs of boxers on the wall, and a signed poster of a broadly smiling accordion player. There was a kitchen, and a door beside it that opened on to a narrow flight of stairs, carpeted in a bright floral pattern.

He climbed quietly up to the narrow landing and opened the first door he came to. It was the room at the front. The air was hot and stuffy, and Will opened the glass door on to the balcony to let in the night air. The room itself was small and furnished with things that were too big for it, and shabby, but it was clean and comfortable. Hospitable people lived here. There was a little shelf of books, a magazine on the table, a couple of photographs in frames.

Will left and looked in the other rooms: a little bathroom, a bedroom with a double bed.

Something made his skin prickle before he opened the last door. His heart raced. He wasn't sure if he'd heard a sound from inside, but something told him that the room wasn't empty. He thought how odd it was that this day had begun with someone outside a darkened room, and himself waiting inside; and now the positions were reversed –

And as he stood wondering, the door burst open and something came hurtling at him like a wild beast.

But his memory had warned him, and he wasn't standing quite close enough to be knocked over. He fought hard: knee, head, fist, and the strength of his arms against it, him, her –

A girl about his own age, ferocious, snarling, with ragged dirty clothes and thin bare limbs.

She realized what he was at the same moment, and snatched herself away from his bare chest, to crouch in the corner of the dark landing like a cat at bay. And there was a cat beside her, to his astonishment: a large wildcat, as tall as his knee, fur on end, teeth bared, tail erect.

She put her hand on the cat's back and licked her dry lips, watching his every movement.

Will stood up slowly.

"Who are you?"

"Lyra Silvertongue," she said.

"Do you live here?"

"No," she said vehemently.

"Then what is this place? This city?"

"I don't know."

"Where do you come from?"

"From my world. It's joined on. Where's your dæmon?"

His eyes widened. Then he saw something extraordinary happen to the cat: it leapt into her arms, and when it got there, it had changed shape. Now it was a red-brown stoat with a cream throat and belly, and it glared at him as ferociously as the girl herself. But then another shift in things took place, because he realized that they were both, girl and stoat, profoundly afraid of him, as much as if he'd been a ghost.

"I haven't got a demon," he said. "I don't know what you mean." Then: "Oh! Is that your demon?"

She stood up slowly. The stoat curled himself around her neck and his dark eyes never left Will's face.

"But you're *alive*," she said, half-disbelievingly. "You en't… You en't been…"

"My name's Will Parry," he said. "I don't know what you mean about demons. In my world demon means… It means devil, something evil."

"In your world? You mean *this* en't your world?"

"No. I just found … a way in. Like your world, I suppose. It must be joined on."

She relaxed a little, but she still watched him intensely, and he stayed calm and quiet as if she were a strange cat he was making friends with.

"Have you seen anyone else in this city?" he went on.

"No."

"How long have you been here?"

"Dunno. A few days. I can't remember."

"So why did you come here?"

"I'm looking for Dust," she said.

"Looking for dust? What, gold dust? What sort of dust?"

She narrowed her eyes and said nothing. He turned away to go downstairs.

"I'm hungry," he said. "Is there any food in the kitchen?"

"I dunno…" she said, and followed, keeping her distance from him.

In the kitchen Will found the ingredients for a casserole of chicken and onions and peppers, but they hadn't been cooked, and in the heat they were smelling bad. He swept them all into the dustbin.

"Haven't you eaten anything?" he said, and opened the fridge.

Lyra came to look.

"I didn't know this was here," she said. "Oh! It's cold…"

Her dæmon had changed again, and become a huge brightly-coloured butterfly, which fluttered into the fridge briefly and out again at once to settle on her shoulder. The butterfly raised and lowered his wings slowly. Will felt he shouldn't stare, though his head was ringing with the strangeness of it.

"Haven't you seen a fridge before?" he said.

He found a can of cola and handed it to her before taking out a tray of eggs. She pressed the can between her palms with pleasure.

"Drink it, then," he said.

She looked at it, frowning. She didn't know how to open it. He snapped the lid for her, and the drink frothed out. She licked it suspiciously and then her eyes opened wide.

"This is good?" she said, her voice half-hoping and half-fearful.

"Yeah. They have Coke in this world, obviously. Look, I'll drink some to prove it isn't poison."

He opened another can. Once she saw him drink, she followed his example. She was obviously thirsty. She drank so quickly that the bubbles got up her nose, and she snorted and belched loudly, and scowled when he looked at her.

"I'm going to make an omelette," he said. "D'you want some?"

"I don't know what omelette is."

"Well, watch and you'll see. Or there's a can of baked beans if you like."

"I don't know baked beans."

He showed her the can. She looked for the snap-open top like the one on the cola can.

"No, you have to use a can-opener," he said. "Don't they have can-openers in your world?"

"In my world servants do the cooking," she said scornfully.

"Look in the drawer over there."

She rummaged through the kitchen cutlery while he broke six eggs into a bowl and whisked them with a fork.

"That's it," he said, watching. "With the red handle. Bring it here."

He pierced the tin and showed her how to open it.

"Now get that little saucepan off the hook and tip them in," he told her.

She sniffed the beans, and again an expression of pleasure and suspicion entered her eyes. She tipped the can into the saucepan and licked a finger, watching as Will shook salt and pepper into the eggs and cut a knob of butter from a package in the fridge into a cast-iron pan. He went into the bar to find some matches, and when he came back she was dipping her dirty finger in the bowl of beaten eggs and licking it greedily. Her dæmon, a cat again, was dipping his paw in it too, but he backed away when Will came near.

"It's not cooked yet," Will said, taking it away. "When did you last have a meal?"

"At my father's house on Svalbard," she said. "Days and days ago. I don't know. I found bread and stuff here and ate that."

He lit the gas, melted the butter, poured in the eggs and let them run all over the base of the pan. Her eyes followed everything greedily, watching him pull the eggs up into soft ridges in the centre as they cooked and tilt the pan to let raw egg flow into the space. She watched him, too, looked at his face and his working hands and his bare shoulders and his feet.

When the omelette was cooked he folded it over and cut it in half with the spatula.

"Find a couple of plates," he said, and Lyra obediently did so.

She seemed quite willing to take orders if she saw the sense of them, so he told her to go and clear a table in front of the café. He brought out the food and some knives and forks from a drawer, and they sat down together, a little awkwardly.

She ate hers in less than a minute, and then fidgeted, swinging back and forth on her chair and plucking at the plastic strips of the woven seat while he finished his omelette. Her dæmon changed yet again, and became a goldfinch, pecking at invisible crumbs on the table-top.

Will ate slowly. He'd given her most of the beans, but even so he took much longer than she did. The harbour in front of them, the lights along the empty boulevard, the stars in the dark sky above, all hung in the huge silence as if nothing else existed at all.

And all the time he was intensely aware of the girl. She was small and slight, but wiry, and she'd fought like a tiger; his fist had raised a bruise on her cheek, and she was ignoring it. Her expression was a mixture of the very young – when she first tasted the cola – and a kind of deep sad wariness. Her eyes were pale blue and her hair would be a darkish blonde once it was washed; because she was filthy, and she smelled as if she hadn't washed for days.

"Laura? Lara?" Will said.

"Lyra."

"Lyra … Silvertongue?"

"Yes."

"Where is your world? How did you get here?"

She shrugged. "I walked," she said. "It was all foggy. I didn't know where I was going. At least I knew I was going out of *my* world. But I couldn't see this one till the fog cleared. Then I found myself here."

"What did you say about dust?"

"Dust, yeah. I'm going to find out about it. But this world

seems to be empty. There's no one here to ask. I've been here for ... I dunno, three days, maybe four. And there's no one here."

"But why do you want to find out about dust?"

"Special Dust," she said shortly. "Not ordinary dust, obviously."

The dæmon changed again. He did so in the flick of an eye, and from a goldfinch he became a rat, a powerful pitch-black rat with red eyes. Will looked at him with wide wary eyes, and the girl saw his glance.

"You *have* got a dæmon," she said decisively. "Inside you."

He didn't know what to say.

"You have," she went on. "You wouldn't be human else. You'd be ... half-dead. We seen a kid with his dæmon cut away. You en't like that. Even if you don't know you've got a dæmon, you have. We was scared at first when we saw you. Like you was a night-ghast or something. But then we saw you weren't like that at all."

"We?"

"Me and Pantalaimon. Us. Your dæmon en't *separate* from you. It's you. A part of you. You're part of each other. En't there *anyone* in your world like us? Are they all like you, with their dæmons all hidden away?"

Will looked at the two of them, the skinny pale-eyed girl with her black rat-dæmon now sitting in her arms, and felt profoundly alone.

"I'm tired. I'm going to bed," he said. "Are you going to stay in this city?"

"Dunno. I've got to find out more about what I'm looking for. There must be some scholars in this world. There must be *someone* who knows about it."

"Maybe not in this world. But I came here out of a place called Oxford. There's plenty of scholars there, if that's what you want."

"Oxford?" she cried. "That's where I come from!"

"Is there an Oxford in your world, then? You never came from my world."

"No," she said decisively. "Different worlds. But in my world there's an Oxford too. We're both speaking English, en't we? Stands to reason there's other things the same. How did you get through? Is there a bridge, or what?"

"Just a kind of window in the air."

"Show me," she said.

It was a command, not a request. He shook his head.

"Not now," he said. "I want to sleep. Anyway it's the middle of the night."

"Then show me in the morning!"

"All right, I'll show you. But I've got my own things to do. You'll have to find your scholars by yourself."

"Easy," she said. "I know all about scholars."

He put the plates together and stood up.

"I cooked," he said, "so you can wash the dishes."

She looked incredulous. "Wash the dishes?" she scoffed. "There's millions of clean ones lying about! Anyway I'm not a servant. I'm not going to wash them."

"So I won't show you the way through."

"I'll find it by myself."

"You won't, it's hidden. You'd never find it. Listen. I don't know how long we can stay in this place. We've got to eat, so we'll eat what's here, but we'll tidy up afterwards and keep the place clean, because we ought to. You wash these dishes. We've got to treat this place *right*. Now I'm going to bed. I'll have the other room. I'll see you in the morning."

He went inside, cleaned his teeth with a finger and some toothpaste from his tattered bag, fell on the double bed and was asleep in a moment.

Lyra waited till she was sure he was asleep, and then took the dishes into the kitchen and ran them under the tap, rubbing hard with a cloth until they looked clean. She did the same with the knives and forks, but the procedure didn't work with the omelette pan, so she tried a bar of yellow soap on it, and picked at it stubbornly until it looked as clean as she thought it was going to. Then she dried everything on another cloth and stacked it neatly on the draining board.

Because she was still thirsty and because she wanted to try opening a tin again she snapped open another cola and took it upstairs. She listened outside Will's door and, hearing nothing, tiptoed into the other room and took out the alethiometer from under her pillow.

She didn't need to be close to Will to ask about him, but she wanted to look anyway, and she turned his door handle as quietly as she could before going in.

There was a light on the sea front outside shining straight up into the room, and in the glow reflected from the ceiling she looked down at the sleeping boy. He was frowning, and his face glistened with sweat. He was strong and stocky, not as formed as a grown man, of course, because he wasn't much older than she was, but he'd be powerful one day. How much easier if his dæmon had been visible! She wondered what its form might be, and whether it was fixed yet. Whatever its form was, it would express a nature that was savage, and courteous, and unhappy.

She tiptoed to the window. In the glow from the street lamp she carefully set the hands of the alethiometer, and relaxed her mind into the shape of a question. The needle began to sweep around the dial in a series of pauses and swings almost too fast to watch.

She had asked: *What is he? A friend or an enemy?*

The alethiometer answered: *He is a murderer.*

When she saw the answer, she relaxed at once. He could find food, and show her how to reach Oxford, and those were powers that were useful, but he might still have been untrustworthy or cowardly. A murderer was a worthy companion. She felt as safe with him as she'd done with Iorek Byrnison the armoured bear.

She swung the shutter across the open window so the morning sunlight wouldn't strike in on his face, and tiptoed out.

2

Among the Witches

The witch Serafina Pekkala, who had rescued Lyra and the other children from the experimental station at Bolvangar and flown with her to the island of Svalbard, was deeply troubled.

In the atmospheric disturbances that followed Lord Asriel's escape from his exile on Svalbard, she and her companions were blown far from the island and many miles out over the frozen sea. Some of them managed to stay with the damaged balloon of Lee Scoresby, the Texan aëronaut, but Serafina herself was tossed high into the banks of fog that soon came rolling in from the gap that Lord Asriel's experiment had torn in the sky.

When she found herself able to control her flight once more, her first thought was of Lyra; for she knew nothing of the fight between the false bear-king and the true one, Iorek Byrnison, nor of what had happened to Lyra after that.

So she began to search for her, flying through the cloudy gold-tinged air on her branch of cloud-pine, accompanied by her dæmon Kaisa the snow-goose. They moved back towards Svalbard and south a little, soaring for several hours under a sky turbulent with strange lights and shadows. Serafina Pekkala knew from the unsettling tingle of the light on her skin that it came from another world.

After some time had passed, Kaisa said, "Look! A witch's dæmon, lost…"

Serafina Pekkala looked through the fog-banks and saw a tern, circling and crying in the chasms of misty light. They wheeled and flew towards him. Seeing them come near, he darted up in alarm, but Serafina Pekkala signalled friendship, and he dropped down beside them.

Serafina Pekkala said, "What clan are you from?"

"Taymyr," he told her. "My witch is captured… Our companions have been driven away! I am lost…"

"Who has captured your witch?"

"The woman with the monkey-dæmon, from Bolvangar… Help me! Help us! I am so afraid!"

"Was your clan allied with the child-cutters?"

"Yes, until we found out what they were doing… After the fight at Bolvangar they drove us off, but my witch was taken prisoner… They have her on a ship… What can I do? She is calling to me and I can't find her! Oh, help, help me!"

"Quiet," said Kaisa the goose-dæmon. "Listen down below."

They glided lower, listening with keen ears, and Serafina Pekkala soon made out the beat of a gas-engine, muffled by the fog.

"They can't navigate a ship in fog like this," Kaisa said. "What are they doing?"

"It's a smaller engine than that," said Serafina Pekkala, and as she spoke there came a new sound from a different direction: a low brutal shuddering blast, like some immense sea creature calling from the depths. It roared for several seconds and then stopped abruptly.

"The ship's foghorn," said Serafina Pekkala.

They wheeled low over the water and cast about again for the sound of the engine. Suddenly they found it, for the fog seemed to have patches of different density, and the witch darted up out of sight just in time as a launch came chugging slowly through the swathes of damp air. The swell was slow and oily, as if the water was reluctant to rise.

They swung around and above, the tern-dæmon keeping close like a child to its mother, and watched the steersman adjust the course slightly as the foghorn boomed again. There was a light mounted on the bow, but all it lit up was the fog a few yards in front.

Serafina Pekkala said to the lost dæmon: "Did you say there are still some witches helping these people?"

"I think so – a few renegade witches from Volgorsk – unless they've fled too," he told her. "What are you going to do? Will you look for my witch?"

"Yes. But stay with Kaisa for now."

Serafina Pekkala flew down towards the launch, leaving the dæmons out of sight above, and alighted on the counter just behind the steersman. His seagull-dæmon squawked, and the man turned to look.

"You taken your time, en't you?" he said. "Get up ahead and guide us in on the port side."

She took off again at once. It had worked: they still had some witches helping them, and he thought she was one. Port was left, she remembered, and the port light was red. She cast about in the fog until she caught its hazy glow no more than a hundred yards away. She darted back and hovered above the launch calling directions to the steersman, who slowed the craft down to a crawling pace and brought it in to the gangway-ladder that hung just above the water-line. The steersman called, and a sailor threw a line from above, and another hurried down the ladder to make it fast to the launch.

Serafina Pekkala flew up to the ship's rail, and retreated to the shadows by the lifeboats. She could see no other witches, but they were probably patrolling the skies; Kaisa would know what to do.

Below, a passenger was leaving the launch and climbing the ladder. The figure was fur-swathed, hooded, anonymous; but as it reached the deck, a golden monkey-dæmon swung himself lightly up on the rail and glared around, his black eyes radiating malevolence. Serafina caught her breath: the figure was Mrs Coulter.

A dark-clothed man hurried out on deck to greet her, and looked around as if he were expecting someone else as well.

"Lord Boreal –" he began.

But Mrs Coulter interrupted: "He has gone on elsewhere. Have they started the torture?"

"Yes, Mrs Coulter," was the reply, "but –"

"I ordered them to wait," she snapped. "Have they taken to disobeying me? Perhaps there should be more discipline on this ship."

She pushed her hood back. Serafina Pekkala saw her face clearly in the yellow light: proud, passionate, and to the witch, so young.

"Where are the other witches?" she demanded.

The man from the ship said, "All gone, ma'am. Fled to their homeland."

"But a witch guided the launch in," said Mrs Coulter. "Where has she gone?"

Serafina shrank back; obviously the sailor in the launch hadn't heard the latest state of things. The cleric looked around, bewildered, but Mrs Coulter was too impatient, and after a cursory glance above and along the deck, she shook her head and hurried in with her dæmon through the open door that cast a yellow nimbus on the air. The man followed.

Serafina Pekkala looked around to check her position. She was concealed behind a ventilator on the narrow area of decking between the rail and the central superstructure of the ship; and on this level, facing forward below the bridge and the funnel, was a saloon from which windows, not portholes, looked out on three sides. That was where the people had gone in. Light spilled thickly from the windows on to the fog-pearled railing, and dimly showed up the foremast and the canvas-covered hatch. Everything was wringing wet and beginning to freeze into stiffness. No one could see Serafina where she was; but if she wanted to see any more, she would have to leave her hiding-place.

That was too bad. With her pine branch she could escape, and with her knife and her bow she could fight. She hid the branch behind the ventilator and slipped along the deck until she reached the first window. It was fogged with condensation and impossible to see through, and Serafina could hear no voices, either. She withdrew to the shadows again.

There was one thing she could do; she was reluctant, because it was desperately risky, and it would leave her exhausted; but it seemed there was no choice. It was a kind of magic she could work to make herself unseen. True invisibility was impossible, of course: this was mental magic, a kind of fiercely-held modesty that could make the spell-worker not invisible but simply unnoticed. Holding it with the right degree of intensity she could pass through a crowded room, or walk beside a solitary traveller, without being seen.

So now she composed her mind and brought all her concentration to bear on the matter of altering the way she held herself so as to deflect attention completely. It took some minutes before she was confident. She tested it by stepping out of her hiding-place and into the path of a sailor coming along the deck

33

with a bag of tools. He stepped aside to avoid her without looking at her once.

She was ready. She went to the door of the brightly-lit saloon and opened it, finding the room empty. She left the outer door ajar so that she could flee through it if she needed to, and saw a door at the far end of the room that opened on to a flight of stairs leading down into the bowels of the ship. She descended, and found herself in a narrow corridor hung with white-painted pipework, and illuminated with anbaric bulkhead lights, which led straight along the length of the hull, with doors opening off it on both sides.

She walked quietly along, listening, until she heard voices. It sounded as if some kind of council was in session.

She opened the door and walked in.

A dozen or so people were seated around a large table. One or two of them looked up for a moment, gazed at her absently, and forgot her at once. She stood quietly near the door and watched. The meeting was being chaired by an elderly man in the robes of a Cardinal, and the rest of them seemed clerics of one sort or another, apart from Mrs Coulter, who was the only woman present. Mrs Coulter had thrown her furs over the back of the chair, and her cheeks were flushed in the heat of the ship's interior.

Serafina Pekkala looked around carefully, and saw someone else in the room as well: a thin-faced man with a frog-dæmon, seated to one side at a table laden with leather-bound books and loose piles of yellowed paper. She thought at first that he was a clerk or a secretary, until she saw what he was doing: he was intently gazing at a golden instrument like a large watch or a compass, stopping every minute or so to note down what he found. Then he would open one of the books, search laboriously through the index, and look up a reference before writing that down too and turning back to the instrument.

Serafina looked back to the discussion at the table, because she heard the word *witch*.

"She knows something about the child," said one of the clerics. "She confessed that she knows something. All the witches know something about her."

"I am wondering what Mrs Coulter knows," said the Cardinal. "Is there something she should have told us before, I wonder?"

"You will have to speak more plainly than that," said Mrs Coulter icily. "You forget I am a woman, Your Eminence, and thus not so subtle as a prince of the Church. What is this truth that I should have known about the child?"

The Cardinal's expression was full of meaning, but he said nothing. There was a pause and then another cleric said almost apologetically:

"It seems that there is a prophecy. It concerns the child, you see, Mrs Coulter. All the signs have been fulfilled. The circumstances of her birth, to begin with. The gyptians know something about her too – they speak of her in terms of witch-oil and marsh-fire, uncanny, you see – hence her success in leading the gyptian men to Bolvangar. And then there's her astonishing feat of deposing the bear-king Iofur Raknison – this is no ordinary child. Fra Pavel can tell us more, perhaps…"

He glanced at the thin-faced man reading the alethiometer, who blinked, rubbed his eyes, and looked at Mrs Coulter.

"You may be aware that this is the only alethiometer left, apart from the one in the child's possession," he said. "All the others have been acquired and destroyed, by order of the Magisterium. I learn from this instrument that the child was given hers by the Master of Jordan College, and that she learned to read it by herself, and that she can use it without the books of readings. If it were possible to disbelieve the alethiometer, I would do so, because to use the instrument without the books is simply inconceivable to me. It takes decades of diligent study to reach any sort of understanding. She began to read it within a few weeks of acquiring it, and now she has an almost complete mastery. She is like no human scholar I can imagine."

"Where is she now, Fra Pavel?" said the Cardinal.

"In the other world," said Fra Pavel. "It is already late."

"The witch knows!" said another man, whose muskrat-dæmon gnawed unceasingly at a pencil. "It's all in place but for the witch's testimony! I say we should torture her again!"

"What is this prophecy?" demanded Mrs Coulter, who had been getting increasingly angry. "How dare you keep it from me?"

Her power over them was visible. The golden monkey glared round the table, and none of them could look him in the face.

Only the Cardinal did not flinch. His dæmon, a macaw, lifted a foot and scratched her head.

"The witch has hinted at something extraordinary," the Cardinal said. "I dare not believe what I think it means. If it's true, it places on us the most terrible responsibility men and women have ever faced. But I ask you again, Mrs Coulter – what do *you* know of the child and her father?"

Mrs Coulter's face was chalk-white with fury.

"How dare you interrogate me?" she spat. "And how dare you keep from me what you've learned from the witch? And finally, how dare you assume that I am keeping something from you? D'you think I'm on her side? Or perhaps you think I'm on her father's side? Perhaps you think I should be tortured like the witch. Well, we are all under your command, Your Eminence. You have only to snap your fingers and you could have me torn apart. But if you searched every scrap of flesh for an answer you wouldn't find one, because I know nothing of this prophecy, nothing whatever. And I demand that you tell me what *you* know. My child, my own child, conceived in sin and born in shame, but my child nonetheless, and you keep from me what I have every right to know!"

"Please," said another of the clerics nervously. "Please, Mrs Coulter; the witch hasn't spoken yet; we shall learn more from her. Cardinal Sturrock himself says that she's only hinted at it."

"And suppose the witch doesn't reveal it?" Mrs Coulter said. "What then? We guess, do we? We shiver and quail and guess?"

Fra Pavel said: "No, because that is the question I am now preparing to put to the alethiometer. We shall find the answer, whether from the witch or from the books of readings."

"And how long will that take?"

He raised his eyebrows wearily and said, "A considerable time. It is an immensely complex question."

"But the witch would tell us at once," said Mrs Coulter.

And she rose to her feet. As if in awe of her, most of the men did too. Only the Cardinal and Fra Pavel remained seated. Serafina Pekkala stood back, fiercely holding herself unseen. The golden monkey was gnashing his teeth, and all his shimmering fur was standing on end.

Mrs Coulter swung him up to her shoulder.

"So let us go and ask her," she said.

She turned and swept out into the corridor. The men hastened to follow her, jostling and shoving past Serafina Pekkala, who had only time to stand quickly aside, her mind in a turmoil. The last to go was the Cardinal.

Serafina took a few seconds to compose herself, because her agitation was beginning to make her visible. Then she followed the clerics down the corridor and into a smaller room, bare and white and hot, where they were all clustered around the dreadful figure in the centre: a witch bound tightly to a steel chair, with agony on her grey face and her legs twisted and broken.

Mrs Coulter stood over her. Serafina took up a position by the door, knowing that she could not stay unseen for long; this was too hard.

"Tell us about the child, witch," said Mrs Coulter.

"No!"

"You will suffer."

"I have suffered enough."

"Oh, there is more suffering to come. We have a thousand years of experience in this Church of ours. We can draw out your suffering endlessly. Tell us about the child," Mrs Coulter said, and reached down to break one of the witch's fingers. It snapped easily.

The witch cried out, and for a clear second Serafina Pekkala became visible to everyone, and one or two of the clerics looked at her, puzzled and fearful; but then she controlled herself again, and they turned back to the torture.

Mrs Coulter was saying, "If you don't answer I'll break another finger, and then another. What do you know about the child? Tell me."

"All right! Please, please, no more!"

"Answer then."

There came another sickening crack, and this time a flood of sobbing broke from the witch. Serafina Pekkala could hardly hold herself back. Then came these words, in a shriek:

"No, no! I'll tell you! I beg you, no more! The child who was to come… The witches knew who she was before you did… We found out her name…"

"We know her name. What name do you mean?"

"Her true name! The name of her destiny!"

"What is this name? Tell me!" said Mrs Coulter.

"No … no…"

"And how? Found out how?"

"There was a test… If she was able to pick out one spray of cloud-pine from many others, she would be the child who would come, and it happened at our Consul's house at Trollesund, when the child came with the gyptian men… The child with the bear…"

Her voice gave out.

Mrs Coulter gave a little exclamation of impatience, and there came another loud slap, and a groan.

"But what was your prophecy about this child?" Mrs Coulter went on, and her voice was all bronze now, and ringing with passion. "And what is this name that will make her destiny clear?"

Serafina Pekkala moved closer, even among the tight throng of men around the witch, and none of them felt her presence at their very elbows. She must end this witch's suffering, and soon, but the strain of holding herself unseen was enormous. She trembled as she took the knife from her waist.

The witch was sobbing, "She is the one who came before, and you have hated and feared her ever since! Well, now she has come again, and you failed to find her… She was there on Svalbard – she was with Lord Asriel, and you lost her. She escaped, and she will be –"

But before she could finish, there came an interruption.

Through the open doorway there flew a tern, mad with terror, and it beat its wings brokenly as it crashed to the floor and struggled up and darted to the breast of the tortured witch, pressing itself against her, nuzzling, chirruping, crying, and the witch called in anguish: "Yambe-Akka! Come to me, come to me!"

No one but Serafina Pekkala understood. Yambe-Akka was the

goddess who came to a witch when she was about to die.

And Serafina was ready. She became visible at once, and stepped forward smiling happily, because Yambe-Akka was merry and light-hearted and her visits were gifts of joy. The witch saw her and turned up her tear-stained face, and Serafina bent to kiss it, and slid her knife gently into the witch's heart. The tern-dæmon looked up with dim eyes and vanished.

And now Serafina Pekkala would have to fight her way out.

The men were still shocked, disbelieving, but Mrs Coulter recovered her wits almost at once.

"Seize her! Don't let her go!" she cried, but Serafina was already at the door, with an arrow nocked in her bowstring. She swung up the bow and loosed the arrow in less than a second, and the Cardinal fell choking and kicking to the floor.

Out, along the corridor to the stairs, turn, nock, loose; and another man fell, and already a loud jarring bell was filling the ship with its clangour.

Up the stairs and out on to the deck. Two sailors barred her way, and she said, "Down there! The prisoner has got loose! Get help!"

That was enough to puzzle them, and they stood undecided, which gave her time to dodge past and seize her cloud-pine from where she had hidden it behind the ventilator.

"Shoot her!" came a cry in Mrs Coulter's voice from behind, and at once three rifles fired, and the bullets struck metal and whined off into the fog, as Serafina leapt on the branch and urged it up like one of her own arrows. A few seconds later she was in the air, in the thick of the fog, safe, and then a great goose-shape glided out of the wraiths of grey to her side.

"Where to?" he said.

"Away, Kaisa, away," she said. "I want to get the stench of these people out of my nose."

In truth, she didn't know where to go or what to do next. But there was one thing she knew for certain: there was an arrow in her quiver that would find its mark in Mrs Coulter's throat.

They turned south, away from that troubling other-world gleam in the fog, and as they flew a question began to form more clearly in Serafina's mind. What was Lord Asriel doing?

Because all the events that had overturned the world had their origin in his mysterious activities.

The problem was that the usual sources of her knowledge were natural ones. She could track any animal, catch any fish, find the rarest berries; and she could read the signs in the pine marten's entrails, or decipher the wisdom in the scales of a perch, or interpret the warnings in the crocus-pollen; but these were children of nature, and they told her natural truths.

For knowledge about Lord Asriel, she had to go elsewhere. In the port of Trollesund, their consul Dr Lanselius maintained his contact with the world of men and women, and Serafina Pekkala sped there through the fog to see what he could tell her. Before she went to his house she circled over the harbour, where wisps and tendrils of mist drifted ghostlike on the icy water, and watched as the pilot guided in a large vessel with an African registration. There were several other ships riding at anchor outside the harbour. She had never seen so many.

As the short day faded, she flew down and landed in the back garden of the consul's house. She tapped on the window, and Dr Lanselius himself opened the door, a finger to his lips.

"Serafina Pekkala, greetings," he said. "Come in quickly, and welcome. But you had better not stay long." He offered her a chair at the fireside, having glanced through the curtains out of a window that fronted the street, and said, "You'll have some wine?"

She sipped the golden Tokay and told him of what she had seen and heard aboard the ship.

"Do you think they understood what she said about the child?" he asked.

"Not fully, I think. But they know she is important. As for that woman, I'm afraid of her, Dr Lanselius. I shall kill her, I think, but still I'm afraid of her."

"Yes," he said. "So am I."

And Serafina listened as he told her of the rumours that had swept the town. Amid the fog of rumour, a few facts had begun to emerge clearly.

"They say that the Magisterium is assembling the greatest army ever known, and this is an advance party. And there are unpleasant rumours about some of the soldiers, Serafina Pekkala. I've heard about Bolvangar, and what they were doing there – cutting children's dæmons away, the most evil work I've ever heard of – well, it seems there is a regiment of warriors who have been treated in the same way. Do you know the word *zombi*? They fear nothing, because they're mindless. There are some in this town now. The authorities keep them hidden, but word gets out, and the townspeople are terrified of them."

"What of the other witch–clans?" said Serafina Pekkala. "What news do you have of them?"

"Most have gone back to their homelands. All the witches are waiting, Serafina Pekkala, with fear in their hearts, for what will happen next."

"And what do you hear of the church?"

"They're in complete confusion. You see, they don't know what Lord Asriel intends to do."

"Nor do I," she said, "and I can't imagine what it might be. What do *you* think he's intending, Dr Lanselius?"

He gently rubbed the head of his serpent-dæmon with his thumb.

"He is a scholar," he said after a moment, "but scholarship is not his ruling passion. Nor is statesmanship. I met him once, and I thought he had an ardent and powerful nature, but not a despotic one. I don't think he wants to rule... I don't know, Serafina Pekkala. I suppose his servant might be able to tell you. He is a man called Thorold, and he was imprisoned with Lord Asriel in the house on Svalbard. It might be worth a visit there to see if he can tell you anything; but of course, he might have gone into the other world with his master."

"Thank you. That's a good idea... I'll do it. And I'll go at once."

She said farewell to the consul and flew up through the gathering dark to join Kaisa in the clouds.

Serafina's journey to the north was made harder by the confusion in the world around her. All the Arctic peoples had been thrown into panic, and so had the animals, not only by the fog and the magnetic variations but by unseasonal crackings of ice and stirrings in the soil. It was as if the earth itself, the permafrost, were slowly awakening from a long dream of being frozen.

In all this turmoil, where sudden shafts of uncanny brilliance lanced down through rents in towers of fog and then vanished as quickly, where herds of musk-ox were seized by the urge to gallop south and then wheeled immediately to the west or the north again, where tight-knit skeins of geese disintegrated into a honking chaos as the magnetic fields they flew by wavered and snapped this way and that, Serafina Pekkala set her cloud-pine and flew north, to the house on the headland in the wastes of Svalbard.

There she found Lord Asriel's servant Thorold fighting off a group of cliff-ghasts.

She saw the movement before she came close enough to see what was happening. A swirl of lunging leathery wings, and a malevolent *yowk-yowk-yowk* resounding in the snowy courtyard; and a single figure swathed in furs, firing a rifle into the midst of them with a gaunt dog-dæmon snarling and snapping beside him whenever one of the filthy things flew low enough.

She didn't know the man, but a cliff-ghast was an enemy always. She swung round above and loosed a dozen arrows into the mêlée. With shrieks and gibberings the gang – too loosely organized to be called a troop – circled, saw their new opponent, and fled in confusion. A minute later the skies were bare again, and their dismayed *yowk-yowk-yowk* echoed distantly off the mountains before dwindling into silence.

Serafina flew down to the courtyard and alighted on the trampled, blood-sprinkled snow. The man pushed his hood back, still holding his rifle warily, because a witch was an enemy sometimes, and she saw an elderly man, long-jawed and grizzled and steady-eyed.

"I am a friend of Lyra's," she said. "I hope we can talk. Look: I lay my bow down."

"Where is the child?" he said.

"In another world. I'm concerned for her safety. And I need to know what Lord Asriel is doing."

He lowered the rifle and said, "Step inside, then. Look: I lay my rifle down."

The formalities exchanged, they went indoors. Kaisa glided through the skies above, keeping watch, while Thorold brewed some coffee and Serafina told him of her involvement with Lyra.

"She was always a wilful child," he said when they were seated at the oaken table in the glow of a naphtha lamp. "I'd see her every year or so when his lordship visited his college. I was fond of her, mind, you couldn't help it. But what her place was in the wider scheme of things, I don't know."

"What was Lord Asriel planning to do?"

"You don't think he told me, do you, Serafina Pekkala? I'm his manservant, that's all. I clean his clothes and cook his meals and keep his house tidy. I may have learned a thing or two in the years I been with his lordship, but only by picking 'em up accidental. He wouldn't confide in me any more than in his shaving-mug."

"Then tell me the thing or two you've learned by accident," she insisted.

Thorold was an elderly man, but he was healthy and vigorous, and he felt flattered by the attention of this young witch and her beauty, as any man would. He was shrewd, though, too, and he knew the attention was not really on him, but on what he knew; and he was honest, so he did not draw out his telling for much longer than he needed.

"I can't tell you precisely what he's doing," he said, "because all the philosophical details are beyond my grasp. But I can tell you what drives his lordship, though he doesn't know I know. I've seen this in a hundred little signs. Correct me if I'm wrong, but the witch-people have different gods from ours, en't that right?"

"Yes, that's true."

"But you know about our God? The God of the church, the one they call the Authority?"

"Yes, I do."

"Well, Lord Asriel has never found hisself at ease in the doctrines of the church, so to speak. I've seen a spasm of disgust cross his face when they talk of the sacraments, and atonement, and redemption, and suchlike. It's death among our people, Serafina Pekkala, to challenge the church, but Lord Asriel's been nursing a rebellion in his heart for as long as I've served him, that's one thing I do know."

"A rebellion against the church?"

"Partly, aye. There was a time when he thought of making it an issue of force, but he turned away from that."

"Why? Was the church too strong?"

"No," said the old servant, "that wouldn't stop my master. Now this might sound strange to you, Serafina Pekkala, but I know the man better than any wife could know him, better than a mother. He's been my master and my study for nigh on forty years. I can't follow him to the height of his thought any more than I can fly, but I can see where he's a-heading even if I can't go after him. No, it's my belief he turned away from a rebellion against the church not because the church was too strong, but because it was too weak to be worth the fighting."

"So … what is he doing?"

"I think he's a-waging a higher war than that. I think he's aiming a rebellion against the highest power of all. He's gone a-searching for the dwelling place of the Authority Himself, and he's a-going to destroy Him. That's what I think. It shakes my heart to voice it, ma'am. I hardly dare think of it. But I can't put together any other story that makes sense of what he's doing."

Serafina sat quiet for a few moments, absorbing what Thorold had said.

Before she could speak, he went on:

"Course, anyone setting out to do a grand thing like that would be the target of the church's anger. Goes without saying. It'd be the most gigantic blasphemy, that's what they'd say. They'd have him before the Consistorial Court and sentenced to death before you could blink. I've never spoke of it before and I shan't again; I'd be afraid to speak it aloud to you if you weren't a witch and beyond the power of the church; but that makes sense, and nothing else does. He's a-going to find the Authority and kill Him."

"Is that possible?" said Serafina.

"Lord Asriel's life has been filled with things that were impossible. I wouldn't like to say there was anything he couldn't do. But on the face of it, Serafina Pekkala, yes, he's stark mad. If angels couldn't do it, how can a man dare to think about it?"

"Angels? What are angels?"

"Beings of pure spirit, the church says. The church teaches that some of the angels rebelled before the world was created, and got flung out of heaven and into hell. They failed, you see, that's the point. They couldn't do it. And they had the power of angels. Lord Asriel is just a man, with human power, no more than that. But his ambition is limitless. He dares to do what men and women don't even dare to think. And look what he's done already: he's torn open the sky, he's opened the way to another world. Who else has ever done that? Who else could think of it? So with one part of me, Serafina Pekkala, I say he's mad, wicked, deranged. Yet with another part I think, he's Lord Asriel, he's not like other men. Maybe… If it was ever going to be possible, it'd be done by him and by no one else."

"And what will you do, Thorold?"

"I'll stay here and wait. I'll guard this house till he comes back and tells me different, or till I die. And now I might ask you the same question, ma'am."

"I'm going to make sure the child is safe," she said. "It might be that I have to pass this way again, Thorold. I'm glad to know that you will still be here."

"I won't budge," he told her.

She refused Thorold's offer of food, and said goodbye.

A minute or so later she joined her goose-dæmon again, and the dæmon kept silence with her as they soared and wheeled above the foggy mountains. She was deeply troubled, and there was no need to explain: every strand of moss, every icy puddle, every midge in her homeland thrilled against her nerves and called her back. She felt fear for them, but fear for herself too, for she was having to change; these were human affairs she was inquiring into, this was a human matter; Lord Asriel's god was not hers. Was she becoming human? Was she losing her witch-hood?

If she were, she could not do it alone.

"Home now," she said. "We must talk to our sisters, Kaisa. These events are too big for us alone."

And they sped through the roiling banks of fog towards Lake Enara, and home.

In the forested caves beside the lake they found the others of their clan, and Lee Scoresby, too. The aëronaut had struggled to keep his balloon aloft after the crash of Svalbard, and the witches had guided him to their homeland, where he had begun to repair the damage to his basket and the gas-bag.

"Ma'am, I'm very glad to see you," he said. "Any news of the little girl?"

"None, Mr Scoresby. Will you join our council tonight and help us discuss what to do?"

The Texan blinked with surprise, for no man had ever been known to join a witch-council.

"I'd be greatly honoured," he said. "I may have a suggestion or two of my own."

All through that day the witches came, like flakes of black snow on the wings of a storm, filling the skies with the darting flutter of their silk and the swish of air through the needles of their cloud-pine branches. Men who hunted in the dripping forests or fished among melting ice-floes heard the sky-wide whisper through the fog, and if the sky was clear they would look up to see the witches flying, like scraps of darkness drifting on a secret tide.

By evening the pines around the lake were lit from below by a hundred fires, and the greatest fire of all was built in front of the gathering-cave. There, once they had eaten, the witches assembled. Serafina Pekkala sat in the centre, the crown of little scarlet flowers nestling among her fair hair. On her left sat Lee Scoresby, and on her right, a visitor: the queen of the Latvian witches, whose name was Ruta Skadi.

She had arrived only an hour before, to Serafina's surprise. Serafina had thought Mrs Coulter beautiful, for a short-life; but Ruta Skadi was as lovely as Mrs Coulter, with an extra dimension of the mysterious, the uncanny. She had trafficked with spirits, and it showed. She was vivid and passionate, with large black eyes; it was said that Lord Asriel himself had been her lover. She wore heavy gold earrings and a crown on her black curly hair ringed with the fangs of snow-tigers. Serafina's dæmon Kaisa had learned from Ruta Skadi's dæmon that she had killed the tigers herself in order to punish the Tartar tribe who worshipped them, because the tribesmen had failed to do her honour when she had visited their territory. Without their tiger-gods the tribe declined into fear and melancholy, and begged her to allow them to worship her instead, only to be rejected with contempt; for what good would their worship do her, she asked? It had done nothing for the tigers. Such was Ruta Skadi: beautiful, proud and pitiless.

Serafina was not sure why she had come, but she made her welcome, and etiquette demanded that she should sit on Serafina's right. When they were all assembled, Serafina began to speak.

"Sisters! You know why we have come together: we must decide what to do about these new events. The universe is broken wide, and Lord Asriel has opened the way from this world to another. Should we concern ourselves with it, or live our lives as we have done until now, looking after our own affairs? Then there is the matter of the child Lyra Belacqua, now called Lyra Silvertongue by King Iorek Byrnison. She chose the right cloud-pine spray at the house of Dr Lanselius: she is the child we have always expected, and now she has vanished.

"We have two guests, who will tell us their thoughts. First we shall hear Queen Ruta Skadi."

Ruta Skadi stood. Her white arms gleamed in the firelight, her eyes glittered so brightly that even the furthest witch could see the play of expression on her vivid face.

"Sisters," she began, "let me tell you what is happening, and who it is that we must fight. For there is a war coming. I don't know who will join with us, but I know whom we must fight. It is the Magisterium, the church. For all its history – and that's not long by our lives, but it's many, many of theirs – it's tried to suppress and control every natural impulse. And when it can't control them, it cuts them out. Some of you have seen what they did at Bolvangar. And that was horrible, but it is not the only such place, not the only such practice. Sisters, you know only the north: I have travelled in the south lands. There are churches there, believe me, that cut their children too, as the people of Bolvangar did – not in the same way, but just as horribly – they cut their sexual organs, yes, both boys and girls – they cut them with knives so that they shan't feel. That is what the church does, and every church is the same: control, destroy, obliterate every good feeling. So if a war comes, and the church is on one side of it, we must be on the other, no matter what strange allies we find ourselves bound to.

"What I propose is that our clans join together and go north to explore this new world, and see what we can discover there. If the child is not to be found in our world, it's because she will have gone after Lord Asriel already. And Lord Asriel is the key to this, believe me. He was my lover once, and I would willingly join forces with him, because he hates the church and all it does.

"That is what I have to say."

Ruta Skadi spoke passionately, and Serafina admired her power and her beauty. When the Latvian queen sat down, Serafina turned to Lee Scoresby.

"Mr Scoresby is a friend of the child's, and thus a friend of ours," she said. "Would you tell us your thoughts, sir?"

The Texan got to his feet, whiplash-lean and courteous. He looked as if he were not conscious of the strangeness of the occasion, but he was. His hare-dæmon Hester crouched beside him, her ears flat along her back, her golden eyes half-closed.

"Ma'am," he said, "I have to thank you all first for the kindness you've shown to me, and the help you extended to an aëronaut battered by winds that came from another world. I won't trespass long on your patience.

"When I was travelling north to Bolvangar with the gyptians, the child Lyra told me about something that happened in the college she used to live in, back in Oxford. Lord Asriel had shown the other scholars the severed head of a man called Stanislaus Grumman, and that kinda persuaded them to give him some money to come north and find out what had happened.

"Now the child was so sure of what she'd seen that I didn't like to question her too much. But what she said made a kind of memory come to my mind, except that I couldn't reach it clearly. I knew something about this Dr Grumman. And it was only on the flight here from Svalbard that I remembered what it was. It was an old hunter from Tungusk who told me. It seems that Grumman knew the whereabouts of some kind of object that gives protection to whoever holds it. I don't want to belittle the magic that you witches can command, but this thing, whatever it is, has a kind of power that outclasses anything I've ever heard of.

"And I thought I might postpone my retirement to Texas, because of my concern for that child, and search for Dr Grumman. You see, I don't think he's dead. I think Lord Asriel was fooling those scholars.

"So I'm going to Nova Zembla, where I last heard of him alive, and I'm going to search for him. I cain't see the future, but I can see the present clear enough. And I'm with you in this war, for what my bullets are worth. But that's the task I'm going to take on, ma'am," he concluded, turning back to Serafina Pekkala: "I'm going to seek out Stanislaus Grumman, and find out what he knows, and if I can find that object he knows of, I'll take it to Lyra."

Serafina said, "Have you been married, Mr Scoresby? Have you any children?"

"No, ma'am, I have no child, though I would have liked to be a father. But I understand your question, and you're right: that little girl has had bad luck with her true parents, and maybe I can make it up to her. Someone has to do it, and I'm willing."

"Thank you, Mr Scoresby," she said.

And she took off her crown, and plucked from it one of the little scarlet flowers that, while she wore them, remained as fresh as if they had just been picked.

"Take this with you," she said, "and whenever you need my help, hold it in your hand and call to me. I shall hear you, wherever you are."

"Why, thank you, ma'am," he said, surprised. He took the little flower and tucked it carefully into his breast pocket.

"And we shall call up a wind to help you to Nova Zembla," Serafina Pekkala told him. "Now, sisters, who would like to speak?"

The council proper began. The witches were democratic, up to a point; every witch, even the youngest, had the right to speak, but only their queen had the power to decide. The talk lasted all night, with many passionate voices for open war at once, and some others urging caution, and a few, though those were the wisest, suggesting a mission to all the other witch-clans to urge them to join together for the first time.

Ruta Skadi agreed with that, and Serafina sent out messengers at once. As for what they should do immediately, Serafina picked out twenty of her finest fighters and ordered them to prepare to fly north with her, into the new world that Lord Asriel had opened, and search for Lyra.

"What of you, Queen Ruta Skadi?" Serafina said finally. "What are your plans?"

"I shall search for Lord Asriel, and learn what he's doing from his own lips. And it seems that the way he's gone is northwards too. May I come the first part of the journey with you, sister?"

"You may, and welcome," said Serafina, who was glad to have her company.

So they agreed.

But soon after the council had broken up, an elderly witch came to Serafina Pekkala and said, "You had better listen to what Juta Kamainen has to say, Queen. She's headstrong, but it might be important."

The young witch Juta Kamainen – young by witch standards, that is; she was only just over a hundred years old – was stubborn and embarrassed, and her robin-dæmon was agitated, flying from her shoulder to her hand and circling high above her before settling again briefly on her shoulder. The witch's cheeks were plump and red; she had a vivid and passionate nature. Serafina didn't know her very well.

"Queen," said the young witch, unable to stay silent under

Serafina's gaze, "I know the man Stanislaus Grumman. I used to love him. But I hate him now with such a fervour that if I see him, I shall kill him. I would have said nothing, but my sister made me tell you."

She glanced with hatred at the elder witch, who returned her look with compassion: she knew about love.

"Well," said Serafina, "if he is still alive, he'll have to stay alive until Mr Scoresby finds him. You had better come with us into the new world, and then there'll be no danger of your killing him first. Forget him, Juta Kamainen. Love makes us suffer. But this task of ours is greater than revenge. Remember that."

"Yes, Queen," said the young witch humbly.

And Serafina Pekkala and her twenty-one companions and Queen Ruta Skadi of Latvia prepared to fly into the new world, where no witch had ever flown before.

3

A Children's World

Lyra was awake early. She'd had a horrible dream: she had been given the vacuum flask she'd seen her father Lord Asriel show to the Master and Scholars of Jordan College.

When that had really happened, Lyra had been hiding in the wardrobe, and she'd watched as Lord Asriel opened the flask to show the Scholars the severed head of Stanislaus Grumman the lost explorer; but in her dream, Lyra had to open the flask herself, and she didn't want to. In fact she was terrified. But she had to do it, whether she wanted to or not, and she felt her hands weakening with dread as she unclipped the lid, and heard the air rush into the frozen chamber. Then she lifted the lid away, nearly choking with fear, but knowing she had to, she had to do it. And there was nothing inside. The head had gone. There was nothing to be afraid of.

But she awoke all the same, crying and sweating, in the hot little bedroom facing the harbour, with the moonlight streaming through the window, and lay in someone else's bed clutching someone else's pillow, with the ermine-Pantalaimon nuzzling her and making soothing noises. Oh, she was so frightened! And how odd it was, that in real life she had been eager to see the head of Stanislaus Grumman, and begged Lord Asriel to open the flask again and let her look, and yet in her dream she was so terrified.

When morning came she asked the alethiometer what the dream meant, but all it said was *It was a dream about a head.*

She thought of waking the strange boy, but he was so deeply asleep that she decided not to. Instead she went down to the kitchen and tried to make an omelette, and twenty minutes later she sat down at a table on the pavement and ate the blackened, gritty thing with great pride while the sparrow-Pantalaimon pecked at the bits of shell.

She heard a sound behind her, and there was Will, heavy-eyed with sleep.

"I can make omelette," she said. "I'll make you some if you like."

He looked at her plate and said, "No, I'll have some cereal. There's still some milk in the fridge that's all right. They can't have been gone very long, the people who lived here."

She watched him shake corn flakes into a bowl and pour milk on them: something else she'd never seen before.

He carried the bowl outside and said, "If you don't come from this world, where's your world? How did you get here?"

"Over a bridge. My father made this bridge, and … I followed him across. But he's gone somewhere else, I don't know where. I don't care. But while I was walking across there was so much fog, and I got lost, I think. I walked around in the fog for days just eating berries and stuff I found. Then one day the fog cleared and we was up on that cliff back there –"

She gestured behind her. Will looked along the shore, past the lighthouse, and saw the coast rising in a great series of cliffs that disappeared into the haze of the distance.

"And we saw the town here, and came down, but there was no one here. At least there were things to eat and beds to sleep in. We didn't know what to do next."

"You sure this isn't another part of your world?"

"Course. This en't my world, I know that for certain."

Will remembered his own absolute certainty, on seeing the patch of grass through the window in the air, that it wasn't in his world, and he nodded.

"So there's three worlds at least that are joined on," he said.

"There's millions and millions," Lyra said. "This other dæmon told me. He was a witch's dæmon. No one can count how many worlds there are, all in the same space, but no one could get from one to another before my father made this bridge."

"What about the window I found?"

"I dunno about that. Maybe all the worlds are starting to move into one another."

"And why are you looking for dust?"

She looked at him coldly. "I might tell you some time," she said.

"All right. But how are you going to look for it?"

"I'm going to find a scholar who knows about it."

"What, any scholar?"

"No. An experimental theologian," she said. "In my Oxford, they were the ones who knew about it. Stands to reason it'll be the same in your Oxford. I'll go to Jordan College first, because Jordan had the best ones."

"I never heard of experimental theology," he said.

"They know all about elementary particles and fundamental forces," she explained. "And anbaromagnetism, stuff like that. Atomcraft."

"What–magnetism?"

"Anbaromagnetism. Like anbaric. Those lights," she said, pointing up at the ornamental street light, "they're anbaric."

"We call them electric."

"Electric… That's like electrum. That's a kind of stone, a

jewel, made out of gum from trees. There's insects in it, sometimes."

"You mean amber," he said, and they both said, "Anbar…"

And each of them saw their own expression on the other's face. Will remembered that moment for a long time afterwards.

"Well, electromagnetism," he went on, looking away. "Sounds like what we call physics, your experimental theology. You want scientists, not theologians."

"Ah," she said warily. "I'll find 'em."

They sat in the wide clear morning, with the sun glittering placidly on the harbour, and each of them might have spoken next, because they were both burning with questions; but then they heard a voice from further along the harbour front, towards the casino gardens.

They both looked there, startled. It was a child's voice, but there was no one in sight.

Will said to Lyra quietly, "How long did you say you'd been here?"

"Three days, four, I lost count. I never seen anyone. There's no one here. I looked almost everywhere."

But there was. Two children, one a girl of Lyra's age and the other a younger boy, came out of one of the streets leading down to the harbour. They were carrying baskets, and they both had red hair. They were about a hundred yards away when they saw Will and Lyra at the café table.

Pantalaimon changed from a goldfinch to a mouse and ran up Lyra's arm to the pocket of her shirt. He'd seen that these new children were like Will: neither of them had a dæmon visible.

The two children wandered up and sat at a table nearby.

"You from Ci'gazze?" the girl said.

Will shook his head.

"From Sant'Elia?"

"No," said Lyra. "We're from somewhere else."

The girl nodded. This was a reasonable reply.

"What's happening?" said Will. "Where are the grown-ups?"

The girl's eyes narrowed. "Didn't the Spectres come to your city?" she said.

"No," Will said. "We just got here. We don't know about Spectres. What is this city called?"

"Ci'gazze," the girl said suspiciously. "Cittàgazze, all right."

"Cittàgazze," Lyra repeated. "Ci'gazze. Why do the grown-ups have to leave?"

"Because of the Spectres," the girl said with weary scorn. "What's your name?"

"Lyra. And he's Will. What's yours?"

"Angelica. My brother is Paolo."

"Where've you come from?"

"Up the hills. There was a big fog and storm and everyone was frightened, so we all run up in the hills. Then when the fog cleared the grown-ups could see with telescopes that the city was full of Spectres, so they couldn't come back. But the kids, we ain afraid of Spectres, all right. There's more kids coming down. They be here later, but we're first."

"Us and Tullio," said little Paolo proudly.

"Who's Tullio?"

Angelica was cross: Paolo shouldn't have mentioned him; but the secret was out now.

"Our big brother," she said. "He ain with us. He's hiding till he can... He's just hiding."

"He's gonna get –" Paolo began, but Angelica smacked him hard, and he shut his mouth at once, pressing his quivering lips together.

"What did you say about the city?" said Will. "It's full of Spectres?"

"Yeah, Ci'gazze, Sant'Elia, all cities, the Spectres go where the people are. Where you from?"

"Winchester," said Will.

"I never heard of it. They ain got Spectres there?"

"No. I can't see any here either."

"Course not!" she crowed. "You ain grown up! When we grow up we see Spectres."

"I ain afraid of Spectres, all right," the little boy said, thrusting forward his grubby chin. "Kill the buggers."

"En't the grown-ups going to come back at all?" said Lyra.

"Yeah, in a few days," said Angelica. "When the Spectres go somewhere else. We like it when the Spectres come, 'cause we can run about in the city, do what we like, all right."

"But what do the grown-ups think the Spectres will do to them?" Will said.

"Well, when a Spectre catch a grown-up, that's bad to see. They eat the life out of them there and then, all right. I don't want to be grown-up, for sure. At first they know it's happening, and they're afraid, they cry and cry, they try and look away and pretend it ain happening, but it is. It's too late. And no one ain gonna go near them, they on they own. Then they get pale and they stop moving. They still alive, but it's like they been eaten out from inside. You look in they eyes, you see the back of they heads. Ain nothing there."

The girl turned to her brother and wiped his nose on the sleeve of his shirt.

"Me and Paolo's going to look for ice creams," she said. "You want to come and find some?"

"No," said Will, "we got something else to do."

"Goodbye, then," she said, and Paolo said, "Kill the Spectres!"

"Goodbye," said Lyra.

As soon as Angelica and the little boy had vanished, Pantalaimon appeared from Lyra's pocket, his mouse-head ruffled and bright-eyed.

He said to Will, "They don't know about this window you found."

It was the first time Will had heard him speak, and he was almost more startled by that than by anything else he'd seen so far. Lyra laughed at his astonishment.

"He – but he spoke – do all dæmons talk?" Will said.

"Course they do!" said Lyra. "Did you think he was just a *pet*?"

Will rubbed his hair and blinked. Then he shook his head. "No," he said, addressing Pantalaimon. "You're right, I think. They don't know about it."

"So we'd better be careful how we go through," Pantalaimon said.

It was only strange for a moment, talking to a mouse. Then it was no more strange than talking into a telephone, because he was really talking to Lyra. But the mouse was separate; there was something of Lyra in his expression, but something else too. It was too hard to work out, when there were so many strange things happening at once. Will tried to bring his thoughts together.

"You got to find some clothes first," he said to Lyra, "before you go into my Oxford."

"Why?" she said stubbornly.

"Because you can't go and talk to people in my world looking like that, they wouldn't let you near them. You got to look as if you fit in. You got to go about camouflaged. I *know*, see. I've been doing it for years. You better listen to me or you'll get caught, and if they find out where you come from, and the window, and everything... Well, this is a good hiding-place, this world. See,

61

I'm… I got to hide from some men. This is the best hiding-place I could dream of, and I don't want it found out. So I don't want you giving it away by looking out of place or as if you don't belong. I got my own things to do in Oxford, and if you give me away, I'll kill you."

She swallowed. The alethiometer never lied: this boy was a murderer, and if he'd killed before, he could kill her too. She nodded seriously, and she meant it.

"All right," she said.

Pantalaimon had become a lemur, and was gazing at him with disconcerting wide eyes. Will stared back, and the dæmon became a mouse once more and crept into her pocket.

"Good," he said. "Now while we're here, we'll pretend to these other kids that we just come from somewhere in their world. It's good there aren't any grown-ups about. We can just come and go and no one'll notice. But in my world, you got to do as I say. And the first thing is you better wash yourself. You need to look clean, or you'll stand out. We got to be camouflaged everywhere we go. We got to look as if we belong there so naturally that people don't even notice us. So go and wash your hair for a start. There's some shampoo in the bathroom. Then we'll go and find some different clothes."

"I dunno how," she said. "I never washed my hair. The house-keeper done it at Jordan, and then I never needed to after that."

"Well, you'll just have to work it out," he said. "Wash yourself all over. In my world people are clean."

"H'mm," said Lyra, and went upstairs. A ferocious rat-face glared at him over her shoulder, but he looked back coldly.

Part of him wanted to wander about this sunny silent morning exploring the city, and another part trembled with anxiety for his mother, and another part was still numb with shock at the death he'd caused. And overhanging them all there was the task he had to do. But it was good to keep busy, so while he waited for Lyra he cleaned the working surfaces in the kitchen, and washed the floor, and emptied the rubbish into the bin he found in the alley outside.

Then he took the green leather writing-case from his shopping bag and looked at it longingly. As soon as he'd shown Lyra how to get through the window into his Oxford, he'd come back and look at what was inside; but in the meanwhile, he tucked it under the mattress of the bed he'd slept in. In this world, it was safe.

When Lyra came down, clean and wet, they left to look for some clothes for her. They found a department store, shabby like everywhere else, with clothes in styles that looked a little old-fashioned to Will's eye, but they found Lyra a tartan skirt and a green sleeveless blouse with a pocket for Pantalaimon. She refused to wear jeans: refused even to believe Will when he told her that most girls did.

"They're trousers," she said. "I'm a girl. Don't be stupid."

He shrugged; the tartan skirt looked unremarkable, which was the main thing. Before they left, Will dropped some coins in the till behind the counter.

"What you doing?" she said.

"Paying. You have to pay for things. Don't they pay for things in your world?"

"They don't in this one! I bet those other kids en't paying for a thing."

"They might not, but I do."

"If you start behaving like a grown-up, the Spectres'll get you," she said, but she didn't know whether she could tease him yet, or whether she should be afraid of him.

In the daylight, Will could see how ancient the buildings in the heart of the city were, and how near to ruin some of them had come. Holes in the road had not been repaired; windows were broken, plaster was peeling. And yet there had once been a beauty and grandeur about this place: through carved archways they could see spacious courtyards filled with greenery, and there were great buildings that looked like palaces, for all that the steps were cracked and the door frames loose from the walls. It looked as if rather than knock a building down and build a new one, the citizens of Ci'gazze preferred to patch it up indefinitely.

At one point they came to a tower standing on its own in a little square. It was the oldest building they'd seen: a simple battlemented tower four storeys high. Something about its stillness in the bright sun was intriguing, and both Will and Lyra felt drawn to the half-open door at the top of the broad steps; but they didn't speak of it, and they went half-reluctantly on.

When they reached the broad boulevard with the palm trees, he told her to look for a little café on a corner, with green-painted metal tables on the pavement outside. She found it within a minute. It looked smaller and shabbier by daylight, but it was the same place, with the zinc-topped bar, the espresso machine, the half-finished plate of risotto, now beginning to smell bad in the warm air.

"Is it in here?" she said.

"No. It's in the middle of the road. Make sure there's no other kids around…"

But they were alone. Will took her to the central reservation under the palm trees, and looked around to get his bearings.

"I think it was about here," he said. "When I came through I could just about see that big hill behind the white house up there, and looking this way there was the café there, and…"

"What's it look like? I can't see anything."

"You won't mistake it. It doesn't look like anything you've ever seen."

He cast up and down. Had it vanished? Had it closed? He couldn't see it anywhere.

And then suddenly he had it. He moved back and forth, watching the edge. Just as he'd found the night before, on the Oxford side of it, you could only see it at all from one side: when you moved behind it, it was invisible. And the sun on the grass beyond it was just like the sun on the grass on this side, except unaccountably different.

"Here it is," he said, when he was sure.

"Ah! I see it!"

She was agog: she looked as astounded as he'd looked himself to hear Pantalaimon talk. Her dæmon, unable to remain inside her pocket, had come out to be a wasp, and he buzzed up to the hole and back several times, while she rubbed her still slightly wet hair into spikes.

"Keep to one side," he told her. "If you stand in front of it people'd just see a pair of legs, and that *would* make 'em curious. I don't want anyone noticing."

"What's that noise?"

"Traffic. It's part of the Oxford ring road. It's bound to be busy. Get down and look at it from the side. It's the wrong time of day to go through, really, there's far too many people about. But it'd be hard to find somewhere to go if we went through in the middle of the night. At least once we're through we can blend in easy. You go through first. Just duck through quickly and then move away from the window."

She had a little blue rucksack that she'd been carrying since they left the café, and she unslung it and held it in her arms before crouching to look through.

"Ah –" she gasped. "And that's your world? That don't look like any part of Oxford. You sure you was in Oxford?"

"Course I'm sure. When you go through, you'll see a road

right in front of you. Go to the left, and then a little further along you take the road that goes down to the right. That leads to the city centre. Make sure you can see where this window is, and remember, all right? It's the only way back."

"Right," she said. "I won't forget."

Taking her rucksack in her arms, she ducked through the window in the air and vanished. Will crouched down to see where she went.

And there she was, standing on the grass in his Oxford with Pan still as a wasp on her shoulder, and no one, as far as he could tell, had seen her appear. Cars and trucks raced past a few feet beyond, and no driver, at this busy junction, would have time to gaze sideways at an odd-looking bit of air, even if they could see it, and the traffic screened the window from anyone looking across from the far side.

There was a squeal of brakes, a shout, a bang. He flung himself down to look.

Lyra was lying on the grass. A car had braked so hard that a van had struck it from behind, and knocked the car forward anyway, and there was Lyra, lying still –

Will darted through after her. No one saw him come; all eyes were on the car, the crumpled bumper, the van driver getting out, and on the little girl.

"I couldn't help it – she ran out in front –" said the car driver, a middle-aged woman. "*You* were too close," she said, rounding on the van driver.

"Never mind that," he said, "how's the kid?"

The van driver was addressing Will, who was on his knees beside Lyra. Will looked up and around, but there was nothing for it; he was responsible. On the grass next to him, Lyra was moving her head about, blinking hard. Will saw the wasp-Pantalaimon crawling dazedly up a grass stem beside her.

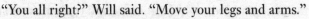

"You all right?" Will said. "Move your legs and arms."

"Stupid!" said the woman from the car. "Just ran out in front. Didn't look once. What am I supposed to do?"

"You still there, love?" said the van driver.

"Yeah," muttered Lyra.

"Everything working?"

"Move your feet and hands," Will insisted.

She did. There was nothing broken.

"She's all right," said Will, "I'll look after her. She's fine."

"D'you know her?" said the truck driver.

"She's my sister," said Will. "It's all right. We just live round the corner. I'll take her home."

Lyra was sitting up now, and as she was obviously not badly hurt, the woman turned her attention back to the car. The rest of the traffic was moving around the two stationary vehicles, and as they went past the drivers looked curiously at the little scene, as people always do. Will helped Lyra up: the sooner they moved away, the better. The woman and the van driver had realized that their argument ought to be handled by their insurance companies, and were exchanging addresses, when the woman saw Will helping Lyra to limp away.

"Wait!" she called. "You'll be witnesses. I need your name and address."

"I'm Mark Ransom," said Will, turning back, "and my sister's Lisa. We live at 26 Bourne Close."

"Postcode?"

"I can never remember," he said. "Look, I want to get her home."

"Hop in the cab," said the van driver, "and I'll take you round."

"No, it's no trouble, it'd be quicker to walk, honest."

Lyra wasn't limping badly. She walked away with Will, back

67

along the grass under the hornbeam trees, and turned around the first corner they came to.

They sat on a low garden wall.

"You hurt?" Will said.

"Banged me leg. And when I fell down it shook me head," she said.

But she was more concerned about what was in the rucksack. She felt inside it and brought out a heavy little bundle wrapped in black velvet and unfolded it. Will's eyes widened to see the alethiometer: the tiny symbols painted around the face, the golden hands, the questing needle, the heavy richness of the case took his breath away.

"What's that?" he said.

"It's my alethiometer. It's a truth-teller. A symbol-reader. I hope it en't broken…"

But it was unharmed. Even in her trembling hands the long needle swung steadily. She put it away and said, "I never seen so many carts and things… I never guessed they was going so fast."

"They don't have cars and vans in your Oxford?"

"Not so many. Not like these ones. I wasn't used to it. But I'm all right now."

"Well be careful from now on. If you go and walk under a bus or get lost or something, they'll realize you're not from this world, and start looking for the way through…"

He was far more angry than he needed to be. Finally he said:

"All right, look. If you pretend you're my sister, that'll be a disguise for me, because the person they're looking for hasn't got a sister. And if I'm with you I can show you how to cross roads without getting killed."

"All right," she said humbly.

"And money. I bet you haven't – well, how could you have any money? How are you going to get around and eat and so on?"

"I have got money," she said, and shook some gold coins out of her purse.

Will looked at them incredulously.

"Is that gold? It is, isn't it? Well, that would get people asking questions, and no mistake. You're just not safe. I'll give you some money. Put those coins away and keep them out of sight. And remember – you're my sister, and your name's Lisa Ransom."

"Lizzie. I pretended to call myself Lizzie before. I can remember that."

"All right, Lizzie then. And I'm Mark. Don't forget."

"All right," she said peaceably.

Her leg was going to be painful; already it was red and swollen where the car had struck it, and a dark massive bruise was forming. What with the bruise on her cheek where he'd struck her the night before, she looked as if she'd been badly treated, and that worried him too: suppose some police officer should become curious?

He tried to put it out of his mind, and they set off together, crossing at the traffic lights and casting just one glance back at the window under the hornbeam trees. They couldn't see it at all. It was quite invisible, and the traffic was flowing again.

In Summertown, ten minutes' walk down the Banbury Road, Will stopped in front of a bank.

"What are you doing?" said Lyra.

"I'm going to get some money. I probably better not do it too often, but they won't register it till the end of the working day, I shouldn't think."

He put his mother's bank card into the automatic dispenser and tapped out her PIN number. Nothing seemed to be going wrong, so he withdrew a hundred pounds, and the machine gave it up without a hitch. Lyra watched open-mouthed. He gave her a twenty-pound note.

"Use that later," he said. "Buy something and get some change. Let's find a bus into town."

Lyra let him deal with the bus, and sat very quiet, watching the houses and gardens of the city that was hers and not hers. It was like being in someone else's dream. They got off in the city centre next to an old stone church, which she did know, opposite a big department store which she didn't.

"It's all changed," she said. "Like… That en't the Cornmarket? And this is the Broad. There's Balliol. And Bodley's Library, down there. But where's Jordan?"

Now she was trembling badly. It might have been delayed reaction from the accident, or present shock from finding an entirely different building in place of the Jordan College she knew as home.

"That en't right," she said. She spoke quietly, because Will had told her to stop pointing out so loudly the things that were wrong. "This is a different Oxford."

"Well, we knew that," he said.

He wasn't prepared for Lyra's wide-eyed helplessness. He couldn't know how much of her childhood had been spent running about streets almost identical with these, and how proud she'd been of belonging to Jordan College, whose scholars were the cleverest, whose coffers the richest, whose beauty the most splendid of all; and now it simply wasn't there, and she wasn't Lyra of Jordan any more; she was a lost little girl in a strange world, belonging nowhere.

"Well," she said shakily. "If it en't there…"

It was going to take longer than she'd thought, that was all.

4

Trepanning

As soon as Lyra had gone her way, Will found a phone box and dialled the number of the lawyer's office on the letter he held.

"Hello? I want to speak to Mr Perkins."

"Who's calling, please?"

"It's in connection with Mr John Parry. I'm his son."

"Just a moment, please…"

A minute went by and then a man's voice said, "Hello. This is Alan Perkins. Who am I speaking to?"

"William Parry. Excuse me for calling. It's about my father Mr John Parry. You send money every three months from my father to my mother's bank account."

"Yes…"

"Well, I want to know where my father is, please. Is he alive or dead?"

"How old are you, William?"

"Twelve. I want to know about him."

"Yes… Has your mother, is she, does she know you're phoning me?"

Will thought carefully.

"No," he said. "But she's not in very good health. She can't tell me very much and I want to know."

"Yes, I see. Where are you now? Are you at home?"

"No, I'm … I'm in Oxford."

"On your own?"

"Yes."

"And your mother's not well, you say?"

"No."

"Is she in hospital or something?"

"Something like that. Look, can you tell me or not?"

"Well, I can tell you something, but not much and not right now, and I'd rather not do it over the phone. I'm seeing a client in five minutes… Can you find your way to my office at about half-past two?"

"No," Will said. It would be too risky: the lawyer might have heard by then that he was wanted by the police. He thought quickly, and went on, "I've got to catch a bus to Nottingham and I don't want to miss it. But what I want to know, you can tell me over the phone, can't you? All I want to know is, is my father alive, and if he is, where I can find him. You can tell me that, can't you?"

"It's not quite as simple as that. I can't really give out private information about a client unless I'm sure the client would want me to. And I'd need some proof of who you were, anyway."

"Yes, I understand, but can you just tell me whether he's alive or dead?"

"Well… No, that wouldn't be confidential. Unfortunately I can't tell you anyway, because I don't know."

"What?"

"The money comes from a family trust. He left instructions to pay it until he told me to stop. I haven't heard from him from that day to this. What it boils down to is that he's… Well, I suppose he's vanished. That's why I can't answer your question."

"Vanished? Just … lost?"

"It's a matter of public record, actually. Look, why don't you come into the office and –"

"I can't. I'm going to Nottingham."

"Well, write to me or get your mother to write and I'll let you know what I can. But you must understand, I can't do very much over the phone."

"Yes, I suppose so. All right. But can you tell me where he disappeared?"

"As I say, it's a matter of public record. There were several newspaper stories at the time. You know he was an explorer?"

"My mother's told me some things, yes…"

"Well, he was leading an expedition and it just disappeared. About ten years ago."

"Where?"

"The far north. Alaska, I think. You can look it up in the public library. Why don't you –"

But at that point Will's money ran out, and he hadn't got any more change. The dialling tone purred in his ear. He put the phone down and looked around.

What he wanted above all was to speak to his mother. He had to stop himself dialling Mrs Cooper's number, because if he heard his mother's voice it would be very hard not to go back to her, and that would put them both in danger. But he could send her a postcard.

He chose a view of the city, and wrote, "Dear Mum, I am safe and well, and I will see you again soon. I hope everything is all right. I love you. Will." Then he addressed it and bought a stamp and held the card close to him for a minute before dropping it in the letter box.

It was mid-morning, and he was in the main shopping street, where buses shouldered their way through crowds of pedestrians. He began to realize how exposed he was; for it was a weekday, when a child of his age should have been in school. Where could he go?

It didn't take him long to hide. Will could vanish easily enough, because he was good at it; he was even proud of his skill. The way he did it was similar to the way Serafina Pekkala had made herself invisible on the ship: he made himself intensely inconspicuous. He made himself part of the background.

So now, knowing the sort of world he lived in, he went into a stationery shop and bought a ballpoint, a pad of paper, and a clipboard. Schools often sent groups of kids off to do a shopping survey, or something of the sort, and if he seemed to be on a project like that he wouldn't look as if he was at a loose end.

Then he wandered along, pretending to be making notes, and kept his eyes open for the public library.

Meanwhile, Lyra was looking for somewhere quiet to consult the alethiometer. In her own Oxford there would have been a dozen places within five minutes' walk, but this Oxford was so disconcertingly different, with patches of poignant familiarity right next to the downright outlandish: why had they painted those yellow lines on the road? What were those little white patches dotting every pavement? (In her own world, they had never heard of chewing gum.) What could those red and green lights mean at the corner of the road? It was all much harder to read than the alethiometer.

But here were St John's College gates, which she and Roger had once climbed after dark to plant fireworks in the flowerbeds; and that particular worn stone at the corner of Catte Street – there were the initials SP that Simon Parslow had scratched, the very same ones! She'd seen him do it! Someone in this world with the same initials must have stood here idly and done exactly the same.

There might be a Simon Parslow in this world.

Perhaps there was a Lyra.

A chill ran down her back, and mouse-shaped Pantalaimon shivered in her pocket. She shook herself; there were mysteries enough without imagining more.

The other way in which this Oxford differed from hers was in the vast numbers of people swarming on every pavement, in and out of every building; people of every sort, women dressed like men, Africans, even a group of Tartars meekly following their leader, all neatly dressed and hung about with little black cases. She glared at them fearfully at first, because they had no dæmons, and in her world they would have been regarded as ghasts, or worse.

But (this was the strangest thing) they all looked fully alive. These creatures moved about cheerfully enough, for all the world as though they were human, and Lyra had to concede that human was what they probably were, and that their dæmons were inside them as Will's was.

After wandering about for an hour taking the measure of this mock-Oxford, she felt hungry and bought a bar of chocolatl with her twenty-pound note. The shopkeeper looked at her oddly, but he was from the Indies and didn't understand her accent, perhaps, although she asked very clearly. With the change she bought an apple from the Covered Market, which was much more like the proper Oxford, and walked up towards the park. There she found herself outside a grand building, a real Oxford-looking building that didn't exist in herworld at all, though it wouldn't have looked out of place. She sat on the grass outside to eat, and regarded the building approvingly.

She discovered that it was a museum. The doors were open, and inside she found stuffed animals and fossil skeletons and cases of minerals, just like the Royal Geological Museum she'd visited with Mrs Coulter in her London. At the back of the great iron and glass hall was the entrance to another part of the museum, and because it was nearly deserted, she went through and looked around. The alethiometer was still the most urgent thing on her mind, but in this second chamber she found herself surrounded by things she knew well: there were showcases filled with Arctic clothing, just like her own furs – with sledges and walrus ivory carvings and seal-hunting harpoons – with a thousand and one jumbled trophies and relics and objects of magic and tools and weapons, and not only from the Arctic, as she saw, but from every part of this world.

Well, how strange. Those caribou-skin furs were *exactly* the same as hers, but they'd tied the traces on that sledge completely wrong. But here was a photogram showing some Samoyed hunters, the very doubles of the ones who'd caught Lyra and sold her to Bolvangar: look! They were the same men! And even that rope had frayed and been re-knotted in precisely the same spot, and she knew it intimately, having been tied up in that very sledge for several agonizing hours… What were these mysteries? Was there only one world after all, which spent its time dreaming of others?

And then she came across something that made her think of the alethiometer again. In an old glass case with a black-painted wooden frame there were a number of human skulls, and some of them had holes in them: some at the front, some on the side, some on the top. The one in the centre had two. This process, it said in spidery writing on a card, was called trepanning. The card also said that all the holes had been made during the owners' lifetimes, because the bone had healed and grown smooth around the edge. One, however, hadn't: the hole had been made by a bronze arrow-head which was still in it, and its edges were sharp and broken, so you could tell it was different.

This was just what the northern Tartars did. And what Stanislaus Grumman had had done to himself, according to the Jordan scholars who'd known him. Lyra looked around quickly, saw no one nearby, and took out the alethiometer.

She focused her mind on the central skull and asked: What sort of person did this skull belong to, and why did he have those holes made in it?

As she stood concentrating in the dusty light that filtered through the glass roof and slanted down past the upper galleries, she didn't notice that she was being watched.

A powerful-looking man in his sixties, wearing a beautifully-tailored linen suit and holding a panama hat, stood on the gallery above and looked down over the iron railing.

His grey hair was brushed neatly back from his smooth, tanned, barely wrinkled forehead. His eyes were large, dark and long-lashed and intense, and every minute or so his sharp, dark-pointed tongue peeped out at the corner of his lips and flicked across them moistly. The snowy handkerchief in his breast pocket was scented with some heavy cologne like those hot-house plants so rich you can smell the decay at their roots.

He had been watching Lyra for some minutes. He had moved along the gallery above as she moved about below, and when she stood still by the case of skulls, he watched her closely, taking in all of her: her rough untidy hair, the bruise on her cheek, the new clothes, her bare neck arched over the alethiometer, her bare legs.

He shook out the breast pocket handkerchief and mopped his forehead, and then made for the stairs.

Lyra, absorbed, was learning strange things. These skulls were unimaginably old; the cards in the case said simply "Bronze Age", but the alethiometer, which never lied, said that the man whose skull it was had lived thirty-three thousand two hundred and fifty-four years before the present day, and that he had been a sorcerer, and that the hole had been made to let the gods into his head. And then the alethiometer, in the casual way it sometimes had of answering a question Lyra hadn't asked, added that there was a good deal more Dust around the trepanned skulls than around the one with the arrow-head.

What in the world could that mean? Lyra came out of the focused calm she shared with the alethiometer and drifted back to the present moment, to find herself no longer alone. Gazing into the next case was an elderly man in a pale suit, who smelled sweetly. He reminded her of someone, but she couldn't think who.

He became aware of her staring at him, and looked up with a smile.

"You're looking at the trepanned skulls?" he said. "What strange things people do to themselves."

"Mm," she said expressionlessly.

"D'you know, people still do that?"

"Yeah," she said.

"Hippies, you know, people like that. Actually you're far too young to remember hippies. They say it's more effective than taking drugs."

Lyra had put the alethiometer in her rucksack, and was wondering how she could get away: she still hadn't asked it the main question, and now this old man was having a conversation with her. He seemed nice enough, and he certainly smelled nice. He was closer now. His hand brushed hers as he leaned across the case.

"Makes you wonder, doesn't it? No anaesthetic, no disinfectant, probably done with stone tools. They must have been tough, mustn't they? I don't think I've seen you here before. I come here quite a lot. What's your name?"

"Lizzie," she said comfortably.

"Lizzie. Hello, Lizzie. I'm Charles. Do you go to school in Oxford?"

She wasn't sure how to answer.

"No," she said.

"Just visiting? Well, you've chosen a wonderful place to look at. What are you specially interested in?"

She was more puzzled by this man than by anyone she'd met for a long time. On the one hand he was kind and friendly and very clean and smartly dressed, but on the other hand Pantalaimon, inside her pocket, was plucking at her attention and begging her to be careful, because he was half-remembering something too; and from somewhere she sensed, not a smell, but the idea of a smell, and it was the smell of dung, of putrefaction. She was reminded of Iofur Raknison's palace, where the air was perfumed but the floor was thick with filth.

"What am I interested in?" she said. "Oh, all sorts really. Those skulls I got interested in just now, when I saw them there. I shouldn't think anyone would want that done. It's horrible."

"No, I wouldn't enjoy it myself, but I promise you it does happen. I could take you to meet someone who's done it," he said, looking so friendly and helpful that she was very nearly tempted. But then out came that little dark tongue-point, as quick as a snake's, flick-moisten, and she shook her head.

"I got to go," she said. "Thank you for offering, but I better not. Anyway I got to go now because I'm meeting someone. My friend," she added. "Who I'm staying with."

"Yes, of course," he said kindly. "Well, it was nice talking to you. Bye-bye, Lizzie."

"Bye," she said.

"Oh – just in case – here's my name and address," he said, handing her a little slip of card, "just in case you want to know more about things like this."

"Thank you," she said blandly, and put it in the pocket on the back of her rucksack before leaving. She felt he was watching her all the way out.

Once she was outside the museum she turned into the park, which she knew as a field for cricket and other sports, and found a quiet spot under some trees and tried the alethiometer again.

This time she asked where she could find a scholar who knew about Dust. The answer she got was simple: it directed her to a certain room in the tall square building behind her. In fact the answer was so straightforward, and came so abruptly, that Lyra was sure the alethiometer had more to say: she was beginning to sense now that it had moods, like a person, and to know when it wanted to tell her more.

And it did now. What it said was: *You must concern yourself with the boy. Your task is to help him find his father. Put your mind to that.*

She blinked. She was genuinely startled. Will had appeared out of nowhere in order to help her: surely that was obvious. The idea that she had come all this way in order to help him took her breath away.

But the alethiometer still hadn't finished. The needle twitched again, and she read:

Do not lie to the scholar.

She folded the velvet around the alethiometer and thrust it into the rucksack out of sight. Then she stood and looked around for the building where her scholar would be found, and set off towards it, feeling awkward and defiant.

Will found the library easily enough. The reference librarian was perfectly prepared to believe that he was doing some research for a geography project, and helped him find the bound copies of *The Times* index for the year of his birth, which was when his

father had disappeared. Will sat down to look through. Sure
enough, there were several references to John Parry, in
connection with an archaeological expedition.

Each month, he found, was on a separate roll of microfilm. He
threaded each in turn into the projector, scrolled through to find
the stories, and read them with fierce attention. The first story
told of the departure of an expedition to the north of Alaska. The
expedition was sponsored by the Institute of Archaeology at
Oxford University, and it was going to survey an area in which
they hoped to find evidence of early human settlements. It was
accompanied by John Parry, late of the Royal Marines, a
professional explorer.

The second story was dated six weeks later. It said briefly that
the expedition had reached the North American Arctic Survey
Station at Noatak in Alaska.

The third was dated two months after that. It said that there
had been no reply to signals from the Survey Station, and that
John Parry and his companions were presumed missing.

There was a brief series of articles following that, describing
the parties that had set out fruitlessly to look for them, the search
flights over the Bering Sea, the reaction of the Institute of
Archaeology, interviews with relatives...

His heart thudded, because there was a picture of his own
mother. Holding a baby. Him.

The reporter had written a standard tearful-wife-waiting-in-
anguish-for-news story, which Will found disappointingly short
of actual facts. There was a brief paragraph saying that John Parry
had had a successful career in the Royal Marines and had left to
specialize in organizing geographical and scientific expeditions,
and that was all.

There was no other mention in the index, and Will got up
from the microfilm reader baffled. There must be some more

information somewhere else; but where could he go next? And if he took too long searching for it, he'd be traced…

He handed back the rolls of microfilm and asked the librarian, "Do you know the address of the Institute of Archaeology, please?"

"I could find out… What school are you from?"

"St Peter's," said Will.

"That's not in Oxford, is it?"

"No, it's in Hampshire. My class is doing a sort of residential field trip. Kind of environmental study research skills…"

"Oh, I see. What was it you wanted… Archaeology… Here we are."

Will copied down the address and phone number, and since it was safe to admit he didn't know Oxford, asked where to find it. It wasn't far away. He thanked the librarian and set off.

Inside the building Lyra found a wide desk at the foot of the stairs, with a porter behind it.

"Where are you going?" he said.

This was like home again. She felt Pan, in her pocket, enjoying it.

"I got a message for someone on the second floor," she said.

"Who?"

"Dr Lister," she said.

"Dr Lister's on the third floor. If you've got something for him, you can leave it here and I'll let him know."

"Yeah, but this is something he needs right now. He just sent for it. It's not a *thing* actually, it's something I need to tell him."

He looked at her carefully, but he was no match for the bland and vacuous docility Lyra could command when she wanted to; and finally he nodded and went back to his newspaper.

The alethiometer didn't tell Lyra people's names, of course.

She read the name Dr Lister off a pigeonhole on the wall behind him, because if you pretend you know someone, they're more likely to let you in. In some ways Lyra knew Will's world better than he did.

On the second floor she found a long corridor, where one door was open to an empty lecture theatre and another to a smaller room where two scholars stood discussing something at a blackboard. These rooms, the walls of this corridor, were all flat and bare and plain in a way Lyra thought belonged to poverty, not to the scholarship and splendour of Oxford; and yet the brick walls were smoothly painted, and the doors were of heavy wood and the banisters of polished steel, so they were costly. It was just another way in which this world was strange.

She soon found the door the alethiometer had told her about. The label pinned to it said "Dark Matter Research Unit", and under it someone had scribbled R.I.P. Another hand had added in pencil "Director: Lazarus".

Lyra made nothing of that. She knocked, and a woman's voice said, "Come in."

It was a small room, crowded with tottering piles of papers and books, and the whiteboards on the walls were covered in figures and equations. Pinned to the back of the door was a design that looked Chinese. Through an open doorway Lyra could see another room, where some kind of complicated anbaric machinery stood in silence.

For her part, Lyra was a little surprised to find that the scholar she sought was female, but the alethiometer hadn't said a man, and this was a strange world, after all. The woman was sitting at an engine that displayed figures and shapes on a small glass screen, in front of which all the letters of the alphabet had been laid out on grimy little blocks in an ivory tray. The scholar tapped one and the screen became blank.

"Who are you?" she said.

Lyra shut the door behind her. Mindful of what the alethiometer had told her, she tried hard not to do what she normally would have done, and she told the truth.

"Lyra Silvertongue," she answered. "What's your name?"

The woman blinked. She was in her late thirties, Lyra supposed, perhaps a little older than Mrs Coulter, with short black hair and red cheeks. She wore a white coat open over a green shirt and those blue canvas trousers so many people wore in this world.

At Lyra's question the woman ran a hand through her hair and said, "Well, you're the second unexpected thing that's happened today. I'm Doctor Mary Malone. What do you want?"

"I want you to tell me about Dust," said Lyra, having looked around to make sure they were alone. "I know you know about it. I can prove it. You got to tell me."

"Dust? What are you talking about?"

"You might not call it that. It's elementary particles. In my world the scholars call it Rusakov Particles, but normally they call it Dust. They don't show up easily, but they come out of space and fix on people. Not children so much, though. Mostly on grown-ups. And something I only found out today – I was in that museum down the road and there was some old skulls with holes in their heads, like the Tartars make, and there was a lot more Dust round them than round this other one that hadn't got that sort of hole in. When's the Bronze Age?"

The woman was looking at her wide-eyed.

"The Bronze Age? Goodness, I don't know; about five thousand years ago," she said.

"Ah, well, they got it wrong then, when they wrote that label. That skull with the two holes in is thirty-three thousand years old."

She stopped then, because Dr Malone looked as if she was about to faint. The high colour left her cheeks completely, she put one hand to her breast while the other clutched the arm of her chair, and her jaw dropped.

Lyra stood, stubborn and puzzled, waiting for her to recover.

"Who are you?" the woman said at last.

"Lyra Silver –"

"No, where d'you come from? What are you? How do you know things like this?"

Wearily Lyra sighed; she had forgotten how roundabout scholars could be. It was difficult to tell them the truth when a lie would have been so much easier for them to understand.

"I come from another world," she began. "And in that world there's an Oxford like this, only different, and that's where I come from. And –"

"Wait, wait, wait. You come from where?"

"From somewhere else," said Lyra, more carefully. "Not here."

"Oh, somewhere else," the woman said. "I see. Well, I think I see."

"And I got to find out about Dust," Lyra explained. "Because the Church people in my world, right, they're frightened of Dust because they think it's original sin. So it's very important. And my father... No," she said passionately, and even stamped, "that's not what I meant to say. I'm doing it all wrong."

Dr Malone looked at Lyra's desperate frown and clenched fists, at the bruises on her cheek and her leg, and said, "Dear me, child, calm down..."

She broke off and rubbed her eyes, which were red with tiredness.

"Why am I listening to you?" she went on. "I must be crazy. The fact is, this is the only place in the world where you'd get the

85

answer you want, and they're about to close us down... What you're talking about, your Dust, sounds like something we've been investigating for a while now, and what you say about the skulls in the museum gave me a turn, because... Oh, no, this is just too much. I'm too tired. I want to listen to you, believe me, but not now, please. Did I say they were going to close us down? I've got a week to put together a proposal to the funding committee, but we haven't got a hope in hell..."

She yawned widely.

"What was the first unexpected thing that happened today?" Lyra said.

"Oh. Yes. Someone I'd been relying on to back our funding application withdrew his support. I don't suppose it was *that* unexpected, anyway."

She yawned again.

"I'm going to make some coffee," she said. "If I don't I'll fall asleep. You'll have some too?"

She filled an electric kettle, and while she spooned instant coffee into two mugs Lyra stared at the Chinese pattern on the back of the door.

"What's that?" she said.

"It's Chinese. The symbols of the I Ching. D'you know what that is? Do they have that in your world?"

Lyra looked at her narrow-eyed, in case she was being sarcastic. She said: "There are some things the same and some that are different, that's all. I don't know everything about my world. Maybe they got this Ching thing there too."

"I'm sorry," said Dr Malone. "Yes, maybe they have."

"What's dark matter?" said Lyra. "That's what it says on the notice, isn't it?"

Dr Malone sat down again, and hooked another chair out with her ankle for Lyra.

She said, "Dark matter is what my research team is looking for. No one knows what it is. There's more stuff out there in the universe than we can see, that's the point. We can see the stars and the galaxies and the things that shine, but for it all to hang together and not fly apart, there needs to be a lot more of it – to make gravity work, you see. But no one can detect it. So there are lots of different research projects trying to find out what it is, and this is one of them."

Lyra was all focused attention. At last the woman was talking seriously.

"And what do you think it is?" she asked.

"Well, what *we* think it is…" she began, as the kettle boiled, so she got up and made the coffee as she continued: "We think it's some kind of elementary particle. Something quite different from anything discovered so far. But they're very hard to detect… Where do you go to school? Do you study physics?"

Lyra felt Pantalaimon nip her hand, warning her not to get cross. It was all very well the alethiometer telling her to be truthful, but she knew what would happen if she told the whole truth. She had to tread carefully, and just avoid direct lies.

"Yes," she said, "I know a little bit. But not about dark matter."

"Well, we're trying to detect this almost undetectable thing among the noise of all the other particles crashing about. Normally they put detectors hundreds of metres underground, but what we've done instead is to set up an electromagnetic field around the detector that shuts out the things we don't want and lets through the ones we do. Then we amplify the signal and put it through a computer."

She handed across a mug of coffee. There was no milk and no sugar, but she did find a couple of ginger biscuits in a drawer, and Lyra took one hungrily.

"And we found a particle that fits," Dr Malone went on. "We think it fits. But it's so strange… Why am I telling you this? I shouldn't. It's not published, it's not refereed, it's not even written down. I'm a little crazy this afternoon.

"Well…" she went on, and she yawned for so long that Lyra thought she'd never stop … "our particles are strange little devils and no mistake. We call them shadow-particles, Shadows. You know what nearly knocked me off my chair just now? When you mentioned the skulls in the museum. Because one of our team, you see, is a bit of an amateur archaeologist. And he discovered something one day that we couldn't believe. But we couldn't ignore it, because it fitted in with the craziest thing of all about these Shadows. You know what? They're conscious. That's right. Shadows are particles of consciousness. You ever heard anything so stupid? No wonder we can't get our grant renewed."

She sipped her coffee. Lyra was drinking in every word like a thirsty flower.

"Yes," Dr Malone went on, "they know we're here. They answer back. And here goes the crazy part: you can't see them unless you expect to. Unless you put your mind in a certain state. You have to be confident and relaxed at the same time. You have to be capable – where's that quotation…"

She reached into the muddle of papers on her desk, and found a scrap on which someone had written with a green pen. She read:

"'…capable of being in uncertainties, mysteries, doubts, without any irritable reaching after fact and reason –' You have to get into that state of mind. That's from the poet Keats, by the way. I found it the other day. So you get yourself in the right state of mind, and then you look at the Cave –"

"The cave?" said Lyra.

"Oh, sorry. The computer. We call it the Cave. Shadows on

the walls of the Cave, you see, from Plato. That's our archaeologist again. He's an all-round intellectual. But he's gone off to Geneva for a job interview, and I don't suppose for a moment he'll be back… Where was I? OK, the Cave, that's right. Once you're linked up to it, if you *think*, the Shadows respond. There's no doubt about it. The Shadows flock to your thinking like birds…"

"What about the skulls?"

"I was coming to that. Oliver Payne, him, my colleague, was fooling about one day testing things with the Cave. And it was so odd. It didn't make any sense in the way a physicist would expect. He got a piece of ivory, just a lump, and there were no Shadows with that. It didn't react. But a carved ivory chess piece did. A big splinter of wood off a plank didn't, but a wooden ruler did. And a carved wooden statuette had more… I'm talking about elementary particles here, for goodness' sake. Little minute lumps of scarcely anything. *They knew what these objects were*. Anything that was associated with human workmanship and human thought was surrounded by Shadows…

"And then Oliver, Dr Payne, got some fossil skulls from a friend at the museum and tested them to see how far back in time the effect went. There was a cut-off point about thirty, forty thousand years ago. Before that, no Shadows. After that, plenty. And that's about the time, apparently, that modern human beings first appeared. I mean, you know, our remote ancestors, but people no different from us, really…"

"It's Dust," said Lyra authoritatively. "That's what it is."

"But you see, you can't say this sort of thing in a funding application if you want to be taken seriously. It does not make sense. It cannot exist. It's impossible, and if it isn't impossible it's irrelevant, and if it isn't either of those things it's embarrassing."

"I want to see the Cave," said Lyra.

She stood up.

Dr Malone was running her hands through her hair and blinking hard to keep her tired eyes clear.

"Well, I can't see why not," she said. "We might not have a Cave tomorrow. Come along through."

She led Lyra into the other room. It was larger, and crowded with electronic equipment.

"This is it. Over there," she said, pointing to a screen which was glowing with an empty grey, "that's where the detector is, behind all that wiring. To see the Shadows you have to be linked up to some electrodes. Like for measuring brain waves."

"I want to try it," said Lyra.

"You won't see anything. Anyway I'm tired. It's too complicated."

"Please! I know what I'm doing!"

"Do you, now. I wish I did. *No*, for heaven's sake. This is an expensive, difficult scientific experiment. You can't come charging in here and expect to have a go as if it was a pinball machine… Where *do* you come from, anyway? Shouldn't you be at school? How did you find your way in here?"

And she rubbed her eyes again, as if she was only just waking up.

Lyra was trembling. *Tell the truth*, she thought. "I found my way in with this," she said, and took out the alethiometer.

"What in the world is that? A compass?"

Lyra let her take it. Dr Malone's eyes widened as she felt the weight.

"Dear Lord, it's made of gold. Where on earth –"

"I think it does what your Cave does. That's what I want to find out. If I can answer a question truly," said Lyra desperately, "something you know the answer to and I don't, can I try your Cave then?"

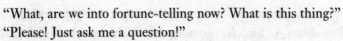

"What, are we into fortune-telling now? What is this thing?"

"Please! Just ask me a question!"

Dr Malone shrugged. "Oh, all right," she said. "Tell me... Tell me what I was doing before I took up this business."

Eagerly Lyra took the alethiometer from her and turned the winding-wheels. She could feel her mind reaching for the right pictures even before the hands were pointing at them, and she sensed the longer needle twitching to respond. As it began to swing round the dial her eyes followed it, watching, calculating, seeing down the long chains of meaning to the level where the truth lay.

Then she blinked and sighed and came out of her temporary trance.

"You used to be a nun," she said. "I wouldn't have guessed that. Nuns are supposed to stay in their convents for ever. But you stopped believing in church things and they let you leave. This en't like my world at all, not a bit."

Dr Malone sat down in the only chair, staring.

Lyra said, "That's true, en't it?"

"Yes. And you found out from that..."

"From my alethiometer. It works by Dust, I think. I came all this way to find out more about Dust, and it told me to come to you. So I reckon your dark matter must be the same thing. *Now* can I try your Cave?"

Dr Malone shook her head, but not to say no, just out of helplessness. She spread her hands. "Very well," she said. "I think I'm dreaming. I might as well carry on."

She swung round in her chair and pressed several switches, bringing an electrical hum and the sound of a computer's cooling fan into the air; and at the sound of them, Lyra gave a little muffled gasp. It was because the sound in that room was the same sound she'd heard in that dreadful glittering chamber at

Bolvangar, where the silver guillotine had nearly parted her and Pantalaimon. She felt him quiver in her pocket, and gently squeezed him for reassurance.

But Dr Malone hadn't noticed; she was too busy adjusting switches and tapping the letters in another of those ivory trays. As she did, the screen changed colour, and some small letters and figures appeared on it.

"Now you sit down," she said, and gave the chair to Lyra. Then she opened a small jar and said, "I need to put some gel on your skin to help the electrical contact. It washes off easily. Hold still, now."

Dr Malone took six wires, each ending in a flat pad, and attached them to various places on Lyra's head. Lyra sat determinedly still, but she was breathing quickly, and her heart was beating hard.

"All right, you're all hooked up," said Dr Malone. "The room's full of Shadows. The universe is full of Shadows, come to that. But this is the only way we can see them, when you make your mind empty and look at the screen. Off you go."

Lyra looked. The glass was dark and blank. She saw her own reflection dimly, but that was all. As an experiment she pretended that she was reading the alethiometer, and imagined herself asking: What does this woman know about Dust? What questions is *she* asking?

She mentally moved the alethiometer's hands around the dial, and as she did, the screen began to flicker. Astonished, she came out of her concentration, and the flicker died. She didn't notice the ripple of excitement that made Dr Malone sit up: she frowned and sat forward and began to concentrate again.

This time the response came instantaneously. A stream of dancing lights, for all the world like the shimmering curtains of the aurora, blazed across the screen. They took up patterns that were held for a moment only to break apart and form again, in different shapes, or different colours; they looped and swayed, they sprayed apart, they burst into showers of radiance that suddenly swerved this way or that like a flock of birds changing direction in the sky. And as Lyra watched, she felt the same sense, as of trembling on the brink of understanding, that she remembered from the time when she was beginning to read the alethiometer.

She asked another question: Is *this* Dust? Is it the same thing making these patterns and moving the needle of the alethiometer?

The answer came in more loops and swirls of light. She guessed it meant yes. Then another thought occurred to her, and she turned to speak to Dr Malone, and saw her open-mouthed, hand to her head.

"What?" she said.

The screen faded. Dr Malone blinked.

"What is it?" Lyra said again.

"Oh – you've just put on the best display I've ever seen, that's all," said Dr Malone. "What were you doing? What were you thinking?"

"I was thinking you could get it clearer than this," Lyra said.

"Clearer? That's the clearest it's ever been!"

"But what does it mean? Can you read it?"

"Well," said Dr Malone, "you don't *read* it in the sense of reading a message, it doesn't work like that. What's happening is that the Shadows are responding to the attention that you pay them. That's revolutionary enough: it's our consciousness that they respond to, you see."

"No," Lyra explained, "what I mean is, those colours and shapes up there. They could do other things, those Shadows. They could make any shapes you wanted. They could make pictures if you wanted them to. Look."

And she turned back and focused her mind again, but this time she pretended to herself that the screen was the alethiometer, with all thirty-six symbols laid out round the edge. She knew them so well now that her fingers automatically twisted in her lap as she moved the imaginary hands to point at the candle (for understanding), the alpha and omega (for language), and the ant (for diligence), and framed the question: What would these people have to do in order to understand the language of the Shadows?

The screen responded as quickly as thought itself, and out of the welter of lines and flashes a series of pictures formed with perfect clarity: compasses, alpha and omega again, lightning, angel. Each picture flashed up a different number of times, and then came a different three: camel, garden, moon.

Lyra saw their meanings clearly, and unfocused her mind to explain. This time, when she turned around, she saw that Dr Malone was sitting back in her chair, white-faced, clutching the edge of the table.

"What it says," Lyra told her, "it's saying in my language, right, the language of pictures. Like the alethiometer. But what it says is that it could use ordinary language too, words, if you fixed it up like that. You could fix this so it put words on the screen. But you'd need a lot of careful figuring with numbers – that was the compasses, see – and the lightning meant anbaric, I mean electric power, more of that. And the angel – that's all about messages. There's things it wants to say. But when it went on to that second bit… It meant Asia, almost the furthest east but not quite. I dunno what country that would be – China, maybe… And there's a way they have in that country of talking to Dust, I mean Shadows, same as you got here and I got with the – I got with pictures, only their way uses sticks. I think it meant that picture on the door, but I didn't understand it really. I thought

94

when I first saw it there was something important about it, only I didn't know what. So there must be lots of ways of talking to Shadows."

Dr Malone was breathless.

"The I Ching," she said. "Yes, it's Chinese. A form of divination – fortune-telling, really… And yes, they use sticks. It's only up there for decoration," she said, as if to reassure Lyra that she didn't really believe in it. "You're telling me that when people consult the I Ching, they're getting in touch with Shadow-particles? With dark matter?"

"Yeah," said Lyra. "There's lots of ways, like I said. I hadn't realized before. I thought there was only one."

"Those pictures on the screen…" Dr Malone began.

Lyra felt a flicker of a thought at the edge of her mind, and turned back to the screen. She had hardly begun to formulate a question when more pictures flashed up, succeeding each other so quickly that Dr Malone could hardly follow them; but Lyra knew what they were saying, and turned back to her.

"It says that *you're* important, too," she told the scientist. "It says you got something important to do. I dunno what, but it wouldn't say that unless it was true. So you probably ought to get it using words, so you can understand what it says."

Dr Malone was silent. Then she said:

"All right, where *do* you come from?"

Lyra twisted her mouth. She realized that Dr Malone, who until now had acted out of exhaustion and despair, would never normally have shown her work to a strange child who turned up from nowhere, and that she was beginning to regret it. But Lyra had to tell the truth.

"I come from another world," she said. "It's true. I came through to this one. I was … I had to run away, because people in my world were chasing me, to kill me. And the alethiometer comes from … from the same place. The Master of Jordan College gave it me. In *my* Oxford there's a Jordan College, but there en't one here. I looked. And I found out how to read the alethiometer by myself. I got a way of making my mind go blank, and I just see what they mean straight away. Just like you said about … doubts and mysteries and that. So when I looked at the Cave I done the same thing and it works just the same way, so my Dust and your Shadows are the same, too. So…"

Dr Malone was fully awake now. Lyra picked up the alethiometer and folded its velvet cloth over it, like a mother protecting her child, before putting it back in her rucksack.

"So anyway," she said, "you could make this screen so it could talk to you in words, if you wanted. Then you could talk to the Shadows like I talk to the alethiometer. But what I want to know is, why do the people in my world hate it? Dust, I mean, Shadows. Dark matter. They want to destroy it. They think it's evil. But I think what *they* do is evil. I seen them do it. So what is it, Shadows? Is it good or evil, or what?"

Dr Malone rubbed her face and made her cheeks even redder than they were.

"Everything about this is *embarrassing*," she said. "D'you know how embarrassing it is to mention good and evil in a scientific laboratory? Have you any idea? One of the reasons I became a scientist was not to have to think about that kind of thing."

"You *got* to think about it," said Lyra severely. "You can't investigate Shadows, Dust, whatever it is, without thinking about that kind of thing, good and evil and such. And it said you got to, remember. You can't refuse. When are they going to close this place down?"

"The funding committee decides at the end of the week… Why?"

"'Cause you got tonight then," said Lyra. "You could fix this engine thing to put words on the screen instead of pictures like I made. You could do that easy. Then you could show 'em and they'd have to give you the money to carry on. And you could find out all about Dust, or Shadows, and tell me. You see," she went on a little haughtily, like a duchess describing an unsatisfactory housemaid, "the alethiometer won't exactly tell me what I need to know. But you could find out for me. Else I could probably do that Ching thing, with the sticks. But pictures are easier to work. I think so, anyway. I'm going to take this off now," she added, and pulled at the electrodes on her head.

Dr Malone gave her a tissue to wipe off the gel, and folded up the wires.

"So you're going?" she said. "Well, you've given me a strange hour, and no mistake."

"Are you going to make it do words?" Lyra said, gathering up her rucksack.

"It's about as much use as completing the funding application, I dare say," said Dr Malone. "No, listen. I want you to come back tomorrow. Can you do that? About the same time? I want you to show someone else."

Lyra narrowed her eyes. Was this a trap?

"Well, all right," she said. "But remember, there's things I need to know."

"Yes. Of course. You *will* come?"

"Yes," said Lyra. "If I say I will, I will. I could help you, I expect."

And she left. The porter at the desk looked up briefly and then went back to his paper.

"The Nuniatak dig," said the archaeologist, swinging his chair round. "You're the second person in a month to ask me about that."

"Who was the other one?" said Will, on his guard at once.

"I think he was a journalist, I'm not sure."

"Why did he want to know about it?" he said.

"In connection with one of the men who disappeared on that trip. It was the height of the cold war when the expedition vanished. Star Wars. You're probably too young to remember that. The Americans and the Russians were building enormous radar installations all across the Arctic... Anyway, what can I do for you?"

"Well," said Will, trying to keep calm, "I was just trying to find out about that expedition, really. For a school project about prehistoric people. And I read about this expedition that disappeared, and I got curious."

"Well, you're not the only one, as you see. There was a big to-do about it at the time. I looked it all up for the journalist. It was a preliminary survey, not a proper dig. You can't do a dig till you know whether it's worth spending time on it, so this group went out to look at a number of sites and make a report. Half a dozen blokes altogether. Sometimes on an expedition like this you combine forces with people from another discipline, you know, geologists or whatever, to split the cost. They look at their stuff and we look at ours. In this case there was a physicist on the team. I think he was looking at high-level atmospheric particles. The aurora, you know, the northern lights. He had balloons with radio transmitters, apparently.

"And there was another man with them. An ex-Marine, a sort of professional explorer. They were going up into some fairly wild territory, and polar bears are always a danger in the Arctic. Archaeologists can deal with some things, but we're not trained to shoot, and someone who can do that and navigate and make camp and do all the sort of survival stuff is very useful.

"But then they all vanished. They kept in radio contact with a local survey station, but one day the signal didn't come, and nothing more was heard. There'd been a blizzard, but that was nothing unusual. The search expedition found their last camp, more or less intact, though the bears had eaten their stores, but no sign of the people whatsoever.

"And that's all I can tell you, I'm afraid."

"Yes," said Will. "Thank you. Umm ... that journalist," he went on, stopping at the door, "you said he was interested in one of the men. Which one was it?"

"The explorer type. A man called Parry."

"What did he look like? The journalist, I mean?"

"What d'you want to know that for?"

"Because…" Will couldn't think of a plausible reason. He shouldn't have asked. "No reason. I just wondered."

"As far as I can remember, he was a big blond man. Very pale hair."

"Right, thanks," Will said, and turned to go.

The man watched him leave the room, saying nothing, frowning a little. Will saw him reach for the phone, and left the building quickly.

He found he was shaking. The journalist, so called, was one of the men who'd come to his house: a tall man with such fair hair that he seemed to have no eyebrows or eyelashes. He wasn't the one Will had knocked down the stairs: he was the one who'd appeared at the door of the living room as Will ran down and jumped over the body.

But he wasn't a journalist.

There was a large museum nearby. Will went in, holding his clipboard as if he were working, and sat down in a gallery hung with paintings. He was trembling hard and feeling sick, because pressing at him was the knowledge that he'd killed someone, he was a murderer. He'd kept it at bay till now, but it was closing in. He'd taken away the man's life.

He sat still for half an hour, and it was one of the worst half hours he'd ever spent. People came and went, looking at the paintings, talking in quiet voices, ignoring him; a gallery attendant stood in the doorway for a few minutes, hands behind his back, and then slowly moved away; and Will wrestled with the horror of what he'd done, and didn't move a muscle.

Gradually he grew calmer. He'd been defending his mother. They were frightening her: given the state she was in, they were persecuting her. He had a right to defend his home. His father would have wanted him to do that. He did it because it was the good thing to do. He did it to stop them stealing the green leather case. He did it so he could find his father; and didn't he have a right to do that? All his childish games came back to him, with himself and his father rescuing each other from avalanches or fighting pirates. Well, now it was real. "I'll find you," he said in his mind. "Just help me and I'll find you, and we'll look after Mum, and everything'll be all right…"

And after all he had somewhere to hide now, somewhere so safe no one would ever find him. And the papers from the case (which he still hadn't had time to read) were safe too, under the mattress in Cittàgazze.

Finally he noticed people moving more purposefully, and all in the same direction. They were leaving, because the attendant was telling them that the museum would shut in ten minutes. Will gathered himself and left. He found his way to the High Street, where the solicitor's office was, and wondered about going to see him, despite what he'd said earlier. The man had sounded friendly enough…

But as he made up his mind to cross the street and go in, he stopped suddenly.

The tall man with the pale eyebrows was getting out of a car.

Will turned aside at once, casually, and looked in the window of the jeweller's shop beside him. He saw the man's reflection look around, settle the knot of his tie, and go in to the solicitor's office. As soon as he'd gone in, Will moved away, his heart thudding again. There wasn't anywhere safe. He drifted towards the university library, and waited for Lyra.

5

Airmail Paper

"Will," said Lyra.

She spoke quietly, but he was startled all the same. She was sitting on the bench beside him and he hadn't even noticed.

"Where did you come from?"

"I found my scholar! She's called Dr Malone. And she's got an engine that can see Dust and she's going to make it talk..."

"I didn't see you coming."

"You weren't looking," she said. "You must've been thinking about something else. It's a good thing I found you. Look, it's easy to fool people. Watch..."

Two police officers were strolling towards them, a man and a woman on the beat, in their white summer shirtsleeves, with their radios and their batons and their suspicious eyes. Before they reached the bench, Lyra was on her feet and speaking to them.

"Please, could you tell me where the Museum is?" she said. "Me and my brother was supposed to meet our parents there and we got lost."

The policeman looked at Will, and Will, containing his anger, shrugged as if to say she's right, we're lost, isn't it silly. The man smiled. The woman said: "Which museum? The Ashmolean?"

"Yeah, that one," said Lyra, and pretended to listen carefully as the woman gave her instructions.

Will got up and said "Thanks," and he and Lyra moved away together. They didn't look back, but the police had already lost interest.

"See?" she said. "If they were looking for you, I put 'em off. 'Cause they won't be looking for someone with a sister. I better stay with you from now on," she went on scoldingly once they'd gone round the corner. "You en't safe on your own."

He said nothing. His heart was thumping with rage. They walked along towards a round building with a great leaden dome, set in a square bounded by honey-coloured stone college buildings and a church and wide-crowned trees above high garden walls. The afternoon sun drew the warmest tones out of it all, and the air felt rich with it, almost the colour itself of heavy golden wine. All the leaves were still, and in this little square even the traffic noise was hushed.

She finally became aware of Will's feelings, and said, "What's the matter?"

"If you speak to people you just attract their attention," he said, with a shaking voice. "You should just keep quiet and still and they overlook you. I've been doing it all my life. I know how to do it. Your way, you just – you make yourself visible. You shouldn't do that. You shouldn't play at it. You're not being serious."

"You think so?" she said, and her anger flashed. "You think I don't know about lying and that? I'm the best liar there ever was. But I en't lying to you, and I never will, I swear it. You're in danger, and if I hadn't done that just then, you'd've been caught. Didn't you see 'em looking at you? 'Cause they were. You en't careful enough. If you want my opinion, it's you that en't serious."

"If I'm not serious, what am I doing hanging about waiting for you when I could be miles away? Or hiding out of sight, safe in that other city? I've got my own things to do, but I'm hanging about here so I can help you. Don't tell me I'm not serious."

"You *had* to come through," she said, furious. No one should speak to her like this: she was an aristocrat. She was Lyra. "You had to, else you'd never find out anything about your father. You done it for yourself, not for me."

They were quarrelling passionately, but in subdued voices, because of the quiet in the square and the people who were wandering past nearby. When she said this, though, Will stopped altogether. He had to lean against the college wall beside him. The colour had left his face.

"What do you know about my father?" he said very quietly.

She replied in the same tone. "I don't know anything. All I know is you're looking for him. That's all I asked about."

"Asked *who*?"

"The alethiometer, of course."

It took a moment for him to remember what she meant. And then he looked so angry and suspicious that she took it out of her rucksack and said, "All right, I'll show you."

And she sat down on the stone kerb around the grass in the middle of the square and bent her head over the golden instrument and began to turn the hands, her fingers moving almost too quickly to see, and then pausing for several seconds while the slender needle whipped around the dial flicking to a stop here and there, and then turning the hands to new positions just as quickly. Will looked around carefully, but there was no one near to see; a group of tourists looked up at the domed building, an ice-cream vendor wheeled his cart along the pavement, but their attention was elsewhere.

Lyra blinked and sighed, as if she were waking after a sleep.

"Your mother's ill," she said quietly. "But she's safe. There's this lady looking after her. And you took some letters and ran away. And there was a man, I think he was a thief, and you killed him. And you're looking for your father, and –"

"All right, shut up," said Will. "That's enough. You've got no right to look into my life like that. Don't ever do that again. That's just spying."

"I know when to stop asking," she said. "See, the alethiometer's like a person, almost. I sort of know when it's going to be cross or when there's things it doesn't want me to know. I kind of feel it. But when you come out of nowhere yesterday, I had to ask it who you were or I might not have been safe. I had to. And it said…" She lowered her voice even more. "It said you was a murderer, and I thought good, that's all right, he's someone I can trust. But I didn't ask more than that till just now, and if you don't want me to ask any more, I promise I won't. This en't like a private peepshow. If I done nothing but spy on people it'd stop working. I know that as well as I know my own Oxford."

"You could have asked me instead of that thing. Did it say whether my father was alive or dead?"

"No, because I didn't ask."

They were both sitting by this time. Will put his head in his hands with weariness.

"Well," he said finally, "I suppose we'll have to trust each other."

"That's all right. I trust you."

Will nodded grimly. He was so tired, and there was not the slightest possibility of sleep in this world. Lyra wasn't usually so perceptive, but something in his manner made her think: he's afraid, but he's mastering his fear, like Iorek Byrnison said we had to do; like I did by the fish-house at the frozen lake.

105

"And Will," she added, "I won't give you away, not to anyone. I promise."

"Good."

"I done that before. I betrayed someone. And it was the worst thing I ever did. I thought I was saving his life actually, only I was taking him right to the most dangerous place there could be. I hated myself for that, for being so stupid. So I'll try very hard not to be careless or forget and betray you."

He said nothing. He rubbed his eyes and blinked hard to try and wake himself up.

"We can't go back through the window till much later," he said. "We shouldn't have come through in daylight anyway. We can't risk anyone seeing. And now we've got to hang around for hours…"

"I'm hungry," Lyra said.

Then he said, "I know! We can go to the cinema!"

"The what?"

"I'll show you. We can get some food there too."

There was a cinema near the city centre, ten minutes' walk away. Will paid for them both to get in, and bought hot dogs and popcorn and Coke, and they carried the food inside and sat down just as the film was beginning.

Lyra was entranced. She had seen projected photograms, but nothing in her world had prepared her for the cinema. She wolfed down the hot dog and the popcorn, gulped the Coca-Cola, and gasped and laughed with delight at the characters on the screen. Luckily it was a noisy audience, full of children, and her excitement wasn't conspicuous. Will closed his eyes at once and went to sleep.

He woke when he heard the clatter of seats as people moved out, and blinked in the light. His watch showed a quarter past eight. Lyra came away reluctantly.

"That's the best thing I ever saw in my whole life," she

said. "I dunno why they never invented this in my world. We
got some things better than you, but this was better than
anything we got."

Will couldn't even remember what the film had been. It was
still light outside, and the streets were busy.

"D'you want to see another one?"

"Yeah!"

So they went to the next cinema, a few hundred yards away
around the corner, and did it again. Lyra settled down with her
feet on the seat, hugging her knees, and Will let his mind go
blank. When they came out this time, it was nearly eleven
o'clock: much better.

Lyra was hungry again, so they bought hamburgers from a
mobile stall and ate them as they walked along, something else
new to her.

"We always sit down to eat. I never seen people just walking
along eating before," she told him. "There's so many ways this
place is different. The traffic, for one. I don't like it. I like the
cinema, though, and hamburgers. I like them a lot. And that
scholar, Dr Malone, she's going to make that engine use words. I
just know she is. I'll go back there tomorrow and see how she's
getting on. I bet I could help her. I could probably get the scholars
to give her the money she wants, too. You know how my father did
it? Lord Asriel? He played a trick on them…"

As they walked up the Banbury Road, she told him about the
night she hid in the wardrobe and watched Lord Asriel show the
Jordan scholars the severed head of Stanislaus Grumman in the
vacuum flask. And since Will was such a good audience, she went
on and told him the rest of her story, from the time she escaped
from Mrs Coulter's flat to the horrible moment when she realized
she'd led Roger to his death on the icy cliffs of Svalbard. Will
listened without comment, but attentively, with sympathy. Her

account of a voyage in a balloon, of armoured bears and witches, of a vengeful arm of the Church, seemed all of a piece with his own fantastic dream of a beautiful city on the sea, empty and silent and safe: it couldn't be true, it was as simple as that.

But eventually they reached the ring road, and the hornbeam trees. There was very little traffic now: a car every minute or so, no more than that. And there was the window. Will felt himself smiling. It was going to be all right.

"Wait till there's no cars coming," he said. "I'm going through now."

And a moment later he was on the grass under the palm trees, and a second or two afterwards Lyra followed.

They felt as if they were home again. The wide warm night, and the scent of flowers and the sea, and the silence, bathed them like soothing water.

Lyra stretched and yawned, and Will felt a great weight lift off his shoulders. He had been carrying it all day, and he hadn't noticed how it had nearly pressed him into the ground; but now he felt light and free and at peace.

And then Lyra gripped his arm. In the same second he heard what had made her do it.

Somewhere in the little streets beyond the café, something was screaming.

Will set off at once towards the sound, and Lyra followed behind as he plunged down a narrow alley shadowed from the moonlight. After several twists and turns they came out into the square in front of the stone tower they'd seen that morning.

Twenty or so children were facing inwards in a semicircle at the base of the tower, and some of them had sticks in their hands, and some were throwing stones at whatever they had trapped against the wall. At first Lyra thought it was another child, but coming from inside the semicircle was a horrible high wailing that wasn't human at all. And the children were screaming too, in fear as well as hatred.

Will ran up to the children and pulled the first one back. It was a boy of about his own age, a boy in a striped T-shirt. As he turned Lyra saw the wild white rims around his pupils, and then the other children realized what was happening and stopped to look. Angelica and her little brother were there too, stones in hand, and all the children's eyes glittered fiercely in the moonlight.

They fell silent. Only the high wailing continued, and then both Will and Lyra saw what it was: a tabby cat, cowering against the wall of the tower, its ear torn and its tail bent. It was the cat Will had seen in Sunderland Avenue, the one like Moxie, the one that had led him to the window.

As soon as he saw her he flung the boy he was holding aside. The boy fell to the ground and was up in a moment, furious, but the others held him back. Will was already kneeling by the cat.

And then she was in his arms. She fled to his breast and he cradled her close and stood to face the children, and Lyra thought for a crazy second that his dæmon had appeared at last.

"What are you hurting this cat for?" he demanded, and they couldn't answer. They stood trembling at Will's anger, breathing heavily, clutching their sticks and their stones, and they couldn't speak.

But then Angelica's voice came clearly: "You ain from here! You ain from Ci'gazze! You didn' know about Spectres, you don' know about cats either. You ain like us!"

The boy in the striped T-shirt whom Will had thrown down was trembling to fight, and if it hadn't been for the cat in Will's arms he would have flown at Will with fists and teeth and feet, and Will would have gladly joined battle: there was a current of electric hatred between the two of them that only violence could earth. But the boy was afraid of the cat.

"Where you come from?" he said contemptuously.

"Doesn't matter where we come from. If you're scared of this cat I'll take her away from you. If she's bad luck to you she'll be good luck for us. Now get out of the way."

For a moment Will thought their hatred would overcome their fear, and he was preparing to put the cat down and fight, but then came a low thunderous growl from behind the children, and they turned to see Lyra standing with her hand on the shoulders of a great spotted leopard whose teeth shone white as he snarled. Even Will, who recognized Pantalaimon, was frightened for a second. Its effect on the children was dramatic: they turned and fled at once. A few seconds later the square was empty.

But before they left, Lyra looked up at the tower. A growl from Pantalaimon prompted her, and just briefly she saw someone there on the very top, looking down over the battlemented rim, and not a child either, but a young man, with curly hair.

Half an hour later they were in the flat above the café. Will had found a tin of condensed milk, and the cat had lapped it hungrily and then begun to lick her wounds. Pantalaimon had become cat-formed out of curiosity, and at first the cat had bristled with suspicion, but she soon realized that whatever Pantalaimon was, he was neither a true cat nor a threat, and proceeded to ignore him.

Lyra watched Will tending this one with fascination. The only animals she had been close to in her world (apart from the armoured bears) were working animals of one sort or another: cats were for keeping Jordan College clear of mice, not for making pets of.

"I think her tail's broken," Will said. "I don't know what to do about that. Maybe it'll heal by itself. I'll put some honey on her ear. I read about that somewhere; it's antiseptic…"

It was messy, but at least it kept her occupied licking it off, and the wound was getting cleaner all the time.

"You sure this is the one you saw?" she said.

"Oh, yes. And if they're all so frightened of cats there wouldn't be any in this world anyway. She probably couldn't find her way back."

"They were just crazy," Lyra said. "They would have killed her. I never seen kids being like that."

"I have," said Will.

But his face had closed: he didn't want to talk about it, and she knew better than to ask. She knew she wouldn't even ask the alethiometer.

She was very tired, so presently she went to bed, and slept at once.

A little later, when the cat had curled up to sleep, Will took a cup of coffee and the green leather writing-case, and sat on the balcony. There was enough light coming through the window for him to read by, and he wanted to look at the papers.

There weren't many. As he'd thought, they were letters, written on airmail paper in black ink. These very marks were made by the hand of the man he wanted so much to find; he moved his fingers over and over them, and pressed them to his face, trying to get closer to the essence of his father. Then he started to read.

Fairbanks, Alaska
Wednesday 19 June 1985
My darling – the usual mixture of efficiency and chaos – all the stores are here but the physicist, a genial dimwit called Nelson, hasn't made any arrangements for carrying his damn balloons up into the

mountains – having to twiddle our thumbs while he scrabbles around for transport. But it means I had a chance to talk to an old boy I met last time, a gold-miner called Jake Petersen – tracked him down to a dingy bar and under the sound of the baseball game on the TV I asked him about the anomaly. He wouldn't talk there – took me back to his apartment – with the help of a bottle of Jack Daniels he talked for a long time – hadn't seen it himself but he'd met an Eskimo who had – and this chap said it was a doorway into the spirit world – they'd known about it for centuries – part of the initiation of a medicine-man involved going through and bringing back a trophy of some kind – though some never came back – however, old Jake did have a map of the area, and he'd marked on it where his pal told him the thing was. (Just in case: it's at 69°02'11"N, 157°12'19"W, on a spur of Lookout Ridge a mile or two north of the Colville River.) We then got on to other Arctic legends – the Norwegian ship that's been drifting unmanned for sixty years – stuff like that. The archaeologists are a decent crew, keen to get to work, containing their impatience with Nelson and his balloons. None of them has ever heard of the anomaly, and believe me I'm going to keep it like that. My fondest love to you both. Johnny.

Umiat, Alaska
Saturday 22 June 1985

My darling – so much for what did I call him, a genial dimwit – the physicist Nelson is nothing of the sort, and if I'm not mistaken he's actually looking for the anomaly himself. The holdup in Fairbanks was orchestrated by him, would you believe – knowing that the rest of the team wouldn't want to wait for anything less than an unarguable reason like no transport, he personally sent ahead and cancelled the vehicles that had been ordered. I found this out by accident and I was going to ask him what the hell he was playing at when I overheard him talking on the radio to someone – describing the anomaly, no less, except

112

he didn't know the location – later on I bought him a drink, played the bluff soldier, old Arctic hand, more things in heaven and earth line – pretended to tease him with the limitations of science – bet you can't explain Bigfoot, etc – watching him closely – then sprung the anomaly on him – Eskimo legend of a doorway into spirit world – invisible – somewhere near Lookout Ridge, would you believe, where we're heading for, fancy that. And you know he was jolted rigid. He knew exactly what I meant. I pretended not to notice and went on to witchcraft, told him the Zaire leopard story – so I hope he's got me down as a superstitious military blockhead. But I'm right, Elaine, he's looking for it too. The question is, do I tell him or not? Got to work out what his game is. Fondest love to both – Johnny.

Colville Bar, Alaska
24 June 1985

Darling – I won't get a chance to post another letter for a while – this is the last town before we take to the hills – the Brooks Range – the archaeologists are fizzing to get up there. One chap is convinced he'll find evidence of much earlier habitation than anyone suspected – I said how much earlier, and why was he convinced – he told me of some narwhal ivory carvings he'd found on a previous dig – Carbon 14 dated to some incredible age, way outside the range of what was previously assumed – anomalous, in fact. Wouldn't it be strange if they'd come through my *anomaly, from some other world – talking of which, the physicist Nelson is my closest buddy now – kids me along, drops hints to imply that he knows that I know that he knows, etc – and I pretend to be bluff Major Parry, stout fellow in a crisis but not too much between the ears, what – but I know he's after it. For one thing, although he's a bona fide academic his funding actually comes from the Ministry of Defence – I know the financial codes they use – and for another his so-called weather balloons are nothing of the sort – I looked in the crate – a radiation suit if ever I've seen one. A rum*

113

do, my darling. I shall stick to my plan – take the archaeologists to their spot and go off by myself for a few days to look for the anomaly – if I bump into Nelson wandering about on Lookout Ridge I'll play it by ear.

Later – *A real bit of luck. I met Jake Petersen's pal the Eskimo, Matt Kigalik. Jake had told me where to find him but I hadn't dared to hope he'd be there. He told me the Soviets had been looking for the anomaly too – he'd come across a man earlier this year high up in the range and watched him for a couple of days without being seen, because he guessed what he was doing, and he was right, and the man turned out to be Russian, a spy; he didn't tell me more than that. I got the impression he bumped him off. But he described the thing to me. It's like a gap in the air, a sort of window. You look through it and you see another world. But it's not easy to find because that part of the other world looks just like this – rocks and moss and so forth. It's on the north side of a small creek fifty paces or so to the west of a tall rock shaped like a standing bear, and the position Jake gave me is not quite right – it's nearer 12"N than 11.*

Wish me luck my darling. I'll bring you back a trophy from the spirit world – I love you for ever – kiss the boy for me – Johnny.

Will found his head ringing.

His father was describing exactly what he himself had found under the hornbeam trees. He too had found a window – he even used the same word for it! So Will must be on the right track. And this knowledge was what the men had been searching for... So it was dangerous, too.

Will had been a year old when that letter was written. Six years after that had come the morning in the supermarket when he realized his mother was in terrible danger, and he had to protect her; and then slowly in the months that followed came his growing realization that the danger was in her mind, and he had to protect her all the more.

And then, brutally, the revelation that not all the danger had been in her mind after all. There really was someone after her. After these letters, this information.

He had no idea what it meant. But he felt deeply happy that he had something so important to share with his father; that John Parry and his son Will had each, separately, discovered this extraordinary thing. When they met they could talk about it, and his father would be proud that Will had followed in his footsteps.

The night was quiet and the sea was still. He folded the letters away and fell asleep.

6

Lighted Fliers

 "**G**rumman?" said the black-bearded fur-trader. "From the Berlin Academy? Reckless. I met him five years back over at the northern end of the Urals. I thought he was dead."

Sam Cansino, an old acquaintance and a Texan like Lee Scoresby, sat in the naphtha-laden, smoky bar of the Samirsky Hotel and tossed back a shot-glass of bitingly cold vodka. He nudged the plate of pickled fish and black bread towards Lee, who took a mouthful and nodded for Sam to tell him more.

"He'd walked into a trap that fool Yakovlev laid," the fur-trader went on, "and cut his leg open to the bone. Instead of using regular medicines, he insisted on using the stuff the bears use – bloodmoss – some kind of lichen, it ain't a true moss; anyway, he was lying on a sledge alternately roaring with pain and calling out instructions to his men – they were taking star-sights, and they had to get the measurements right or he'd lash them with his tongue, and boy, he had a tongue like barbed wire. A lean man, tough, powerful, curious about everything. You know he was a Tartar, by initiation?"

"You don't say," said Lee Scoresby, tipping more vodka into Sam's glass. His dæmon Hester crouched at his elbow on the bar,

116

eyes half-closed as usual, ears flat along her back.

Lee had arrived that afternoon, borne to Nova Zembla by the wind the witches had called up, and once he'd stowed his equipment he'd made straight for the Samirsky Hotel, near the fish-packing station. This was a place where many Arctic drifters stopped to exchange news or look for employment or leave messages for one another, and Lee Scoresby had spent several days there in the past, waiting for a contract or a passenger or a fair wind, so there was nothing unusual in his conduct now.

And with the vast changes they sensed in the world around them, it was natural for people to gather and talk. With every day that passed came more news: the river Yenisei was free of ice, and at this time of year, too; part of the ocean had drained away, exposing strange regular formations of stone on the sea-bed; a squid a hundred feet long had snatched three fishermen out of their boat and torn them apart...

And the fog continued to roll in from the north, dense and cold and occasionally drenched with the strangest imaginable light, in which great forms could be vaguely seen, and mysterious voices heard.

Altogether it was a bad time to work, which was why the bar of the Samirsky Hotel was full.

"Did you say Grumman?" said the man sitting just along the bar, an elderly man in seal-hunter's rig, whose lemming-dæmon looked out solemnly from his pocket. "He was a Tartar all right. I was there when he joined that tribe. I saw him having his skull drilled. He had another name, too; a Tartar name; I'll think of it in a minute."

"Well, how about that," said Lee Scoresby. "Let me buy you a drink, my friend. I'm looking for news of this man. What tribe was it he joined?"

"The Yenisei Pakhtars. At the foot of the Semyonov range.

Near a fork of the Yenisei and the, I forget what it's called, a river that comes down from the hills. There's a rock the size of a house at the landing stage."

"Ah, sure," said Lee. "I remember it now. I've flown over it. And Grumman had his skull drilled, you say? Why was that?"

"He was a shaman," said the old seal-hunter. "I think the tribe recognized him as a shaman before they adopted him. Some business, that drilling. It goes on for two nights and a day. They use a bow-drill, like for lighting a fire."

"Ah, that accounts for the way his team was obeying him," said Sam Cansino. "They were the roughest bunch of scoundrels I ever saw, but they ran round doing his bidding like nervous children. I thought it was his cursing that did it. If they thought he was a shaman it'd make even more sense. But you know, that man's curiosity was as powerful as a wolf's jaws; he would *not* let go. He made me tell him every scrap I knew about the land thereabouts, and the habits of wolverines and foxes. And he was in some pain from that damn trap of Yakovlev's; leg laid open, and he was writing the results of that bloodmoss, taking his temperature, watching the scar form, making notes on every damn thing… A strange man. There was a witch who wanted him for a lover, but he turned her down."

"Is that so?" said Lee, thinking of the beauty of Serafina Pekkala.

"He shouldn't have done that," said the seal-hunter. "A witch offers you her love, you should take it. If you don't, it's your own fault if bad things happen to you. It's like having to make a choice: a blessing or a curse. The one thing you can't do is choose neither."

"He might have had a reason," said Lee.

"If he had any sense, it will have been a good one."

"He was headstrong," said Sam Cansino.

"Maybe faithful to another woman," Lee guessed. "I heard something else about him; I heard he knew the whereabouts of some magic object, I don't know what it might be, that could protect anyone who held it. Did you ever hear that story?"

"Yes, I heard that," said the seal-hunter. "He didn't have it himself, but he knew where it was. There was a man who tried to make him tell, but Grumman killed him."

"His dæmon, now," said Sam Cansino, "that was curious. She was an eagle, a black eagle with a white head and breast, of a kind I'd never set eyes on, and I didn't know how she might be called."

"She was an osprey," said the barman, listening in. "You're talking about Stan Grumman? His dæmon was an osprey. A fish-eagle."

"What happened to him?" said Lee Scoresby.

"Oh, he got mixed up in the Skraeling wars over to Beringland. Last I heard he'd been shot," said the seal-hunter. "Killed outright."

"I heard they beheaded him," said Lee Scoresby.

"No, you're both wrong," said the barman, "and I know, because I heard it from an Inuit who was with him. Seems that they were camped out on Sakhalin somewhere and there was an avalanche. Grumman was buried under a hundred tons of rock. This Inuit saw it happen."

"What I can't understand," said Lee Scoresby, offering the bottle round, "is what the man was doing. Was he prospecting for rock-oil, maybe? Or was he a military man? Or was it something philosophical? You said something about measurements, Sam. What would that be?"

"They were measuring the starlight. And the aurora. He had a passion for the aurora. I think his main interest was in ruins, though. Ancient things."

"I know who could tell you more," said the seal-hunter. "Up the mountain they have an observatory belonging to the Imperial Muscovite Academy. They'd be able to tell you. I know he went up there more than once."

"What d'you want to know for anyway, Lee?" said Sam Cansino.

"He owes me some money," said Lee Scoresby.

This explanation was so satisfying that it stopped their curiosity at once. The conversation turned to the topic on everyone's lips: the catastrophic changes taking place around them, which no one could see.

"The fishermen," said the seal-hunter, "they say you can sail right up into that new world."

"There's a new world?" said Lee.

"As soon as this damn fog clears we'll see right into it," the seal-hunter told them confidently. "When it first happened, I was out in my kayak and looking north, just by chance. I'll never forget what I saw. Instead of the earth curving down over the horizon it went straight on. I could see for ever, and as far as I could see, there was land and shoreline, mountains, harbours, green trees and fields of corn, for ever into the sky. I tell you, friends, that was something worth toiling fifty years to see, a sight like that. I would have paddled up the sky into that calm sea without a backward glance; but then came the fog…"

"Ain't never seen a fog like this," grumbled Sam Cansino. "Reckon it's set in for a month, maybe more. But you're out of luck if you want money from Stanislaus Grumman, Lee; the man's dead."

"Ah! I got his Tartar name!" said the seal-hunter. "I just remembered what they called him during the drilling. It sounded like Jopari."

"Jopari? That's no kind of name I've ever heard of," said Lee.

"Might be Nipponese, I suppose. Well, if I want my money, maybe I can chase up his heirs and assigns. Or maybe the Berlin Academy can square the debt. I'll go ask at the observatory, see if they have an address I can apply to."

The observatory was some distance to the north, and Lee Scoresby hired a dog-sledge and driver. It wasn't easy to find someone willing to risk the journey in the fog, but Lee was persuasive, or his money was; and eventually an old Tartar from the Ob region agreed to take him there, after a lengthy bout of haggling.

The driver didn't rely on a compass, or he would have found it impossible. He navigated by other signs, his Arctic fox-dæmon for one, who sat at the front of the sledge keenly scenting the way. Lee, who carried his compass everywhere, had realized already that the earth's magnetic field was as disturbed as everything else.

The old driver said, as they stopped to brew coffee, "This happen before, this thing."

"What, the sky opening? That happened before?"

"Many thousand generation. My people remember. All long time ago, many thousand generation."

"What do they say about it?"

"Sky fall open, and spirits move between this world and that world. All the lands move. The ice melt, then freeze again. The spirits close up the hole after a while. Seal it up. But witches say the sky is thin there, behind the northern lights."

"What's going to happen, Umaq?"

"Same thing as before. Make all same again. But only after big trouble, big war. Spirit war."

The driver wouldn't tell him any more, and soon they moved on, tracking slowly over undulations and hollows and past outcrops of dim rock, dark through the pallid fog, until the old man said:

"Observatory up there. You walk now. Path too crooked for sledge. You want go back, I wait here."

"Yeah, I want to go back when I've finished, Umaq. You make yourself a fire, my friend, and sit and rest a spell. I'll be three, four hours maybe."

Lee Scoresby set off, with Hester tucked into the breast of his coat, and after half an hour's stiff climb found a clump of buildings suddenly above him as if they'd just been placed there by a giant hand. But the effect was only due to a momentary lifting of the fog, and after a minute it closed in again. He saw the great dome of the main observatory, a smaller one a little way off, and between them a group of administration buildings and domestic quarters. No lights showed, because the windows were blacked out permanently so as not to spoil the darkness for their telescopes.

A few minutes after he arrived, Lee was talking to a group of astronomers eager to learn what news he could bring them, and there are few natural philosophers as frustrated as astronomers in a fog. He told them about everything he'd seen, and once that topic had been thoroughly dealt with, he asked about Stanislaus Grumman. The astronomers hadn't had a visitor in weeks, and they were keen to talk.

"Grumman? Yes, I'll tell you something about him," said the Director. "He was an Englishman, in spite of his name. I remember –"

"Surely not," said his deputy. "He was a member of the Imperial German Academy. I met him in Berlin. I was sure he was German."

"No, I think you'll find he was English. His command of that language was immaculate, anyway," said the Director. "But I agree, he was certainly a member of the Berlin Academy. He was a geologist –"

"No, no, you're wrong," said someone else. "He did look at the earth, but not as a geologist. I had a long talk with him once. I suppose you'd call him a palaeo-archaeologist."

They were sitting, five of them, around a table in the room that served as their common room, living and dining room, bar, recreation room and more or less everything else. Two of them were Muscovites, one was a Pole, one a Yoruba and one a Skraeling. Lee Scoresby sensed that the little community was glad to have a visitor, if only because he introduced a change of conversation. The Pole had been the last to speak, and then the Yoruba interrupted:

"What do you mean, a palaeo-archaeologist? Archaeologists already study what's old; why do you need to put another word meaning *old* in front of it?"

"His field of study went back much further than you'd expect, that's all. He was looking for remains of civilizations from twenty, thirty thousand years ago," the Pole replied.

"Nonsense!" said the Director. "Utter nonsense! The man was pulling your leg. Civilizations thirty thousand years old? Ha! Where is the evidence?"

"Under the ice," said the Pole. "That's the point. According to Grumman, the earth's magnetic field changed dramatically at various times in the past, and the earth's axis actually moved too, so that temperate areas became ice-bound."

"How?" said the Yoruba.

"Oh, he had some complex theory. The point was, any evidence there might have been for very early civilizations was long since buried under the ice. He claimed to have some photograms of unusual rock formations…"

"Ha! Is that all?" said the Director.

"I'm only reporting, I'm not defending him," said the Pole.

"How long had you known Grumman, gentlemen?" Lee Scoresby asked.

"Well, let me see," said the Director. "It was seven years ago I met him for the first time."

"He made a name for himself a year or two before that, with his paper on the variations in the magnetic pole," said the Yoruba. "But he came out of nowhere. I mean no one had known him as a student or seen any of his previous work…"

They talked on for a while, contributing reminiscences and offering suggestions as to what might have become of Grumman, though most of them thought he was probably dead. While the Pole wentto brew some more coffee, Lee's hare-dæmon Hester said to him quietly:

"Check out the Skraeling, Lee."

The Skraeling had spoken very little. Lee had thought he was naturally taciturn, but prompted by Hester he casually glanced across during the next break in the conversation to see the man's dæmon, a snowy owl, glaring at him with bright orange eyes. Well, that was what owls looked like, and they did stare; but Hester was right, and there was a hostility and suspicion in the dæmon that the man's face showed nothing of.

And then Lee saw something else: the Skraeling was wearing a ring with the Church's symbol engraved on it. Suddenly he realized the reason for the man's silence. Every philosophical research establishment, so he'd heard, had to include on its staff a representative of the Magisterium, to act as a censor and suppress the news of any heretical discoveries.

So, realizing this, and remembering something he'd heard Lyra say, Lee asked:

"Tell me, gentlemen – do you happen to know if Grumman ever looked into the question of Dust?"

And instantly a silence fell in the stuffy little room, and everyone's attention focused on the Skraeling, though no one looked at him directly. Lee knew that Hester would remain inscrutable, with her eyes half-closed and her ears flat along her back, and he put on a cheerful innocence as he looked from face to face.

Finally he settled on the Skraeling, and said, "I beg your pardon – have I asked about something it's forbidden to know?"

The Skraeling said, "Where did you hear mention of this subject, Mr Scoresby?"

"From a passenger I flew across the sea a while back," Lee said easily. "They never said what it was, but from the way it was mentioned it seemed like the kind of thing Dr Grumman might have enquired into. I took it to be some kind of celestial thing, like the aurora. But it puzzled me, because as an aëronaut I know the skies pretty well, and I'd never come across this stuff. What is it, anyhow?"

"As you say, a celestial phenomenon," said the Skraeling. "It has no practical significance."

Presently Lee decided it was time to leave; he had learned no more, and he didn't want to keep Umaq waiting. He left the astronomers to their fog-bound observatory and set off down the track, feeling his way along by following his dæmon, whose eyes were closer to the ground.

And when they were only ten minutes down the path, something swept past his head in the fog and dived at Hester. It was the Skraeling's owl-dæmon.

But Hester sensed her coming and flattened herself in time, and the owl's claws just missed. Hester could fight: her claws were sharp, too, and she was tough and brave. Lee knew that the Skraeling himself must be close by, and reached for the revolver at his belt.

"Behind you, Lee," Hester said, and he whipped round, diving, as an arrow hissed over his shoulder.

He fired at once. The Skraeling fell, grunting, as the bullet thudded into his leg. A moment later the owl-dæmon, wheeling on silent wings, swooped with a clumsy fainting movement at his side, and half-lay on the snow, struggling to fold her wings.

Lee Scoresby cocked his pistol and held it to the man's head.

"Right, you damn fool," he said. "What did you try that for? Can't you see we're all in the same trouble now this thing's happened to the sky?"

"It's too late," said the Skraeling.

"Too late for what?"

"Too late to stop. I have already sent a messenger bird. The Magisterium will know of your enquiries, and they will be glad to know about Grumman –"

"What about him?"

"The fact that others are looking for him. It confirms what we thought. And that others know of Dust. You are an enemy of the church, Lee Scoresby. By their fruits shall ye know them. By their questions shall ye see the serpent gnawing at their heart..."

The owl was making soft hooting sounds, and raising and dropping her wings fitfully. Her bright orange eyes were filming over with pain. There was a gathering red stain in the snow around the Skraeling: even in the fog-thick dimness Lee could see that the man was going to die.

"Reckon my bullet must have hit an artery," he said. "Let go my sleeve and I'll make a tourniquet."

"No!" said the Skraeling harshly. "I am glad to die! I shall have the martyr's palm! You will not deprive me of that!"

"Then die if you want to. Just tell me this –"

But he never had the chance to complete his question, because with a bleak little shiver the owl-dæmon disappeared. The

Skraeling's soul was gone. Lee had once seen a painting in which a saint of the church was shown being attacked by assassins. While they bludgeoned his dying body, the saint's dæmon was borne upwards by cherubs and offered a spray of palm, the badge of a martyr. The Skraeling's face now bore the same expression as the saint's in the picture: an ecstatic straining towards oblivion. Lee dropped him in distaste.

Hester clicked her tongue.

"Should a reckoned he'd send a message," she said. "Take his ring."

"What the hell for? We ain't thieves, are we?"

"No, we're renegades," she said. "Not by our choice, but by his malice. Once the church learns about this, we're done for anyway. Take every advantage we can in the meantime. Go on, take the ring and stow it away, and mebbe we can use it."

Lee saw the sense, and took the ring off the dead man's finger. Peering into the gloom, he saw that the path was edged by a steep drop into rocky darkness, and he rolled the Skraeling's body over. It fell for a long time before he heard any impact. Lee had never enjoyed violence, and he hated killing, although he'd had to do it three times before.

"No sense in thinking that," said Hester. "He didn't give us a choice, and we didn't shoot to kill. Damn it, Lee, he wanted to die. These people are insane."

"I guess you're right," he said, and put the pistol away.

At the foot of the path they found the driver, with the dogs harnessed and ready to move.

"Tell me, Umaq," Lee said as they set off back to the fish-packing station, "you ever hear of a man called Grumman?"

"Oh, sure," said the driver. "Everybody know Dr Grumman."

"Did you know he had a Tartar name?"

"Not Tartar. You mean Jopari? Not Tartar."

"What happened to him? Is he dead?"

"You ask me that, I have to say I don't know. So you never know the truth from me."

"I see. So who can I ask?"

"You better ask his tribe. Better go to Yenisei, ask them."

"His tribe... You mean the people who initiated him? Who drilled his skull?"

"Yes. You better ask them. Maybe he not dead, maybe he is. Maybe neither dead nor alive."

"How can he be neither dead nor alive?"

"In spirit world. Maybe he in spirit world. Already I say too much. Say no more now."

And he did not.

But when they returned to the station, Lee went at once to the docks and looked for a ship that could give him passage to the mouth of the Yenisei.

Meanwhile, the witches were searching too. The Latvian queen Ruta Skadi flew with Serafina Pekkala's company for many days and nights, through fog and whirlwind, over regions devastated by flood or landslide. It was certain that they were in a world none of them had known before, with strange winds, strange scents in the air, great unknown birds that attacked them on sight and had to be driven off with volleys of arrows; and when they found land to rest on, the very plants were strange.

Still, some of those plants were edible, and there were small creatures not unlike rabbits that made a tasty meal, and there was no shortage of water. It might have been a good land to live in, but for the spectral forms that drifted like mist over the grasslands and congregated near streams and low-lying water. In some lights they were hardly there at all, just visible as a drifting quality in the light, a rhythmic evanescence, like veils of transparency turning before a mirror. The witches had never seen anything like them before, and mistrusted them at once.

"Are they alive, do you think, Serafina Pekkala?" said Ruta Skadi, as they circled high above a group of the things that stood motionless at the edge of a tract of forest.

"Alive or dead, they're full of malice," Serafina replied. "I can feel that from here. And unless I knew what weapon could harm them, I wouldn't want to go closer than this."

The Spectres seemed to be earthbound, without the power of flight, luckily for the witches. Later that day, they saw what the Spectres could do.

It happened at a river-crossing, where a dusty road went over a low stone bridge beside a stand of trees. The late afternoon sun slanted across the grassland, drawing an intense green out of the ground and a dusty gold out of the air, and in that rich oblique light the witches saw a band of travellers making for the bridge, some on foot, some in horse-drawn carts, two of them riding horses. They hadn't seen the witches, for they had no reason to look up, but they were the first people the witches had seen in this world, and Serafina was about to fly down to speak to them when they heard a cry of alarm.

It came from the rider on the leading horse. He was pointing at the trees, and as the witches looked down they saw a stream of those spectral forms pouring across the grass, seeming to flow with no effort towards the people, their prey.

The people scattered. Serafina was shocked to see the leading rider turn tail at once and gallop away, without staying to help his comrades, and the second rider did the same, escaping as fast as he could in another direction.

"Fly lower and watch, sisters," Serafina told her companions. "But don't interfere till I command."

They saw that the little band contained children as well,

some riding in the carts, some walking beside them. And it was clear that the children couldn't see the Spectres, and the Spectres weren't interested in them: they made instead for the adults. One old woman seated on a cart held two little children on her lap, and Ruta Skadi was angered by her cowardice: because she tried to hide behind them, and thrust them out towards the Spectre that approached her, as if offering them up to save her own life.

The children pulled free of the old woman and jumped down from the cart, and now like the other children around them ran to and fro in fright, or stood and clung together weeping as the Spectres attacked the adults. The old woman in the cart was soon enveloped in a transparent shimmer that moved busily, working and feeding in some invisible way that made Ruta Skadi sick to watch. The same fate attacked every adult in the party apart from the two who had fled on their horses.

Fascinated and horrified, Serafina Pekkala flew down even closer. There was a father with his child who had tried to ford the river to get away, but a Spectre had caught up with them, and as the child clung to the father's back, crying, the man slowed down and stood waist-deep in the water, arrested and helpless.

What was happening to him? Serafina hovered above the water a few feet away, gazing horrified. She had heard from travellers in her own world of the legend of the vampyre, and she thought of that as she watched the Spectre busy gorging on – something, some quality the man had, his soul, his dæmon perhaps; for in this world, evidently, dæmons were inside, not outside. His arms slackened under the child's thighs, and the child fell into the water behind him and grabbed vainly at his hand, gasping, crying, but the man only turned his head slowly and looked down with perfect indifference at his little son drowning beside him.

That was too much for Serafina. She swooped lower and

plucked the child from the water, and as she did so, Ruta Skadi cried out: "Be careful, sister! Behind you –"

And Serafina felt just for a moment a hideous dullness at the edge of her heart, and reached out and up for Ruta Skadi's hand, which pulled her away from the danger. They flew higher, the child screaming and clinging to her waist with sharp fingers, and Serafina saw the Spectre behind her, a drift of mist swirling on the water, casting about for its lost prey. Ruta Skadi shot an arrow into the heart of it, with no effect at all.

Serafina put the child down on the river bank, seeing that it was in no danger from the Spectres, and they retreated to the air again. The little band of travellers had halted for good now; the horses cropped the grass or shook their heads at flies, the children were howling or clutching one another and watching from a distance, and every adult had fallen still. Their eyes were open; some were standing, though most had sat down; and a terrible stillness hung over them. As the last of the Spectres drifted away, sated, Serafina flew down and alighted in front of a woman sitting on the grass, a strong healthy-looking woman whose cheeks were red and whose fair hair was glossy.

"Woman?" said Serafina. There was no response. "Can you hear me? Can you see me?"

She shook her shoulder. With an immense effort the woman looked up. She scarcely seemed to notice. Her eyes were vacant, and when Serafina pinched the skin of her forearm, she merely looked down slowly and then away again.

The other witches were moving through the scattered wagons, looking at the victims in dismay. The children, meanwhile, were gathering on a little knoll some way off, staring at the witches and whispering together fearfully.

"The horseman's watching," said a witch.

She pointed up to where the road led through a gap in the

hills. The rider who'd fled had reined in his horse and turned round to look back, shading his eyes to see what was going on.

"We'll speak to him," said Serafina, and sprang into the air.

However the man had behaved when faced with the Spectres, he was no coward. As he saw the witches approach he unslung the rifle from his back and kicked the horse forward on to the grass, where he could wheel and fire and face them in the open; but Serafina Pekkala alighted slowly and held her bow out before laying it on the ground in front of her.

Whether or not they had that gesture here, its meaning was unmistakable. The man lowered the rifle from his shoulder and waited, looking from Serafina to the other witches, and up to their dæmons too, who circled in the skies above. Women, young and ferocious, dressed in scraps of black silk and riding pine-branches through the sky – there was nothing like that in his world, but he faced them with calm wariness. Serafina, coming closer, saw sorrow in his face as well, and strength. It was hard to reconcile with the memory of his turning tail and running while his companions perished.

"Who are you?" he said.

"My name is Serafina Pekkala. I am the queen of the witches of Lake Enara, which is in another world. What is your name?"

"Joachim Lorenz. Witches, you say? Do you treat with the devil then?"

"If we did, would that make us your enemy?"

He thought for a few moments, and settled his rifle across his thighs. "It might have done, once," he said, "but times have changed. Why have you come to this world?"

"Because the times have changed. What are those creatures who attacked your party?"

"Well, the Spectres..." he said, shrugging, half astonished. "Don't you know the Spectres?"

"We've never seen them in our world. We saw you making your escape, and we didn't know what to think. Now I understand."

"There's no defence against them," said Joachim Lorenz. "Only the children are untouched. Every party of travellers has to include a man and a woman on horseback, by law, and they have to do what we did, or else the children will have no one to look after them. But times are bad now; the cities are thronged with Spectres, and there used to be no more than a dozen or so in each place."

Ruta Skadi was looking around. She saw the other rider moving back towards the wagons, and saw that it was, indeed, a woman. The children were running to meet her.

"But tell me what you're looking for," Joachim Lorenz went on. "You didn't answer me before. You wouldn't have come here for nothing. Answer me now."

"We're looking for a child," said Serafina, "a young girl from our world. Her name is Lyra Belacqua, called Lyra Silvertongue. But where she might be, in a whole world, we can't guess. You haven't seen a strange child, on her own?"

"No. But we saw angels the other night, making for the Pole."

"Angels?"

"Troops of them in the air, armed and shining. They haven't been so common in the last years, though in my grandfather's time they passed through this world often, or so he used to say."

He shaded his eyes and gazed down towards the scattered wagons, the halted travellers. The other rider had dismounted now, and was comforting some of the children.

Serafina followed his gaze and said, "If we camp with you tonight and keep guard against the Spectres, will you tell us more about this world, and these angels you saw?"

"Certainly I will. Come with me."

The witches helped to move the wagons further along the road, over the bridge and away from the trees where the Spectres had come from. The stricken adults had to stay where they were, though it was painful to see the little children clinging to a mother who no longer responded to them, or tugging the sleeve of a father who said nothing and gazed into nothing and had nothing in his eyes. The younger children couldn't understand why they had to leave their parents. The older ones, some of whom had already lost parents of their own and who had seen it before, simply looked bleak and stayed dumb. Serafina picked up the little boy who'd fallen in the river, and who was crying out for his daddy, reaching back over Serafina's shoulder to the silent figure still standing in the water, indifferent. Serafina felt his tears on her bare skin.

The horsewoman, who wore rough canvas breeches and rode like a man, said nothing to the witches. Her face was grim. She moved the children on, speaking sternly, ignoring their tears. The evening sun suffused the air with a golden light in which every detail was clear and nothing was dazzling, and the faces of the children and the man and woman too seemed immortal and strong and beautiful.

Later, as the embers of a fire glowed in a circle of ashy rocks and the great hills lay calm under the moon, Joachim Lorenz told Serafina and Ruta Skadi about the history of his world.

It had once been a happy one, he explained. The cities were spacious and elegant, the fields well-tilled and fertile. Merchant ships plied to and fro on the blue oceans, and fishermen hauled in brimming nets of cod and tunny, bass and mullet; the forests ran with game, and no children went hungry. In the courts and squares of the great cities ambassadors from Brasil and Benin, from Eireland and Corea mingled with tabaco-sellers, with commedia players from Bergamo, with dealers in fortune-bonds.

At night masked lovers met under the rose-hung colonnades or in the lamp-lit gardens, and the air stirred with the scent of jasmine and throbbed to the music of the wire-strung mandarone.

The witches listened wide-eyed to this tale of a world so like theirs, and yet so different.

"But it went wrong," he said. "Three hundred years ago, it all went wrong. Some people reckon the philosophers' Guild of the Torre degli Angeli, the Tower of the Angels, in the city we have just left, they're the ones to blame. Others say it was a judgement on us for some great sin, though I never heard any agreement about what that sin was. But suddenly out of nowhere there came the Spectres, and we've been haunted ever since. You've seen what they do. Now imagine what it is to live in a world with Spectres in it. How can we prosper, when we can't rely on anything continuing as it was? At any moment a father might be taken, or a mother, and the family fall apart; a merchant might be taken, and his enterprise fail, and all his clerks and factors lose their employment; and how can lovers trust their vows? All the trust and all the virtue fell out of our world when the Spectres came."

"Who are these philosophers?" said Serafina. "And where is this Tower you speak of?"

"In the city we left – Cittàgazze. The city of magpies. You know why it's called that? Because magpies steal, and that's all we can do now. We create nothing, we have built nothing for hundreds of years, all we can do is steal from other worlds. Oh yes, we know about other worlds. Those philosophers in the Torre degli Angeli discovered all we need to know about that subject. They have a spell which, if you say it, lets you walk through a door that isn't there, and find yourself in another world. Some say it's not a spell but a key that can open even

135

where there isn't a lock. Who knows? Whatever it is, it let the Spectres in. And the philosophers use it still, I understand. They pass into other worlds and steal from them and bring back what they find. Gold and jewels, of course, but other things too, like ideas, or sacks of corn, or pencils. They are the source of all our wealth," he said bitterly, "that Guild of thieves."

"Why don't the Spectres harm children?" asked Ruta Skadi.

"That is the greatest mystery of all. In the innocence of children there's some power that repels the Spectres of Indifference. But it's more than that. Children simply don't see them, though we can't understand why. We never have. But Spectre-orphans are common, as you can imagine, children whose parents have been taken; they gather in bands and roam the country, and sometimes they hire themselves out to adults to look for food and supplies in a Spectre-ridden area, and sometimes they simply drift about and scavenge.

"So that is our world. Oh, we managed to live with this curse. They're true parasites: they won't kill their host, though they drain most of the life out of him. But there was a rough balance – till recently, till the great storm. Such a storm it was; it sounded as if the whole world was breaking and cracking apart; there hadn't been a storm like that in memory.

"And then there came a fog that lasted for days and covered every part of the world that I know of, and no one could travel; and when the fog cleared, the cities were full of the Spectres, hundreds and thousands of them. So we fled to the hills and out to sea, but there's no escaping them this time wherever we go. As you saw for yourselves.

"Now it's your turn. You tell me about your world, and why you've left it to come to this one."

Serafina told him truthfully as much as she knew. He was an honest man, and there was nothing that needed concealing from him. He listened closely, shaking his head with wonder, and when she had finished, he said:

"I told you about the power they say our philosophers have, of opening the way to other worlds. Well, some think that occasionally they leave a doorway open, out of forgetfulness; I wouldn't be surprised if travellers from other worlds found their way here from time to time. We know that angels pass through, after all."

"Angels?" said Serafina. "You mentioned them before. We have never heard of angels. What are they?"

"You want to know about angels?" said Joachim Lorenz. "Very well. Their name for themselves is *bene elim*, I'm told. Some call them Watchers, too. They're not beings of flesh like us, they're beings of spirit; or maybe their flesh is finer-drawn than ours, lighter and clearer, I wouldn't know; but they're not like us. They carry messages from heaven, that's their calling. We see them sometimes in the sky, passing through this world on the way to another, shining like fireflies way, way up high. On a still night you can even hear their wingbeats. They have concerns different from ours, though in the ancient days they came down and had dealings with men and women, and they bred with us, too, some say.

"And when the fog came, after the great storm, I was beset in the hills behind the city of Sant'Elia, on my way homewards. I took refuge in a shepherd's hut by a spring next to a birch wood, and all night long I heard voices above me in the fog, cries of alarm and anger, and wingbeats too, closer than I'd ever heard them before; and towards dawn there was the sound of a skirmish of arms, the whoosh of arrows, and the clang of swords. I daredn't go out and see, though I was powerfully curious, for I was afraid. I was stark terrified, if you want to know. When the sky was as light as it ever got during that fog, I ventured to look out, and I saw a great figure lying wounded by the spring. I felt as if I was seeing things I had no right to see – sacred things. I had to look away, and when I looked again the figure was gone.

"That's the closest I ever came to an angel. But as I told you, we saw them the other night, way high aloft among the stars, making for the Pole, like a fleet of mighty ships under sail... Something is happening, and we don't know down here what it may be. There could be a war breaking out. There was a war in heaven once, oh, thousands of years ago, immense ages back, but I don't know what the outcome was. It wouldn't be impossible if there was another. But the devastation would be enormous, and the consequences for us... I can't imagine it.

"Though," he went on, sitting up to stir the fire, "the end of it might be better than I fear. It might be that a war in heaven would sweep the Spectres from this world altogether, and back into the pit they come from. What a blessing that would be, eh! How fresh and happy we could live, free of that fearful blight!"

Though Joachim Lorenz looked anything but hopeful as he stared into the flames. The flickering light played over his face, but there was no play of expression in his strong features; he looked grim and sad.

Ruta Skadi said, "The Pole, sir. You said these angels were making for the Pole. Why would they do that, do you know? Is that where heaven lies?"

"I couldn't say. I'm not a learned man, you can see that plain enough. But the north of our world, well, that's the abode of spirits, they say. If angels were mustering, that's where they'd go, and if they were going to make an assault on heaven, I dare say that's where they'd build their fortress and sally out from."

He looked up, and the witches followed his eyes. The stars in this world were the same as theirs: the Milky Way blazed bright across the dome of the sky, and innumerable points of starlight dusted the dark, almost matching the moon for brightness...

"Sir," said Serafina, "did you ever hear of Dust?"

"Dust? I guess you mean it in some other sense than that dust on the roads. No, I never did. But look – there's a troop of angels now…"

He pointed to the constellation of Ophiucus. And sure enough, something was moving through it, a tiny cluster of lighted beings. And they didn't drift; they moved with the purposeful flight of geese or swans.

Ruta Skadi stood up.

"Sister, it's time I parted from you," she said to Serafina. "I'm going up to speak to these angels, whatever they may be. If they're going to Lord Asriel, I'll go with them. If not, I'll search on by myself. Thank you for your company, and go well."

They kissed, and Ruta Skadi took her cloud-pine branch and sprang into the air. Her dæmon Sergi, a bluethroat, sped out of the dark alongside her.

"We're going high?" he said.

"As high as those lighted fliers in Ophiucus. They're going swiftly, Sergi. Let's catch them!"

And she and her dæmon raced upwards, flying quicker than sparks from a fire, the air rushing through the twigs on her branch and making her black hair stream out behind. She didn't look back at the little fire in the wide darkness, at the sleeping children and her witch-companions. That part of her journey was over, and besides, those glowing creatures ahead of her were no larger yet, and unless she kept her eye on them they were easily lost against the great expanse of starlight.

So she flew on, never losing sight of the angels, and gradually as she came closer they took on a clearer shape.

They shone not as if they were burning but as if, wherever they were and however dark the night, sunlight was shining on them. They were like humans, but winged, and much taller; and as they were naked, the witch could see that three of them were male, two female. Their wings sprang from their shoulder blades, and their backs and chests were deeply muscled. Ruta Skadi stayed behind them for some way, watching, measuring their strength in case she should need to fight them. They weren't armed, but on the other hand they were flying easily within their power, and might even outstrip her if it came to a chase.

Making her bow ready, just in case, she sped forward and flew alongside them, calling:

"Angels! Halt and listen to me! I am the witch Ruta Skadi, and I want to talk to you!"

They turned. Their great wings beat inwards, slowing them, and their bodies swung downwards till they were standing upright inthe air, holding their position by the beating of their wings. They surrounded her, five huge forms glowing in the dark air, lit by an invisible sun.

She looked around, sitting her pine-branch proud and unafraid, though her heart was beating with the strangeness of it, and her dæmon fluttered to sit close to the warmth of her body.

Each angel-being was distinctly an individual, and yet they had more in common with each other than with any human she had seen. What they shared was a shimmering, darting play of intelligence and feeling that seemed to sweep over them all simultaneously. They were naked, but she felt naked in front of their glance, it was so piercing and went so deep.

Still, she was unashamed of what she was, and she returned their gaze with head held high.

"So you are angels," she said, "or Watchers, or *bene elim*. Where are you going?"

"We are following a call," said one.

She was not sure which one had spoken. It might have been any or all of them at once.

"Whose call?" she said.

"A man's."

"Lord Asriel's?"

"It may be."

"Why are you following his call?"

"Because we are willing to," came the reply.

"Then wherever he is, you can guide me to him as well," she ordered them.

Ruta Skadi was four hundred and sixteen years old, with all the pride and knowledge of an adult witch-queen. She was wiser by far than any short-lived human, but she had not the slightest idea of how like a child she seemed beside these ancient beings. Nor did she know how far their awareness spread out beyond her like filamentary tentacles to the remotest corners of universes she had never dreamed of; nor that she saw them as human-formed only because her eyes expected to. If she were to perceive their true form, they would seem more like architecture than organism, like huge structures composed of intelligence and feeling.

But they expected nothing else: she was very young.

At once they beat their wings and surged forward, and she darted with them, surfing on the turbulence their pinions caused in the air and relishing the speed and power it added to her flight.

They flew throughout the night. The stars wheeled around them, and faded and vanished as the dawn seeped up from the east. The world burst into brilliance as the sun's rim appeared, and then they were flying through blue sky and clear air, fresh and sweet and moist.

In the daylight the angels were less visible, though to any eye their strangeness was clear. The light Ruta Skadi saw them by was stillnot that of the sun now climbing the sky, but some other light from somewhere else.

Tirelessly they flew on and on, and tirelessly she kept pace. She felt a fierce joy possessing her, that she could command these immortal presences. And she rejoiced in her blood and flesh, in the rough pine bark she felt next to her skin, in the beat of her heart and the life of all her senses, and in the hunger she was feeling now, and in the presence of her sweet-voiced bluethroat dæmon, and in the earth below her and the lives of every creature, plant and animal both; and she delighted in being of the same substance as them, and in knowing that when she died her flesh would nourish other lives as they had nourished her. And she rejoiced, too, that she was going to see Lord Asriel again.

Another night came, and still the angels flew on. And at some point the quality of the air changed, not for the worse or the better, but changed nonetheless, and Ruta Skadi knew that they'd passed out of that world and into another. How it had happened she couldn't guess.

"Angels!" she called, as she sensed the change. "How have we left the world I found you in? Where was the boundary?"

"There are invisible places in the air," came the answer, "gateways into other worlds. We can see them, but you cannot."

Ruta Skadi couldn't see the invisible gateway, but she didn't need to: witches could navigate better than birds. As soon as the angel spoke, she fixed her attention on three jagged peaks below her, and memorized their configuration exactly. Now she could find it again, if she needed to, despite what the angels might think.

They flew on further, and presently she heard an angel-voice:

"Lord Asriel is in this world, and there is the fortress he's building…"

They had slowed, and were circling like eagles in the middle airs. Ruta Skadi looked where one angel was pointing. The first faint glimmer of light was tinting the east, though all the stars above shone as brilliantly as ever against the profound velvet black of the high heavens. And on the very rim of the world, where the light was increasing moment by moment, a great mountain range reared its peaks – jagged spears of black rock, mighty broken slabs and sawtooth ridges piled in confusion like the wreckage of a universal catastrophe. But on the highest point, which as she looked was touched by the first rays of the morning sun and outlined in brilliance, stood a regular structure: a huge fortress whose battlements were formed of single slabs of basalt half a hill in height, and whose extent was to be measured in flying-time.

Beneath this colossal fortress, fires glared and furnaces smoked in the darkness of early dawn, and from many miles away Ruta Skadi heard the clang of hammers and the pounding of great mills. And from every direction, she could see more flights of angels winging towards it, and not only angels, but machines too: steel-winged craft gliding like albatrosses, glass cabins under flickering dragonfly-wings, droning zeppelins like huge bumble bees – all making for the fortress that Lord Asriel was building on the mountains at the edge of the world.

"And is Lord Asriel there?" she said.

"Yes, he is there," the angels replied.

"Then let's fly there to meet him. And you must be my guard of honour."

Obediently they spread their wings, and set their course towards the gold-rimmed fortress, with the eager witch flying before them.

7

The Rolls Royce

Lyra woke early to find the morning quiet and warm, as if the city never had any other weather than this calm summer. She slipped out of bed and downstairs and, hearing some children's voices out on the water, went to see what they were doing.

Three boys and a girl were splashing across the sunlit harbour in a couple of pedal-boats, racing towards the steps. As they saw Lyra they slowed for a moment, but then the race took hold of them again. The winners crashed into the steps so hard that one of them fell into the water, and then he tried to climb into the other craft and tipped that over too, and then they all splashed about together as if the fear of the night before had never happened. They were younger than most of the children by the Tower, Lyra thought, and she joined them in the water, with Pantalaimon as a little silver fish glittering beside her. She never found it hard to talk to other children, and soon they were gathered round her, sitting in pools of water on the warm stone, their shirts drying quickly in the sun. Poor Pantalaimon had to creep into her pocket again, frog-shaped in the cool damp cotton.

"What you going to do with that cat?"

"Can you really take the bad luck away?"

"Where you come from?"

"Your friend, he ain afraid of Spectres?"

"Will en't afraid of anything," Lyra said. "Nor'm I. What you scared of cats for?"

"You don't know about cats?" the oldest boy said incredulously. "Cats, they got the devil in them, all right. You got to kill every cat you see. They bite you and put the devil in you too. And what was you doing with that big pard?"

She realized he meant Pantalaimon in his leopard-shape, and shook her head innocently.

"You must have been dreaming," she said. "There's all kinds of things look different in the moonlight. But me and Will, we don't have Spectres where we come from, so we don't know much about 'em."

"If you can't see 'em, you're safe," said a boy. "You see 'em, you know they can get you. That's what my pa said, then they got him. He missed them that time."

"And they're here, all round us now?"

"Yeah," said the girl. She reached out a hand and grabbed a fistful of air, crowing, "I got one now!"

"They can't hurt you," one of the boys said. "So we can't hurt them, all right."

"And there's always been Spectres in this world?" said Lyra.

"Yeah," said one boy, but another said, "No, they came a long time ago. Hundreds of years."

"They came because of the Guild," said the third.

"The what?" said Lyra.

"They never!" said the girl. "My granny said they came because people were bad, and God sent them to punish us."

"Your granny don' know nothing," said a boy. "She got a beard, your granny. She's a goat, all right."

"What's the Guild?" Lyra persisted.

"You know the Torre degli Angeli," said a boy, "the stone tower, right, well it belongs to the Guild, and there's a secret place in there. The Guild, they're men who know all kind of things. Philosophy, alchemy, all kind of things they know. And they were the ones who let the Spectres in."

"That ain true," said another boy. "They came from the stars."

"It *is*! This is what happened, all right: this Guild man hundreds of years ago was taking some metal apart. Lead. He was going to make it into gold. And he cut it and cut it smaller and smaller till he came to the smallest piece he could get. There ain nothing smaller than that. So small you couldn't see it, even. But he cut that too, and inside the smallest little bit, there was all the Spectres packed in twisted over and folded up so tight they took up no space at all. But once he cut it, bam! They whooshed out, and they been here ever since. That's what my pappa said."

"Is there any Guild men in the tower now?" said Lyra.

"No! They run away like everyone else," said the girl.

"There ain no one in the tower. That's haunted, that place," said a boy. "That's why the cat came from there. We ain gonna go in there, all right. Ain no kids gonna go in there. That's scary."

"The Guild men ain afraid to go in there," said another.

"They got special magic, or something. They're greedy, they live off the poor people," said the girl. "The poor people do all the work, and the Guild men just live there for nothing."

"But there en't anyone in the tower now?" Lyra said. "No grown-ups?"

"No grown-ups in the city at all!"

"They wouldn't dare, all right."

But she had seen a young man up there. She was convinced of it. And there was something in the way these children spoke: as a practised liar, she knew liars when she met them, and they were lying about something.

And suddenly she remembered: little Paolo had mentioned that he and Angelica had an elder brother Tullio who was in the city too, and Angelica had hushed him... Could the young man she'd seen have been their brother?

She left them to rescue their boats and pedal back to the beach, and went inside to make some coffee and see if Will was awake. But he was still asleep, with the cat curled up at his feet, and Lyra was impatient to see her scholar again; so she wrote a note and left it on the floor by his bedside, and took her rucksack and went off to look for the window.

The way she took led her through the little square they'd come to the night before. But it was empty now, and the sunlight dusted the front of the ancient tower and showed up the blurred carvings beside the doorway: human-like figures with folded wings, their features eroded by centuries of weather, but somehow in their stillness expressing power and compassion and intellectual force.

"Angels," said Pantalaimon, a cricket on her shoulder.

"Maybe Spectres," Lyra said.

"No! They said this was something *angeli*," he insisted. "Bet that's angels."

"Shall we go in?"

They looked up at the great oak door on its ornate black hinges. The half-dozen steps up to it were deeply worn, and the door itself stood slightly open. There was nothing to stop Lyra going in except her own fear.

She tiptoed to the top of the steps and looked through the opening. A dark stone-flagged hall was all she could see, and not much of that; but Pantalaimon was fluttering anxiously on her shoulder, just as he had when they'd played the trick on the skulls in the crypt at Jordan College, and she was a little wiser now. This was a bad place. She ran down the steps and out of the square, making for the bright sunlight of the palm-tree boulevard. And as soon as she was sure there was no one looking, she went straight across to the window and through into Will's Oxford.

Forty minutes later she was inside the physics building once more, arguing with the porter; but this time she had a trump card.

"You just ask Dr Malone," she said sweetly. "That's all you got to do, ask her. She'll tell you."

The porter turned to his telephone, and Lyra watched pityingly as he pressed the buttons and spoke into it. They didn't give him a proper lodge to sit in, like a real Oxford college, just a big wooden counter, as if it was a shop.

"All right," said the porter, turning back. "She says go on up. Mind you don't go anywhere else."

"No, I won't," she said demurely, a good little girl doing what she was told.

At the top of the stairs, though, she had a surprise, because just as she passed a door with a symbol indicating woman on it, it opened and there was Dr Malone silently beckoning her in.

She entered, puzzled. This wasn't the laboratory, it was a washroom, and Dr Malone was agitated.

She said, "Lyra – there's someone else in the lab – police officers or something – they know you came to see me yesterday – I don't know what they're after but I don't like it – what's going on?"

"How do they know I came to see you?"

"I don't know! They didn't know your name, but I knew who they meant –"

"Oh. Well, I can lie to them. That's easy."

"But *what is going on*?"

A woman's voice spoke from the corridor outside:

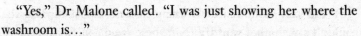

"Dr Malone? Have you seen the child?"

"Yes," Dr Malone called. "I was just showing her where the washroom is…"

There was no need for her to be so anxious, thought Lyra, but perhaps she wasn't used to danger.

The woman in the corridor was young and dressed very smartly, and she did try to smile when Lyra came out, but her eyes remained hard and suspicious.

"Hello," she said. "You're Lyra, are you?"

"Yeah. What's your name?"

"I'm Sergeant Clifford. Come along in."

Lyra thought this young woman had a nerve, acting as if it was her own laboratory, but she nodded meekly. That was the moment when she first felt a twinge of regret. She knew she shouldn't be here; she knew what the alethiometer wanted her to do, and it was not this. She stood doubtfully in the doorway.

In the room already there was a tall powerful man with white eyebrows. Lyra knew what scholars looked like, and neither of these two was a scholar.

"Come in, Lyra," said Sergeant Clifford again. "It's all right. This is Inspector Walters."

"Hello, Lyra," said the man. "I've been hearing all about you from Dr Malone here. I'd like to meet you, and ask you a few questions, if that's all right."

"What sort of questions?" she said.

"Nothing difficult," he said, smiling. "Come and sit down, Lyra."

He pushed a chair towards her. Lyra sat down carefully, and heard the door close itself. Dr Malone was standing nearby. Pantalaimon, cricket-formed in Lyra's breast pocket, was agitated: she could feel him against her breast, and hoped the tremor didn't show. She thought to him to keep still.

"Where d'you come from, Lyra?" said Inspector Walters.

If she said Oxford, they'd easily be able to check. But she couldn't say another world, either; these people were dangerous; they'd want to know more at once. She thought of the only other name she knew of in this world: the place Will had come from.

"Winchester," she said.

"You've been in the wars, haven't you, Lyra?" said the inspector. "How did you get those bruises? There's a bruise on your cheek, and another on your leg – has someone been knocking you about?"

"No," said Lyra.

"Do you go to school, Lyra?"

"Yeah. Sometimes," she added.

"Shouldn't you be at school today?"

She said nothing. She was feeling more and more uneasy. She looked at Dr Malone, whose face was tight and unhappy.

"I just came here to see Dr Malone," Lyra said.

"Are you staying in Oxford, Lyra? Where are you staying?"

"With some people," she said. "Just friends."

"What's their address?"

"I don't know exactly what it's called. I can find it, easy, but I can't remember the name of the street."

"Who are these people?"

"Just friends of my father," she said.

"Oh, I see. How did you find Dr Malone?"

"'Cause my father's a physicist and he knows her."

It was going more easily now, she thought. She began to relax into it and lie more fluently.

"And she showed you what she was working on, did she?"

"Yeah. The engine with the screen… Yes, all that."

"You're interested in that sort of thing, are you? Science and so on?"

"Yeah. Physics, especially."

"You going to be a scientist when you grow up?"

That sort of question deserved a blank stare, which it got. He wasn't disconcerted. His pale eyes looked briefly at the young woman, and then back to Lyra.

"And were you surprised at what Dr Malone showed you?"

"Well, sort of, but I knew what to expect."

"Because of your father?"

"Yeah. 'Cause he's doing the same kind of work."

"Yes, quite. Do you understand it?"

"Some of it."

"Your father's looking into dark matter, then?"

"Yes."

"Has he got as far as Dr Malone?"

"Not in the same way. He can do some things better, but that engine with the words on the screen, he hasn't got one of those."

"Is Will staying with your friends as well?"

"Yes, he –"

And she stopped. She knew at once she'd made a horrible mistake.

So did they, and they were on their feet in a moment to stop her running out, but somehow Dr Malone was in the way, and the sergeant tripped and fell, blocking the way of the inspector. It gave Lyra time to dart out and slam the door shut behind her, and run full tilt for the stairs.

Two men in white coats came out of a door, and she bumped into them and suddenly Pantalaimon was a crow, shrieking and flapping, and he startled them so much they fell back and she pulled free of their hands and raced down the last flight of stairs into the lobby just as the porter put the phone down and lumbered along behind his counter calling out: "Oy! Stop there! You!"

151

But the flap he had to lift was at the other end, and she got to the revolving door before he could come out and catch her.

And behind her, the lift doors were opening, and the pale-haired man was running out, so fast, so strong –

And the door wouldn't turn! Pantalaimon shrieked at her: they were pushing the wrong side!

She cried out in fear and darted out and into the other compartment, hurling her little weight against the heavy glass, willing it to turn, and got it to move just in time to avoid the grasp of the porter, who then got in the way of the pale-haired man, so Lyra could dash out and away before they got through.

Across the road, ignoring the cars, the brakes, the squeal of tyres; into this gap between tall buildings, and then another road, with cars from both directions, but she was quick, dodging bicycles, always with the pale-haired man just behind her – oh, he was frightening!

Into a garden – over a fence – through some bushes – Pantalaimon skimming overhead, a swift, calling to her which way to go; crouching down behind a coal-bunker as the pale man's footsteps came racing past, and she couldn't hear him panting, he was so fast, and so fit; and Pantalaimon said, "Back now – go back to the road –"

So she crept out of her hiding-place and ran back across the grass, out through the garden gate, into the open spaces of the Banbury Road again; and once again she dodged across, and once again tyres squealed on the road; and then she was running up Norham Gardens, a quiet tree-lined road of tall Victorian houses near the Park.

She stopped to gain her breath. There was a tall hedge in front of one of the gardens, with a low wall at its foot, and she sat there tucked closely in under the privet.

"She helped us!" Pantalaimon said. "Dr Malone got in their

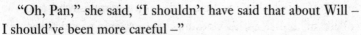

way. She's on our side, not theirs."

"Oh, Pan," she said, "I shouldn't have said that about Will – I should've been more careful –"

"Shouldn't have come," he said severely.

"I know. That too…"

But she hadn't got time to berate herself, because Pantalaimon fluttered to her shoulder, and then said, "Look out – behind –" and immediately changed to a cricket again and dived into her pocket.

She stood, ready to run, and saw a large dark-blue car gliding silently to the pavement beside her. She was braced to dart in either direction, but the car's rear window rolled down, and there looking out was a face she recognized.

"Lizzie," said the old man from the Museum. "How nice to see you again. Can I give you a lift anywhere?"

And he opened the door and moved up to make room beside him. Pantalaimon nipped her breast through the thin cotton, but she got in at once, clutching the rucksack, and the man leaned across her and pulled the door shut.

"You look as if you're in a hurry," he said. "Where d'you want to go?"

"Up Summertown," she said, "please."

The driver was wearing a peaked cap. Everything about the car was smooth and soft and powerful, and the smell of the old man's cologne was strong in the enclosed space. The car pulled out from the pavement and moved away with no noise at all.

"So what have you been up to, Lizzie?" the old man said. "Did you find out more about those skulls?"

"Yeah," she said, twisting to see out of the rear window. There was no sign of the pale-haired man. She'd got away! And he'd never find her now she was safe in a powerful car with a rich man like this. She felt a little hiccup of triumph.

"I made some enquiries too," he said. "An anthropologist friend of mine tells me that they've got several others in the collection, as well as the ones on display. Some of them are very old indeed. Neanderthal, you know."

"Yeah, that's what I heard too," Lyra said, with no idea what he was talking about.

"And how's your friend?"

"What friend?" said Lyra, alarmed: had she told him about Will too?

"The friend you're staying with."

"Oh. Yes. She's very well, thank you."

"What does she do? Is she an archaeologist?"

"Oh… She's a physicist. She studies dark matter," said Lyra, still not quite in control. This was a harder world to tell lies in than she'd thought. And something else was nagging at her: this old man was familiar in some long-lost way, and she just couldn't place it.

"Dark matter?" he was saying. "How fascinating! I saw something about that in *The Times* this morning. The universe is full of this mysterious stuff, and nobody knows what it is! And your friend is on the track of it, is she?"

"Yes. She knows a lot about it."

"And what are you going to do later on, Lizzie? Are you going in for physics too?"

"I might," said Lyra. "It depends."

The chauffeur coughed gently, and slowed the car down.

"Well, here we are in Summertown," said the old man. "Where would you like to be dropped?"

"Oh – just up past these shops – I can walk from there," said Lyra. "Thank you."

"Turn left into South Parade, and pull up on the right, could you, Allan," said the old man.

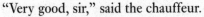

"Very good, sir," said the chauffeur.

A minute later the car came to a silent halt outside a public library. The old man held open the door on his side, so that Lyra had to climb past his knees to get out. There was a lot of space, but somehow it was awkward, and she didn't want to touch him, nice as he was.

"Don't forget your rucksack," he said, handing it to her.

"Thank you," she said.

"I'll see you again, I hope, Lizzie," he said. "Give my regards to your friend."

"Goodbye," she said, and lingered on the pavement till the car had turned the corner and gone out of sight before she set off towards the hornbeam trees. She had a feeling about that pale-haired man, and she wanted to ask the alethiometer.

Will was reading his father's letters again. He sat on the terrace hearing the distant shouts of children diving off the harbour mouth, and read the clear handwriting on the flimsy airmail sheets, trying to picture the man who'd penned it, and looking again and again at the reference to the baby, to himself.

He heard Lyra's running footsteps from some way off. He put the letters in his pocket and stood up, and almost at once Lyra was there, wild-eyed, with Pantalaimon a snarling savage wildcat, too distraught to hide. She who seldom cried was sobbing with rage; her chest was heaving, her teeth were grinding, and she flung herself at him, clutching his arms, and cried, "Kill him! Kill him! I want him dead! I wish Iorek was here – oh, Will, I done wrong, I'm so sorry –"

"What? What's the matter?"

"That old man – he en't nothing but a low thief – he *stole* it, Will! He stole my alethiometer! That stinky old man with his rich clothes and his servant driving the car – oh, I done such wrong

155

things this morning – oh, I…"

And she sobbed so passionately he thought that hearts really did break, and hers was breaking now, for she fell to the ground wailing and shuddering, and Pantalaimon beside her became a wolf and howled with bitter grief.

Far off across the water, children stopped what they were doing and shaded their eyes to see. Will sat down beside Lyra and shook her shoulder.

"Stop! Stop crying!" he said. "Tell me from the beginning. What old man? What happened?"

"You're going to be so angry – I promised I wouldn't give you away, I *promised* it, and then…" she sobbed, and Pantalaimon became a young clumsy dog with lowered ears and wagging tail, squirming with self-abasement; and Will understood that Lyra had done something that she was too ashamed to tell him about, and he spoke to the dæmon.

"What *happened*? Just tell me," he said.

Pantalaimon said, "We went to the scholar, and there was someone else there, a man and a woman – and they tricked us – they asked a lot of questions and then they asked about you, and before we could stop we gave it away that we knew you, and then we ran away –"

Lyra was hiding her face in her hands, pressing her head down against the pavement. Pantalaimon was flickering from shape to shape in his agitation: dog, bird, cat, snow-white ermine.

"What did the man look like?" said Will.

"Big," said Lyra's muffled voice, "and ever so strong, and pale eyes…"

"Did he see you come back through the window?"

"No, but…"

"Well, he won't know where we are, then."

"But the alethiometer!" she cried, and she sat up fiercely, her face rigid with emotion, like a Greek mask.

"Yeah," said Will. "Tell me about that."

Between sobs and teeth-grindings she told him what had happened: how the old man had seen her using the alethiometer in the Museum the day before, and how he'd stopped the car today and she'd got in to escape from the pale man, and how the car had pulled up on that side of the road so she'd had to climb past him to get out, and how he must have swiftly taken the alethiometer as he'd passed her the rucksack…

He could see how devastated she was, but not why she should feel guilty. And then she said:

"And Will, please, I done something very bad. Because the alethiometer told me I had to stop looking for Dust, and I had to help you. I had to help you find your father. And I *could*, I could take you to wherever he is, if I had it. But I wouldn't listen. I just done what I wanted to do, and I shouldn't…"

He'd seen her use it, and he knew it could tell her the truth. He turned away. She seized his wrist, but he broke away from her and walked to the edge of the water. The children were playing again across the harbour. Lyra ran up to him and said, "Will, I'm so sorry –"

"What's the use of that? I don't care if you're sorry or not. You did it."

"But Will, we got to help each other, you and me, because there en't anyone else!"

"I can't see how."

"Nor can I, but…"

She stopped in mid-sentence, and a light came into her eyes. She turned and raced back to her rucksack, abandoned on the pavement, and rummaged through it feverishly.

"I know who he is! And where he lives! Look!" she said, and held up a little slip of white card. "He gave this to me in the

157

Museum! We can go and get it back!"

Will took the card and read:

Sir Charles Latrom, CBE
Limefield House
Old Headington
Oxford

"He's a sir," he said. "A knight. That means people will automatically believe him and not us. What did you want me to do anyway? Go to the police? The police are after me! Or if they weren't yesterday they will be by now. And if *you* go, they know who you are now, and they know you know me, so that wouldn't work either."

"We could steal it. We could go to his house and steal it. I know where Headington is, there's a Headington in my Oxford too. It en't far. We could walk there in an hour, easy."

"You're stupid."

"Iorek Byrnison would go there straight away and rip his head off. I wish he was here. He'd –"

But she fell silent. Will was just looking at her, and she quailed. She would have quailed in the same way if the armoured bear had looked at her like that, because there was something not unlike Iorek in Will's eyes, young as they were.

"I never heard anything so stupid in my life," he said. "You think we can just go to his house and creep in and steal it? You need to think. You need to use your bloody brain. He's going to have all kinds of burglar alarms and stuff, if he's a rich man, there'll be bells that go off and special locks and lights with infra-red switches that come on automatically –"

"I never heard of those things," Lyra said. "We en't got 'em in my world. I couldn't know that, Will."

"All right, then think of this: he's got a whole house to hide it in, and how long would any burglar have to look through every cupboard and drawer and hiding-place in a whole house? Those men who came to my house had hours to look around, and they never found what they were looking for, and I bet he's got a whole lot bigger house than we have. And probably a safe, too. So even if we did get into his house we'd never find it in time before the police came."

She hung her head. It was all true.

"What we going to do then?" she said.

He didn't answer. But it was *we*, for certain. He was bound to her now whether he liked it or not.

He walked to the water's edge, and back to the terrace, and back to the water again. He beat his hands together, looking for an answer, but no answer came, and he shook his head angrily.

"Just … go there," he said. "Just go there and see him. It's no good asking your scholar to help us, either, not if the police have been to her. She's bound to believe them rather than us. At least if we get into his house we'll see where the main rooms are. That'll be a start."

Without another word he went inside and put the letters under the pillow in the room he'd slept in. Then, if he were caught, they'd never have them.

Lyra was waiting on the terrace, with Pantalaimon perched on her shoulder as a sparrow. She was looking more cheerful.

"We're going to get it back all right," she said. "I can feel it."

He said nothing. They set off for the window.

It took an hour and a half to walk to Headington. Lyra led the way, avoiding the city centre, and Will kept watch all around, saying nothing. It was much harder for Lyra now than it had been even in the Arctic, on the way to Bolvangar, for then she'd had the gyptians and Iorek Byrnison with her, and even if the tundra was full of danger, you knew the danger when you saw it. Here, in the city that was both hers and not hers, danger could look friendly, and treachery smiled and smelt sweet; and even if they weren't going to kill her or part her from Pantalaimon, they had robbed her of her only guide. Without the alethiometer, she was … just a little girl, lost.

Limefield House was the colour of warm honey, and half the front of it was covered in Virginia creeper. It stood in a large well-tended garden, with a shrubbery at one side and a gravel drive sweeping up to the front door. The Rolls Royce was parked in front of a double garage to the left. Everything Will could see spoke of wealth and power, the sort of informal settled superiority that some upper-class English people still took for granted. There was something about it that made him grit his teeth, and he didn't know why, until suddenly he remembered an occasion when he was very young – his mother had taken him to a house not unlike this – they'd dressed in their best clothes and he'd had to be on his best behaviour, and an old man and woman had made his mother cry and they'd left the house and she was still crying…

Lyra saw him breathing fast and clenching his fists, and was sensible enough not to ask why: it was something to do with him, not with her. Presently he took a deep breath.

"Well," he said, "might as well try."

He walked up the drive, and Lyra followed close behind. They felt very exposed.

The door had an old-fashioned bell-pull, like those in Lyra's world, and Will didn't know where to find it till Lyra showed him. When they pulled it, the bell jangled a long way off inside the house.

The man who opened the door was the servant who'd been driving the car, only now he didn't have his cap on. He looked at

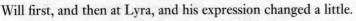

Will first, and then at Lyra, and his expression changed a little.

"We want to see Sir Charles Latrom," Will said.

His jaw was jutting as it had done last night facing the stone-throwing children by the tower. The servant nodded.

"Wait here," he said. "I'll tell Sir Charles."

He closed the door. It was solid oak, with two heavy locks, and bolts top and bottom, though Will thought that no sensible burglar would try the front door anyway. And there was a burglar alarm prominently fixed to the front of the house, and a large spotlight at each corner; they'd never be able to get near it, let alone break in.

Steady footsteps came to the door, and then it opened again. Will looked up at the face of this man who had so much that he wanted even more, and found him disconcertingly smooth and calm and powerful, not in the least guilty or ashamed.

Sensing Lyra beside him impatient and angry, Will said quickly:

"Excuse me, but Lyra thinks that when she had a lift in your car earlier on, she left something in it by mistake."

"Lyra? I don't know a Lyra. What an unusual name. I know a child called Lizzie. And who are you?"

Cursing himself for forgetting, Will said, "I'm her brother. Mark."

"I see. Hello, Lizzie, or Lyra. You'd better come in."

He stood aside. Neither Will nor Lyra was quite expecting this, and they stepped inside uncertainly. The hall was dim, and smelt of beeswax and flowers. Every surface was polished and clean, and a mahogany cabinet against the wall contained dainty porcelain figures. Will saw the servant standing in the background, as if he were waiting to be called.

"Come into my study," said Sir Charles, and held open another door off the hall.

He was being courteous, even welcoming, but there was an edge to his manner that put Will on guard. The study was large and comfortable in a cigar-smoke and leather-armchair sort of way, and seemed to be full of bookshelves, pictures, hunting trophies. There were three or four glass-fronted cabinets containing antique scientific instruments – brass microscopes, telescopes covered in green leather, sextants, compasses; it was clear why he wanted the alethiometer.

"Sit down," said Sir Charles, and indicated a leather sofa. He sat at the chair behind his desk, and went on, "Well? What have you got to say?"

"You stole –" began Lyra hotly, but Will looked at her, and she stopped.

"Lyra thinks she left something in your car," he said again. "We've come to get it back."

"Is this the object you mean?" he said, and took a velvet cloth from his drawer in the desk. Lyra stood up. He ignored her and unfolded the cloth, disclosing the golden splendour of the alethiometer resting in his palm.

"Yes!" Lyra burst out, and reached for it.

But he closed his hand. The desk was wide, and she couldn't reach; and before she could do anything else, he swung around and placed the alethiometer in a glass-fronted cabinet before locking it and dropping the key in his waistcoat pocket.

"But it isn't yours, Lizzie," he said. "Or Lyra, if that's your name."

"It is mine! It's my alethiometer!"

He shook his head, sadly and heavily, as if he were reproaching her and it was a sorrow to him, but he was doing it for her own good.

"I think at the very least there's considerable doubt about the matter," he said.

"But it is hers!" said Will. "Honestly! She's shown it to me! I know it's hers!"

"You see, I think you'd have to prove that," he said. "I don't have to prove anything, because it's in my possession. It's assumed to be mine. Like all the other items in my collection. I must say, Lyra, I'm surprised to find you so dishonest –"

"I en't dishonest!" Lyra cried.

"Oh, but you are. You told me your name was Lizzie. Now I learn it's something else. Frankly, you haven't got a hope of convincing anyone that a precious piece like this belongs to you. I tell you what. Let's call the police."

He turned his head to call for the servant.

"No, wait –" said Will, before Sir Charles could speak, but Lyra ran round the desk, and from nowhere Pantalaimon was in her arms, a snarling wildcat baring his teeth and hissing at the old man. Sir Charles blinked at the sudden appearance of the dæmon, but hardly flinched.

"You don't even know what it is you stole," Lyra stormed. "You seen me using it and you thought you'd steal it, and you did. But you – you're worse than my mother – at least she knows it's important – you're just going to put it in a case and do nothing with it! You ought to die! If I can, I'll make someone kill you. You're not worth leaving alive. You're –"

She couldn't speak. All she could do was spit full in his face, so she did, with all her might.

Will sat still, watching, looking around, memorizing where everything was.

Sir Charles calmly shook out a silk handkerchief and mopped himself.

"Have you *any* control over yourself?" he said. "Go and sit down, you filthy brat."

Lyra felt tears shaken out of her eyes by the trembling of her body, and threw herself on to the sofa. Pantalaimon, his thick cat's tail erect, stood on her lap with his blazing eyes fixed on the old man.

Will sat silent and puzzled. Sir Charles could have thrown them out long before this. What was he playing at?

And then he saw something so bizarre he thought he had imagined it. Out of the sleeve of Sir Charles's linen jacket, past the snowy white shirt-cuff, came the emerald head of a snake. Its black tongue flickered this way, that way, and its mailed head with its gold-rimmed black eyes moved from Lyra to Will and back again. She was too angry to see it at all, and Will saw it only for a moment before it retreated again up the old man's sleeve, but it made his eyes widen with shock.

Sir Charles moved to the window seat and calmly sat down, arranging the crease in his trousers.

"I think you'd better listen to me instead of behaving in this uncontrolled way," he said. "You really haven't any choice. The instrument is in my possession, and will stay there. I want it. I'm a collector. You can spit and stamp and scream all you like, but by the time you've persuaded anyone else to listen to you, I shall have plenty of documents to prove that I bought it. I can do that very easily. And then you'll never get it back."

They were both silent now. He hadn't finished. A great puzzlement was slowing Lyra's heartbeat, and making the room very still.

"However," he went on, "there's something I want even more. And I can't get it myself, so I'm prepared to make a deal with you. You fetch the object I want, and I'll give you back the – what did you call it?"

"Alethiometer," said Lyra hoarsely.

"Alethiometer. How interesting. Aletheia, truth – those emblems – yes, I see."

"What's this thing you want?" said Will. "And where is it?"

"It's somewhere I can't go, but you can. I'm perfectly well aware that you've found a doorway somewhere. I guess it's not too far from Summertown, where I dropped Lizzie, or Lyra, this morning. And that through the doorway is another world, one with no grown-ups in it. Right so far? Well, you see, the man who made that doorway has got a knife. He's hiding in that other world right now, and he's extremely afraid. He has reason to be. If he's where I think he is, he's in an old stone tower which has angels carved around the doorway. The Torre degli Angeli.

"So that's where you have to go, and I don't care how you do it, but I want that knife. Bring it to me, and you can have the alethiometer. I shall be sorry to lose it, but I'm a man of my word. That's what you have to do: bring me the knife."

8

The Tower of the Angels

W

ill said, "Who is this man who's got the knife?"

They were in the Rolls Royce, driving up through Oxford. Sir Charles sat in the front, half turned round, and Will and Lyra sat in the back, with Pantalaimon a mouse now, soothed in Lyra's hands.

"Someone who has no more right to the knife than I have to the alethiometer," said Sir Charles. "Unfortunately for all of us, the alethiometer is in my possession, and the knife is in his."

"How do you know about that other world anyway?"

"I know many things that you don't. What else would you expect? I am a good deal older, and considerably better informed. There are a number of doorways between this world and that; those who know where they are can easily pass back and forth. In Cittàgazze there's a Guild of learned men, so-called, who used to do so all the time."

"You en't from this world at all!" said Lyra suddenly. "You're from there, en't you?"

And again came that strange nudge at her memory. She was almost certain she'd seen him before.

"No, I'm not," he said.

Will said, "If we've got to get the knife from that man, we

need to know more about him. He's not going to just give it to us, is he?"

"Certainly not. It's the one thing keeping the Spectres away. It's not going to be easy by any means."

"The Spectres are afraid of the knife?"

"Very much so."

"Why do they only attack grown-ups?"

"You don't need to know that now. It doesn't matter. Lyra," Sir Charles said, turning to her, "tell me about your remarkable friend."

He meant Pantalaimon. And as soon as he said it, Will realized that the snake he'd seen concealed in the man's sleeve was a dæmon too, and that Sir Charles must come from Lyra's world. He was asking about Pantalaimon to put them off the track: so he didn't realize that Will had seen his own dæmon.

Lyra lifted Pantalaimon close to her breast, and he became a black rat, whipping his tail round and round her wrist and glaring at Sir Charles with red eyes.

"You weren't supposed to see him," she said. "He's my dæmon. You think you en't got dæmons in this world, but you have. Yours'd be a dung beetle."

He said, "If the Pharaohs of Egypt were content to be represented by a scarab, so am I. Well, you're from yet another world. How interesting. Is that where the alethiometer comes from, or did you steal it on your travels?"

"I was given it," said Lyra furiously. "The Master of Jordan College in my Oxford gave it me. It's mine by right. And you wouldn't know what to do with it, you stupid stinky old man, you'd never read it in a hundred years. It's just a toy to you. But I *need* it, and so does Will. We'll get it back, don't worry."

"We'll see," said Sir Charles. "This is where I dropped you before. Shall we let you out here?"

"No," said Will, because he could see a police car further down the road. "You can't come into Ci'gazze because of the Spectres, so it doesn't matter if you know where the window is. Take us further up towards the Ring Road."

"As you wish," said Sir Charles, and the car moved on. "When, or if, you get the knife, call my number and Allan will come to pick you up."

They said no more till the chauffeur drew the car to a halt. As they got out, Sir Charles wound his window down and said to Will:

"By the way, if you can't get the knife, don't bother to return. Come to my house without it and I'll call the police. I imagine they'll be there at once when I tell them your real name. It is William Parry, isn't it? Yes, I thought so. There's a very good photo of you in today's paper."

And the car pulled away. Will was speechless.

Lyra was shaking his arm. "It's all right," she said, "he won't tell anyone else. He would have done already if he was going to. Come on."

Ten minutes later they stood in the little square at the foot of the Tower of the Angels. Will had told her about the snake-dæmon, and she had stopped still in the street, tormented again by the half-memory. Who was the old man? Where had she seen him? It was no good; the memory wouldn't come clear.

"I didn't want to tell *him*," Lyra said quietly, "but I saw a man up there last night. He looked down when the kids were making all that noise…"

"What did he look like?"

"Young, with curly hair. Not old at all. But I only saw him for a moment, at the very top, over those battlements. I thought he might be… You remember Angelica and Paolo, and he said they had an older brother, and he'd come into the city as well, and she made Paolo stop telling us, as if it was a secret? Well, I thought it might be him. He might be after this knife as well. And I reckon all the kids know about it. I think that's the real reason why they come back in the first place."

"Mmm," he said, looking up. "Maybe."

She remembered the children talking earlier that morning: no children would go in the tower, they'd said; there were scary things in there; and she remembered her own feeling of unease as she and Pantalaimon had looked through the open door before leaving the city. Maybe that was why they needed a grown man to go in there. Her dæmon was fluttering around her head now, moth-formed in the bright sunlight, whispering anxiously.

"Hush," she whispered back, "there en't any choice, Pan. It's our fault. We got to make it right, and this is the only way."

Will walked off to the right, following the wall of the tower. At the corner a narrow cobbled alley led between it and the next building, and Will went down there too, looking up, getting the measure of the place. Lyra followed. He stopped under a window at the second-storey level, and said to Pantalaimon:

"Can you fly up there? Can you look in?"

He became a sparrow at once and set off. He could only just reach it; Lyra gasped and gave a little cry when he was at the window sill, and he perched there for a second or two before diving down again. She sighed and took deep breaths like someone rescued from drowning. Will frowned, puzzled.

"It's hard," she explained; "when your dæmon goes away from you, it hurts…"

"Sorry. Did you see anything?" he said.

"Stairs," said Pantalaimon, "stairs and dark rooms. There were swords hung on the wall, and spears and shields, like a museum. And I saw the man. He was … dancing."

"Dancing?"

"Moving to and fro ... waving his hand about. Or as if he was fighting something invisible... I just saw him through an open door. Not clearly."

"Fighting a Spectre?" Lyra guessed.

But they couldn't guess any better, so they moved on. Behind the tower a high stone wall, topped with broken glass, enclosed a small garden with formal beds of herbs around a fountain (once again Pantalaimon flew up to look); and then there was an alley on the other side, bringing them back to the square. The windows around the tower were small and deeply-set, like frowning eyes.

"We'll have to go in the front then," said Will.

He climbed the steps and pushed the door wide. Sunlight struck in, and the heavy hinges creaked. He took a step or two inside, and seeing no one, went in further. Lyra followed close behind. The floor was made of stone flags worn smooth over centuries, and the air inside was cool.

Will looked at a flight of steps going downwards, and went far enough down to see that it opened into a wide low-ceilinged room with an immense cold furnace at one end, where the plaster walls were black with soot; but there was no one there, and he went up to the entrance hall again, where he found Lyra with her finger to her lips, looking up.

"I can hear him," she whispered. "He's talking to himself, I reckon."

Will listened hard, and heard it too: a low crooning murmur interrupted occasionally by a harsh laugh or a short cry of anger. It sounded like the voice of a madman.

Will blew out his cheeks and set off to climb the staircase. It was made of blackened oak, immense and broad, with steps as worn as the flagstones: far too solid to creak underfoot. The light diminished as they climbed, because the only illumination was the small deep-set window on each landing. They climbed up one floor, stopped and listened, climbed the next, and the sound of the man's voice was now mixed with that of halting, rhythmic footsteps. It came from a room across the landing, whose door stood ajar.

Will tiptoed to it and pushed it open another few inches so he could see.

It was a large room with cobwebs thickly clustered on the ceiling. The walls were lined with bookshelves containing badly preserved volumes with the bindings crumbling and flaking, or distorted with damp. Several of them lay thrown out of the shelves, open on the floor or the wide dusty tables, and others had been thrust back higgledy-piggledy.

In the centre of the room, a young man was – dancing. Pantalaimon was right: it looked exactly like that. He had his back to the door, and he'd shuffle to one side, then to the other, and all the time his right hand moved in front of him as if he was clearing a way through some invisible obstacles. In that hand was a knife, not a special-looking knife, just a dull blade about eight inches long, and he'd thrust it forward, slice it sideways, feel forward with it, jab up and down, all in the empty air.

He moved as if to turn, and Will withdrew. He put a finger to his lips and beckoned to Lyra, and led her to the stairs and up to the next floor.

"What's he doing?" she whispered.

He described it as well as he could.

"He sounds mad," said Lyra. "Is he thin, with curly hair?"

"Yes. Red hair, like Angelica's. He certainly looks mad. I don't know, I think this is odder than Sir Charles said. Let's look further up before we speak to him."

She didn't question, but let him lead them up a further

staircase to the top storey. It was much lighter up here, because a white-painted flight of steps led up to the roof – or rather, to a wood-and-glass structure like a little greenhouse. Even at the foot of the steps they could feel the heat it was absorbing.

And as they stood there, they heard a groan from above.

They jumped. They'd been sure there was only one man in the Tower. Pantalaimon was so startled that he changed at once from a cat to a bird, and flew to Lyra's breast. Will and Lyra realized as he did so that they'd seized each other's hand, and let go slowly.

"Better go and see," Will whispered. "I'll go first."

"I ought to go first," she whispered back, "seeing it's my fault."

"Seeing it's your fault, you got to do as I say."

She twisted her lip, but fell in behind him.

He climbed up into the sun. The light in the glass structure was blinding. It was as hot as a greenhouse, too, and Will could neither see nor breathe easily. He found a door handle and turned it and stepped out quickly, holding his hand up to keep the sun out of his eyes.

He found himself on a roof of lead, enclosed by the battle-mented parapet. The glass structure was set in the centre, and the lead sloped slightly downwards all round towards a gutter inside the parapet, with square drainage holes in the stone for rainwater.

Lying on the lead, in the full sun, was an old man with white hair. His face was bruised and battered, and one eye was closed, and as they saw when they got closer, his hands were tied behind him.

He heard them coming, and groaned again, and tried to turn over to shield himself.

"It's all right," said Will quietly, "we aren't going to hurt you. Did the man with the knife do this?"

"Mmm," the old man grunted.

"Let's undo the rope. He hasn't tied it very well…"

It was clumsily and hastily knotted, and it fell away quickly once Will had seen how to work it. They helped the old man to get up and took him over to the shade of the parapet.

"Who are you?" Will said. "We didn't think there were two people here. We thought there was only one."

"Giacomo Paradisi," the old man muttered through broken teeth. "I am the bearer. No one else. That young man stole it from me. There are always fools who take risks like that for the sake of the knife. But this one is desperate. He is going to kill me…"

"No he en't," Lyra said. "What's the bearer? What's that mean?"

"I hold the subtle knife on behalf of the Guild. Where has he gone?"

"He's downstairs," said Will. "We came up past him. He didn't see us. He was waving it about in the air…"

"Trying to cut through. He won't succeed. When he –"

"Watch out," Lyra said.

Will turned. The young man was climbing up into the little wooden shelter. He hadn't seen them yet, but there was nowhere to hide, and as they stood up he saw the movement and whipped round to face them.

Immediately Pantalaimon became a bear, and reared up on his hind legs. Only Lyra knew that he wouldn't be able to touch the other man, and certainly the other blinked and stared for a second, but Will saw that he hadn't really registered it. The man was crazy. His curly red hair was matted, his chin was flecked with spit, and the whites of his eyes showed all round the pupils.

And he had the knife, and they had no weapons at all.

Will stepped up the lead, away from the old man, crouching, ready to jump or fight or leap out of the way.

The young man sprang forward and slashed at him with the knife, left – right – left, coming closer and closer, making Will back away till he was trapped in the angle where two sides of the tower met.

Lyra was scrambling towards the man from behind, with the loose rope in her hand. Will darted forward suddenly, just as he'd done to the man in his house, and with the same effect: his antagonist tumbled backwards unexpectedly, falling over Lyra to crash on to the lead. It was all happening too quickly for Will to be frightened. But he did have time to see the knife fly from the man's hand and sink at once into the lead some feet away, point first, with no more resistance than if it had fallen into butter. It plunged as far as the hilt and stopped suddenly.

And the young man twisted over and reached for it at once, but Will flung himself on his back and seized his hair. He had learned to fight at school: there had been plenty of occasion for it, once the other children had sensed that there was something the matter with his mother. And he'd learned that the object of a school fight was not to gain points for style but to force your enemy to give in, which meant hurting him more than he was hurting you. He knew that you had to be willing to hurt someone else, too, and he'd found out that not many people were, when it came to it; but he knew that he was.

So this wasn't unfamiliar to him, but he hadn't fought against a nearly-grown man armed with a knife before, and at all costs he must keep him away from picking it up now that he'd dropped it.

He twisted his fingers into the young man's thick damp hair and wrenched back as hard as he could. The man grunted and flung himself sideways, but Will hung on even tighter, and his opponent roared with pain and anger. He pushed up and then threw himself backwards, crushing Will between himself and the parapet, and that was too much: all the breath left Will's body, and in the shock his hands loosened. The man pulled free.

Will dropped to his knees in the gutter, winded badly, but he couldn't stay there. He pushed himself up to his knees, and then tried to stand – and in doing so, he thrust his foot through one of the drainage holes. For a horrible second he thought there was nothing there behind him. His fingers scraped desperately on the warm lead. But nothing happened; his left leg was thrust out into empty space, but the rest of him was safe.

He pulled his foot back inside the parapet and scrambled to his feet. The man had reached his knife again, but he didn't have time to pull it out of the lead before Lyra leapt on to his back, scratching, kicking, biting like a wildcat; but she missed the hold on his hair that she was trying for, and he threw her off. And when he got up, he had the knife in his hand.

Lyra had fallen to one side, with Pantalaimon a wildcat now, fur raised, teeth bared, beside her. Will faced the man directly, and saw him clearly for the first time. There was no doubt: he was Angelica's brother all right, and he was vicious. All his mind was focused on Will, and the knife was in his hand.

But Will wasn't harmless either.

He'd seized the rope when Lyra dropped it, and now he wrapped it around his left hand for protection against the knife. He moved sideways between the young man and the sun, so that his antagonist had to squint and blink. Even better, the glass structure threw brilliant reflections into his eyes, and Will could see that for a moment he was almost blinded.

He leapt to the man's left, away from the knife, holding his left hand high, and kicked hard at the man's knee. He'd taken care to aim, and his foot connected well. The man went down with a loud grunt, and twisted away awkwardly.

Will leapt after him, hitting with both hands and kicking again and again, kicking whatever parts he could reach, driving the man back and back towards the glass house. If he could get him to the top of the stairs…

This time the man fell more heavily, and his right hand with the knife in it came down on the lead at Will's feet. Will stamped on it at once, hard, crushing the man's fingers between the hilt and the lead, and then wrapped the rope more tightly around his hand and stamped a second time. The man yelled and let go of the knife. At once Will kicked it away, his shoe connecting with the hilt, luckily for him, and it spun across the lead and came to rest in the gutter just beside a drainage hole. The rope had come loose around his hand once more, and there seemed to be a surprising amount of blood from somewhere sprinkled on the lead and on his own shoes. The man was pulling himself up –

"Look out!" shouted Lyra, but Will was ready.

At the moment when the man was off balance he threw himself at him, crashing as hard as he could into the man's midriff. The man fell backwards into the glass, which shattered at once, and the flimsy wooden frame went too. He sprawled among the wreckage half over the stairwell, and grabbed the door frame, but it had nothing to support it any more, and it gave way. He fell downwards, and more glass fell all around him.

And Will darted back to the gutter, and picked up the knife, and the fight was over. The young man, cut and battered, clambered up the steps, and saw Will standing above him holding the knife, and stared with a sickly anger and then turned and fled.

"Ah," said Will, sitting down. "Ah."

Something was badly wrong, and he hadn't noticed it. He

dropped the knife and hugged his left hand to himself. The tangle of rope was sodden with blood, and when he pulled it away –

"Your fingers!" Lyra breathed. "Oh, Will –"

His little finger and the finger next to it fell away with the rope.

His head swam. Blood was pulsing strongly from the stumps where his fingers had been, and his jeans and shoes were sodden already. He had to lie back and close his eyes for a moment. The pain wasn't that great, and a part of his mind registered that with a dull surprise: it was like a persistent deep hammer-thud more than the bright sharp clarity when you cut yourself superficially.

He'd never felt so weak. He supposed he had gone to sleep for a moment. Lyra was doing something to his arm. He sat up to look at the damage, and felt sick. The old man was somewhere close by, but Will couldn't see what he was doing, and meanwhile Lyra was talking to him.

"If only we had some bloodmoss," she was saying, "what the bears use, I could make it better, Will, I could – look, I'm going to tie this bit of rope round your arm, to stop the bleeding, 'cause I can't tie it round where your fingers were, there's nothing to tie it to – hold still –"

He let her do it, and looked around for his fingers. There they were, curled like a bloody quotation mark on the lead. He laughed.

"Hey," she said, "stop that. Get up now. Mr Paradisi's got some medicine, some salve, I dunno what it is. You got to come downstairs. That other man's gone – we seen him run out the door. He's gone now. You beat him. Come on, Will – come on –"

Nagging and cajoling, she urged him down the steps, and they picked their way through the shattered glass and splintered wood and into a small cool room off the landing. The walls were lined with shelves of bottles, jars, pots, pestles and mortars and chemists' balances. Under the dirty window was a stone sink, where the old man was pouring something with a shaky hand from a large bottle into a smaller one.

"Sit down and drink this," he said, and filled a small glass with a dark liquid.

Will sat down and took the glass. The first mouthful hit the back of his throat like fire. Lyra took the glass to stop it falling as Will gasped.

"Drink it all," the old man commanded.

"What is it?"

"Plum brandy. Drink."

Will sipped it more cautiously. Now his hand was really beginning to hurt.

"Can you heal him?" said Lyra, her voice desperate.

"Oh, yes, we have medicines for everything. You, girl, open that drawer in the table and bring out a bandage."

Will saw the knife lying on the table in the centre of the room, but before he could pick it up the old man was limping towards him with a bowl of water.

"Drink again," the old man said.

Will held the glass tightly and closed his eyes while the old man did something to his hand. It stung horribly, but then he felt the rough friction of a towel on his wrist, and something mopping the wound more gently. Then there was a coolness for a moment, and it hurt again.

"This is precious ointment," the old man said. "Very difficult to obtain. Very good for wounds."

It was a dusty, battered tube of ordinary antiseptic cream, such as Will could have bought in any chemist's shop in his world. The old man was handling it as if it were made of myrrh. Will looked away.

And while the man was dressing the wound, Lyra felt Pantalaimon calling to her silently to come and look out of the window. He was a kestrel perching on the open window-frame, and his eyes had caught a movement below. She joined him, and saw a familiar figure: the girl Angelica was running towards her elder brother Tullio, who stood with his back against the wall on the other side of the narrow street, waving his arms in the air as if trying to keep a flock of bats from his face. Then he turned away and began to run his hands along the stones in the wall, looking closely at each one, counting them, feeling the edges, hunching up his shoulders as if warding off something behind him, shaking his head.

Angelica was desperate, and so was little Paolo behind her, and they reached their brother and seized his arms and tried to pull him away from whatever was troubling him.

And Lyra realized with a jolt of sickness what was happening: the man was being attacked by Spectres. Angelica knew it, though she couldn't see them, of course, and little Paolo was crying and striking at the empty air to try and drive them off; but it didn't help, and Tullio was lost. His movements became more and more lethargic, and presently they stopped altogether. Angelica clung to him, shaking and shaking his arm, but nothing woke him; and Paolo was crying his brother's name over and over as if that would bring him back.

Then Angelica seemed to feel Lyra watching her, and she looked up. For a moment their eyes met. Lyra felt a jolt as if the girl had struck her a physical blow, because the hatred in her eyes was so intense, and then Paolo saw her looking and looked up too, and his little boy's voice cried, "We'll kill you! You done this to Tullio! We gonna kill you, all right!"

The two children turned and ran, leaving their stricken brother, and Lyra, frightened and guilty, withdrew inside the room again and shut the window. The others hadn't heard.

Giacomo Paradisi was dabbing more ointment on the wounds, and Lyra tried to put what she'd seen out of her mind, and focused on Will.

"You got to tie something round his arm," Lyra said, "to stop the bleeding. It won't stop otherwise."

"Yes, yes, I know," said the old man, but sadly.

Will kept his eyes averted while they did up a bandage, and drank the plum brandy sip by sip. Presently he felt soothed and distant, though his hand was hurting abominably.

"Now," said Giacomo Paradisi, "here you are, take the knife, it is yours."

"I don't want it," said Will. "I don't want anything to do with it."

"You haven't got the choice," said the old man. "You are the bearer now."

"I thought you said *you* was?" said Lyra.

"My time is over," he said. "The knife knows when to leave one hand and settle in another, and I know how to tell. You don't believe me? Look!"

He held up his own left hand. The little finger and the finger next to it were missing, just like Will's.

"Yes," he said, "me too. I fought and lost the same fingers, the badge of the bearer. And I did not know either, in advance."

Lyra sat down, wide-eyed. Will held on to the dusty table with his good hand. He struggled to find words.

"But I – we only came here because – there was a man who stole something of Lyra's, and he wanted the knife, and he said if we brought him that, then he'd…"

"I know that man. He is a liar, a cheat. He wouldn't give you anything, make no mistake. He wants the knife, and once he has it he will betray you. He will never be bearer. The knife is yours by right."

With a heavy reluctance, Will turned to the knife itself. He pulled it towards him. It was an ordinary-looking dagger, with a double-sided blade of dull metal about eight inches long, a short cross-piece of the same metal, and a handle of rosewood. As he looked at it more closely, he saw that the rosewood was inlaid with golden wires, forming a design he didn't recognize till he turned the knife around and saw an angel, with wings folded. On the other side was a different angel, with wings upraised. The wires stood out a little from the surface, giving a firm grip, and as he picked it up he felt that it was light in his hand and strong and beautifully balanced, and that the blade was not dull after all. In fact, a swirl of cloudy colours seemed to live just under the surface of the metal: bruise-purples, sea-blues, earth-browns, cloud-greys, and the deep green under heavy-foliaged trees, the clustering shades at the mouth of a tomb as evening falls over a deserted graveyard – if there was such a thing as shadow-coloured, it was the blade of the subtle knife.

But the edges were different. In fact the two edges differed from each other. One was clear bright steel, merging a little way back into those subtle shadow-colours, but steel of an incomparable sharpness. Will's eye shrank back from looking at it, so sharp did it seem. The other edge was just as keen, but silvery in colour, and Lyra, who was looking at it over Will's shoulder, said:

"I seen that colour before! That's the same as the blade they was going to cut me and Pan apart with – that's just the same!"

"This edge," said Giacomo Paradisi, touching the steel with the handle of a spoon, "will cut through any material in the world. Look."

And he pressed the silver spoon against the blade. Will, holding the knife, felt only the slightest resistance as the tip of the spoon's handle fell to the table, cut clean off.

"The other edge," the old man went on, "is more subtle still. With it you can cut an opening out of this world altogether. Try it now. Do as I say – you are the bearer. You have to know. No one can teach you but me, and I have not much time left. Stand up and listen."

Will pushed his chair back and stood, holding the knife loosely. He felt dizzy, sick, rebellious.

"I don't want –" he began, but Giacomo Paradisi shook his head.

"Be silent! You don't want – you don't want – you have no choice! Listen to me, because time is short. Now hold the knife out ahead of you – like that. It's not only the knife that has to cut, it's your own mind. You have to think it. So do this: put your mind out at the very tip of the knife. Concentrate, boy. Focus your mind. Don't think about your wound. It will heal. Think about the knife tip. That is where you are. Now feel with it, very gently. You're looking for a gap so small you could never see it with your eyes, but the knife tip will find it, if you put your mind there. Feel along the air till you sense the smallest little gap in the world…"

Will tried to do it. But his head was buzzing and his left hand throbbed horribly and he saw his two fingers again, lying on the roof, and then he thought of his mother, his poor mother… What would she say? How would she comfort him? How could he ever comfort her? And he put the knife down on the table and crouched low hugging his wounded hand, and cried. It was all too much to bear. The sobs racked his throat and his chest and the tears dazzled him, and he should be crying for her, the poor frightened unhappy dear beloved, he'd left her, he'd left her…

He was desolate. But then he felt the strangest thing, and brushed the back of his right wrist across his eyes to find Pantalaimon's head on his knee. The dæmon, in the form of a wolfhound, was gazing up at him with melting, sorrowing eyes, and then he gently licked Will's wounded hand again and again, and laid his head on Will's knee once more.

Will had no idea of the taboo in Lyra's world preventing one person from touching another's dæmon, and if he hadn't touched Pantalaimon before, it was politeness that had held him back and not knowledge. Lyra, in fact, was breathtaken. Her dæmon had done it on his own initiative, and now he withdrew, and fluttered to her shoulder as the smallest of moths. The old man was watching with interest but not incredulity. He'd seen dæmons before, somehow; he'd travelled to other worlds too.

Pantalaimon's gesture had worked. Will swallowed hard and stood up again, wiping the tears out of his eyes.

"All right," he said, "I'll try again. Tell me what to do."

This time he forced his mind to do what Giacomo Paradisi said, gritting his teeth, trembling with exertion, sweating. Lyra was bursting to interrupt, because she knew this process. So did Dr Malone, and so did the poet Keats, whoever he was, and all of them knew you couldn't get it by straining towards it. But she held her tongue and clasped her hands.

"Stop," said the old man gently. "Relax. Don't push. This is a subtle knife, not a heavy sword. You're gripping it too tight. Loosen your fingers. Let your mind wander down your arm to your wrist and then into the handle, and out along the blade, no hurry, go gently, don't force it. Just wander. Then along to the very tip, where the edge is sharpest of all. You become the tip of the knife. Just do that now. Go there and feel that, and then come back."

Will tried again. Lyra could see the intensity in his body, saw his jaw working, and then saw an authority descend over it, calming and relaxing and clarifying. The authority was Will's own – or his dæmon's, perhaps. How he must miss having a dæmon! The loneliness of it… No wonder he'd cried; and it was right of Pantalaimon to do what he'd done, though it had felt so strange to her. She reached up to her beloved dæmon, and, ermine-shaped, he flowed on to her lap.

They watched together as Will's body stopped trembling. No less intense, he was focused differently now, and the knife looked different too. Perhaps it was those cloudy colours along the blade, or perhaps it was the way it sat so naturally in Will's hand, but the little movement he was making with the tip now looked purposeful instead of random. He felt this way, then turned the knife over and felt the other, always feeling with the silvery edge; and then he seemed to find some little snag in the empty air.

"What's this? Is this it?" he said hoarsely.

"Yes. Don't force it. Come back now, come back to yourself."

Lyra imagined she could see Will's soul flowing back along the blade to his hand, and up his arm to his heart. He stood back, dropped his hand, blinked.

"I felt something there," he said to Giacomo Paradisi. "The knife was just slipping through the air at first and then I felt it…"

"Good. Now do it again. This time, when you feel it, slide the knife in and along. Make a cut. Don't hesitate. Don't be surprised. Don't drop the knife."

Will had to crouch and take two or three deep breaths and put his left hand under his other arm before he could go on. But he was intent on it; he stood up again after a couple of seconds, the knife held forward already.

This time it was easier. Having felt it once, he knew what to search for again, and he felt the curious little snag after less than a minute. It was like delicately searching out the gap between one stitch and the next with the point of a scalpel. He touched, withdrew, touched again to make sure, and then did as the old man had said, and cut sideways with the silver edge.

It was a good thing that Giacomo Paradisi had reminded him not to be surprised. He kept careful hold of the knife, and put it down on the table before giving in to his astonishment. Lyra was on her feet already, speechless, because there in the middle of the dusty little room was a window just like the one under the hornbeam trees: a gap in mid-air through which they could see another world.

And because they were high in the tower, they were high above north Oxford. Over a cemetery, in fact, looking back towards the city. There were the hornbeam trees a little way ahead of them; there were houses, trees, roads, and in the distance the towers and spires of the city.

If they hadn't already seen the first window, they would have thought this was some kind of optical trick. Except that it wasn't only optical; air was coming through it; they could smell the traffic fumes, which didn't exist in the world of Cittàgazze. Pantalaimon changed into a swallow and flew through, delighting in the open air, and then snapped up an insect before darting back through to Lyra's shoulder again.

Giacomo Paradisi was watching with a curious, sad smile. Then he said, "So much for opening. Now you must learn to close."

Lyra stood back to give Will room, and the old man came to stand beside him.

"For this you need your fingers," he said. "One hand will do. Feel for the edge as you felt with the knife to begin with. You won't find it unless you put your soul into your fingertips. Touch very delicately, feel again and again till you find the edge. Then you pinch it together. That's all. Try."

But Will was trembling. He couldn't get his mind back to the delicate balance he knew it needed, and he got more and more frustrated. Lyra could see what was happening.

She stood up and took his right arm and said, "Listen, Will, sit down, I'll tell you how to do it. Just sit down for a minute, 'cause your hand hurts and it's taking your mind off it. It's bound to. It'll ease off in a little while."

The old man raised both his hands and then changed his mind, shrugged, and sat down again.

Will sat down and looked at Lyra. "What am I doing wrong?" he said.

He was bloodstained, trembling, wild-eyed. He was living on the edge of his nerves: clenching his jaw, tapping his foot, breathing fast.

"It's your wound," she said. "*You* en't wrong at all. You're doing it right, but your hand won't let you concentrate on it. I don't know an easy way of getting round that, except maybe if you didn't try to shut it out…"

"What d'you mean?"

"Well, you're trying to do two things with your mind, both at once. You're trying to ignore the pain *and* close that window. I remember when I was reading the alethiometer once when I was frightened, and maybe I was used to it by that time, I don't know, but I was still frightened all the time I was reading it. Just sort of relax your mind and say yes, it does hurt, I know. Don't try and shut it out."

His eyes closed briefly. His breathing slowed a little.

"All right," he said. "I'll try that."

And this time it was much easier. He felt for the edge, found it within a minute, and did as Giacomo Paradisi had told him: pinched the edges together. It was the easiest thing in the world. He felt a brief, calm exhilaration, and then the window was gone. The other world was shut.

The old man handed him a leather sheath, backed with stiff horn, with buckles to hold the knife in place, because the slightest sideways movement of the blade would have cut through the thickest leather. Will slid the knife into it and buckled it as tight as he could with his clumsy hand.

"This should be a solemn occasion," Giacomo Paradisi said. "If we had days and weeks I could begin to tell you the story of the subtle knife, and the Guild of the Torre degli Angeli, and the whole sorry history of this corrupt and careless world. The Spectres are our fault, our fault alone. They came because my predecessors, alchemists, philosophers, men of learning, were making an enquiry into the deepest nature of things. They became curious about the bonds that held the smallest particles of matter together. You know what I mean by a bond? Something that binds?

"Well, this was a mercantile city. A city of traders and bankers. We thought we knew about bonds. We thought a bond was something negotiable, something that could be bought and sold and exchanged and converted… But about these bonds, we were wrong. We undid them, and we let the Spectres in."

Will said, "Where do the Spectres come from? Why was the window left open under those trees, the one we first came in through? Are there other windows in the world?"

"Where the Spectres come from is a mystery. From another world; from the darkness of space; who knows? What matters is that they are here, and they have destroyed us. Are there other windows into this world? Yes, a few, because sometimes a knife-bearer might be careless or forgetful, without time to stop and close as he should. And the window you came through, under the hornbeam trees … I left that open myself, in a moment of unforgivable foolishness. The man you spoke of – I thought to tempt him through and into the city where he would fall victim to the Spectres. But I think that he is too clever for a trick like that. He wants the knife. Please, never let him get it."

Will and Lyra shared a glance.

"Well," the old man finished, spreading his hands, "all I can do is hand the knife on to you and show you how to use it, which I have done, and tell you what the rules of the Guild used to be, before it decayed. First, never open without closing. Second, never let anyone else use the knife. It is yours alone. Third, never use it for a base purpose. Fourth, keep it secret. If there are other rules, I have forgotten them, and if I've forgotten them it is because they don't matter. You have the knife. You are the bearer. You should not be a child. But our world is crumbling, and the mark of the bearer is unmistakable. I don't even know your name. Now go. I shall die very soon, because I know where there are poisonous drugs, and I don't intend to wait for the Spectres to come in, as they will once the knife has left. Go."

"But, Mister Paradisi –" Lyra began, but he shook his head and went on:

"There is no time. You have come here for a purpose, and maybe you don't know what that purpose is, but the angels do who brought you here. Go. You are brave, and your friend is clever. And you have the knife. Go."

"You en't really going to poison yourself?" said Lyra, distressed.

"Come on," said Will.

"And what did you mean about angels?" she went on.

Will tugged her arm.

"Come on," he said again. "We got to go. Thank you, Mr Paradisi."

He held out his bloodstained dusty right hand, and the old man shook it gently. He shook Lyra's hand too, and nodded to Pantalaimon, who lowered his ermine-head in acknowledgement.

Clutching the knife in its leather sheath, Will led the way down the broad dark stairs and out of the tower. The sunlight was hot in the little square, and the silence was profound. Lyra looked all around, with immense caution, but the street was empty. And it would be better not to worry Will about what she'd seen; there was quite enough to worry about already. She led him away from the street where she'd seen the children, where the stricken Tullio was still standing, as still as death.

"I wish –" Lyra said when they had nearly left the square, stopping to look back up. "It's horrible, thinking of ... and his poor teeth was all broken, and he could hardly see out his eye... He's just going to swallow some poison and die now, and I wish..."

She was on the verge of tears.

"Hush," said Will. "It won't hurt him. He'll just go to sleep. It's better than the Spectres, he said."

"Oh, what we going to do, Will?" she said. "What we going to do? You're hurt so bad, and that poor old man... I hate this place, I really do, I'd burn it to the ground. What we going to do now?"

"Well," he said, "that's easy. We've got to get the alethiometer back, so we'll have to steal it. That's what we're going to do."

9
Theft

irst they went back to the café, to recover and rest and change their clothes. It was clear that Will couldn't go everywhere covered in blood, and the time of feeling guilty about taking things from shops was over; so he gathered a complete set of new clothes and shoes, and Lyra, demanding to help, and watching in every direction for the other children, carried them back to the café.

Lyra put some water on to boil, and Will took it up to the bathroom and stripped to wash from head to foot. The pain was dull and unrelenting, but at least the cuts were clean, and having seen what the knife could do, he knew that no cuts could be cleaner; but the stumps where his fingers had been were bleeding freely. When he looked at them he felt sick, and his heart beat faster, and that in turn seemed to make the bleeding even worse. He sat on the edge of the bath and closed his eyes and breathed deeply several times.

Presently he felt calmer and set himself to washing. He did the best he could, drying himself on the increasingly bloodied towels, and then dressed in his new clothes, trying not to make them bloody too.

"You're going to have to tie my bandage again," he said to

Lyra. "I don't care how tight you make it as long as it stops the bleeding."

She tore up a sheet and wrapped it round and round, clamping it down over the wounds as tight as she could. He gritted his teeth, but he couldn't help tears. He brushed them away without a word, and she said nothing.

When she'd finished he said, "Thank you." Then he said, "Listen. I want you to take something in your rucksack for me, in case we can't come back here. It's only letters. You can read them if you want."

He took out the green leather writing-case and handed her the sheets of airmail paper.

"I won't read them unless –"

"I don't mind. Else I wouldn't have said."

She folded the letters up, and he lay on the bed, pushed the cat aside, and fell asleep.

Much later that night, Will and Lyra crouched in the lane that ran along beside the tree-shaded shrubbery in Sir Charles's garden. On the Cittàgazze side, they were in a grassy park surrounding a classical villa that gleamed white in the moonlight. They'd taken a long time to get to Sir Charles's house, moving mainly in Cittàgazze, with frequent stops to cut through and check their position in Will's world, closing the windows as soon as they knew where they were.

Not with them but not far behind came the tabby cat. She had slept since they'd rescued her from the stone-throwing children, and now she was awake again she was reluctant to leave them, as if she thought that wherever they were, she was safe. Will was far from sure about that, but he had enough on his mind without the cat, and he ignored her. All the time he was growing more familiar with the knife, more certain in his command of it; but his wound was hurting worse than before, with a deep unceasing throb, and the bandage Lyra had freshly tied after he woke up was already soaked.

He cut a window in the air not far from the white-gleaming villa, and they came through to the quiet lane in Headington to work out exactly how to get to the study where Sir Charles had put the alethiometer. There were two floodlights illuminating his garden, and lights were on in the front windows of the house, though not in the study. Only moonlight lit this side, and the study window was dark.

The lane ran down through trees to another road at the far end, and it wasn't lighted. It would have been easy for an ordinary burglar to get unobserved into the shrubbery and thus to the garden, except that there was a strong iron fence twice as high as Will, with spikes on the top, running the length of Sir Charles's property. However, it was no barrier to the subtle knife.

"Hold this bar while I cut it," Will whispered. "Catch it when it falls."

Lyra did as he said, and he cut through four bars altogether, enough for them to pass through without difficulty. Lyra laid them one by one on the grass, and then they were through, and moving among the bushes.

Once they had a clear sight of the side of the house, with the creeper-shaded window of the study facing them across the smooth lawn, Will said quietly:

"I'm going to cut through into Ci'gazze here, and leave the window open, and move in Ci'gazze to where I think the study is, and then cut back through to this world. Then I'll take the alethiometer out of that cabinet thing and I'll close that window and then I'll come back to this one. You stay here in this world and keep watch. As soon as you hear me call you,

you come through this window into Ci'gazze and then I'll close it up again. All right?"

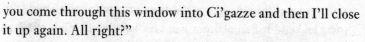

"Yeah," she whispered. "Me and Pan'll both look out."

Her dæmon was a small tawny owl, almost invisible in the dappled shadows under the trees. His wide pale eyes took in every movement.

Will stood back and held out the knife, searching, touching the air with the most delicate movements, until after a minute or so he found a point at which he could cut. He did it swiftly, opening a window through into the moon-drenched parkland of Ci'gazze, and then stood back, estimating how many steps it would take him in this world to reach the study, and memorizing the direction.

Then without a word he stepped through and vanished.

Lyra crouched down nearby. Pantalaimon was perched on a branch above her head, turning this way and that, silent. She could hear traffic from Headington behind her, and the quiet footsteps of someone going along the road at the end of the lane, and even the weightless movement of insects among the twigs and leaves at her feet.

A minute went by, and another. Where was Will now? She strained to look through the window of the study, but it was just a dark mullioned square overhung with creeper. Sir Charles had sat inside it on the window-seat only that morning, and crossed his legs, and arranged the creases in his trousers. Where was the cabinet in relation to the window? Would Will get inside without disturbing anyone in the house? Lyra could hear her heart beating, too.

Then Pantalaimon made a soft noise, and at the same moment a different sound came from the front of the house to Lyra's left. She couldn't see the front, but she could see a light sweeping across the trees, and heard a deep crunching sound: the sound of tyres on gravel. She hadn't heard the car's engine at all.

She looked for Pantalaimon, and he was already gliding ahead silently, as far as he could go from her. He turned in the darkness and swooped back to settle on her fist.

"Sir Charles is coming back," he whispered. "And there's someone with him."

He took off again, and this time Lyra followed, tiptoeing over the soft earth with the utmost care, crouching down behind the bushes, finally going on hands and knees to look between the leaves of a laurel.

The Rolls Royce stood in front of the house, and the chauffeur was moving around to the passenger side to open the door. Sir Charles stood waiting, smiling, offering his arm to the woman who was getting out, and as she came into view Lyra felt a blow at her heart, the worst blow since she'd escaped from Bolvangar, because Sir Charles's guest was her mother, Mrs Coulter.

Will stepped carefully across the moonlit grass in Cittàgazze, counting his paces, holding in his mind as clearly as he could a memory of where the study was and trying to locate it with reference to the villa, which stood nearby, stucco-white and columned in a formal garden with statues and a fountain. And he was aware of how exposed he was in this moon-drenched parkland.

When he thought he was in the right spot, he stopped and held out the knife again, feeling forward carefully. These little invisible gaps were anywhere, but not everywhere, or any slash of the knife would open a window.

He cut a small opening first, no bigger than his hand, and looked through. Nothing but darkness on the other side: he couldn't see where he was. He closed that one, turned through ninety degrees, and opened another. This time he found fabric in

194

front of him – heavy green velvet: the curtains of the study. But where were they in relation to the cabinet? He had to close that one too, turn the other way, try again. Time was passing.

The third time was better: he found he could see the whole of the study in the dim light through the open door to the hall. There was the desk, the sofa, the cabinet! He could see a faint gleam along the side of a brass microscope. And there was no one in the room, and the house was silent. It couldn't be better.

He carefully estimated the distance, closed that window, stepped forward four paces, and held up the knife again. If he was right, he'd be in exactly the right spot to reach through, cut through the glass in the cabinet, take out the alethiometer and close the window behind him.

He cut a window at the right height. The glass of the cabinet door was only a hand's breadth in front of it. He put his face close, looking intently at this shelf and that, from top to bottom.

The alethiometer wasn't there.

At first Will thought he'd got the wrong cabinet. There were four of them in the room – he'd counted that morning, and memorized where they were – tall square cases made of dark wood, with glass sides and fronts and velvet-covered shelves, made for displaying valuable objects of porcelain or ivory or gold. Could he have simply opened a window in front of the wrong one? But on the top shelf was that bulky instrument with the brass rings: he'd made a point of noticing that. And on the shelf in the middle, where Sir Charles had placed the alethiometer, there was a space. This was the right cabinet, and the alethiometer wasn't there.

Will stepped back a moment and took a deep breath.

He'd have to go through properly and look around. Opening windows here and there at random would take all night. He closed the window in front of the cabinet, opened another to look at the rest of the room, and when he'd taken careful stock, he closed that one and opened a larger one behind the sofa through which he could easily get out in a hurry if he needed to.

His hand was throbbing brutally by this time, and the bandage was trailing loose. He wound it round as best he could and tucked the end in, and then went through into Sir Charles's house completely and crouched behind the leather sofa, the knife in his right hand, listening carefully.

Hearing nothing, he stood up slowly and looked around the room. The door to the hall was half-open, and the light that came through was quite enough to see by. The cabinets, the bookshelves, the pictures were all there, as they had been that morning, undisturbed.

He stepped out on the silent carpet and looked into each of the cabinets in turn. It wasn't there. Nor was it on the desk among the neatly piled books and papers, nor on the mantelpiece among the invitation cards to this opening or that reception, nor on the cushioned window-seat, nor on the octagonal table behind the door.

He moved back to the desk, intending to try the drawers, but with the heavy expectation of failure; and as he did so, he heard the faint crunch of tyres on gravel. It was so quiet that he half-thought he was imagining it, but he stood stock still, straining to listen. It stopped.

Then he heard the front door open.

He went at once to the sofa again, and crouched behind it, next to the window that opened on to the moon-silvered grass in Cittàgazze. And no sooner had he got there than he heard footsteps in that other world, lightly running over the grass, and looked through to see Lyra racing towards him. He was just in time to wave and put his finger to his lips, and she slowed, realizing that he was aware Sir Charles had returned.

"I haven't got it," he whispered when she came up. "It wasn't
there. He's probably got it with him. I'm going to listen and see
if he puts it back. Stay here."

"No! It's worse!" she said, and she was nearly in a genuine
panic. "*She's* with him – Mrs Coulter – my mother – I dunno
how she got here, but if she sees me I'm dead, Will, I'm lost – and
I know who *he* is now! I remember where I seen him before! Will,
he's called Lord Boreal! I seen him at Mrs Coulter's cocktail
party, when I ran away! And he must have known who I was, all
the time…"

"Ssh. Don't stay here if you're going to make a noise."

She mastered herself, and swallowed hard, and shook her
head.

"Sorry. I want to stay with you," she whispered. "I want to
hear what they say."

"Hush now…"

Because he could hear voices in the hall. The two of them
were close enough to touch, he in his world, she in Cittàgazze,
and seeing Will's trailing bandage, Lyra tapped him on the arm
and mimed tying it up again. He held out his hand for her to do
it, crouching meanwhile with his head cocked sideways, listening
hard.

A light came on in the room. He heard Sir Charles speaking
to the servant, dismissing him, coming into the study, closing the
door.

"May I offer you a glass of Tokay?" he said.

A woman's voice, low and sweet, replied, "How kind of you,
Carlo. I haven't tasted Tokay for many years."

"Have the chair by the fireplace."

There was the faint glug of wine being poured, a tinkle of
decanter on glass-rim, a murmur of thanks, and then Sir Charles
seated himself on the sofa, inches away from Will.

"Your good health, Marisa," he said, sipping. "Now, suppose you tell me what you want."

"I want to know where you got the alethiometer."

"Why?"

"Because Lyra had it, and I want to find her."

"I can't imagine why you would. She is a repellent brat."

"I'll remind you that she's my daughter."

"Then she is even more repellent, because she must have resisted your charming influence on purpose. No one could do it by accident."

"Where is she?"

"I'll tell you, I promise. But you must tell me something first."

"If I can," she said, in a different tone that Will thought might be a warning. Her voice was intoxicating: soothing, sweet, musical, and young, too. He longed to know what she looked like, because Lyra had never described her, and the face that went with this voice must be remarkable. "What do you want to know?"

"What is Asriel up to?"

There was a silence then, as if the woman were calculating what to say. Will looked back through the window at Lyra, and saw her face, moonlit and wide-eyed with fear, biting her lip to keep silent, and straining to hear, as he was.

Finally Mrs Coulter said, "Very well, I'll tell you. Lord Asriel is gathering an army, with the purpose of completing the war that was fought in heaven aeons ago."

"How medieval. However, he seems to have some very modern powers. What has he done to the magnetic pole?"

"He found a way of blasting open the barrier between our world and others. It caused profound disturbances to the earth's magnetic field, and that must resonate in this world too... But

198

how do you know about that? Carlo, I think you should answer some questions of mine. What is this world? And how did you bring me here?"

"It is one of millions. There are openings between them, but they're not easily found. I know a dozen or so, but the places they open into have shifted, and that must be due to what Asriel's done. It seems that we can now pass directly from this world to our own, and probably to many others too. Previously, there was one world that acted as a sort of crossroads, and all the doorways opened into that. So you can imagine how surprised I was to see you, when I came through today, and how delighted that I could bring you here directly, without the risk of going through Cittàgazze."

"Cittàgazze? What is that?"

"The crossroads. A world in which I have an interest, my dear Marisa. But one too dangerous for us to visit at the moment."

"Why is it dangerous?"

"Dangerous for adults. Children can go there freely."

"What? I must know about this, Carlo," said the woman, and Will could hear her passionate impatience. "This is at the heart of everything, this difference between children and adults! It contains the whole mystery of Dust! This is why I must find the child. And the witches have a name for her – I nearly had it, so nearly, from a witch in person, but she died too quickly. I must find the child. She has the answer, somehow, and I *must* have it…"

"And you shall. This instrument will bring her to me – never fear. And once she's given me what I want, you can have her. But tell me about your curious bodyguard, Marisa. I've never seen soldiers like that. Who are they?"

"Men, that's all. But … they've undergone intercision. They have no dæmons, so they have no fear and no imagination and no free will, and they'll fight till they're torn apart."

"No dæmons... Well, that's very interesting. I wonder if I might suggest a little experiment, if you can spare one of them? I'd like to see whether the Spectres are interested in them. If they're not, we might be able to travel in Cittàgazze after all."

"Spectres? What are they?"

"I'll explain later, my dear. They are the reason adults can't go into the world. Dust – children – Spectres – dæmons – intercision... Yes, it might very well work. Have some more wine."

"I want to know *everything*," she said, over the sound of wine being poured. "And I'll hold you to that. Now tell me: what are you doing in this world? Is this where you come when we thought you were in Brasil or the Indies?"

"I found my way here a long time ago. It was too good a secret to reveal, even to you, Marisa. I've made myself very comfortable, as you can see. Being part of the Council of State at home made it easy for me to see where the power lay here.

"As a matter of fact, I became a spy, though I never told my masters all I knew. The security services in this world were pre-occupied for years with the Soviet Union – we know it as Muscovy. And although that threat has receded, there are still listening-posts and machines trained in that direction, and I'm still in touch with those who run the spies.

"And I heard recently about a profound disturbance in the earth's magnetic field. The security services are alarmed. Every nation that does research into fundamental physics – what we call experimental theology – is turning to its scientists urgently to discover what's going on. Because they know that *something* is happening. And they suspect it has to do with other worlds.

"They do have a few clues to this, as a matter of fact. There is some research being done into Dust. Oh, yes, they know it here as well. There is a team in this very city working on it. And another thing: there was a man who disappeared ten or twelve years ago, in the north, and the security services think he was in possession of some knowledge they badly need – specifically, the location of a doorway between the worlds, such as the one you came through earlier today. The one he found is the only one they know about: you can imagine I haven't told them what I know. When this new disturbance began, they set out to look for this man.

"And naturally, Marisa, I myself am curious. And I am keen to add to my knowledge."

Will sat frozen, with his heart thudding so hard he was afraid the adults would hear it. Sir Charles was talking about his own father! So that was who the men were, and what they were looking for!

But all the time, he was conscious of something else in the room as well as the voices of Sir Charles and the woman. There was a shadow moving across the floor, or that part of it he could see beyond the end of the sofa and past the legs of the little octagonal table. But neither Sir Charles nor the woman was moving. The shadow moved in a quick darting prowl, and it disturbed Will greatly. The only light in the room was a standard lamp beside the fireplace, so the shadow was clear and definite, but it never stopped long enough for Will to make out what it was.

Then two things happened. First, Sir Charles mentioned the alethiometer.

"For example," he said, continuing what he'd been saying, "I'm very curious about this instrument. Suppose you tell me how it works."

And he placed the alethiometer on the octagonal table at the end of the sofa. Will could see it clearly; he could almost reach it.

The second thing that happened was that the shadow fell still.

The creature that was the source of it must have been perched on the back of Mrs Coulter's chair, because the light streaming over it threw its shadow clearly on the wall. And the moment it stopped, he realized it was the woman's dæmon: a crouching monkey, turning its head this way and that, searching for something.

Will heard an intake of breath from Lyra behind him as she saw it too. He turned silently and whispered:

"Go back to the other window, and come through into his garden. Find some stones and throw them at the study so they look away for a moment, and then I can get the alethiometer. Then run back to the other window and wait for me."

She nodded, and turned and ran away silently over the grass. Will turned back.

The woman was saying: "…the Master of Jordan College is a foolish old man. Why he gave it to her I can't imagine; you need several years of intensive study to make any sense of it at all. And now you owe me some information, Carlo. How did you find it? And where is the child?"

"I saw her using it in a museum in the city. I recognized her, of course, having seen her at your cocktail party all that time ago, and I realized she must have found a doorway. And then I realized that I could use it for a purpose of my own. So when I came across her a second time, I stole it."

"You're very frank."

"No need to be coy; we're both grown up."

"And where is she now? What did she do when she found it was missing?"

"She came to see me, which must have taken some nerve, I imagine."

"She doesn't lack nerve. And what are you going to do with it? What is this purpose of yours?"

"I told her that she could have it back, provided she got something for me – something I couldn't get myself."

"And what is that?"

"I don't know whether you –"

And that was the moment when the first stone smashed into the study window.

It broke with a satisfying crash of glass, and instantly the monkey-shadow leapt from the chair back as the adults gasped. There came another crash, and another, and Will felt the sofa move as Sir Charles got up.

Will leaned forward and snatched the alethiometer from the little table, thrust it into his pocket, and darted back through the window. As soon as he was on the grass in Cittàgazze he felt in the air for those elusive edges, calming his mind, breathing slowly, conscious all the time that only feet away there was horrible danger.

Then came a screech, not human, not animal, but worse than either, and he knew it was that loathsome monkey. By that time he'd got most of the window closed, but there was still a small gap at the level of his chest – and then he leapt back, because into that gap there came a small furry golden hand with black fingernails, and then a face: a nightmare face. The golden monkey's teeth were bared, his eyes glaring, and such a concentrated malevolence blazed from him that Will felt it almost like a spear.

Another second, and he would have been through, and that would have been the end; but Will was still holding the knife, and he brought it up at once and slashed left, right, across the monkey's face – or where the face would have been if the monkey hadn't withdrawn just in time. That gave Will the moment he needed to seize the edges of the window and press them shut.

His own world had vanished, and he was alone in the moonlit parkland in Cittàgazze, panting and trembling and horribly frightened.

But now there was Lyra to rescue. He ran back to the first window, the one he'd opened into the shrubbery, and looked through. The dark leaves of laurels and holly obscured the view, but he reached through and thrust them aside to see the side of the house clearly, with the broken study window sharp in the moonlight.

As he watched, he saw that monkey leaping around the corner of the house, scampering over the grass with the speed of a cat, and then saw Sir Charles and the woman following close behind. Sir Charles was carrying a pistol. The woman herself was beautiful – Will saw that with shock – lovely in the moonlight, her brilliant dark eyes wide with enchantment, her slender shape light and graceful; but as she snapped her fingers, the monkey stopped at once and leapt up into her arms, and he saw that the sweet-faced woman and the evil monkey were one being.

But where was Lyra?

The adults were looking around, and then the woman put the monkey down, and it began to cast this way and that on the grass as if it were scenting or looking for footprints. There was silence from all around. If Lyra were in the shrubbery already, she wouldn't be able to move without making a noise which would give her away at once.

Sir Charles adjusted something on his pistol with a soft click: the safety catch. He peered into the shrubbery, seeming to look directly at Will, and then his eyes travelled on past.

Then both of the adults looked to their left, for the monkey had heard something. And in a flash it leapt forward to where Lyra must be, and a moment later it would have found her –

And at that moment the tabby cat sprang out of the shrubbery and on to the grass, and hissed.

The monkey heard, and twisted in mid-air as if with astonishment; though he was hardly as astonished as Will himself. The monkey fell on his paws, facing the cat, and the cat arched her back, tail raised high, and stood sideways on, hissing, challenging, spitting.

And the monkey leapt for her. The cat reared up, slashing with needle-paws left and right too quick to see, and then Lyra was beside Will, tumbling through the window with Pantalaimon beside her. And the cat screamed and the monkey screamed too as the cat's claws raked his face; and then the monkey turned and leapt into Mrs Coulter's arms, and the cat shot away into the bushes of her own world, and vanished.

And Will and Lyra were through the window, and Will felt once again for the almost intangible edges in the air and pressed them swiftly together, closing the window all along its length as through the diminishing gap came the sound of feet among twigs and cracking branches –

And then there was only a hole the size of Will's hand, and then it was shut, and the whole world was silent. He fell to his knees on the dewy grass, and fumbled for the alethiometer.

"Here," he said to Lyra.

She took it. With shaking hands he slid the knife back into its sheath. Then he lay down trembling in all his limbs and closed his eyes, and felt the moonlight bathing him with silver, and felt Lyra undoing his bandage and tying it up again with delicate gentle movements.

"Oh, Will," he heard her say, "thank you for what you done, for all of it…"

"I hope the cat's all right," he muttered. "She's like my Moxie. She's probably gone home now. In her own world again. She'll be all right now."

"You know what I thought? I thought she was your dæmon,

for a second. She done what a good dæmon would have done, anyway. We rescued her and she rescued us. Come on, Will, don't lie on the grass, it's wet. You got to come and lie down in a proper bed else you'll catch cold. We'll go in that big house over there. There's bound to be beds and food and stuff. Come on, I'll make a new bandage, I'll put some coffee on to cook, I'll make some omelette, whatever you want, and we'll sleep… We'll be safe now we've got the alethiometer back, you'll see. I'll do nothing now except help you find your father, I promise…"

She helped him up, and they walked slowly through the garden towards the great white-gleaming house under the moon.

10
The Shaman

Lee Scoresby disembarked at the port in the mouth of the Yenisei River, and found the place in chaos, with fishermen trying to sell their meagre catches of unknown kinds of fish to the canning factories, with ship-owners angry about the harbour charges the authorities had raised to cope with the floods, and with hunters and fur-trappers drifting into town unable to work because of the rapidly thawing forest and the disordered behaviour of the animals.

It was going to be hard to make his way into the interior along the road, that was certain; for in normal times the road was simply a cleared track of frozen earth, and now that even the permafrost was melting, the surface was a swamp of churned mud.

So Lee put his balloon and equipment into storage, and with his dwindling gold hired a boat with a gas-engine and bought several tanks of fuel and some stores, and set off up the swollen river.

He made slow progress at first. Not only was the current swift, but the waters were laden with all kinds of debris: tree trunks, brushwood, drowned animals, and once the bloated corpse of a man. He had to pilot carefully and keep the little engine beating hard to make any headway.

He was heading for the village of Grumman's tribe. For guidance he had only his memory of having flown over the country some years before, but that memory was good, and he had little difficulty in finding the right course among the swift-running streams, even though some of the banks had vanished under the milky-brown flood waters. The temperature had disturbed the insects, and a cloud of midges made every outline hazy. Lee smeared his face and hands with jimson-weed ointment and smoked a succession of pungent cigars, which kept the worst at bay.

As for Hester, she sat taciturn in the bow, her long ears flat against her skinny back and her eyes narrowed. He was used to her silence, and she to his. They spoke when they needed to.

On the morning of the third day, Lee steered the little craft up a creek that joined the main stream, flowing down from a line of low hills that should have been deep under snow, but now were patched and streaked with brown. Soon the stream was flowing between low pines and spruce, and after a few miles they came to a large round rock, the height of a house, where Lee drew in to the bank and tied up.

"There was a landing stage here," he said to Hester. "Remember the old seal-hunter in Nova Zembla who told us about it? It must be six feet under now."

"I hope they had sense enough to build the village high, then," she said, hopping ashore.

No more than half an hour later he laid his pack down beside the wooden house of the village headman and turned to salute the little crowd that had gathered. He used the gesture universal in the north to signify friendship, and laid his rifle down at his feet.

An old Siberian Tartar, his eyes almost lost in the wrinkles around them, laid his bow down beside it. His wolverine-dæmon twitched her nose at Hester, who flicked an ear in response, and then the headman spoke.

Lee replied, and they moved through half a dozen languages before finding one they could talk in.

"My respects to you and your tribe," Lee said. "I have some smokeweed, which is not worthy, but I would be honoured to present it to you."

The headman nodded in appreciation, and one of his wives received the bundle Lee removed from his pack.

"I am seeking a man called Grumman," Lee said. "I heard tell he was a kinsman of yours by adoption. He may have acquired another name, but the man is European."

"Ah," said the headman, "we have been waiting for you."

The rest of the villagers, gathered in the thin steaming sunlight on the muddy ground in the middle of the houses, couldn't understand the words but they saw the headman's pleasure. Pleasure, and relief, Lee felt Hester think.

The headman nodded several times.

"We have been expecting you," he said again. "You have come to take Dr Grumman to the other world."

Lee's eyebrows rose, but he merely said, "As you say, sir. Is he here?"

"Follow me," said the headman.

The other villagers fell aside respectfully. Understanding Hester's distaste for the filthy mud she had to lope through, Lee scooped her up in his arms and shouldered his pack, following the headman along a forest path to a hut ten long bow-shots from the village, in a clearing in the larches.

The headman stopped outside the wood-framed, skin-covered hut. The place was decorated with boar-tusks and the antlers of elk and reindeer, but they weren't merely hunting trophies, for they had been hung with dried flowers and carefully

209

plaited sprays of pine, as if for some ritualistic purpose.

"You must speak to him with respect," the headman said quietly. "He is a shaman. And his heart is sick."

Suddenly Lee felt a shiver go down his back, and Hester stiffened in his arms, for they saw that they had been watched all the time. From among the dried flowers and the pine-sprays a bright yellow eye looked out. It was a dæmon, and as Lee watched, she turned her head, and delicately took a spray of pine in her powerful beak and drew it across the space like a curtain.

The headman called out in his own tongue, addressing the man by the name the old seal-hunter had told him: Jopari. A moment later the door opened.

Standing in the doorway, gaunt, blazing-eyed, was a man dressed in skins and furs. His black hair was streaked with grey, his jaw jutted strongly, and his osprey-dæmon sat glaring on his fist.

The headman bowed three times and withdrew, leaving Lee alone with the shaman-academic he'd come to find.

"Dr Grumman," he said. "My name's Lee Scoresby. I'm from the country of Texas, and I'm an aëronaut by profession. If you'd let me sit and talk a spell, I'll tell you what brings me here. I am right, ain't I? You *are* Dr Stanislaus Grumman, of the Berlin Academy?"

"Yes," said the shaman. "And you're from Texas, you say. The winds have blown you a long way from your homeland, Mr Scoresby."

"Well, there are strange winds blowing through the world now, sir."

"Indeed. The sun is warm, I think. You'll find a bench inside my hut. If you help me bring it out we can sit in this agreeable light, and talk out here. I have some coffee, if you would care to share it."

"Most kind, sir," said Lee, and carried out the wooden bench himself while Grumman went to the stove and poured the scalding drink into two tin cups. His accent was not German, to Lee's ears, but English, of England. The Director of the Observatory had been right.

When they were seated, Hester narrow-eyed and impassive beside Lee and the great osprey-dæmon glaring into the full sun, Lee began. He started with his meeting at Trollesund with John Faa, Lord of the gyptians, and told how they recruited Iorek Byrnison the bear and journeyed to Bolvangar, and rescued Lyra and the other children; and then he spoke of what he'd learned both from Lyra and from Serafina Pekkala in the balloon as they flew towards Svalbard.

"You see, Dr Grumman, it seemed to me, from the way the little girl described it, that Lord Asriel just brandished this severed head packed in ice at the scholars there and frightened them so much with it they didn't look closely. That's what made me suspect you might still be alive. And clearly, sir, you have a kind of specialist knowledge of this business. I've been hearing about you all along the Arctic seaboard, about how you had your skull pierced, about how your subject of study seems to vary between digging on the ocean bed and gazing at the northern lights, about how you suddenly appeared, like as it might be out of nowhere, about ten-twelve years ago, and that's all mighty interesting. But something's drawn me here, Dr Grumman, beyond simple curiosity. I'm concerned about the child. I think she's important, and so do the witches. If there's anything you know about her and about what's going on, I'd like you to tell me. As I said, something's given me the conviction that you can, which is why I'm here.

"But unless I'm mistaken, sir, I heard the village headman say that I had come to take you to another world. Did I get it wrong, or is that truly what he said? And one more question for you, sir: what was that name he called you by? Was that some kind of tribal name, some magician's title?"

Grumman smiled briefly, and said, "The name he used is my own true name, John Parry. Yes, you have come to take me to the other world. And as for what brought you here, I think you'll find it was this."

And he opened his hand. In the palm lay something that Lee could see, but not understand. He saw a ring of silver and turquoise, a Navajo design, he saw it clearly and he recognized it as his own mother's, he knew its weight and the smoothness of the stone and the way the silversmith had folded the metal over more closely at the corner where the stone was chipped, and he knew how the chipped corner had worn smooth, because he had run his fingers over it many, many times, years and years ago in his boyhood in the sagelands of his native country.

He found himself standing. Hester was trembling, standing upright, ears pricked. The osprey had moved without Lee's noticing between him and Grumman, defending her man, but Lee wasn't going to attack; he felt undone; he felt like a child again, and his voice was tight and shaky as he said:

"Where did you get that?"

"Take it," said Grumman, or Parry. "Its work is done. It summoned you. Now I don't need it."

"But how –" said Lee, lifting the beloved thing from Grumman's palm. "I don't understand how you can have – did you – how did you get this? I ain't seen this thing for forty years."

"I am a shaman. I can do many things you don't understand. Sit down, Mr Scoresby. Be calm. I'll tell you what you need to know."

Lee sat again, holding the ring, running his fingers over it again and again.

"Well," he said, "I'm shaken, sir. I think I need to hear what you can tell me."

"Very well," said Grumman, "I'll begin. My name, as I told you, is Parry, and I was not born in this world. Lord Asriel is not the first by any means to travel between the worlds, though he's the first to open the way so spectacularly. In my own world I was a soldier and then an explorer. Twelve years ago I was accompanying an expedition to a place in my world that corresponds with your Beringland. My companions had other intentions, but I was looking for something I'd heard about from old legends: a rent in the fabric of the world, a hole that had appeared between our universe and another. Well, some of my companions got lost. In searching for them, I and two others walked through this hole, this doorway, without even seeing it, and left our world altogether. At first we didn't realize what had happened. We walked on till we found a town, and then there was no mistaking it: we were in a different world.

"Well, try as we might, we could not find that first doorway again. We'd come through it in a blizzard, and you are an old Arctic hand: you know what that means.

"So we had no choice but to stay in that new world. And we soon discovered what a dangerous place it was. It seemed that there was a strange kind of ghoul or apparition haunting it, something deadly and implacable. My two companions died soon afterwards, victims of the Spectres, as the things are called.

"The result was that I found their world an abominable place, and I couldn't wait to leave it. The way back to my own world was barred for ever. But there were other doorways into other worlds, and a little searching found the way into this.

"So here I came. And I discovered a marvel as soon as I did, Mr Scoresby, for worlds differ greatly, and in this world I saw my dæmon for the first time. Yes, I hadn't known of Sayan Kötör here till I entered yours. People here cannot conceive of worlds where dæmons are a silent voice in the mind and no more. Can you imagine my astonishment, in turn, at learning that part of my own nature was female, and bird-formed, and beautiful?

"So with Sayan Kötör beside me, I wandered through the northern lands, and I learned a good deal from the peoples of the Arctic, like my good friends in the village down there. What they told me of this world filled some gaps in the knowledge I'd acquired in mine, and I began to see the answer to many mysteries.

"I made my way to Berlin under the name of Grumman. I told no one about my origins; it was my secret. I presented a thesis to the Academy, and defended it in debate, which is their method. I was better informed than the Academicians, and I had no difficulty in gaining membership.

"So with my new credentials I could begin to work in this world, where I found myself, for the most part, greatly contented. I missed some things about my own world, to be sure. Are you a married man, Mr Scoresby? No? Well, I was; and I loved my wife dearly, as I loved my son, my only child, a little boy not yet one year old when I wandered out of my world. I missed them terribly. But I might search for a thousand years, and never find the way back. We were sundered for ever.

"However, my work absorbed me. I sought other forms of knowledge; I was initiated into the skull-cult; I became a shaman. And I have made some useful discoveries: I have found a way of making an ointment from bloodmoss, for example, that preserves all the virtues of the fresh plant.

"I know a great deal about this world now, Mr Scoresby. I know, for example, about Dust. I see from your expression that you have heard the term. It is frightening your theologians to death, but they are the ones who frighten me. I know what Lord Asriel is doing, and I know why, and that's why I summoned you here. I am going to help him, you see, because the task he's undertaken is the greatest in human history. The greatest in thirty-five thousand years of human history, Mr Scoresby.

"I can't do very much myself. My heart is diseased beyond the powers of anyone in this world to cure it. I have one great effort left in me, perhaps. But I know something Lord Asriel doesn't, something he needs to know if his effort is to succeed.

"You see, I was intrigued by that haunted world where the Spectres fed on human consciousness. I wanted to know what they were, how they had come into being. And as a shaman, I can discover things in the spirit where I cannot go in the body, and I spent much time in trance, exploring that world. I found that the philosophers there, centuries ago, had created a tool for their own undoing: an instrument they called the subtle knife. It had many powers – more than they'd guessed when they made it, far more than they know even now – and somehow, in using it, they had let the Spectres into their world.

"Well, I know about the subtle knife, and what it can do. And I know where it is, and I know how to recognize the one who must use it, and I know what he must do in Lord Asriel's cause. I hope he's equal to the task. So I have summoned you here, and you are to fly me northwards, into the world Asriel has opened, where I expect to find the bearer of the subtle knife.

"That is a dangerous world, mind. Those Spectres are worse than anything in your world or mine. We shall have to be careful and courageous. I shall not return, and if you want to see your country again, you'll need all your courage, all your craft, all your luck.

"That's your task, Mr Scoresby. That is why you sought me out."

And the shaman fell silent. His face was pallid, with a faint sheen of sweat.

"This is the craziest damn idea I ever heard in my life," said Lee.

He stood up in his agitation and walked a pace or two this way, a pace or two that, while Hester watched unblinking from the bench. Grumman's eyes were half-closed; his dæmon sat on his knee, watching Lee warily.

"Do you want money?" Grumman said after a few moments. "I can get you some gold. That's not hard to do."

"Damn, I didn't come here for gold," said Lee hotly. "I came here … I came here to see if you were alive, like I thought you were. Well, my curiosity's kinda satisfied on that point."

"I'm glad to hear it."

"And there's another angle to this thing, too," Lee added, and told Grumman of the witch-council at Lake Enara, and the resolution the witches had sworn to. "You see," he finished, "that little girl Lyra… Well, she's the reason I set out to help the witches in the first place. You say you brought me here with that Navajo ring. Maybe that'sso and maybe it ain't. What I know is, I came here because I thought I'd be helping Lyra. I ain't never seen a child like that. If I had a daughter of my own, I hope she'd be half as strong and brave and good. Now I'd heard that you knew of some object, I didn't know what it might be, that confers a protection on anyone who holds it. And from what you say, I think it must be this subtle knife.

"So this is my price for taking you into the other world, Dr Grumman: not gold, but the subtle knife, and I don't want it for myself, I want it for Lyra. You have to swear you'll get her under the protection of that object, and then I'll take you wherever you want to go."

The shaman listened closely, and said, "Very well, Mr Scoresby; I swear. Do you trust my oath?"

"What will you swear by?"

"Name anything you like."

Lee thought, and then said, "Swear by whatever it was made you turn down the love of the witch. I guess that's the most important thing you know."

Grumman's eyes widened, and he said, "You guess well, Mr Scoresby. I'll gladly swear by that. I give you my word that I'll make certain the child Lyra Belacqua is under the protection of the subtle knife. But I warn you: the bearer of that knife has his own task to do, and it may be that his doing it will put her into even greater danger."

Lee nodded soberly. "Maybe so," he said, "but whatever little chance of safety there is, I want her to have it."

"You have my word. And now I must go into the new world, and you must take me."

"And the wind? You ain't been too sick to observe the weather, I guess?"

"Leave the wind to me."

Lee nodded. He sat on the bench again and ran his fingers over and over the turquoise ring while Grumman gathered the few goods he needed into a deerskin bag, and then the two of them went back down the forest track to the village.

The headman spoke at some length. More and more of the villagers came out to touch Grumman's hand, to mutter a few words, and to receive what looked like a blessing in return. Lee, meanwhile, was looking at the weather. The sky was clear to the south, and a fresh-scented breeze was just lifting the twigs and stirring the pine-tops. To the north the fog still hung over the heavy river, but it was the first time for days that there seemed to be a promise of clearing it.

At the rock where the landing-stage had been he lifted Grumman's pack into the boat, and filled the little engine, which fired at once. He cast off, and with the shaman in the bow, the boat sped down with the current, darting under the trees and skimming out into the main river so fast that Lee was afraid for Hester, crouching just inside the gunwale; but she was a seasoned traveller, he should have known that; why was he so damn jumpy?

They reached the port at the river-mouth to find every hotel, every lodging-house, every private room commandeered by soldiers. Not just any soldiers, either: these were troops of the Imperial Guard of Muscovy, the most ferociously-trained and lavishly-equipped army in the world, and one sworn to uphold the power of the Magisterium.

Lee had intended to rest a night before setting off, because Grumman looked in need of it, but there was no chance of finding a room.

"What's going on?" he said to the boatman when he returned the hired boat.

"We don't know. The regiment arrived yesterday and commandeered every billet, every scrap of food, and every ship in the town. They'd have had this boat too if you hadn't taken it."

"D'you know where they're going?"

"North," said the boatman. "There's a war going to be fought, by all accounts, the greatest war ever known."

"North, into that new world?"

"That's right. And there's more troops coming – this is just the advance guard. There won't be a loaf of bread or a gallon of spirit left in a week's time. You did me a favour taking this boat – the price has already doubled…"

There was no sense in resting up now, even if they could find a place. Full of anxiety about his balloon, Lee went at once to the warehouse where he'd left it, with Grumman beside him. The man was keeping pace. He looked sick, but he was tough.

The warehouse-keeper, busy counting out some spare engine

parts to a requisitioning sergeant of the Guard, looked up briefly from his clip-board.

"Balloon – too bad – requisitioned yesterday," he said. "You can see how it is. I've got no choice."

Hester flicked her ears, and Lee understood what she meant.

"Have you delivered the balloon yet?" he said.

"They're going to collect it this afternoon."

"No they're not," said Lee, "because I have an authority that trumps the Guard."

And he showed the warehouseman the ring he'd taken from the finger of the dead Skraeling on Nova Zembla. The sergeant, beside him at the counter, stopped what he was doing and saluted at the sight of the Church's token, but for all his discipline he couldn't prevent a flicker of puzzlement passing over his face.

"So we'll have the balloon right now," said Lee, "and you can set some men to fill it. And I mean at once. And that includes food, and water, and ballast."

The warehouseman looked at the sergeant, who shrugged, and then hurried away to see to the balloon. Lee and Grumman withdrew to the wharf, where the gas-tanks were, to supervise the filling and talk quietly.

"Where did you get that ring?" said Grumman.

"Off a dead man's finger. Kinda risky using it, but I couldn't see another way of getting my balloon back. You reckon that sergeant suspected anything?"

"Of course he did. But he's a disciplined man. He won't question the Church. If he reports it at all, we'll be away by the time they can do anything about it. Well, I promised you a wind, Mr Scoresby; I hope you like it."

The sky was blue overhead now, and the sunlight was bright. To the north fog-banks still hung like a mountain range over the sea, but the breeze was pushing them back and back, and Lee was impatient for the air again.

As the balloon filled and began to swell up beyond the edge of the warehouse roof, Lee checked the basket, and stowed all his equipment with particular care; for in the other world, who knew what turbulence they'd meet? His instruments, too, he fixed to the framework with close attention, even the compass, whose needle was swinging around the dial quite uselessly. Finally he lashed a score of sandbags around the basket for ballast.

When the gas-bag was full and leaning northwards in the buffeting breeze, and the whole apparatus straining against the stout ropes anchoring it down, Lee paid the warehouseman with the last of his gold, and helped Grumman into the basket. Then he turned to the men at the ropes to give the order to let go.

But before they could do so, there was an interruption. From the alley at the side of the warehouse came the noise of pounding boots, moving at the double, and a shout of command:

"Halt!"

The men at the ropes paused, some looking that way, some looking to Lee, and he called sharply:

"Let go! Cast off!"

Two of the men obeyed, and the balloon lurched up, but the other two had their attention on the soldiers, who were moving at the double around the corner of the building. Those two men still held their ropes fast around the bollards, and the balloon lurched sickeningly sideways. Lee grabbed at the suspension-ring; Grumman was holding it too, and his dæmon had her claws tight around it.

Lee shouted, "Let go, you damn fools! She's going up!"

Because the buoyancy of the gas-bag was too great, and the men, haul as they might, couldn't hold it back. One let go, and his rope lashed itself loose from the bollard; but the other man, feeling the rope lift, instinctively clung on instead of letting go.

Lee had seen this happen once before, and dreaded it. The poor man's dæmon, a heavy-set husky, howled with fear and pain from the ground as the balloon surged up towards the sky, and five endless seconds later it was over; the man's strength failed; he fell, half-dead, and crashed into the water.

But the soldiers had their rifles up already. A volley of bullets whistled past the basket, one striking a spark from the suspension-ring and making Lee's hands sting with the impact, but none of them did any damage. By the time they fired their second shot, the balloon was almost out of range, hurtling up into the blue and speeding out over the sea. Lee felt his heart lift with it. He'd said once to Serafina Pekkala that he didn't care for flying, that it was only a job, but he hadn't meant it. Soaring upwards, with a fair wind behind and a new world in front: what could be better in this life?

He let go the suspension-ring and saw that Hester was crouching in her usual corner, eyes half-closed. From far below and a long way back came another futile volley of rifle-fire. The town was receding fast, and the broad sweep of the river-mouth was glittering in the sunlight below them.

"Well, Dr Grumman," he said, "I don't know about you, but I feel better in the air. I wish that poor man had let go of the rope, though. It's so damned easy to do, and if you don't let go at once there's no hope for you."

"Thank you, Mr Scoresby," said the shaman. "You managed that very well. Now we settle down and fly. I would be grateful for those furs; the air is still cold."

11
The Belvedere

In the great white villa in the park Will slept uneasily, plagued with dreams that were filled with anxiety and with sweetness in equal measure, so that he struggled to wake up and yet longed for sleep again. When his eyes were fully open he felt so drowsy that he could scarcely move, and then he sat up to find his bandage loose and his bed crimson.

He struggled out of bed and made his way through the heavy dust-filled sunlight and silence of the great house down to the kitchen. He and Lyra had slept in servants' rooms under the attic, not feeling welcomed by the stately four-poster beds in the grand rooms further down, and it was a long unsteady walk.

"Will —" she said at once, her voice full of concern, and she turned from the stove to help him to a chair.

He felt dizzy. He supposed he'd lost a lot of blood; well, there was no need to suppose, with the evidence all over him. And the wounds were still bleeding.

"I was just making some coffee," she said. "Do you want that first, or shall I do another bandage? I can do whichever you want. And there's eggs in the cold cabinet, but I can't find any baked beans."

"This isn't a baked beans kind of house. Bandage first. Is there any hot water in the tap? I want to wash. I hate being covered in this…"

She ran some hot water and he stripped to his underpants. He was too faint and dizzy to feel embarrassed, but Lyra became embarrassed for him, and went out. He washed as best he could and then dried himself on the tea-towels that hung on a line by the stove.

When she came back she'd found some clothes for him, just a shirt and canvas trousers and a belt. He put them on and she tore a fresh tea-towel into strips and bandaged him tightly again. She was badly worried about his hand: not only were the wounds bleeding freely still, but the rest of the hand was swollen and red. But he said nothing about it, and neither did she.

Then she made the coffee and toasted some stale bread, and they took it into the grand room at the front of the house, overlooking the city. When he'd eaten and drunk he felt a little better.

"You better ask the alethiometer what to do next," he said. "Have you asked it anything yet?"

"No," she said. "I'm only going to do what you ask, from now on. I thought of doing it last night, but I never did. And I won't either unless you ask me to."

"Well, you better do it now," he said. "There's as much danger here as there is in my world, now. There's Angelica's brother for a start. And if –"

He stopped, because she began to say something, but she stopped as soon as he did. Then she collected herself and went on:

"Will, there was something that happened yesterday that I didn't tell you. I should've, but there was just so many other things going on. I'm sorry…"

And she told him everything she'd seen through the window of the Tower while Giacomo Paradisi was dressing his wound: Tullio being beset by the Spectres, Angelica seeing her at the window and her look of hatred, and Paolo's threat.

"And d'you remember," she went on, "when she first spoke to us? Her little brother said something about what they were all doing. He said 'He's gonna get –' and she wouldn't let him finish, she smacked him, remember? I bet he was going to say Tullio was after the knife, and that's why all the kids came here. 'Cause if they had the knife, they could do anything, they could even grow up without being afraid of Spectres."

"What did it look like, when he was attacked?" Will said. To her surprise he was sitting forward, his eyes demanding and urgent.

"He…" She tried to remember exactly: "He started counting the stones in the wall. He sort of felt all over them… But he couldn't keep it up. In the end he sort of lost interest and stopped. Then he was just still," she finished, and seeing Will's expression she said: "Why?"

"Because … I think maybe they come from my world after all, the Spectres. If they make people behave like that, I wouldn't be surprised at all if they came from my world. And when the Guild men opened their first window, if it was into my world, the Spectres could have gone through then."

"But you don't have Spectres in your world! You never heard of them, did you?"

"Maybe they're not called Spectres. Maybe we call them something else."

Lyra wasn't sure what he meant, but she didn't want to press him. His cheeks were red and his eyes were hot.

"Anyway," she went on, turning away, "the important thing is that Angelica saw me in the window. And now she knows we've got the knife, she'll tell all of 'em. She'll think it's our fault that her brother was attacked by Spectres. I'm sorry, Will. I should've told you earlier. But there was just so many other things…"

"Well," he said, "I don't suppose it would have made any difference. He was torturing the old man, and once he knew how to use the knife he'd have killed both of us if he could. We had to fight him."

"I just feel bad about it, Will. I mean, he was her brother. And I bet if we were them we'd have wanted the knife too."

"Yes," he said, "but we can't go back and change what happened. We had to get the knife to get the alethiometer back, and if we could have got it without fighting, we would."

"Yeah, we would," she said.

Like Iorek Byrnison, Will was a fighter truly enough, so she was prepared to agree with him when he said it would be better not to fight: she knew it wasn't cowardice that spoke, but strategy. He was calmer now, and his cheeks were pale again. He was looking into the middle distance and thinking.

Then he said, "It's probably more important now to think about Sir Charles and what he'll do, or Mrs Coulter. Maybe if she's got this special bodyguard they were talking about, these soldiers who'd had their dæmons cut away, maybe Sir Charles is right and they'll be able to ignore the Spectres. You know what I think? I think what they eat, the Spectres, is people's dæmons."

"But children have dæmons too. And they don't attack children. It can't be that."

"Then it must be the difference between children's dæmons and grown-ups'," Will said. "There *is* a difference, isn't there? You told me grown-ups' dæmons don't change shape. It must be something to do with that. If these soldiers of hers haven't got dæmons at all, maybe it has the same effect…"

"Yeah!" she said. "Could be. And *she* wouldn't be afraid of Spectres anyway. She en't afraid of anything. And she's so clever, Will, honest, and she's so ruthless and cruel, she could boss them,

225

I bet she could. She could command them like she does people and they'd have to obey her, I bet. Lord Boreal is strong and clever, but she'll have him doing what she wants in no time. Oh, Will, I'm getting scared again, thinking what she might do… I'm going to ask the alethiometer, like you said. Thank goodness we got that back, anyway."

She unfolded the velvet bundle and ran her hands lovingly over the heavy gold.

"I'm going to ask about your father," she said, "and how we can find him. See, I put the hands to point at –"

"No. Ask about my mother first. I want to know if she's all right."

Lyra nodded, and turned the hands before laying the alethiometer in her lap and tucking her hair behind her ears to look down and concentrate. Will watched the light needle swing purposefully round the dial, darting and stopping and darting on as swiftly as a swallow feeding, and he watched Lyra's eyes, so blue and fierce and full of clear understanding.

Then she blinked and looked up.

"She's safe still," she said. "This friend that's looking after her, she's ever so kind. No one knows where your mother is, and the friend won't give her away."

Will hadn't realized how worried he'd been. At this good news, he felt himself relax, and as a little tension left his body, he felt the pain of his wound more sharply.

"Thank you," he said. "All right, now ask about my father –"

But before she could even begin, they heard a shout from outside.

They looked out at once. At the lower edge of the park in front of the first houses of the city there was a belt of trees, and something was stirring there. Pantalaimon became a lynx at once and padded to the open door, gazing fiercely down.

"It's the children," he said.

They both stood up. The children were coming out of the trees, one by one, maybe forty or fifty of them. Many of them were carrying sticks. At their head was the boy in the striped T-shirt, and it wasn't a stick that he was carrying: it was a pistol.

"There's Angelica," Lyra whispered, pointing.

Angelica was beside the leading boy, tugging at his arm, urging him on. Just behind them her little brother Paolo was shrieking with excitement, and the other children, too, were yelling and waving their fists in the air. Two of them were lugging heavy rifles. Will had seen children in this mood before, but never so many of them, and the ones in his town didn't carry guns.

They were shouting, and Will managed to make out Angelica's voice high over them all: "You killed my brother and you stole the knife! You murderers! You made the Spectres get him! You killed him and we'll kill you! You ain gonna get away! We gonna kill you same as you killed him!"

"Will, you could cut a window!" Lyra said urgently, clutching his good arm. "We could get away, easy –"

"Yeah, and where would we be? In Oxford, a few yards from Sir Charles's house, in broad daylight. Probably in the main street in front of a bus. I can't just cut through anywhere and expect to be safe – I've got to look first and see where we are, and that'd take too long. There's a forest or woods or something behind this house. If we can get up there in the trees we'll be safer."

Lyra looked out of the window, furious. "I should have killed her yesterday!" she said. "She's as bad as her brother. I'd like to –"

"Stop talking and come on," said Will.

He checked that the knife was strapped to his belt, and Lyra put on her little rucksack with the alethiometer and the letters from Will's father. They ran through the echoing hall, along the corridor and into the kitchen, through the scullery and into a cobbled court beyond it. A gate in the wall led out into a kitchen garden, where beds of vegetables and herbs lay baking under the morning sun.

The edge of the wood was a few hundred yards away, up a slope of grass that was horribly exposed. On a knoll to the left, closer than the trees, stood a little building, a circular temple-like structure with an upper storey open like a balcony for viewing the city from.

"Let's run," said Will, though he felt less like running than like lying down and closing his eyes.

With Pantalaimon flying above to keep watch, they set off across the grass. But it was tussocky and ankle-high, and Will couldn't run more than a few steps before he felt too dizzy to carry on. He slowed to a walk.

Lyra looked back. The children hadn't seen them yet; they were still at the front of the house; maybe they'd take a while to look through all the rooms...

But Pantalaimon chirruped in alarm. There was a boy standing at an open window on the second floor of the villa, pointing at them. They heard a shout.

"Come *on*, Will," Lyra said.

She tugged at his good arm, helping him, lifting him. He tried to respond, but he didn't have the strength. He could only walk.

"All right," he said, "we can't get to the trees. Too far away. So we'll go to that temple place. If we shut the door maybe we can hold them out for long enough to cut through after all..."

Pantalaimon darted ahead, and Lyra gasped and called to him breathlessly, making him pause. Will could almost see the bond between them, the dæmon tugging and the girl responding. He

228

stumbled through the thick grass with Lyra running ahead to see, and then back to help, and then ahead again, until they reached the stone pavement around the temple.

The door under the little portico was unlocked, and they ran inside to find themselves in a bare circular room with several statues of goddesses in niches around the wall. In the very centre a spiral staircase of wrought iron led up through an opening to the floor above. There was no key to lock the door, so they clambered up the staircase and on to the floorboards of an upper level that was really a viewing place, where people could come to take the air and look out over the city; for there were no windows or walls, simply a series of open arches all the way round supporting the roof. In each archway a window sill at waist height was broad enough to lean on, and below them the pantiled roof ran down in a gentle slope all around to the gutter.

As they looked out they could see the forest behind, tantalizingly close; and the villa below them, and beyond that the open park and then the red-brown roofs of the city, with the Tower rising to the left. There were carrion crows wheeling in the air above the grey battlements, and Will felt a jolt of sickness as he realized what had drawn them there.

But there was no time to take in the view; first they had to deal with the children, who were racing up towards the temple, screaming with rage and excitement. The leading boy slowed down and held up his pistol, and fired two or three wild shots towards the temple, and then they came on again, yelling:

"Thiefs!"

"Murderers!"

"We gonna kill you!"

"You got our knife!"

"You don' come from here!"

"You gonna die!"

Will took no notice. He had the knife out already, and swiftly cut a small window to see where they were – only to recoil at once. Lyra looked too, and fell back in disappointment. They were fifty feet or so in the air, high above a main road busy with traffic.

"Of course," Will said bitterly, "we came up a slope… Well, we're stuck. We'll have to hold them off, that's all."

Another few seconds and the first children were crowding in through the door. The sound of their yelling echoed in the temple and reinforced their wildness; and then came a gunshot, enormously loud, and another, and the screaming took another tone, and then the stairs began to shake as the first ones climbed up.

Lyra was crouching paralysed against the wall, but Will still had the knife in his hand. He scrambled over to the opening in the floor and reached down and sliced through the iron of the top step as if it were paper. With nothing to hold it up, the staircase began to bend under the weight of the children crowding on it, and then it swung down and fell with a huge crash. More screams, more confusion; and again the gun went off, but this time by accident, it seemed, because someone had been hit, and the scream was of pain this time, and Will looked down to see a tangle of writhing bodies, covered in plaster and dust and blood.

They weren't individual children: they were a single mass, like a tide. They surged below him and leaped up in fury, snatching, threatening, screaming, spitting, but they couldn't reach.

Then someone called, and they looked to the door, and those who could move surged out towards it, leaving several pinned beneath the iron stairs or dazed and struggling to get up from the rubble-strewn floor.

Will soon realized why they'd run out. There was a scrabbling sound from the roof outside the arches, and he ran to the window sill to see the first pair of hands grasping the edge of the pantiles and pulling up. Someone was pushing from behind, and then came another head and another pair of hands, as they clambered over the shoulders and backs of those below and swarmed up on to the roof like ants.

But the pantiled ridges were hard to walk on, and the first ones scrambled up on hands and knees, their wild eyes never leaving Will's face. Lyra had joined him, and Pantalaimon was snarling as a leopard, paws on the sill, making the first children hesitate. But still they came on, more and more of them.

Someone was shouting "Kill! Kill! Kill!" and then others joined in, louder and louder, and those on the roof began to stamp and thump the tiles in rhythm, but they didn't quite dare come closer, faced by the snarling dæmon. Then a tile broke, and the boy standing on it slipped and fell, but the one beside him picked up the broken piece and hurled it at Lyra.

She ducked, and it shattered on the column beside her, showering her with broken pieces. Will had noticed the rail around the edge of the opening in the floor, and cut two sword-length pieces of it, and he handed one to Lyra now; and she swung it round as hard as she could and into the side of the first boy's head. He fell at once, but then came another, and it was Angelica, red-haired, white-faced, crazy-eyed; she scrambled up on to the sill, but Lyra jabbed the length of rail at her fiercely and she fell back again.

Will was doing the same. The knife was in its sheath at his waist, and he struck and swung and jabbed with the iron rail, and while several children fell back, others kept replacing them, and more and more were clambering up on to the roof from below.

Then the boy in the striped T-shirt appeared, but he'd lost the pistol, or perhaps it was empty. However, his eyes and Will's locked together, and each of them knew what was going to happen: they were going to fight, and it was going to be brutal and deadly.

"Come on," said Will, passionate for the battle, "come on then…"

Another second, and they would have fought.

But then the strangest thing appeared: a great white snow-goose swooping low, his wings spread wide, calling and calling so loud that even the children on the roof heard through their savagery and turned to see.

"Kaisa!" cried Lyra joyfully, for it was Serafina Pekkala's dæmon.

The snow-goose called again, a piercing whoop that filled the sky, and then wheeled and turned an inch away from the boy in the striped T-shirt. The boy fell back in fear and slid down and over the edge, and then others began to cry in alarm too, because there was something else in the sky, and as Lyra saw the little black shapes sweeping out of the blue she cheered and shouted with glee.

"Serafina Pekkala! Here! Help us! Here we are! In the temple –"

And with a hiss and rush of air a dozen arrows, and then another dozen swiftly after, and then another dozen loosed so quickly that they were all in the air at once, shot at the temple roof above the gallery and landed with a thunder of hammer-blows. Astonished and bewildered, the children on the roof felt all the aggression leave them in a moment, and horrible fear rushed in to take its place: what were these black-garbed women rushing at them in the air? How could it happen? Were they ghosts? Were they a new kind of Spectre?

And whimpering and crying they jumped off the roof, some of them falling clumsily and dragging themselves away limping and others rolling down the slope and dashing for safety, but a mob

no longer; just a lot of frightened shame-faced children. A
minute after the snow-goose had appeared, the last of the
children left the temple and the only sound was the rush of air in
the branches of the circling witches above.

Will looked up in wonder, too amazed to speak, but Lyra was
leaping and calling with delight:

"Serafina Pekkala! How did you find us? Thank you, thank
you! They was going to kill us! Come down and land…"

But Serafina and the others shook their heads, and flew up
again, to circle high above. The snow-goose dæmon wheeled and
flew down towards the roof, beating his great wings inwards to
help him slow down, and landed with a clatter on the pantiles
below the sill.

"Greetings, Lyra," he said. "Serafina Pekkala can't come to
the ground, and nor can the others. The place is full of Spectres
– a hundred or more surrounding the building, and more
drifting up over the grass. Can't you see them?"

"No! We can't see 'em at all!"

"Already we've lost one witch. We can't risk any more. Can
you get down from this building?"

"If we jump off the roof like they done. But how did you find
us? And where –"

"Enough now. There's more trouble coming, and bigger. Get
down as best you can and then make for the trees."

They climbed over the sill and moved sideways down through
the broken tiles to the gutter. It wasn't high, and below it was
grass, with a gentle slope away from the building. First Lyra
jumped and then Will followed, rolling over and trying to protect
his hand, which was bleeding freely again and hurting badly. His
sling had come loose and trailed behind him, and as he tried to
roll it up, the snow-goose landed on the grass at his side.

"Lyra, who is this?" Kaisa said.

"It's Will. He's coming with us –"

"Why are the Spectres avoiding you?" The goose-dæmon was speaking directly to Will.

By this time Will was hardly surprised by anything, and he said, "I don't know. We can't see them. No, wait!" And he stood up, struck by a thought. "Where are they now?" he said. "Where's the nearest one?"

"Ten paces away, down the slope," said the dæmon. "They don't want to come any closer, that's obvious."

Will took the knife out and looked in that direction, and he heard the dæmon hiss with surprise.

But Will couldn't do what he intended, because at the same moment a witch landed her branch on the grass beside him. He was taken aback not so much by her flying as by her astounding gracefulness, the fierce cold lovely clarity of her gaze, and by the pale bare limbs, so youthful, and yet so far from being young.

"Your name is Will?" she said.

"Yes, but –"

"Why are the Spectres afraid of you?"

"Because of the knife. Where's the nearest one? Tell me! I want to kill it!"

But Lyra came running before the witch could answer.

"Serafina Pekkala!" she cried, and she threw her arms around the witch and hugged her so tightly that the witch laughed out loud, and kissed the top of her head. "Oh, Serafina, where did you come from like that? We were – those kids – they were *kids*, and they were going to kill us – did you see them? We thought we were going to die, and – oh, I'm so glad you came! I thought I'd never see you again!"

Serafina Pekkala looked over Lyra's head to where the Spectres were obviously clustering a little way off, and then looked at Will.

"Now listen," she said, "there's a cave in these woods not far away. Head up the slope and then along the ridge to the left. We might be able to carry Lyra for a little way, but you're too big: you'll have to go on foot. The Spectres won't follow – they don't see us while we're in the air, and they're afraid of you. We'll meet you there – it's a half-hour walk."

And she leapt into the air again. Will shaded his eyes to watch her and the other ragged elegant figures wheel in the air and dart up over the trees.

"Oh, Will, we'll be safe now! It'll be all right now Serafina Pekkala's here!" said Lyra. "I never thought I'd see her again – she came just at the right time, didn't she? Just like before, at Bolvangar…"

Chattering happily, as if she'd already forgotten the fight, she led the way up the slope towards the forest. Will followed in silence. His hand was throbbing badly, and with each throb a little more blood was leaving him. He held it up across his chest and tried not to think about it.

It took not half an hour but an hour and three-quarters, because Will had to stop and rest several times. When they reached the cave they found a fire, a rabbit roasting, and Serafina Pekkala stirring something in a small iron pot.

"Let me see your wound," was the first thing she said to Will, and he dumbly held out his hand.

Pantalaimon, cat-formed, watched curiously, but Will looked away. He didn't like the sight of his mutilated fingers.

The witches spoke softly to each other, and then Serafina Pekkala said, "What weapon made this wound?"

Will reached for the knife and handed it to her silently. Her companions looked at it with wonder and suspicion, for they had never seen such a blade before, with such an edge on it.

"This will need more than herbs to heal. It will need a spell," said Serafina Pekkala. "Very well, we'll prepare one. It will be ready when the moon rises. In the meantime, you shall sleep."

She gave him a little horn cup, containing a hot potion whose bitterness was moderated by honey, and presently he lay back and fell deeply asleep. The witch covered him with leaves, and turned to Lyra, who was still gnawing the rabbit.

"Now, Lyra," she said, "tell me who this boy is, and what you know about this world, and about this knife of his."

So Lyra took a deep breath and began.

12
Screen Language

"Tell me again," said Dr Oliver Payne, in the little laboratory overlooking the park. "Either I didn't hear you or you're talking nonsense. A child from another world?"

"That's what she said. All right, it's nonsense, but *listen* to it, Oliver, will you?" said Dr Mary Malone. "She knew about Shadows. She calls them – it – she calls it Dust, but it's the same thing. It's our Shadow-particles. And I'm telling you, when she was wearing the electrodes linking her to the Cave, there was the most extraordinary display on the screen: pictures, symbols… She had an instrument too, a sort of compass thing made of gold, with different symbols all round the rim. And she said she could read that in the same way, and she knew about the state of mind, too, she knew it intimately."

It was mid-morning. Lyra's scholar Dr Malone was red-eyed from lack of sleep, and her colleague, who'd just returned from Geneva, was impatient to hear more, and sceptical, and preoccupied.

"And the point was, Oliver, she was communicating with them. They *are* conscious. And they can respond. And you remember your skulls? Well, she told me about some skulls in the Pitt-Rivers Museum – she'd found out with her compass thing that they were much older than the Museum said, and there were Shadows –"

"Wait a minute. Give me some sort of *structure* here. What are you saying? You saying she's confirmed what we know already, or that she's telling us something new?"

"Both. I don't know. But suppose something happened thirty, forty thousand years ago. There were Shadow-particles around before then, obviously – they've been around since the Big Bang – but there was no physical way of amplifying their effects at *our* level, the anthropic level. The level of human beings. And then something happened, I can't imagine what, but it involved evolution. Hence your skulls – remember? No Shadows before that time, lots afterwards? And the skulls the child found in the Museum, that she tested with her compass-thing. She told me the same thing. What I'm saying is that around that time, the human brain became the ideal vehicle for this amplification process. Suddenly we became conscious."

Dr Payne tilted his plastic mug and drank the last of his coffee.

"Why should it happen particularly at that time?" he said. "Why suddenly thirty-five thousand years ago?"

"Oh, who can say? We're not palaeontologists. I don't know, Oliver, I'm just speculating. Don't you think it's at least possible?"

"And this policeman. Tell me about him."

Dr Malone rubbed her eyes. "His name was Walters," she said. "He said he was from the Special Branch. I thought that was politics or something?"

"Terrorism, subversion, intelligence… All that. Go on. What did he want? Why did he come here?"

"Because of the girl. He said he was looking for a boy of about the same age, he didn't tell me why, and this boy had been seen in the company of the girl who came here. But he had something else in mind as well, Oliver, he *knew* about the research, he even asked –"

The telephone rang. She broke off, shrugging, and Dr Payne answered it. He spoke briefly and put it down, and said, "We've got a visitor."

"Who?"

"Not a name I know. Sir Somebody Something. Listen, Mary, I'm off, you realize that, don't you?"

"They offered you the job."

"Yes. I've got to take it. You must see that."

"Well, that's the end of this, then."

He spread his hands helplessly, and said, "To be frank … I can't see any point in the sort of stuff you've just been talking about. Children from another world and fossil Shadows… It's all too crazy. I just can't get involved. I've got a career, Mary."

"What about the skulls you tested? What about the Shadows around the ivory figurine?"

He shook his head and turned his back. Before he could answer, there came a tap at the door, and he opened it almost with relief.

Sir Charles said, "Good day to you. Dr Payne? Dr Malone? My name is Charles Latrom. It's very good of you to see me without any notice."

"Come in," said Dr Malone, weary, but puzzled. "Did Oliver say *Sir* Charles? What can we do for you?"

"It may be what I can do for you," he said. "I understand you're waiting for the results of your funding application."

"How do you know that?" said Dr Payne.

"I used to be a civil servant. As a matter of fact I was concerned with directing scientific policy. I still have a number of contacts in the field, and I heard… May I sit down?"

"Oh, please," said Dr Malone. She pulled out a chair, and he sat down as if he were in charge of a meeting.

"Thank you. I heard through a friend – I'd better not mention his name; the Official Secrets Act covers all sorts of silly things – I heard that your application was being considered, and what I heard about it intrigued me so much that I must confess I asked to see some of your work. I know I had no business to, except that I still act as a sort of unofficial adviser, so I used that as an excuse. And really, what I saw was quite fascinating."

"Does that mean you think we'll be successful?" said Dr Malone, leaning forward, eager to believe him.

"Unfortunately, no. I must be blunt. They're not minded to renew your grant."

Dr Malone's shoulders slumped. Dr Payne was watching the old man with cautious curiosity.

"Why have you come here now, then?" he said.

"Well, you see, they haven't officially made the decision yet. It doesn't look promising, and I'm being frank with you: they see no prospect of funding work of this sort in the future. However, it might be that if you had someone to argue the case for you, they would see it differently."

"An advocate? You mean yourself? I didn't think it worked like that," said Dr Malone, sitting up. "I thought they went on peer review and so on…"

"It does in principle, of course," said Sir Charles, "but it also helps to know how these committees work in practice. And to know who's on them. Well, here I am. I'm intensely interested in your work, I think it might be very valuable, and it certainly ought to continue. Would you let me make informal representations on your behalf?"

Dr Malone felt like a drowning sailor being thrown a lifebelt. "Why… Well, yes! Good grief, of course! And thank you… I mean, do you really think it'll make a difference? I don't mean to suggest that... I don't know what I mean. Yes, of course!"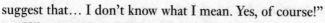

"What would we have to do?" said Dr Payne.

Dr Malone looked at him in surprise. Hadn't Oliver just said he was going to work in Geneva? But he seemed to be understanding Sir Charles better than she was, for a flicker of complicity was passing between them, and Oliver came to sit down too.

"I'm glad you take my point," said the old man. "You're quite right. There is a direction I'd be especially glad to see you taking. And provided we could agree, I might even be able to find you some extra money from another source altogether."

"Wait, wait," said Dr Malone, "wait a minute. The course of this research is a matter for us. I'm perfectly willing to discuss the results, but not the direction. Surely you see —"

Sir Charles spread his hands in a gesture of regret and got to his feet. Oliver Payne stood too, anxious.

"No, please, Sir Charles," he said, "I'm sure Dr Malone will hear you out. Mary, there's no harm in listening, for goodness' sake. And it might make all the difference."

"I thought you were going to Geneva?" she said.

"Geneva?" said Sir Charles. "Excellent place. Lot of scope there. Lot of money, too. Don't let me hold you back."

"No, no, it's not settled yet," said Dr Payne hastily. "There's a lot to discuss — it's all still very fluid. Sir Charles, please sit down. Can I get you some coffee?"

"That would be very kind," said Sir Charles, and sat again, with the air of a satisfied cat.

Dr Malone looked at him clearly for the first time. She saw a man in his late sixties, prosperous, confident, beautifully dressed, used to the very best of everything, used to moving among powerful people and whispering in important ears. Oliver was right: he did want something. And they wouldn't get his support unless they satisfied him.

She folded her arms.

Dr Payne handed him a mug, saying, "Sorry it's rather primitive…"

"Not at all. Shall I go on with what I was saying?"

"Do, please," said Dr Payne.

"Well, I understand that you've made some fascinating discoveries in the field of consciousness. Yes, I know, you haven't published anything yet, and it's a long way – seemingly – from the apparent subject of your research. Nevertheless, word gets around. And I'm especially interested in that. I would be very pleased if, for example, you were to concentrate your researches towards the manipulation of consciousness. Secondly, the many-worlds hypothesis – Everett, you remember, 1957 or thereabouts; I believe you're on the track of something that could take that theory a good deal further. And that line of research might even attract defence funding, which as you may know is still plentiful, even today, and certainly isn't subject to these wearisome application processes.

"Don't expect me to reveal my sources," he went on, holding up his hand as Dr Malone sat forward and tried to speak. "I mentioned the Official Secrets Act; a tedious piece of legislation, but we mustn't be naughty about it. I confidently expect some advances in the many-worlds area. I think you are the people to do it. And thirdly, there is a particular matter connected with an individual. A child."

He paused there, and sipped the coffee. Dr Malone couldn't speak. She'd gone pale, though she couldn't know that, but she did know that she felt faint.

"For various reasons," Sir Charles went on, "I am in contact with the intelligence services. They are interested in a child, a girl, who has an unusual piece of equipment, an antique scientific instrument, certainly stolen, which should be in safer hands than hers. There is also a boy of roughly the same age – twelve or so – who is wanted in connection with a murder. It's a moot point whether a child of that age is capable of murder, of course, but he has certainly killed someone. And he has been seen with the girl.

"Now, Dr Malone, it may be that you have come across one or other of these children. And it may be that you are quite properly inclined to tell the police about what you know. But you would be doing a greater service if you were to let me know privately. I can make sure the proper authorities deal with it efficiently and quickly and with no stupid tabloid publicity. I know that Inspector Walters came to see you yesterday, and I know that the girl turned up – you see, I do know what I'm talking about. I would know, for instance, if you saw her again, and if you didn't tell me, I would know that too. You'd be very wise to think hard about that, and to clarify your recollections of what she said and did when she was here. This is a matter of national security. You understand me.

"Well, there I'll stop. Here's my card so you can get in touch. I shouldn't leave it too long; the funding committee meets tomorrow, as you know. But you can reach me on this number at any time."

He gave a card to Oliver Payne and, seeing Dr Malone with her arms still folded, laid one on the bench for her. Dr Payne held the door for him. Sir Charles set his Panama hat on his head, patted it gently, beamed at them both, and left.

When he'd shut the door again, Dr Payne said, "Mary, are you mad? Where's the sense in behaving like that?"

"I beg your pardon? You're not taken in by that old creep, are you?"

"You can't turn down offers like that! Do you want this project to survive or not?"

"It wasn't an offer," she said hotly, "it was an ultimatum. Do as he says, or close down. And Oliver, for God's sake, all those not-so-subtle threats and hints about national security and so on – can't you see where that would lead?"

"Well, I think I can see it more clearly than you can. If you said no, they wouldn't close this place down. They'd take it over. If they're as interested as he says, they'll want it to carry on. But only on their terms."

"But their terms would be … I mean, *defence* for God's sake – they want to find new ways of killing people. And you heard what he said about consciousness: he wants to *manipulate* it. I'm not going to get mixed up in that, Oliver, never."

"They'll do it anyway, and you'll be out of a job. If you stay, you might be able to influence it in a better direction. And you'd still have your hands on the work! You'd still be involved!"

"But what does it matter to you, anyway?" she said. "I thought Geneva was all settled?"

He ran his hands through his hair and said, "Well, not settled. Nothing's signed. And it would be a different angle altogether, and I'd be sorry to leave here now I think we're really on to something…"

"What are you saying?"

"I'm not saying –"

"You're hinting. What are you getting at?"

"Well…" He walked around the laboratory, spreading his hands, shrugging, shaking his head. "Well, if you don't get in touch with him, I will," he said finally.

She was silent. Then she said, "Oh, I see."

"Mary, I've got to think of –"

"Of course you have."

"It's not that –"

"No, no."

"You don't understand –"

"Yes I do. It's very simple. You promise to do as he says, you get the funding, I leave, you take over as Director. It's not hard to understand. You'd have a bigger budget. Lots of nice new machines. Half a dozen more Ph.D.s under you. Good idea. You do it, Oliver. You go ahead. But that's it for me, I'm off. It stinks."

"You haven't…"

But her expression silenced him. She took off her white coat and hung it on the door, gathered a few papers into a bag, and left without a word. As soon as she'd gone, he took Sir Charles's card and picked up the phone.

Several hours later, just before midnight in fact, Dr Malone parked her car outside the science building and let herself in at the side entrance. But just as she turned to climb the stairs, a man came out of another corridor, startling her so much she nearly dropped her briefcase. He was wearing uniform.

"Where are you going?" he said.

He stood in the way, bulky, his eyes hardly visible under the low brim of his cap.

"I'm going to my laboratory. I work here. Who are you?" she said, a little angry, a little frightened.

"Security. Have you got some ID?"

"What security? I left this building at three o'clock this afternoon and there was only a porter on duty, as usual. I should be asking *you* for identification. Who appointed you? And why?"

"Here's my ID," said the man, showing her a card, too quickly for her to read it. "Where's yours?"

She noticed he had a mobile phone in a holster at his hip. Or was it a gun? No, surely, she was being paranoid. And he hadn't answered her questions. But if she persisted she'd make him suspicious, and the important thing now was to get into the lab: soothe him like a dog, she thought. She fumbled through her bag and found her wallet.

"Will this do?" she said, showing him the card she used to operate the barrier in the car park.

He looked at it briefly.

"What are you doing here at this time of night?" he said.

"I've got an experiment running. I have to check the computer periodically."

He seemed to be searching for a reason to forbid her, or perhaps he was just exercising his power. Finally he nodded and stood aside. She went past, smiling at him, but his face remained blank.

When she reached the laboratory she was still trembling. There had never been any more "security" in this building than a lock on the door and an elderly porter, and she knew why the change had come about. But it meant that she had very little time: she'd have to get it right at once, because once they realized what she was doing, she wouldn't be able to come back again.

She locked the door behind her and lowered the blinds. She switched on the detector and then took a floppy disk from her pocket and slipped it into the computer that controlled the Cave, and within a minute she had begun to manipulate the numbers on the screen, going half by logic, half by guesswork, and half by the program she'd worked on all evening at home; and the complexity of her task was about as baffling as getting three halves to make one whole.

Finally she brushed the hair out of her eyes and put the electrodes on her head, and then flexed her fingers and began to type. She felt intensely self-conscious.

Hello. I'm not sure what I'm doing.
Maybe this is crazy.

The words arranged themselves on the left of the screen, which was the first surprise. She wasn't using a word-processing program of any kind – in fact she was by-passing much of the operating system – and whatever formatting was imposing itself on the words, it wasn't hers. She felt the hairs begin to stir on the back of her neck, and she became aware of the whole of the building around her, the corridors dark, the machines idling, various experiments running automatically, computers monitoring tests and recording the results, the air-conditioning sampling and adjusting the humidity and the temperature, all the ducts and pipework and cabling that were the arteries and the nerves of the building awake and alert ... almost conscious, in fact.

She tried again.

I'm trying to do with words what I've done
before with a state of mind, but

Before she had even finished the sentence the cursor raced across to the right of the screen and printed:

                              Ask a question.

It was almost instantaneous.

She felt as if she had stepped on a space that wasn't there. Her whole being lurched with shock. It took several moments for her to calm down enough to try again. When she did, the answers lashed themselves across the right of the screen almost before she had finished.

Are you Shadows?   Yes.

247

Are you the same as Lyra's Dust?	Yes.
And is that dark matter? Dark matter is conscious?	Yes. Evidently.
What I said to Oliver this morning, my idea about human evolution, is it	Correct. But you need to ask more questions.

She stopped, took a deep breath, pushed her chair back, flexed her fingers. She could feel her heart racing. Every single thing about what was happening was impossible: all her education, all her habits of mind, all her sense of herself as a scientist were shrieking at her silently: this is wrong! It isn't happening! You're dreaming! And yet there they were on the screen: her questions, and answers from some other mind.

She gathered herself and typed again, and again the answers zipped into being with no discernible pause.

The mind that is answering these questions isn't human, is it?	No. But humans have always known us.
Us? There's more than one of you?	Uncountable billions.
But what are you?	Angels.

248

Mary Malone's head rang. She'd been brought up as a
Catholic. More than that: as Lyra had discovered, she had once
been a nun. None of her faith was left to her now, but she knew
about angels. St Augustine had said, "Angel is the name of their
office, not of their nature. If you seek the name of their nature, it
is spirit; if you seek the name of their office, it is angel; from what
they are, spirit, from what they do, angel."

Dizzy, trembling, she typed again:

Angels are creatures of Shadow-matter? Of Dust?	Structures. Complexifications. Yes.
And Shadow-matter is what we have called spirit?	From what we are, spirit; from what we do, matter. Matter and spirit are one.

She shivered. They'd been listening to her thoughts.

And did you intervene in human evolution? Why?	Yes. Vengeance.
Vengeance for – oh! Rebel angels! After the war in Heaven – Satan and the garden of Eden – but it isn't true, is it? Is that what you – but why?	Find the girl and the boy. Waste no more time. You must play the serpent.

She took her hands from the keyboard and rubbed her eyes.
The words were still there when she looked again.

Where	Go to a road called Sunderland Avenue and find a tent. Deceive the guardian and go through. Take provisions for a long journey. You will be protected. The Spectres will not touch you.
But I	Before you go, destroy this equipment.
I don't understand – why me? And what's this journey? And	You have been preparing for this as long as you have lived. Your work here is finished. The last thing you must do in this world is prevent the enemies from taking control of it. Destroy the equipment. Do it now and go at once.

Mary Malone pushed back the chair and stood up, trembling. She pressed her fingers to her temples and discovered the electrodes still attached to her skin. She took them off absently. She might have doubted what she had done, and what she could still see on the screen, but she had passed in the last half-hour or so beyond doubt and belief altogether. Something had happened, and she was galvanized.

She switched off the detector and the amplifier. Then she

bypassed all the safety codes and formatted the computer's hard disk, wiping it clean; and then she removed the interface between the detector and the amplifier, which was on a specially-adapted card, and put the card on the bench and smashed it with the heel of her shoe, there being nothing else heavy to hand. Next she disconnected the wiring between the electromagnetic shield and the detector, and found the wiring plan in a drawer of the filing cabinet and set light to it. Was there anything else she could do? She couldn't do much about Oliver Payne's knowledge of the program, but the special hardware was effectively demolished.

She crammed some papers from a drawer into her briefcase, and finally took down the poster with the I Ching hexagrams and folded it away in her pocket. Then she switched out the light and left.

The security guard was standing at the foot of the stairs, speaking into his telephone. He put it away as she came down and escorted her silently to the side entrance, watching through the glass door as she drove away.

An hour and a half later she drew up her car in a road near Sunderland Avenue. She had had to find it on a map of Oxford; she didn't know this part of town. Up till this moment she had been moving on pent-up excitement, but as she got out of her car in the dark of the small hours, and found the night cool and silent and still all round her, she felt a definite lurch of apprehension. Suppose she was dreaming? Suppose it was all some elaborate joke?

Well, it was too late to worry about that. She was committed. She lifted out the rucksack she'd often taken on camping journeys in Scotland and the Alps, and reflected that at least she knew how to survive out of doors; if the worst came to the worst, she could always run away, take to the hills…

Ridiculous.

But she swung the rucksack on to her back, and left the car and turned into the Banbury Road, and walked the two or three hundred yards up to where Sunderland Avenue ran left from the roundabout. She felt almost more foolish than she had ever felt in her life.

But as she turned the corner and saw those strange childlike trees that Will had seen, she knew that something at least was true about all this. Under the trees on the grass at the far side of the road there was a small square tent of red and white nylon, the sort that electricians put up to keep the rain off while they work, and parked close by was an unmarked white Transit van with darkened glass in the windows.

Better not hesitate. She walked straight across towards the tent. When she was nearly there, the back door of the van swung open, and a policeman stepped out. Without his helmet he looked very young, and the street lamp under the dense green of the leaves above shone full in his face.

"Could I ask where you're going, madam?" he said.

"Into the tent."

"I'm afraid you can't, madam. I've got orders not to let anyone near it."

"Good," she said, "I'm glad they've got the place protected. But I'm from the Department of Physical Sciences – Sir Charles Latrom asked us to make a preliminary survey and then report back before they look at it properly. It's important that it's done now while there aren't many people around – I'm sure you understand the reasons for that."

"Well, yes," he said. "But have you got anything to show who you are?"

"Oh, sure," she said, and swung the rucksack off her back to get at her purse. Among the items she had taken from the drawer in the laboratory was an expired library card of Oliver Payne's.

Fifteen minutes' work at her kitchen table and the photograph from her own passport had produced something she hoped would pass for genuine. The policeman took the laminated card and looked at it closely.

"Dr Olive Payne," he read. "Do you happen to know a Dr Mary Malone?"

"Oh, yes. She's a colleague."

"Do you know where she is now?"

"At home in bed, if she's got any sense. Why?"

"Well, I understand her position in your organization's been terminated, and she wouldn't be allowed through here. In fact we've got orders to detain her if she tries. And seeing a woman, I naturally thought you might be her, if you see what I mean. Excuse me, Dr Payne."

"Ah, I see," said Mary Malone.

The policeman looked at the card once more.

"Still, this seems all right," he said, and handed it back. Nervous, wanting to talk, he went on: "Do you know what's in there under that tent?"

"Well, not at first hand," she said. "That's why I'm here now."

"I suppose it is. All right then, Dr Payne."

He stood back and let her unlace the flap of the tent. She hoped he wouldn't see the shaking of her hands. Clutching the rucksack to her breast, she stepped through. *Deceive the guardian* – well, she'd done that; but she had no idea what she would find inside the tent. She was prepared for some sort of archaeological dig; for a dead body; for a meteorite; but nothing in her life or her dreams had prepared her for that square metre or so in mid-air, or for the silent sleeping city by the sea that she found when she stepped through it.

13

Æsahættr

As the moon rose, the witches began their spell to heal Will's wound.

They woke him and asked him to lay the knife on the ground where it caught a glitter of starlight. Lyra sat nearby stirring some herbs in a pot of boiling water over a fire, and while her companions clapped and stamped and cried in rhythm, Serafina crouched over the knife and sang in a high fierce tone:

"Little knife! They tore your iron
out of mother earth's entrails,
built a fire and boiled the ore,
made it weep and bleed and flood,
hammered it and tempered it,
plunging it in icy water,
heating it inside the forge
till your blade was blood-red, scorching!
Then they made you wound the water
once again, and yet again,
till the steam was boiling fog
and the water cried for mercy.
And when you sliced a single shade
into thirty thousand shadows,

then they knew that you were ready,
then they called you subtle one.
But little knife, what have you done?
Unlocked blood-gates, left them wide!
Little knife, your mother calls you,
from the entrails of the earth,
from her deepest mines and caverns,
from her secret iron womb.
Listen!"

And Serafina stamped again and clapped her hands with the other witches, and they shook their throats to make a wild ululation that tore at the air like claws. Will, seated in the middle of them, felt a chill at the core of his spine.

Then Serafina Pekkala turned to Will himself, and took his wounded hand in both of hers. When she sang this time he nearly flinched, so fierce was her high clear voice, so glittering her eyes; but he sat without moving, and let the spell go on.

"Blood! Obey me! Turn around,
be a lake and not a river.
When you reach the open air,
stop! And build a clotted wall,
build it firm to hold the flood back.
Blood, your sky is the skull-dome,
your sun is the open eye,
your wind the breath inside the lungs,
blood, your world is bounded. Stay there!"

Will thought he could feel all the atoms of his body responding to her command, and he joined in, urging his leaking blood to listen and obey.

She put his hand down and turned to the little iron pot over the fire. A bitter steam was rising from it, and Will heard the liquid bubbling fiercely.

Serafina sang:
"Oak bark, spider-silk,
ground-moss, saltweed –
grip close, bind tight,
hold fast, close up,
bar the door, lock the gate,
stiffen the blood-wall,
dry the gore-flood."

Then the witch took her own knife and split an alder sapling along its whole length. The wounded whiteness gleamed open in the moon. She daubed some of the steaming liquid into the split, and closed up the wood, easing it together from the root to the tip. And the sapling was whole again.

Will heard Lyra gasp, and turned to see another witch holding a squirming struggling hare in her tough hands. The animal was panting, wild-eyed, kicking furiously, but the witch's hands were merciless. In one she held its forelegs and with the other she grasped its hind legs and pulled the frenzied hare out straight, its heaving belly upwards.

Serafina's knife swept across it. Will felt himself grow dizzy, and Lyra was restraining Pantalaimon, hare-formed himself in sympathy, who was bucking and snapping in her arms. The real hare fell still, eyes bulging, breast heaving, entrails glistening.

But Serafina took some more of the decoction and trickled it into the gaping wound, and then closed the wound up with her fingers, smoothing the wet fur over it until there was no wound at all.

The witch holding the animal relaxed her grip and let it gently to the ground, where it shook itself, turned to lick its flank, flicked its ears, and nibbled a blade of grass as if it were completely alone. Suddenly it seemed to become aware of the circle of humans around it, and like an arrow it shot away, whole again, bounding swiftly off into the dark.

Lyra, soothing Pantalaimon, glanced at Will and saw that he knew what it meant: the medicine was ready. He held out his hand, and as Serafina daubed the steaming mixture on the bleeding stumps of his fingers he looked away and breathed in sharply several times, but he didn't flinch.

Once his open flesh was thoroughly soaked, the witch pressed some of the sodden herbs on to the wounds and tied them tight around with a strip of silk.

And that was it; the spell was done.

Will slept deeply through the rest of the night. It was cold, but the witches piled leaves over him, and Lyra slept huddled close behind his back. In the morning Serafina dressed his wound again, and he tried to see from her expression whether it was healing, but her face was calm and impassive.

Once they'd eaten, Serafina told the children that the witches had agreed that since they'd come into this world to find Lyra and be her guardian, they'd help Lyra do what she now knew her task to be: namely, to guide Will to his father.

So they set off; and it was quiet going for the most part. Lyra consulted the alethiometer to begin with, but warily, and learned that they should travel in the direction of the distant mountains they could see across the great bay. Never having been this high above the city, they weren't aware of how the coastline curved, and the mountains had been below the horizon; but now when the trees thinned, or when a slope fell away below them, they could look out to the empty blue sea and to the high blue mountains beyond which were their destination. It seemed a long way to go.

They spoke little. Lyra was busy looking at all the life in the forest, from woodpeckers to squirrels to little green moss-snakes with diamonds down their backs, and Will needed all his energy simply to keep going. Lyra and Pantalaimon discussed him endlessly.

"We *could* look at the alethiometer," Pantalaimon said at one point, when they'd dawdled on the path to see how close they could get to a browsing fawn before it saw them. "We never promised not to. And we could find out all kinds of things for him. We'd be doing it for him, not for us."

"Don't be stupid," Lyra said. "It *would* be us we'd be doing it for, 'cause he'd never ask. You're just greedy and nosy, Pan."

"That makes a change. It's normally you who's greedy and nosy and me who has to warn you not to do things. Like in the retiring room at Jordan. I never wanted to go in there."

"If we hadn't, Pan, d'you think all this would have happened?"

"No. 'Cause the Master would have poisoned Lord Asriel and that would've been the end of it."

"Yeah, I suppose… Who d'you think Will's father is, though? And why's he important?"

"That's what I mean! We could find out in a moment!"

And she looked wistful. "I might have done once," she said, "but I'm changing, I think, Pan."

"No you're not."

"*You* might not be… Hey, Pan, when I change, you'll stop changing. What're you going to be?"

"A flea, I hope."

"No, but don't you get *any* feelings about what you might be?"

"No. I don't want to either."

"You're sulking because I won't do what you want."

He changed into a pig and grunted and squealed and snorted till she laughed at him, and then he changed into a squirrel and darted through the branches beside her.

"Who do *you* think his father is?" Pantalaimon said. "D'you think he could be anyone we've met?"

"Could be. But he's bound to be someone important, almost as important as Lord Asriel. Bound to be. We know what *we're* doing is important, after all."

"We don't know it," Pantalaimon pointed out. "We think it is, but we don't know. We just decided to look for Dust because Roger died."

"We *know* it's important!" Lyra said hotly, and she even stamped. "And so do the witches. They come all this way to look for us just to be my guardian and help me! And we got to help Will find his father. *That's* important. You know it is, too, else you wouldn't have licked him when he was wounded. Why'd you do that, anyway? You never asked me if you could. I couldn't believe it when you did that."

"I did it because he didn't have a dæmon, and he needed one. And if you were half as good at seeing things as you think you are, you'd've known that."

"I did know it really," she said.

They stopped then, because they caught up with Will, who was sitting on a rock beside the path. Pantalaimon became a flycatcher, and as he flew among the branches, Lyra said, "Will, what d'you think those kids'll do now?"

"They won't be following us. They were too frightened of the witches. Maybe they'll just go back to drifting about."

"Yeah, probably… They might want to use the knife, though. They might come after us for that."

"Let them. They're not having it, not now. I didn't want it at first. But if it can kill the Spectres…"

"I never trusted Angelica, not from the beginning," Lyra said virtuously.

"Yes you did," he said.

"Yeah. I did really… I hated it in the end, that city."

"I thought it was heaven, when I first found it. I couldn't imagine anything better than that. And all the time it was full of Spectres, and we never knew…"

"Well, I won't trust kids again," said Lyra. "I thought back at Bolvangar that whatever grown-ups did, however bad it was, kids were different. They wouldn't do cruel things like that. But I en't sure now. I never seen kids like that before, and that's a fact."

"I have," said Will.

"When? In your world?"

"Yeah," he said, awkwardly. Lyra waited and sat still, and presently he went on: "It was when my mother was having one of her bad times. She and me, we lived on our own, see, because obviously my father wasn't there. And every so often she'd start thinking things that weren't true. And having to do things that didn't make sense, not to me, anyway. I mean she had to do them or else get so upset she used to be afraid of everything and so I used to help her. Like touching all the railings in the park, or counting the leaves on a bush, that kind of thing. She used to get better after a while. But I was afraid of anyone finding out she was like that, because I thought they'd take her away, so I used to look after her and hide it. I never told anyone.

"And once she got afraid when I wasn't there to help her. I was at school. And she went out and she wasn't wearing very much, only she didn't know. And some boys from my school, they found her, and they started…"

Will's face was hot. Without being able to help it he found himself walking up and down and looking away from Lyra because his voice was unsteady and his eyes were watering. He went on:

"They were tormenting her just like those kids were at the Tower with the cat… They thought she was mad and they wanted to hurt her, maybe kill her, I wouldn't be surprised. She was just different and they hated her. Anyway I found her and I got her home. And next day in school I fought the boy who was leading them. I fought him and I broke his arm and I think I broke some of his teeth, I don't know. And I was going to fight the rest of them too but I got in trouble and I realized I better stop because they'd find out, I mean the teachers and the authorities, they'd go to my mother and complain about me and then they'd find out about how she was and take her away. So I just pretended to be sorry and told the teachers I wouldn't do it again, and they punished me for fighting and I still said nothing. But I kept her safe, see. No one knew apart from those boys and they knew what I'd do if they said anything; they knew I'd kill them another time. Not just hurt them. And a bit later she got better again. No one knew, ever.

"But after that I never trusted children any more than grown-ups. They're just as keen to do bad things. So I wasn't surprised when those kids in Ci'gazze did that.

"But I was glad when the witches came."

He sat down again with his back to Lyra, and still not looking at her he wiped his hand across his eyes. She pretended not to see.

"Will," she said, "what you said about your mother… And Tullio, when the Spectres got him… And when you said yesterday that you thought the Spectres came from your world…"

"Yes. Because it doesn't make sense, what was happening to her. She's not mad. Those kids might think she was mad and laugh at her and try and hurt her but they were wrong; she wasn't mad. Except that she was afraid of things I couldn't see. And she had to do things that looked crazy, you couldn't see the point of them, but obviously she could. Like her counting all the

261

leaves, or Tullio yesterday touching the stones in the wall. Maybe that was a way of trying to put the Spectres off. If they turned their back on something frightening behind them and tried to get really interested in the stones and how they fitted together, or the leaves on the bush, like if only they could make themselves find that really important, they'd be safe. I don't know. It looks like that. There were real things for her to be frightened of, like those men who came and robbed us, but there was something else as well as them. So maybe we do have the Spectres in my world, only we can't see them and we haven't got a name for them, but they're there, and they keep trying to attack my mother. So that's why I was glad yesterday when the alethiometer said she was all right."

He was breathing fast, and his right hand was gripping the handle of the knife in its sheath. Lyra said nothing, and Pantalaimon kept very still.

"When did you know you had to look for your father?" she said after a while.

"A long time ago," he told her. "I used to pretend he was a prisoner and I'd help him escape. I had long games by myself doing that, it used to go on for days. Or else he was on this desert island and I'd sail there and bring him home. And he'd know exactly what to do about everything, about my mother, especially, and she'd get better and he'd look after her and me and I could just go to school and have friends and I'd have a mother and a father too. So I always said to myself that when I grew up I'd go and look for my father… And my mother used to tell me that I was going to take up my father's mantle. She used to say that to make me feel good. I didn't know what it meant, but it sounded important."

"Didn't you have friends?"

"How could I have friends?" he said, simply puzzled.

262

"Friends… They come to your house and they know your parents and… Sometimes a boy might ask me round to his house, and I might go or I might not, but I could never ask them back. So I never had friends, really. I would have liked… I had my cat," he went on. "I hope she's all right now. I hope someone's looking after her…"

"What about the man you killed?" Lyra said, her heart beating hard. "Who was he?"

"I don't know. If I killed him, I don't care. He deserved it. There were two of them. They kept coming to the house and pestering my mother till she was afraid again, and worse than ever. They wanted to know all about my father, and they wouldn't leave her alone. I'm not sure if they were police or what. I thought at first they were part of a gang or something, and they thought my father had robbed a bank maybe and hidden the money. But they didn't want money, they wanted papers. They wanted some letters that my father had sent. They broke into the house one day and then I saw it would be safer if my mother was somewhere else. See, I couldn't go to the police and ask them for help, because they'd take my mother away. I didn't know what to do.

"So in the end I asked this old lady who used to teach me the piano. She was the only person I could think of. I asked her if my mother could stay with her and I took her there. I think she'll look after her all right. Anyway I went back to the house to look for these letters, because I knew where she kept them, and I got them and the men came to look and broke into the house again. It was night-time, or early morning. And I was hiding at the top of the stairs and Moxie, my cat Moxie, she came out of the bedroom and I didn't see her and nor did the man, and when I knocked into him she tripped him up and he fell right to the bottom of the stairs…

"And I ran away. That's all that happened. So I didn't mean to

263

kill him, but I don't care if I did. I ran away and came to Oxford and then I found that window. And that only happened because I saw the other cat and stopped to watch her, and she found the window first. If I hadn't seen her… Or if Moxie hadn't come out of the bedroom then…"

"Yeah," said Lyra, "that was lucky. And me and Pan were thinking just now, what if I'd never gone into the wardrobe in the retiring room at Jordan and seen the Master put poison in the wine? None of this would have happened either…"

They both sat silent on the moss-covered rock, in the slant of sunlight through the old pines, and thought how many tiny chances had conspired to bring them to this place. Each of those chances might have gone a different way. Perhaps in another world, another Will had not seen the window in Sunderland Avenue, and had wandered on tired and lost towards the Midlands until he was caught. And in another world another Pantalaimon had persuaded another Lyra not to stay in the retiring room, and another Lord Asriel had been poisoned, and another Roger had survived to play with that Lyra for ever on the roofs and in the alleys of another unchanging Oxford.

Presently Will was strong enough to go on, and they moved together along the path, with the great forest quiet around them. They travelled on through the day, resting, moving, resting again, as the trees grew thinner and the land more rocky. Lyra checked the alethiometer: keep going, it said; this is the right direction. At noon they came to a village untroubled by Spectres: goats pastured on the hillside, a grove of lemon trees cast shade on the stony ground, and children playing in the stream called out and ran for their mothers at the sight of the girl in the tattered clothing and the white-faced fierce-eyed boy in the blood stained shirt, and the elegant greyhound that walked beside them.

The grown-ups were wary, but willing to sell some bread and cheese and fruit for one of Lyra's gold coins. The witches kept out of the way, though both children knew they'd be there in a second if any danger threatened. After another round of Lyra's bargaining one old woman sold them two flasks of goatskin and a fine linen shirt, and Will renounced his filthy T-shirt with relief, washing himself in the icy stream and lying to dry in the hot sun afterwards.

Refreshed, they moved on. The land was harsher now; for shade they had to rest in the shadow of rocks, not under wide-spreading trees, and the ground underfoot was hot through the soles of their shoes. The sun pounded at their eyes. They moved more and more slowly as they climbed, and when the sun touched the mountain-rims, and they saw a little valley open below them, they decided to go no further.

They scrambled down the slope, nearly losing their footing more than once, and then had to shove their way through thickets of dwarf rhododendrons, dark glossy leaves and crimson flower-clusters heavy with the hum of bees, before they came out in the evening shade on a wild meadow bordering a stream. The grass was knee-high and thick with cornflowers, gentians, cinquefoil.

Will drank deeply in the stream and then lay down. He couldn't stay awake, and he couldn't sleep either; his head was spinning, a daze of strangeness hung over everything, and his hand was sore and throbbing.

And what was worse, it had begun to bleed again.

Serafina looked at it, and put more herbs on the wound, and tied the silk tighter than ever, but this time her face was troubled. He didn't want to question her, for what would be the point? It was plain to him that the spell hadn't worked, and he could see she knew it too.

As darkness fell he heard Lyra come to lie down close by, and presently he heard a soft purring. Her dæmon, cat-formed, was dozing with folded paws only a foot or two away from him, and Will whispered:

"Pantalaimon?"

The dæmon's eyes opened. Lyra didn't stir. Pantalaimon whispered, "Yes?"

"Pan, am I going to die?"

"The witches won't let you die. Nor will Lyra."

"But the spell didn't work. I keep losing blood. I can't have much left to lose. And it's bleeding again, and it won't stop. I'm frightened…"

"Lyra doesn't think you are."

"Doesn't she?"

"She thinks you're the bravest fighter she ever saw, as brave as Iorek Byrnison."

"I suppose I better try not to seem frightened, then," Will said. He was quiet for a minute or so, and then he said, "I think Lyra's braver than me. I think she's the best friend I ever had."

"She thinks that about you as well," whispered the dæmon.

Presently Will closed his eyes.

Lyra lay unmoving, but her eyes were wide open in the dark, and her heart was beating hard.

When Will next became aware of things it was completely dark, and his hand was hurting more than ever. He sat up carefully and saw a fire burning not far away, where Lyra was trying to toast some bread on a forked stick. There were a couple of birds roasting on a spit as well, and as Will came to sit nearby, Serafina Pekkala flew down.

"Will," she said, "eat these leaves before you have any other food."

She gave him a handful of soft bitter-tasting leaves somewhat like sage, and he chewed them silently and forced them down. They were astringent, but he felt more awake and less cold, and the better for it.

They ate the roasted birds, seasoning them with lemon juice, and then another witch brought some blueberries she'd found below the scree, and then the witches gathered around the fire. They talked quietly; some of them had flown high up to spy, and one had seen a balloon over the sea. Lyra sat up at once.

"Mr Scoresby's balloon?" she said.

"There were two men in it, but it was too far away to see who they were. A storm was gathering behind them."

Lyra clapped her hands. "If Mr Scoresby's coming," she said, "we'll be able to fly, Will! Oh, I hope it's him! I never said goodbye to him, and he was so kind... I wish I could see him again, I really do..."

The witch Juta Kamainen was listening, with her red-breasted robin-dæmon bright-eyed on her shoulder, because the mention of Lee Scoresby had reminded her of the quest he'd set out on. She was the witch who had loved Stanislaus Grumman and whose love he'd turned down, the witch Serafina Pekkala had brought into this world to prevent her from killing him in their own.

Serafina might have noticed, but something else happened: she held up her hand and lifted her head, as did all the other witches. Will and Lyra could hear very faintly to the north the cry of some night bird. But it wasn't a bird: the witches knew it at once for a dæmon. Serafina Pekkala stood up, gazing intently into the sky.

"I think it's Ruta Skadi," she said.

They kept still, tilting their heads to the wide silence, straining to hear.

And then came another cry, closer already, and then a third;

and at that, all the witches seized their branches and leapt into the air. All but two, that is, who stood close by, arrows at their bowstrings, guarding Will and Lyra.

Somewhere in the dark above, a fight was taking place. And only seconds later, it seemed, they could hear the rush of flight, the whiz of arrows, and the grunt and scream of voices raised in pain or anger or command.

And then with a thud so sudden they had no time to jump, a creature fell from the sky at their feet – a beast of leathery skin and matted fur that Lyra recognized as a cliff-ghast, or something similar.

It was broken by the fall, and an arrow protruded from its side, but still it lurched up and lunged with a flopping malice at Lyra. The witches couldn't shoot, because she was in their line of fire, but Will was there first, and with the knife he slashed back-hand and the creature's head came off and rolled over once or twice. The air left its lungs with a gurgling sigh and it fell dead.

They turned their eyes upwards again, for the fight was coming lower, and the firelight glaring up showed a swift-rushing swirl of black silk, pale limbs, green pine-needles, grey-brown scabby leather. How the witches could keep their balance in the sudden turns and halts and forward darts, let alone aim and shoot, was beyond Will's understanding.

Another cliff-ghast and then a third fell in the stream or on the rocks nearby, stark dead; and then the rest fled skirling and chittering into the dark towards the north.

A few moments later Serafina Pekkala landed with her own witches, and with another: a beautiful witch, fierce-eyed and black-haired, whose cheeks were flushed with anger and excitement.

The new witch saw the headless cliff-ghast and spat.

"Not from our world," she said, "nor from this. Filthy

abominations. There are thousands of them breeding like flies…
Who is this? Is this the child Lyra? And who is the boy?"

Lyra returned her gaze stolidly, though she felt a quickening
of her heart, for Ruta Skadi lived so brilliantly in her nerves that
she set up a responding thrill in the nerves of anyone close by.

Then the witch turned to Will, and he felt the same tingle of
intensity, but like Lyra he controlled his expression. He still had
the knife in his hand, and she saw what he'd done with it and
smiled. He thrust it into the earth to clean it of the foul thing's
blood and then rinsed it in the stream.

Ruta Skadi was saying, "Serafina Pekkala, I am learning so
much; all the old things are changing, or dying, or empty. I'm
hungry…"

She ate like an animal, tearing at the remains of the roasted
birds and cramming handfuls of bread into her mouth, washing
it down with deep gulps from the stream. While she ate, some of
the witches carried the dead cliff-ghast away and rebuilt the fire,
and then set up a watch.

The rest came to sit near Ruta Skadi, and to hear what she
could tell them. She told what had happened when she flew up
to meet the angels, and then of her journey to Lord Asriel's
fortress.

"Sisters, it is the greatest castle you can imagine – ramparts of
basalt, rearing to the skies, with wide roads coming from every
direction, and on them cargoes of gunpowder, of food, of
armour-plate; how has he done this? I think he must have been
preparing this for a long time, for aeons. He was preparing this
before we were born, sisters, even though he is so much
younger… But how can that be? I don't know. I can't
understand. I think he commands time, he makes it run fast or
slow according to his will.

"And coming to this fortress are warriors of every kind, from every world. Men and women, yes, and fighting spirits too, and armed creatures such as I had never seen – lizards and apes, great birds with poison spurs, creatures too outlandish to have a name I could guess at. And other worlds have witches, sisters: did you know that? I spoke to witches from a world like ours, but profoundly different, for those witches live no longer than our short-lifes, and there are men among them too, men-witches who fly as we do…"

Her tale was causing the witches of Serafina Pekkala's clan to listen with awe and fear and disbelief. But Serafina believed her, and urged her on.

"Did you see Lord Asriel, Ruta Skadi? Did you find your way to him?"

"Yes, I did, and it was not easy, because he lives at the centre of so many circles of activity, and he directs them all. But I made myself invisible and found my way to his inmost chamber, when he was preparing to sleep."

Every witch there knew what had happened next, and neither Will nor Lyra dreamed of it. So Ruta Skadi had no need to tell, and she went on:

"And then I asked him why he was bringing all these forces together, and if it was true what we'd heard about his challenge to the Authority, and he laughed.

"'Do they speak of it in Siberia, then?' he said, and I told him yes, and on Svalbard, and in every region of the north – our north; and I told him of our pact, and how I'd left our world to seek him and find out.

"And he invited us to join him, sisters. To join his army against the Authority. I wished with all my heart I could pledge us there and then; I would have thrown my clan into the war with a happy heart. He showed me that to rebel was right and just, when you considered what the agents of the Authority did in his name…

And I thought of the Bolvangar children, and the other terrible mutilations I have seen in our own south-lands; and he told me of many more hideous cruelties dealt out in the Authority's name – of how they capture witches, in some worlds, and burn them alive, sisters, yes, witches like ourselves…

"He opened my eyes. He showed me things I never had seen, cruelties and horrors all committed in the name of the Authority, all designed to destroy the joys and the truthfulness of life.

"Oh, sisters, I longed to throw myself and my whole clan into the cause!

"But I knew I must consult you first, and then fly back to our world and talk to Ieva Kasku and Reina Miti and the other witch-queens.

"So I left his chamber invisibly and found my cloud-pine and flew away. But before I'd flown far, a great wind came up and hurled me high into the mountains, and I had to take refuge on a cliff-top. Knowing the sort of creatures who live on cliffs I made myself invisible again, and in the darkness I heard voices.

"It seemed that I'd stumbled on the nesting-place of the oldest of all cliff-ghasts. He was blind, and they were bringing him food: some stinking carrion from far below. And they were asking him for guidance.

"'Grandfather,' they said, 'how far back does your memory go?'

"'Way, way back. Back long before humans,' he said, and his voice was soft and cracked and frail.

"'Is it true that the greatest battle ever known is coming soon, grandfather?'

"'Yes, children,' he said. 'A greater battle than the last one, even. Fine feasting for all of us. These will be days of pleasure and plenty for every ghast in every world.'

"'And who's going to win, grandfather? Is Lord Asriel going to defeat the Authority?'

"'Lord Asriel's army numbers millions,' the old cliff-ghast told them, 'assembled from every world. It's a greater army than the one that fought the Authority before, and it's better led. As for the forces of the Authority, why, they number a hundred times as many. But the Authority is age-old, far older even than me, children, and his troops are frightened, and complacent where they're not frightened. It would be a close fight, but Lord Asriel would win, because he is passionate and daring and he believes his cause is just. Except for one thing, children. He hasn't got Æsahættr. Without Æsahættr, he and all his forces will go down to defeat. And then we shall feast for years, my children!'

"And he laughed and gnawed the stinking old bone they'd brought to him, and the others all shrieked with glee.

"Now you can imagine how I listened hard to hear more about this Æsahættr, but all I could hear over the howling of the wind was a young ghast asking, 'If Lord Asriel needs Æsahættr, why doesn't he call him?'

"And the old ghast said, 'Lord Asriel knows no more about Æsahættr than you do, child! That is the joke! Laugh long and loud –'

"But as I tried to get closer to the foul things to learn more, my power failed, sisters, I couldn't hold myself invisible any longer. The younger ones saw me and shrieked out, and I had to flee, back into this world through the invisible gateway in the air. A flock of them came after me, and those are the last of them, dead over there.

"But it's clear that Lord Asriel needs us, sisters. Whoever this Æsahættr is, Lord Asriel needs us! I wish I could go back to Lord Asriel now and say, Don't be anxious – we're coming – we the witches of the north, and we shall help you win… Let's agree now, Serafina Pekkala, and call a great council of all the witches, every single clan, and make war!"

Serafina Pekkala looked at Will, and it seemed to him that she was asking his permission for something. But he could give no guidance, and she looked back at Ruta Skadi.

"Not us," she said. "Our task now is to help Lyra, and her task is to guide Will to his father. You should fly back, agreed, but we must stay with Lyra."

Ruta Skadi tossed her head impatiently.

"Well, if you must," she said.

Will lay down, because his wound was hurting him – much more now than when it was fresh. His whole hand was swollen. Lyra too lay down, with Pantalaimon curled at her neck, and watched the fire through half-closed lids, and listened sleepily to the murmur of the witches.

Ruta Skadi walked a little way upstream, and Serafina Pekkala went with her.

"Ah, Serafina Pekkala, you should see Lord Asriel," said the Latvian queen quietly. "He is the greatest commander there ever was. Every detail of his forces is clear in his mind. Imagine the daring of it, to make war on the creator! But who do you think this Æsahættr can be? How have we not heard of him? And how can we urge him to join Lord Asriel?"

"Maybe it's not a *him*, sister. We know as little as the young cliff-ghast. Maybe the old grandfather was laughing at his ignorance. The word sounds as if it means *god-destroyer*. Did you know that?"

"Then it might mean us after all, Serafina Pekkala! And if it does, then how much stronger his forces will be when we do join them. Ah, I long for my arrows to kill those fiends from Bolvangar, and every Bolvangar in every world! Sister, why do they do it? In every world, the agents of the Authority are sacrificing children to their cruel god! Why? Why?"

"They are afraid of Dust," said Serafina Pekkala, "though what that is, I don't know."

"And this boy you've found. Who is he? What world does he come from?"

Serafina Pekkala told her all she knew about Will. "I don't know why he's important," she finished, "but we serve Lyra. And her instrument tells that that is her task. And sister, we tried to heal his wound, but we failed. We tried the holding spell, and it didn't work. Maybe the herbs in this world are less potent than ours. It's too hot here for bloodmoss to grow…"

"He's strange," said Ruta Skadi. "He is the same kind as Lord Asriel. Have you looked into his eyes?"

"To tell the truth," said Serafina Pekkala, "I haven't dared."

The two queens sat quietly by the stream. Time went past; stars set, and other stars rose; a little cry came from the sleepers, but it was only Lyra dreaming. The witches heard the rumbling of a storm, and they saw the lightning play over the sea and the foothills, but it was a long way off.

Later Ruta Skadi said, "The girl, Lyra. What of the part she was supposed to play? Is this it? She's important because she can lead the boy to his father? It was more than that, wasn't it?"

"That's what she has to do now. But as for later, yes, far more than that. What we witches have said about the child is that she would put an end to destiny. Well, we know the name that would make her meaningful to Mrs Coulter, and we know that the woman doesn't know it. The witch she was torturing on the ship near Svalbard nearly gave it away, but Yambe-Akka came to her in time.

"But I'm thinking now that Lyra might be what you heard those generals speak of, this Æsahættr. Not the witches, not those angel-beings, but that sleeping child: the final weapon in the war against the Authority. Why else would Mrs Coulter be so anxious to find her?"

"Mrs Coulter was a lover of Lord Asriel's," said Ruta Skadi.

274

"Of course, and Lyra is their child… Serafina Pekkala, if I had borne his child, what a witch she would be! A queen of queens!"

"Hush, sister," said Serafina. "Listen … and what's that light?"

They stood, alarmed that something had slipped past their guard, and saw a gleam of light from the camping-place: not firelight though, nothing remotely like firelight.

They ran back on silent feet, arrows already nocked to their bowstrings, and stopped suddenly.

All the witches were asleep on the grass, and so were Will and Lyra. But surrounding the two children were a dozen or more angels, gazing down at them.

And then Serafina understood something for which the witches had no word: it was the idea of pilgrimage. She understood why these beings would wait for thousands of years and travel vast distances in order to be close to something important, and how they would feel differently for the rest of time, having been briefly in its presence. That was how these creatures looked now, these beautiful pilgrims of rarefied light, standing around the girl with the dirty face and the tartan skirt and the boy with the wounded hand who was frowning in his sleep.

There was a stir at Lyra's neck. Pantalaimon, a snow-white ermine, opened his black eyes sleepily and gazed around unafraid. Later, Lyra would remember it as a dream. Pantalaimon seemed to accept the attention as Lyra's due, and presently he curled up again and closed his eyes.

Finally one of the creatures spread his wings wide. The others, as close as they were, did so too, and their wings interpenetrated with no resistance, sweeping through one another like light through light, until there was a circle of radiance around the sleepers on the grass.

† Then the watchers took to the air, one after another, rising like flames into the sky and increasing in size as they did so, until they were immense; but already they were far away, moving like shooting stars towards the north.

Serafina and Ruta Skadi sprang to their pine-branches and followed them upwards, but they were left far behind.

"Were they like the creatures you saw, Ruta Skadi?" said Serafina as they slowed down in the middle airs, watching the bright flames diminish towards the horizon.

"Bigger, I think, but the same kind. They have no flesh, did you see that? All they are is light. Their senses must be so different from ours… Serafina Pekkala, I'm leaving you now, to call all the witches of our north together. When we meet again, it will be wartime. Go well, my dear…"

They embraced in mid-air, and Ruta Skadi turned and sped southwards.

Serafina watched her go, and then turned to see the last of the gleaming angels disappear far away. She felt nothing but compassion for those great watchers. How much they must miss, never to feel the earth beneath their feet, or the wind in their hair, or the tingle of the starlight on their bare skin! And she snapped a little twig off the pine-branch she flew with, and sniffed the sharp resin smell with greedy pleasure, before flying slowly downwards to join the sleepers on the grass.

14

Alamo Gulch

 Lee Scoresby looked down at the placid ocean to his left, the green shore to his right, and shaded his eyes to search for human life. It was a day and a night since they had left the Yenisei.

"And this is a new world?" he said.

"New to those not born in it," said Stanislaus Grumman. "As old as yours or mine, otherwise. What Asriel's done has shaken everything up, Mr Scoresby, shaken it more profoundly than it's ever been shaken before. These doorways and windows that I spoke of – they open in unexpected places now. It's hard to navigate, but this wind is a fair one."

"New or old, that's a strange world down there," said Lee.

"Yes," said Stanislaus Grumman. "It is a strange world, though no doubt some feel at home there."

"It looks empty," said Lee.

"Not so. Beyond that headland you'll find a city that was once powerful and wealthy. And it's still inhabited by the descendants of the merchants and nobles who built it, though it's fallen on hard times in the past three hundred years…"

A few minutes later, as the balloon drifted on, Lee saw first a lighthouse, then the curve of a stone breakwater, then the towers and domes and red-brown roofs of a beautiful city around a harbour, with a sumptuous building like an opera house in lush gardens, and wide boulevards with elegant hotels and little streets where blossom-bearing trees hung over shaded balconies.

And Grumman was right: there were people there. But as they drifted closer, Lee was surprised to see that they were children. There was not an adult in sight. The children were playing on the beach, or running in and out of cafés, or eating and drinking, or gathering bags full of goods from houses and shops. And there was a group of boys fighting, and a red-haired girl urging them on, and a little boy throwing stones to smash all the windows of a nearby building. It was like a playground the size of a city, with not a teacher in sight; it was a world of children.

But they weren't the only presences there. Lee had to rub his eyes when he saw them first, but there was no doubt about it: columns of mist – or something more tenuous than mist – a thickening of the air… Whatever they were, the city was full of them; they drifted along the boulevards, they entered houses, they clustered in the squares and courtyards. The children moved among them unseeing.

But not unseen. The further they drifted over the city, the more Lee could observe the behaviour of these forms. And it was clear that some of the children were of interest to them, and they followed certain children around: the older children, those who (as far as Lee could see through his telescope) were on the verge of adolescence. There was one boy, a tall thin youth with a shock of black hair, who was so thickly surrounded by the transparent beings that his very outline seemed to shimmer in the air. They were like flies around meat. And the boy had no idea of it, though from time to time he would brush his eyes, or shake his head as if to clear his vision.

"What the hell are those things?" said Lee.

"The people call them Spectres."

"What do they do, exactly?"

"You've heard of vampyres?"

"Oh, in tales."

"The Spectres feast as vampyres feast on blood, but the Spectres' food is attention. A conscious and informed interest in the world. The immaturity of children is less attractive to them."

"They're the opposite of those devils at Bolvangar, then."

"On the contrary. The Oblation Board and the Spectres of Indifference are both bewitched by this truth about human beings: that innocence is different from experience. The Oblation Board fears and hates Dust, and the Spectres feast on it, but it's Dust they're both obsessed by."

"They're clustered around that kid down there…"

"He's growing up. They'll attack him soon, and then his life will become a blank indifferent misery. He's doomed."

"For Pete's sake! Can't we rescue him?"

"No. The Spectres would seize us at once. They can't touch us up here; all we can do is watch and fly on."

"But where are the adults? You don't tell me the whole world is full of children alone?"

"Those children are Spectre-orphans. There are many gangs of them in this world. They wander about living on what they can find when the adults flee. And there's plenty to find, as you can see. They don't starve. It looks as if a multitude of Spectres have invaded this city, and the adults have gone to safety. You notice how few boats there are in the harbour? The children will come to no harm."

"Except for the older ones. Like that poor kid down there…"

"Mr Scoresby, that is the way this world works. And if you want to put an end to cruelty and injustice you must take me further on. I have a job to do."

"Seems to me –" Lee said, feeling for the words – "seems to

me the place you fight cruelty is where you find it, and the place you give help is where you see it needed. Or is that wrong, Dr Grumman? I'm only an ignorant aëronaut. I'm so damn ignorant I believed it when I was told that shamans had the gift of flight, for example. Yet here's a shaman who hasn't."

"Oh, but I have."

"How d'you make that out?"

The balloon was drifting lower, and the ground was rising. A square stone tower rose directly in their path, and Lee didn't seem to have noticed.

"I needed to fly," said Grumman, "so I summoned you, and here I am, flying."

He was fully aware of the peril they were in, but he held back from implying that the aëronaut wasn't. And in perfect time, Lee Scoresby leant over the side of the basket and pulled the cord on one of the bags of ballast. The sand flowed out, and the balloon lifted gently to clear the tower by six feet or so. A dozen or so crows, disturbed, rose cawing around them.

"I guess you are," said Lee. "You have a strange way about you, Dr Grumman. You ever spend any time among the witches?"

"Yes," said Grumman. "And among academicians, and among spirits. I found folly everywhere, but there were grains of wisdom in every stream of it. No doubt there was much more wisdom that I failed to recognize. Life is hard, Mr Scoresby, but we cling to it all the same."

"And this journey we're on? Is that folly or wisdom?"

"The greatest wisdom I know."

"Tell me again what your purpose is: you're going to find the bearer of this subtle knife, and what then?"

"Tell him what his task is."

"And that's a task that includes protecting Lyra," the aëronaut reminded him.

"It will protect all of us."

They flew on, and soon the city was out of sight behind them.

Lee checked his instruments. The compass was still gyrating loosely, but the altimeter was functioning accurately, as far as he could judge, and showed them to be floating about a thousand feet above the seashore and parallel with it. Some way ahead a line of high green hills rose into the haze, and Lee was glad he'd provided plenty of ballast.

But when he made his regular scan of the horizon, he felt a little check at his heart. Hester felt it too, and flicked up her ears, and turned her head so that one gold-hazel eye rested on his face. He picked her up and tucked her in the breast of his coat, and opened the telescope again.

No, he wasn't mistaken. Far to the south (if south it was, the direction they'd come from) another balloon was floating in the haze. The heat-shimmer and the distance made it impossible to see any details, but the other balloon was larger, and flying higher.

Grumman had seen it too.

"Enemies, Mr Scoresby?" he said, shading his eyes to peer into the pearly light.

"There can't be a doubt. I'm uncertain whether to lose ballast and go higher, to catch the quicker wind, or stay low and be less conspicuous. And I'm thankful that thing's not a zeppelin; they could overhaul us in a few hours. No, damn it, Dr Grumman, I'm going higher, because if I was in that balloon I'd have seen this one already; and I'll bet they have keen eyesight."

He set Hester down again, and leaned out to jettison three bags of ballast. The balloon rose at once, and Lee kept the telescope to his eye.

And a minute later he knew for certain they'd been sighted, for there was a stir of movement in the haze, which resolved itself into a line of smoke streaking up and away at an angle from the other balloon; and when it was some distance up, it burst into a flare. It blazed deep red for a moment and then dwindled into a patch of grey smoke, but it was a signal as clear as a tocsin in the night.

"Can you summon a stiffer breeze, Dr Grumman?" said Lee. "I'd like to make those hills by nightfall."

For they were leaving the shoreline now, and their course was taking them out over a wide bay thirty or forty miles across. A range of hills rose on the far side, and now that he'd gained some height Lee saw that they might more truthfully be called mountains.

He turned to Grumman, but found him deep in a trance. The shaman's eyes were closed, and beads of sweat stood out on his forehead as he rocked gently back and forth. A low rhythmic moaning came from his throat, and his dæmon gripped the edge of the basket, equally entranced.

And whether it was the result of gaining height or whether it was the shaman's spell, a breath did stir the air on Lee's face. He looked up to check the gas-bag and saw it sway a degree or two, leaning towards the hills.

But the breeze that moved them more swiftly was working on the other balloon, too. It was no closer, but nor had they left it behind. And as Lee turned the telescope on it again he saw darker, smaller shapes behind it in the shimmering distance. They were grouped purpose-fully, and becoming clearer and more solid every minute.

"Zeppelins," he said. "Well, there's no hiding out here."

He tried to make an estimate of their distance, and a similar calculation about the hills towards which they were flying. Their speed had certainly picked up now, and the breeze was flicking white tips off the waves far below.

Grumman sat resting in a corner of the basket while his

dæmon groomed her feathers. His eyes were closed, but Lee knew he was awake.

"The situation's like this, Dr Grumman," he said. "I do not want to be caught aloft by those zeppelins. There ain't no defence; they'd have us down in a minute. Nor do I want to land in the water, by free choice or not; we could float for a while, but they could pick us off with grenades as easy as fishing.

"So I want to reach those hills, and make a landing. I can see some forest now; we can hide among the trees for a spell, maybe a long time.

"And meanwhile, the sun's going down. We have about three hours to sunset, by my calculation. And it's hard to say, but I think those zeppelins will have closed on us half-way by that time, and we should have got to the far shore of this bay.

"Now you understand what I'm saying. I'm going to take us up into those hills, and then land, because anything else is certain death. They'll have made a connection now between this ring I showed them and the Skraeling I killed on Nova Zembla, and they ain't chasing us this hard to say we left our wallet on the counter.

"So sometime tonight, Dr Grumman, this flight's gonna be over. You ever landed in a balloon?"

"No," said the shaman. "But I trust your skill."

"I'll try and get as high up that range as I can. It's a question of balance, because the further we go, the closer they'll be behind us. If I land when they're too close behind, they'll be able to see where we go, but if I take us down too early we won't find the shelter of those trees. Either way, there's going to be some shooting before long."

Grumman sat impassively, moving a magical token of feathers and beads from one hand to the other in a pattern that Lee could see had some purposeful meaning. His dæmon's eyes never left the pursuing zeppelins.

An hour went by, and another. Lee chewed an unlit cigar and sipped cold coffee from a tin flask. The sun settled lower in the sky behind them, and Lee could see the long shade of evening creep along the shore of the bay and up the lower flanks of the hills ahead while the balloon itself, and the mountain tops, were bathed in gold.

And behind them, almost lost in the sunset glare, the little dots of the zeppelins grew larger and firmer. They had already overtaken the other balloon, and could now be easily seen with the naked eye: four of them in line abreast. And across the wide silence of the bay came the sound of their engines, tiny but clear, an insistent mosquito-whine.

When they were still a few minutes from making the shore at the foot of the hills, Lee noticed something new in the sky behind the zeppelins. A bank of clouds had been building, and a massive thunderhead reared thousands of feet up into the still bright upper sky. How had he failed to notice? If a storm was coming, the sooner they landed the better.

And then a dark green curtain of rain drifted down and hung from the clouds, and the storm seemed to be chasing the zeppelins as they were chasing Lee's balloon, for the rain swept along towards them from the sea, and as the sun finally vanished, a mighty flash came from the clouds, and several seconds later a crash of thunder so loud it shook the very fabric of Lee's balloon, and echoed back for a long time from the mountains.

Then came another flash of lightning, and this time the jagged fork struck down direct from the thunderhead at one of the zeppelins. In a moment the gas was alight: a bright flower of flame blossomed against the bruise-dark clouds, and the craft drifted down slowly, ablaze like a beacon, and floated still blazing on the water.

Lee let out the breath he'd been holding. Grumman was

standing beside him, one hand on the suspension-ring, with lines of exhaustion deep in his face.

"Did *you* bring that storm?" said Lee.

Grumman nodded.

The sky was now coloured like a tiger: bands of gold alternated with patches and stripes of deepest brown-black, and the pattern changed by the minute, for the gold was fading rapidly as the brown-black engulfed it. The sea behind was a patchwork of black water and phosphorescent foam, and the last of the burning zeppelin's flames were dwindling into nothing as it sank.

The remaining three, however, were flying on, buffeted hard but keeping to their course. More lightning flashed around them, and as the storm came closer Lee began to fear for the gas in his own balloon. One strike could have it tumbling to earth in flames, and he didn't suppose the shaman could control the storm so finely as to avoid that.

"Right, Dr Grumman," he said, "I'm going to ignore those zeppelins for now and concentrate on getting us safe into the mountains and on the ground. What I want you to do is sit tight and hold on, and be prepared to jump when I tell you. I'll give you warning, and I'll try to make it as gentle as I can, but landing in these conditions is a matter of luck as much as skill."

"I trust you, Mr Scoresby," said the shaman.

He sat back in a corner of the basket while his dæmon perched on the suspension-ring, her claws dug deep in the leather binding.

The wind was blowing them hard now, and the great gas-bag swelled and billowed in the gusts. The ropes creaked and strained, but Lee had no fear of their giving way. He let go some more ballast, and watched the altimeter closely. In a storm, when the air pressure sank, you had to offset that drop against the altimetric reading, and very often it was a crude rule-of-thumb calculation. Lee ran through the figures, double-checked them, and then released the last of his ballast. The only control he had now was the gas-valve. He couldn't go higher; he could only descend.

He peered intently through the stormy air and made out the great bulk of the hills, dark against the dark sky. From below there came a roaring, rushing sound like the crash of surf on a stony beach, but he knew it for the wind tearing through the leaves on the trees. So far, already! They were moving faster than he'd thought.

And he shouldn't leave it too long before he brought them down. Lee was too cool by nature to rage at fate; his manner was to raise an eyebrow and greet it laconically; but he couldn't help a flicker of despair now, when the one thing he should do – namely fly before the storm and let it blow itself out – was the one thing guaranteed to get them shot down.

He scooped up Hester and tucked her securely into his breast, buttoning the canvas coat up close to keep her in. Grumman sat steady and quiet; his dæmon, wind-torn, clung firmly with her talons deep in the basket-rim and her feathers blown erect.

"I'm going to take us down, Dr Grumman," Lee shouted above the wind. "You should stand and be ready to jump clear. Hold the ring and swing yourself up when I call."

Grumman obeyed. Lee gazed down, ahead, down, ahead, checking each dim glimpse against the next, and blinking the rain out of his eyes; for a sudden squall had brought the heavy drops at them like handfuls of gravel, and the drumming they made on the gas-bag added to the wind-howl and the lash of the leaves below until Lee could hardly even hear the thunder.

"Here we go," he shouted. "You cooked up a fine storm, Mr Shaman."

He pulled at the gas-valve line and lashed it around a cleat to keep it open. As the gas streamed out of the top, invisible far above, the lower curve of the gas-bag withdrew into itself and a fold, and then another, appeared where there had been a bulging sphere only a minute before.

The basket was tossing and lurching so violently it was hard to tell if they were going down, and the gusts were so sudden and wayward that they might easily have been blown a long way skywards without knowing; but after a minute or so Lee felt a sudden snag and knew the grapnel had caught on a branch. It was only a temporary check, so the branch had broken, but it showed how close they were.

He shouted, "Fifty feet above the trees –"

The shaman nodded.

Then came another snag, more violent, and the two men were thrown hard against the rim of the basket. Lee was used to it, and found his balance at once, but the force took Grumman by surprise. However, he didn't lose his grip on the suspension-ring, and Lee could see him safely poised, ready to swing himself clear.

A moment later came the most jolting shock of all as the grapnel found a branch that held it fast. The basket tilted at once and a second later was crashing into the tree-tops, and amid a lashing of wet leaves and the snapping of twigs and the creak of tormented branches it jolted to a precarious halt.

"Still there, Dr Grumman?" Lee called, for it was impossible to see anything.

"Still here, Mr Scoresby."

"Better keep still for a minute till we see the situation clearly," said Lee, for they were wildly swaying in the wind, and he could feel the basket settling with little jerks against whatever was holding them up.

There was still a strong sideways pull from the gas-bag, which was now nearly empty, but which as a result was catching the wind like a sail. It crossed Lee's mind to cut it loose, but if it didn't fly away altogether, it would hang in the tree-tops like a banner and give their position away; much better to take it in, if they could.

There came another lightning-flash, and a second later the thunder crashed. The storm was nearly overhead. The glare showed Lee an oak trunk, with a great white scar where a branch had been torn away, but torn only partially, for the basket was resting on it near the point where it was still attached to the trunk.

"I'm going to throw out a rope and climb down," he shouted. "As soon as our feet touch the ground we can make the next plan."

"I'll follow you, Mr Scoresby," said Grumman. "My dæmon tells me the ground is forty feet down."

And Lee was aware of a powerful flutter of wing-beats as the eagle-dæmon settled again on the basket-rim.

"She can go that far?" he said, surprised, but put that out of his mind and made the rope secure, first to the suspension-ring and then to the branch, so that even if the basket did fall, it wouldn't fall far.

Then, with Hester secure in his breast, he threw the rest of the rope over and clambered down till he felt solid ground beneath his feet. The branches grew thick around the trunk: this was a massive tree, a giant of an oak, and Lee muttered a thank you to it as he tugged on the rope to signal to Grumman that he could descend.

Was there another sound in the tumult? He listened hard. Yes, the engine of a zeppelin, maybe more than one, some way above – it was impossible to tell how high, or which direction it was flying in; but the sound was there for a minute or so, and then it was gone.

The shaman reached the ground.

"Did you hear it?" said Lee.

"Yes. Going higher, into the mountains, I think. Congratulations on landing us safely, Mr Scoresby."

"We ain't finished yet. I want to git that gas-bag under the canopy before daybreak, or it'll show up our position from miles away. You up to some manual labour, Dr Grumman?"

"Tell me what to do."

"All right. I'm going back up the rope and I'll lower some things down to you. One of them's a tent. You can git that set up while I see what I can do up there to hide the balloon."

They laboured for a long time, and in peril at one point, when the branch that had been supporting the basket finally broke and pitched Lee down with it; but he didn't fall far, since the gas-bag still trailed among the tree-tops, and held the basket suspended.

The fall in fact made concealing it easier, since it pulled the lower part of the gas-bag down through the canopy; and working by flashes of lightning, tugging and wrenching and hacking, Lee managed to drag the whole body of the balloon down among the lower branches and out of sight.

The wind was still beating the tree-tops back and forth, but the worst of the rain had passed by the time he decided he could do no more. He clambered down and found that the shaman had not only pitched the tent but had conjured a fire into being, and was brewing some coffee.

"This done by magic?" said Lee, soaked and stiff, easing himself down into the tent and taking the mug Grumman handed him.

"No, you can thank the Boy Scouts for this," said Grumman. "Do they have Boy Scouts in your world? Be prepared. Of all the

289

ways of starting a fire, the best is dry matches. I never travel without them. We could do worse than this as a campsite, Mr Scoresby."

"You heard those zeppelins again?"

Grumman held up his hand. Lee listened, and sure enough, there was that engine-sound, easier to make out now the rain had eased a little.

"They've been over twice now," said Grumman. "They don't know where we are, but they know we're here somewhere."

And a minute later a flickering glow came from somewhere in the direction the zeppelin had flown. It was less bright than lightning, but it was persistent, and Lee knew it for a flare.

"Best put the fire out, Dr Grumman," he said, "sorry as I am to do without it. I think that canopy's thick, but you never know. I'm going to sleep now, wet through or not."

"You will be dry by the morning," said the shaman.

He took a handful of wet earth and pressed it down over the flames, and Lee struggled to lie down in the little tent and closed his eyes.

He had strange and powerful dreams. At one point he was convinced he had awoken to see the shaman sitting cross-legged, wreathed in flames, and the flames were rapidly consuming his flesh to leave only a white skeleton behind, still seated in a mound of glowing ash. Lee looked for Hester in alarm, and found her sleeping, which never happened, for when he was awake, so was she; so when he found her asleep, his laconic whip-tongued dæmon looking so gentle and vulnerable, he was moved by the strangeness of it, and he lay down uneasily beside her, awake in his dream, but really asleep, and he dreamt he lay awake for a long time.

Another dream focused on Grumman, too. Lee seemed to see

the shaman shaking a feather-trimmed rattle, and commanding something to obey him. The something, Lee saw with a touch of nausea, was a Spectre like the ones they'd seen from the balloon. It was tall and nearly invisible, and it invoked such a gut-churning revulsion in Lee that he nearly woke in terror. But Grumman was directing it fearlessly, and coming to no harm either, because the thing listened closely to him and then drifted upwards like a soap bubble until it was lost in the canopy.

Then his exhausting night took another turn, for he was in the cockpit of a zeppelin, watching the pilot. In fact he was sitting in the co-pilot's seat, and they were cruising over the forest, looking down at the wildly tossing tree-tops, a wild sea of leaf and branch. Then that Spectre was in the cabin with them.

Pinioned in his dream, Lee could neither move nor cry out, and he suffered the terror of the pilot as the man became aware of what was happening to him.

The Spectre was leaning over the pilot and pressing what would be its face to his. His dæmon, a finch, fluttered and shrieked and tried to pull away, only to fall half-fainting on the instrument panel. The pilot turned his face to Lee and put out a hand, but Lee had no power of movement. The anguish in the man's eyes was wrenching. Something true and living was being drained from him, and his dæmon fluttered weakly and called in a wild high call, but she was dying.

Then she vanished. But the pilot was still alive. His eyes became filmy and dull, and his reaching hand fell back with a limp thud against the throttle. He was alive but not alive: he was indifferent to everything.

And Lee sat and watched helplessly as the zeppelin flew on directly into a scarp of the mountains that rose up before them. The pilot watched it rear up in the window, but nothing could interest him. Lee pushed back against the seat in horror, but nothing happened to stop it, and at the moment of impact he cried:

"Hester!"

And woke.

He was in the tent, safe, and Hester nibbled his chin. He was sweating. The shaman was sitting cross-legged, but a shiver passed over Lee as he saw that the eagle-dæmon was not there near him. Clearly this forest was a bad place, full of haunting phantasms.

Then he became aware of the light he was seeing the shaman by, because the fire was long out, and the darkness of the forest was profound. Some distant flicker picked out the tree-trunks and the underside of dripping leaves, and Lee knew at once what it was: his dream had been true, and a zeppelin pilot had flown into the hillside.

"Damn, Lee, you're twitching like an aspen leaf. What's the matter with you?" Hester grumbled, and flicked her long ears.

"Ain't you dreaming too, Hester?" he muttered.

"You ain't dreaming, Lee, you're seeing. If I'd a known you was a seer I'd a cured you a long while back. Now you cut it out, you hear?"

He rubbed her head with his thumb and she shook her ears.

And without the slightest transition he was floating in the air alongside the shaman's dæmon, Sayan Kötör the osprey. To be in the presence of another man's dæmon and away from his own affected Lee with a powerful throb of guilt and strange pleasure. They were gliding, as if he too were a bird, on the turbulent updraughts above the forest, and Lee looked round through the dark air, now suffused with a pallid glow from the full moon that occasionally glared through a brief rent in the cloud-cover and made the tree-tops ring with silver.

The eagle-dæmon uttered a harsh scream, and from below

came in a thousand different voices the calls of a thousand birds: the too-whoo of owls, the alarm-shriek of little sparrows, the liquid music of the nightingale. Sayan Kötör was calling them. And in answer they came, every bird in the forest, whether they had been gliding in the hunt on silent wings or roosting asleep, they came fluttering upwards in their thousands through the tumbling air.

And Lee felt whatever bird-nature he was sharing respond with joy to the command of the eagle queen, and whatever human-ness he had left felt the strangest of pleasures: that of offering eager obedience to a stronger power that was wholly right. And he wheeled and turned with the rest of the mighty flock, a hundred different species all turning as one in the magnetic will of the eagle, and saw against the silver cloud-rack the hateful dark regularity of a zeppelin.

They all knew exactly what they must do. And they streamed towards the airship, the swiftest reaching it first, but none so swiftly as Sayan Kötör; the tiny wrens and finches, the darting swifts, the silent-winged owls – within a minute the craft was laden with them, their claws scrabbling for purchase on the oiled silk or puncturing it to gain a hold.

They avoided the engine, though some were drawn into it and dashed to pieces by the slicing propellers. Most of the birds simply perched on the body of the zeppelin, and those that came next seized on to them, until they covered not only the whole body of the craft (now venting hydrogen through a thousand tiny claw-holes) but the windows of the cabin too, and the struts and cables – every square inch of room had a bird, two birds, three or more, clinging to it.

The pilot was helpless. Under the weight of the birds the craft began to sink further and further down, and then another of those sudden cruel scarps appeared, shouldering up out of the night and of course quite invisible to the men inside the zeppelin, who were swinging their guns wildly and firing at random.

At the last moment Sayan Kötör screamed, and a thunder of wing-beats drowned even the roar of the engine as every bird took off and flew away. And the men in the cabin had four or five horrified seconds of knowledge before the zeppelin crashed and burst into flames.

Fire, heat, flames… Lee woke up again, his body as hot as if he'd been lying in the desert sun.

Outside the tent there was still the endless drip-drip of wet leaves on the canvas, but the storm was over. Pale grey light seeped in, and Lee propped himself up to find Hester blinking beside him and the shaman wrapped in a blanket so deeply asleep he might have been dead, had not Sayan Kötör been perched asleep on a fallen branch outside.

The only sound apart from the drip of water was the normal forest birdsong. No engines in the sky, no enemy voices; so Lee thought it might be safe to light the fire, and after a struggle he got it going and brewed some coffee.

"What now, Hester?" he said.

"Depends. There was four of those zeppelins, and he destroyed three."

"I mean, have we discharged our duty?"

She flicked her ears and said, "Don't remember no contract."

"It ain't a contractual thing. It's a moral thing."

"We got one more zeppelin to think about before you start fretting about morals, Lee. There's thirty, forty men with guns all coming for us. Imperial soldiers, what's more. Survival first, morals later."

She was right, of course, and as he sipped the scalding brew and smoked a cigar, with the daylight gradually growing stronger, he wondered what he would do if he were in charge of the one remaining zeppelin. Withdraw and wait for full daylight, no doubt, and fly high enough to scan the edge of the forest over a wide area, so they could see when Lee and Grumman broke cover.

The osprey-dæmon Sayan Kötör awoke, and stretched her great wings above where Lee was sitting. Hester looked up and turned her head this way and that, looking at the mighty dæmon with each golden eye in turn, and a moment later the shaman himself came out of the tent.

"Busy night," Lee remarked.

"A busy day to come. We must leave the forest at once, Mr Scoresby. They are going to burn it."

Lee looked around incredulously at the soaking vegetation and said, "How?"

"They have an engine that throws out a kind of naphtha blended with potash, which ignites when it touches water. The Imperial Navy developed it to use in their war with Nippon. If the forest is saturated, it will catch all the more quickly."

"You can see that, can you?"

"As clearly as you saw what happened to the zeppelins during the night. Pack what you want to carry, and come away now."

Lee rubbed his jaw. The most valuable things he owned were also the most portable, namely the instruments from the balloon, so he retrieved them from the basket, stowed them carefully in a knapsack, and made sure his rifle was loaded and dry; and left the basket, the rigging, and the gasbag where they lay, tangled and twisted among the branches. From now on he was an aëronaut no more, unless by some miracle he escaped with his life and found enough money to buy another balloon. Now he had to move like an insect, along the surface of the earth.

* * *

They smelled the smoke before they heard the flames, because a breeze from the sea was lifting it inland. By the time they reached the edge of the trees they could hear the fire, a deep and greedy roar.

"Why didn't they do this last night?" said Lee. "They could have barbecued us in our sleep."

"I guess they want to catch us alive," Grumman replied, stripping a branch of its leaves so he could use it as a walking-stick, "and they're waiting to see where we leave the forest."

And sure enough the drone of the zeppelin soon became audible even over the sound of the flames and of their own laboured breathing, for they were hurrying now, clambering upwards over roots and rocks and fallen tree-trunks and stopping only to gather breath. Sayan Kötör, flying high, swooped down to tell them how much progress they were making, and how far behind the flames were; though it wasn't long before they could see smoke above the trees behind them, and then a streaming banner of flame.

Small creatures of the forest, squirrels, birds, wild boar, were fleeing with them and a chorus of squealings, shriekings, alarm calls of every sort rose around them. The two travellers struggled on towards the edge of the tree-line, which was not far ahead; and then they reached it, as wave after wave of heat rolled up at them from the roaring billows of flame that now reached fifty feet into the air. Trees blazed like torches; the sap in their veins boiled and split them asunder, the pitch in the conifers caught like naphtha, the twigs seemed to blossom with ferocious orange flowers all in a moment.

Gasping, Lee and Grumman forced themselves up the steep slope of rocks and scree. Half the sky was obscured by smoke and heat-shimmer, but high above there floated the squat shape of the one remaining zeppelin – too far away, Lee thought hopefully, to see them even through binoculars.

The mountainside rose sheer and impassable ahead of them. There was only one route out of the trap they were in, and that was a narrow defile ahead, where a dry river bed emerged from a fold in the cliffs.

Lee pointed, and Grumman said, "My thoughts exactly, Mr Scoresby."

His dæmon, gliding and circling above, tipped her wings and sped to the ravine on a billowing updraught. The men didn't pause, climbing on as quickly as they could, but Lee said:

"Excuse me for asking this if it's impertinent, but I never knew anyone whose dæmon could do that except witches. But you're no witch. Was that something you learned to do, or did it come natural?"

"For a human being, nothing comes naturally," said Grumman. "We have to learn everything we do. Sayan Kötör is telling me that the ravine leads to a pass. If we get there before they see us, we could escape yet."

The eagle swooped down again, and the men climbed on. Hester preferred to find her own way over the rocks, so Lee followed where she led, avoiding the loose stones and moving as swiftly as he could over the larger rocks, making all the time for the little gulch.

Lee was anxious about Grumman, because the other man was pale and drawn and breathing hard. His labours in the night had drained a lot of his energy. How far they could keep going was a question Lee didn't want to face; but when they were nearly at the entrance to the ravine, and actually on the edge of the dried river bed, he heard a change in the sound of the zeppelin.

"They've seen us," he said.

And it was like receiving a sentence of death. Hester stumbled, even sure-footed firm-hearted Hester stumbled and faltered. Grumman leant on the stick he carried and shaded his eyes to look back, and Lee turned to look too.

The zeppelin was descending fast, making for the slope directly below them. It was clear that the pursuers intended to capture them, not kill them, for a burst of gunfire just then would have finished them both in a second. Instead the pilot brought the airship skilfully to a hover just above the ground, at the highest point in the slope where he safely could, and from the cabin door a stream of blue-uniformed men jumped down, their wolf-dæmons beside them, and began to climb.

Lee and Grumman were six hundred yards above them, and not far from the entrance to the ravine. Once they reached it they could hold the soldiers off as long as their ammunition held out: but they had only one rifle.

"They're after me, Mr Scoresby," said Grumman, "not you. If you give me the rifle and surrender yourself, you'll survive. They're disciplined troops. You'll be a prisoner of war."

Lee ignored that, and said, "Git moving. Make the gulch and I'll hold them off from the mouth while you find your way out the other end. I brought you this far, and I ain't going to sit back and let 'em catch you now."

The men below were moving up quickly, for they were fit and rested. Grumman nodded.

"I had no strength left to bring the fourth one down," was all he said, and they moved quickly into the shelter of the gulch.

"Just tell me before you go," said Lee, "because I won't be easy till I know. What side I'm fighting for I cain't tell, and I don't greatly care. Just tell me this: what I'm a-going to do now, is that going to help that little girl Lyra, or harm her?"

"It's going to help her," said Grumman.

"And your oath. You won't forget what you swore to me?"

"I won't forget."

"Because, Dr Grumman, or John Parry, or whatever name you take up in whatever world you end in, you be aware of this. I love that little child like a daughter. If I'd had a child of my own, I couldn't love her more. And if you break the oath, whatever remains of me will pursue whatever remains of you, and you'll spend the rest of eternity wishing you never existed. That's how important that oath is."

"I understand. And you have my word."

"Then that's all I need to know. Go well."

The shaman held out his hand, and Lee shook it. Then Grumman turned and made his way up the gulch, and Lee looked around for the best place to make his stand.

"Not the big boulder, Lee," said Hester. "You cain't see to the right from there, and they could rush us. Take the smaller one."

There was a roaring in Lee's ears that had nothing to do with the conflagration in the forest below, or with the labouring drone of the zeppelin trying to rise again. It had to do with his childhood, and the Alamo. How often he and his companions had played that heroic battle, in the ruins of the old fort, taking turns to be Danes and French! His childhood was coming back to him, with a vengeance. He took out the Navajo ring of his mother's and laid it on the rock beside him. In the old Alamo games, Hester had often been a cougar or a wolf, and once or twice a rattlesnake, but mostly a mockingbird. Now –

"Quit daydreaming and take a sight," she said. "This ain't play, Lee."

The men climbing the slope had fanned out, and were moving more slowly, because they saw the problem as well as he did. They knew they'd have to capture the gulch, and they knew that one man with a rifle could hold them off for a long time. Behind them, to Lee's surprise, the zeppelin was still labouring to rise. Maybe its buoyancy was going, or maybe the fuel was running low, but either way it hadn't taken off yet, and it gave him an idea.

He adjusted his position and sighted along the old Winchester until he had the port engine mounting plumb in view, and fired. The crack raised the soldiers' heads as they climbed towards him, but a second later the engine suddenly roared and then just as suddenly seized and died. The zeppelin lurched over to one side. Lee could hear the other engine howling, but the airship was grounded now.

The soldiers had halted and taken cover as well as they could. Lee could count them, and he did: twenty-five. He had thirty bullets.

Hester crept up close to his left shoulder.

"I'll watch this way," she said.

Crouched on the grey boulder, her ears flat along her back, she looked like a little stone herself, grey-brown and inconspicuous, except for her eyes. Hester was no beauty; she was about as plain and scrawny as a hare could be; but her eyes were marvellously coloured, gold-hazel flecked with rays of deepest peat-brown and forest-green. And now those eyes were looking down at the last landscape they'd ever see: a barren slope of brutal tumbled rocks, and beyond it a forest on fire. Not a blade of grass, not a speck of green to rest on.

Her ears flicked slightly.

"They're talking," she said. "I can hear, but I cain't understand."

"Russian," he said. "They're gonna come up all together and at a run. That would be hardest for us, so they'll do that."

"Aim straight," she said.

"I will. But hell, I don't like taking lives, Hester."

"Ours or theirs."

"No, it's more than that," he said. "It's theirs or Lyra's. I cain't see how, but we're connected to that child, and I'm glad of it."

"There's a man on the left about to shoot," said Hester, and as she spoke a crack came from his rifle, and chips of stone flew off the boulder a foot from where she crouched. The bullet whined off into the gulch, but she didn't move a muscle.

"Well, that makes me feel better about doing this," said Lee, and took careful aim.

He fired. There was only a small patch of blue to aim at, but he hit it. With a surprised cry the man fell back and died.

And then the fight began. Within a minute the crack of rifles, the whine of ricocheting bullets, the smash of pulverizing rock echoed and rang the length of the mountainside and along the hollow gulch behind. The smell of cordite, and the burning smell that came from the powdered rock where the bullets hit, were just variations on the smell of burning wood from the forest, until it seemed that the whole world was burning.

Lee's boulder was soon scarred and pitted, and he felt the thud of the bullets as they hit it. Once he saw the fur on Hester's back ripple as the wind of a bullet passed over it, but she didn't budge. Nor did he stop firing.

That first minute was fierce. And after it, in the pause that came, Lee found that he was wounded: there was blood on the rock under his cheek, and his right hand and the rifle bolt were red.

Hester moved round to look.

"Nothing big," she said. "A bullet clipped your scalp."

"Did you count how many fell, Hester?"

"No. Too busy ducking. Reload while you can, boy."

He rolled down behind the rock and worked the bolt back and forth. It was hot, and the blood that had flowed freely over it from the scalp wound was drying and making the mechanism stiff. He spat on it carefully and it loosened.

Then he hauled himself back into position, and even before he'd set his eye to the sight, he took a bullet.

It felt like an explosion in his left shoulder. For a few seconds he was dazed, and then he came to his senses, with his left arm numb and useless. There was a great deal of pain waiting to spring on him, but it hadn't raised the courage yet, and that thought gave him the strength to focus his mind on shooting again.

He propped the rifle on the dead and useless arm that had been so full of life a minute ago, and sighted with stolid concentration: one shot, two, three, and each found its man.

"How we doing?" he muttered.

"Good shooting," she whispered back, very close to his cheek. "Don't stop. Over by the black boulder..."

He looked, aimed, shot. The figure fell.

"Damn, these are men like me," he said.

"Makes no sense," she said. "Do it anyway."

"Do you believe him? Grumman?"

"Sure. Plumb ahead, Lee."

Crack: another man fell, and his dæmon went out like a candle.

Then there was a long silence. Lee fumbled in his pocket and found some more bullets. As he reloaded he felt something so rare his heart nearly failed; he felt Hester's face pressed to his own, and it was wet with tears.

"Lee, this is my fault," she said.

"Why?"

"The Skraeling. I told you to take his ring. Without that we'd never be in this trouble."

"You think I ever did what you told me? I took it because the witch –"

He didn't finish, because another bullet found him. This time it smashed into his left leg, and before he could even blink, a third one clipped his head again, like a red-hot poker laid along his skull.

"Not long now, Hester," he muttered, trying to hold still.

"The witch, Lee! You said the witch! Remember?"

Poor Hester, she was lying now, not crouching tense and watchful as she'd done all his adult life. And her beautiful gold-brown eyes were growing dull.

"Still beautiful," he said. "Oh, Hester, yeah, the witch. She gave me…"

"Sure she did. The flower…"

"In my breast pocket. Fetch it, Hester, I cain't move."

It was a hard struggle, but she tugged out the little scarlet flower with her strong teeth and laid it by his right hand. With a great effort he closed it in his fist and said, "Serafina Pekkala! Help me, I beg…"

A movement below: he let go the flower, sighted, fired. The movement died.

Hester was failing.

"Hester, don't you go before I do," Lee whispered.

"Lee, I couldn't abide to be anywhere away from you for a single second," she whispered back.

"You think the witch will come?"

"Sure she will. We should have called her before."

"We should have done a lot of things."

"Maybe so –"

Another crack, and this time the bullet went deep somewhere inside, seeking out the centre of his life. He thought: it won't find it there. Hester's my centre. And he saw a blue flicker down below, and strained to bring the barrel over to it.

"He's the one," Hester breathed.

Lee found it hard to pull the trigger. Everything was hard. He had to try three times, and finally he got it. The blue uniform tumbled away down the slope.

Another long silence. The pain nearby was losing its fear of him. It was like a pack of jackals, circling, sniffing, treading closer, and he knew they wouldn't leave him now till they'd eaten him bare.

"There's one man left," Hester muttered. "He's a-making for the zeppelin."

And Lee saw him mistily, one soldier of the Imperial Guard creeping away from his company's defeat.

"I cain't shoot a man in the back," Lee said.

"Shame to die with one bullet left, though."

So he took aim with his last bullet at the zeppelin itself, still roaring and straining to rise with its one engine, and the bullet must have been red-hot; or maybe a burning brand from the forest below was wafted to the airship on an updraught; for the gas suddenly billowed into an orange fireball, and the envelope and the metal skeleton rose a little way and then tumbled down very slowly, gently, but full of a fiery death.

And the man creeping away and the six or seven others who were the only remnant of the Guard, and who hadn't dared come closer to the man holding the ravine, were engulfed by the fire that fell on them.

Lee saw the fireball and heard through the roar in his ears Hester saying, "That's all of 'em, Lee."

He said, or thought, "Those poor men didn't have to come to this, and nor did we."

She said, "We held 'em off. We held out. We're a-helping Lyra."

Then she was pressing her little proud broken self against his face, as close as she could get, and then they died.

15

Bloodmoss

"On," said the alethiometer, "further, higher."

So on they climbed. The witches flew above to spy out the best routes, because the hilly land soon gave way to steeper slopes and rocky footing, and as the sun rose towards noon the travellers found themselves in a tangled land of dry gullies, cliffs, and boulder-strewn valleys where not a single green leaf grew, and where the stridulation of insects was the only sound.

They moved on, stopping only for sips of water from their goatskin flasks, and talking little. Pantalaimon flew above Lyra's head for a while until he tired of that, and then he became a little sure-footed mountain sheep, vain of his horns, leaping among rocks while Lyra scrambled laboriously alongside. Will moved on grimly, screwing up his eyes against the glare, ignoring the worsening pain from his hand, and finally reaching a state in which movement alone was good and stillness bad, so that he suffered more from resting than from toiling on. And since the failure of the witches' spell to stop his bleeding, he thought they were regarding him with fear, too, as if he was marked by some curse greater than their own powers.

At one point they came to a little lake, a patch of intense blue scarcely thirty yards across among the red rocks. They stopped there awhile to drink and refill their flasks, and to soak their aching feet in the icy water. They stayed a few minutes and moved on, and soon afterwards, when the sun was at its highest and hottest, Serafina Pekkala darted down to speak to them. She was agitated.

"I must leave you for a while," she said. "Lee Scoresby needs me. I don't know why. But he wouldn't call if he didn't need my help. Keep going, and I'll find you…"

"Mr Scoresby?" said Lyra, excited and anxious. "But where –"

But Serafina was gone, speeding out of sight before Lyra could finish the question. Lyra reached automatically for the alethiometer to ask what had happened to Lee Scoresby, but she let her hand drop, because she'd promised to do no more than guide Will.

She looked across to him. He was sitting nearby, his hand loosely on his knee still slowly dripping blood, his face scorched by the sun and pale under the burning.

"Will," she said, "do you know why you have to find your father?"

"It's what I've always known. My mother said I'd take up my father's mantle. That's all I know."

"What does that mean, taking up his mantle? What's a mantle?"

"A task, I suppose. Whatever he's been doing, I've got to carry on. It makes as much sense as anything else."

He wiped the sweat out of his eyes with his right hand. What he couldn't say was that he longed for his father as a lost child yearns for home. That comparison wouldn't have occurred to him, because home was the place he kept safe for his mother, not the place others kept safe for him; but it had been five years now since that Saturday morning in the supermarket when the pretend game of hiding from the enemies became desperately real, such a long time in his life, and his heart craved to hear the words, "Well done, well done, my child; no one on earth could have done better; I'm proud of you. Come and rest now…"

Will longed for that so much that he hardly knew he did. It was just part of what everything felt like. So he couldn't express that to Lyra now, though she could see it in his eyes, and that was new for her, too, to be quite so perceptive. The fact was that where Will was concerned, she was developing a new kind of sense, as if he were simply more in focus than anyone she'd known before. Everything about him was clear and close and immediate.

And she might have said that to him, but at that moment a witch flew down.

"I can see someone behind us," she said. "They're a long way back, but they're moving quickly. Shall I go closer and look?"

"Yes, do," said Lyra, "but fly low, and hide, and don't let them see you."

Will and Lyra got painfully to their feet again and clambered on.

"I been cold plenty of times," Lyra said, to take her mind off the pursuers, "but I en't been this hot, ever. Is it this hot in your world?"

"Not where I used to live. Not normally. But the climate's been changing. The summers are hotter than they used to be. They say that people have been interfering with the atmosphere by putting chemicals in it and the weather's going out of control."

"Yeah, well they have," said Lyra, "and it is. And we're here in the middle of it."

He was too hot and thirsty to reply, and they climbed on breathlessly in the throbbing air. Pantalaimon was a cricket now, and sat on Lyra's shoulder, too tired to leap or fly. From time to time the witches would see a spring high up, too high to climb to, and fly up to fill the children's flasks. They would soon have died without water and there was none where they were; any spring that made its way into the air was soon swallowed again among the rocks.

And so they moved on, towards evening.

The witch who flew back to spy was called Lena Feldt. She flew low, from crag to crag, and as the sun was setting and drawing a wild blood-red out of the rocks she came to the little blue lake, and found a troop of soldiers making camp.

But her first glimpse of them told her more than she wanted to know; these soldiers had no dæmons. And they weren't from Will's world, or the world of Cittàgazze, where people's dæmons were inside them, and where they still looked alive: these men were from her own world, and to see them without dæmons was a gross and sickening horror.

Then out of a tent by the lakeside came the explanation. Lena Feldt saw a woman, a short-life, graceful in her khaki hunting clothes and as full of life as the golden monkey who capered along the water's edge beside her.

Lena Feldt hid among the rocks above and watched as Mrs Coulter spoke to the officer in charge, and his men put up tents, made fires, boiled water.

The witch had been among Serafina Pekkala's troop who rescued the children at Bolvangar, and she longed to shoot Mrs Coulter on the spot; but some fortune was protecting the woman, for it was just too far for a bow-shot from where she was, and the witch could get no closer without making herself invisible. So she began to make the spell. It took ten minutes of deep concentration.

Confident at last, Lena Feldt went down the rocky slope towards the lake, and as she walked through the camp one or two blank-eyed soldiers glanced up briefly, but found what they saw too hard to remember, and looked away again. The witch stopped outside the tent Mrs Coulter had gone into, and fitted an arrow to her bowstring.

She listened to the low voice through the canvas, and then moved carefully to the open flap that overlooked the lake.

Inside the tent Mrs Coulter was talking to a man Lena Feldt hadn't seen before: an older man, grey-haired and powerful, with a serpent-dæmon twined around his wrist. He was sitting in a canvas chair beside hers, and she was leaning towards him, speaking softly.

"Of course, Carlo," she was saying, "I'll tell you anything you like. What do you want to know?"

"How do you command the Spectres?" the man said. "I didn't think it possible, but you have them following you like dogs… Are they afraid of your bodyguard? What is it?"

"Simple," she said. "They know I can give them more nourishment if they let me live than if they consume me. I can lead them to all the victims their phantom hearts desire. As soon as you described them to me I knew I could dominate them, and so it turns out. And a whole world trembles in the power of these pallid things! But Carlo," she whispered, "I can please you, too, you know. Would you like me to please you even more?"

"Marisa," he murmured, "it's enough of a pleasure to be close to you…"

"No, it isn't, Carlo; you know it isn't. You know I can please you more than this."

Her dæmon's little black horny hands were stroking the serpent-dæmon. Little by little the serpent loosened herself and began to flow along the man's arm towards the monkey.

The man and the woman were both holding glasses of golden wine, and she sipped hers and leaned a little closer to him.

"Ah," said the man, as the dæmon slipped slowly off his arm and let her weight into the golden monkey's hands. The monkey raised her slowly to his face and ran his cheek softly along her emerald skin. Her tongue flicked blackly this way and that, and the man sighed.

"Carlo, tell me why you're pursuing the boy," Mrs Coulter whispered, and her voice was as soft as the monkey's caress. "Why do you need to find him?"

"He has something I want. Oh, Marisa –"

"What is it, Carlo? What's he got?"

He shook his head. But he was finding it hard to resist; his dæmon was twined gently around the monkey's breast, and running her head through and through the long lustrous fur as his hands moved along her fluid length.

Lena Feldt watched, standing invisibly just two paces from where they sat. Her bowstring was taut, the arrow nocked to it in readiness: she could have pulled and loosed in less than a second, and Mrs Coulter would have been dead before she finished drawing breath. But the witch was curious. She stood still and silent and wide-eyed.

But while she was watching Mrs Coulter, she didn't look behind her across the little blue lake. On the far side of it in the darkness a grove of ghostly trees seemed to have planted itself, a grove that shivered every so often with a tremor like a conscious intention. But they were not trees, of course; and while all the curiosity of Lena Feldt and her dæmon was directed at Mrs Coulter, one of the pallid forms detached itself from its fellows and drifted across the surface of the icy water, causing not a single ripple, until it paused a foot from the rock on which Lena Feldt's dæmon was perched.

310

"You could easily tell me, Carlo," Mrs Coulter was murmuring. "You could whisper it. You could pretend to be talking in your sleep, and who could blame you for that? Just tell me what the boy has, and why you want it. I could get it for you… Wouldn't you like me to do that? Just tell me, Carlo. I don't want it. I want the girl. What is it? Just tell me, and you shall have it."

He gave a soft shudder. His eyes were closed. Then he said, "It's a knife. The subtle knife of Cittàgazze. You haven't heard of it, Marisa? Some people call it *teleutaia makhaira*, the last knife of all. Others call it Æsahættr…"

"What does it do, Carlo? Why is it special?"

"Ah… It's the knife that will cut anything… Not even its makers knew what it could do… Nothing, no one, matter, spirit, angel, air – nothing is invulnerable to the subtle knife. Marisa, it's mine, you understand?"

"Of course, Carlo. I promise. Let me fill your glass…"

And as the golden monkey slowly ran his hands along the emerald serpent again and again, squeezing just a little, lifting, stroking, as Sir Charles sighed with pleasure, Lena Feldt saw what was truly happening: because while the man's eyes were closed, Mrs Coulter secretly tilted a few drops from a small flask into the glass before filling it again with wine.

"Here, darling," she whispered. "Let's drink, to each other…"

He was already intoxicated. He took the glass and sipped greedily, once, again, and again.

And then without any warning Mrs Coulter stood up and turned and looked Lena Feldt full in the face.

"Well, witch," she said, "did you think I don't know how you make yourself invisible?"

Lena Feldt was too surprised to move.

Behind her, the man was struggling to breathe. His chest was heaving, his face was red, and his dæmon was limp and fainting in the monkey's hands. The monkey shook her off in contempt.

Lena Feldt tried to swing her bow up, but a fatal paralysis had touched her shoulder. She couldn't make herself do it. This had never happened before, and she uttered a little cry.

"Oh, it's too late for that," said Mrs Coulter. "Look at the lake, witch."

Lena Feldt turned, and saw her snow-bunting dæmon fluttering and shrieking as if he were in a glass chamber that was being emptied of air, fluttering and falling, slumping, failing, his beak opening widely, gasping in panic. The Spectre had enveloped him.

"No!" she cried, and tried to move towards it, but was driven back by a spasm of nausea. Even in her sickened distress, Lena Feldt could see that Mrs Coulter had more force in her soul than anyone she had ever seen. It didn't surprise her to see that the Spectre was under Mrs Coulter's power: no one could resist that authority. Lena Feldt turned back to the woman in anguish.

"Let him go! Please let him go!" she cried.

"We'll see. Is the child with you? The girl Lyra?"

"Yes!"

"And a boy, too? A boy with a knife?"

"Yes – I beg you –"

"And how many witches have you?"

"Twenty! Let him go, let him go!"

"All in the air? Or do some of you stay on the ground with the children?"

"Most in the air, three or four on the ground always – this is anguish – let him go or kill me now!"

"How far up the mountain are they? Are they moving on, or have they stopped to rest?"

Lena Feldt told her everything. She could have resisted any

312

torture but what was happening to her dæmon now. When Mrs Coulter had learned all she wanted to know about where the witches were, and how they guarded Lyra and Will, she said:

"And now tell me this. You witches know something about the child Lyra. I nearly learned it from one of your sisters, but she died before I could complete the torture. Well, there is no one to save you now. Tell me the truth about my daughter."

Lena Feldt gasped: "She will be the mother – she will be life – mother – she will disobey – she will –"

"Name her! You are saying everything but the most important thing! Name her!" cried Mrs Coulter.

"Eve! Mother of all! Eve, again! Mother Eve!" stammered Lena Feldt, sobbing.

"Ah," said Mrs Coulter.

And she breathed a great sigh, as if the purpose of her life was clear to her at last.

Dimly the witch saw what she had done, and through the horror that was enveloping her she tried to cry out:

"What will you do to her? What will you do?"

"Why, I shall have to destroy her," said Mrs Coulter, "to prevent another Fall… Why didn't I see this before? It was too large to see…"

She clapped her hands together softly, like a child, wide-eyed. Lena Feldt, whimpering, heard her go on:

"Of course. Asriel will make war on the Authority, and then… Of course, of course… As before, so again. And Lyra is Eve. And this time she will not fall. I'll see to that. There will be no Fall…"

And Mrs Coulter drew herself up, and snapped her fingers to the Spectre feeding on the witch's dæmon. The little snow-bunting dæmon lay twitching on the rock as the Spectre moved towards the witch herself, and then whatever Lena Feldt had undergone before was doubled and trebled and multiplied a

313

hundredfold. She felt a nausea of the soul, a hideous and sickening despair, a melancholy weariness so profound that she was going to die of it. Her last conscious thought was disgust at life: her senses had lied to her; the world was not made of energy and delight but of foulness, betrayal, and lassitude. Living was hateful and death was no better, and from end to end of the universe, this was the first and last and only truth.

Thus she stood, bow in hand, indifferent, dead in life.

So Lena Feldt failed to see or to care about what Mrs Coulter did next. Ignoring the grey-haired man slumped unconscious in the canvas chair and his dull-skinned dæmon coiled in the dust, she called the captain of the soldiers and ordered them to get ready for a night-march up the mountain.

Then she went to the edge of the water and called to the Spectres.

They came at her command, gliding like pillars of mist across the water. She raised her arms and made them forget they were earth bound, so that one by one they rose into the air and floated free like malignant thistledown, drifting up into the night and borne by the air-currents towards Will and Lyra and the other witches; but Lena Feldt saw nothing of it.

The temperature dropped quickly after dark, and when Will and Lyra had eaten the last of their dry bread they lay down under an overhanging rock to keep warm and try to sleep. At least, Lyra didn't have to try: she was unconscious in less than a minute, curled tightly around Pantalaimon, but Will couldn't find sleep, no matter how long he lay there. It was partly his hand, which was now throbbing right up to the elbow and uncomfortably swollen, and partly the hard ground, and partly the cold, and partly utter exhaustion, and partly his longing for his mother.

He was afraid for her, of course, and he knew she'd be safer if he was there to look after her; but he wanted her to look after him, too, as she'd done when he was very small; he wanted her to bandage him and tuck him into bed and sing to him and take away all the trouble and surround him with all the warmth and softness and mother-kindness he needed so badly; and it was never going to happen. Part of him was only a little boy still. So he cried, but he lay very still as he did, not wanting to wake Lyra.

But he still wasn't asleep. He was more awake than ever. Finally he uncurled his stiff limbs and got up quietly, shivering, and with the knife at his waist he set off higher up the mountain, to calm his restlessness.

Behind him the sentry-witch's robin-dæmon cocked his head, and she turned from the watch she was keeping to see Will clambering up the rocks. She reached for her pine-branch and silently took to the air, not to disturb him but to see he came to no harm.

He didn't notice. He felt such a need to move and keep moving that he hardly noticed the pain in his hand any more. He felt as if he should walk all night, all day, for ever, because nothing else would calm this fever in his breast. And as if in sympathy with him, a wind was rising. There were no leaves to stir in this wilderness, but the air buffeted his body and made his hair stream away from his face; it was wild outside him and wild within.

He climbed higher and higher, hardly once thinking of how he might find his way back down to Lyra, until he came out on a little plateau almost at the top of the world, it seemed. All around him, on every horizon, the mountains reached no higher. In the brilliant glare of the moon the only colours were stark black and dead white, and every edge was jagged and every surface bare.

The wild wind must have been bringing clouds overhead,

because suddenly the moon was covered, and darkness swept over the whole landscape: thick clouds, too, for no gleam of moonlight shone through them. In less than a minute Will found himself in nearly total darkness.

And at the same moment Will felt a grip on his right arm.

He cried out with shock and twisted away at once, but the grip was tenacious. And Will was savage now. He felt he was at the very end of everything, and if it was the end of his life too, he was going to fight and fight till he fell.

So he twisted and kicked and twisted again, but that hand wouldn't let go; and since it was his right arm being held, he couldn't get at the knife. He tried with his left, but he was being jerked around so much, and his hand was so painful and swollen, that he couldn't reach: he had to fight with one bare wounded hand against a grown man.

He sank his teeth into the hand on his forearm, but all that happened was that the man landed a dizzying blow on the back of his head. Then Will kicked again and again, and some of the kicks connected and some didn't, and all the time he was pulling, jerking, twisting, shoving, and still the grip held him fast.

Dimly he heard his own panting and the man's grunts and harsh breathing; and then by chance he got his leg behind the man's and hurled himself against his chest, and the man fell with Will on top of him, heavily: but never for a moment did that grip slacken, and Will, rolling around violently on the stony ground, felt a heavy fear tighten round his heart: this man would never let him go, and even if he killed him, his corpse would still be holding fast.

But Will was weakening, and he was crying too now, sobbing bitterly as he kicked and tugged and beat at the man with his head and feet, and he knew his muscles would give up soon. And then he noticed the man had fallen still, though his hand still gripped as tight as ever. He was lying there letting Will batter at him with knees and head, and as soon as Will saw that, the last of his strength left him, and he fell helpless beside his opponent, every nerve in his body ringing and dizzy and throbbing.

Will hauled himself up painfully and peered through the deep darkness, and made out a blur of white on the ground beside the man. It was the white breast and head of a great bird, an osprey, a dæmon, and it was lying still. Will tried to pull away, and his feeble tug woke a response from the man, whose hand hadn't loosened.

But he was moving. He was feeling Will's right hand carefully with his free one. Will's hair stood on end.

Then the man said, "Give me your other hand."

"Be careful," said Will.

The man's free hand felt down Will's left arm, and his fingertips moved gently over the wrist and on to the swollen palm and with the utmost delicacy on to the stumps of Will's two lost fingers.

His other hand let go at once, and he sat up.

"You've got the knife," he said. "You're the knife-bearer."

His voice was resonant, harsh, but breathless. Will sensed that he was badly hurt. Had he wounded this dark opponent?

Will was still lying on the stones, utterly spent. All he could see was the man's shape, crouching above him, but he couldn't see his face. The man was reaching sideways for something, and after a few moments a marvellous soothing coolness spread into his hand from the stumps of his fingers, as the man massaged a salve into his skin.

"What are you doing?" Will said.

"Curing your wound. Keep still."

"Who are you?"

"I'm the only man who knows what the knife is for. Hold your hand up like that. Don't move."

The wind was beating more wildly than ever, and a drop or two of rain splashed into Will's face. He was trembling violently, but he propped up his left hand with his right while the man spread more ointment over the stumps and wound a strip of linen tightly around the hand.

And as soon as the dressing was secure, the man slumped sideways and lay down himself. Will, still bemused by the blessed cool numbness in his hand, tried to sit up and look at him. But it was darker than ever. He felt forward with his right hand and found himself touching the man's chest, where the heart was beating like a bird against the bars of a cage.

"Yes," the man said hoarsely. "Try and cure that, go on."

"Are you ill?"

"I'll be better soon. You have the knife, yes?"

"Yes."

"And you know how to use it?"

"Yes, yes. But are you from this world? How do you know about it?"

"Listen," said the man, sitting up with a struggle. "Don't interrupt. If you're the bearer of the knife, you have a task that's greater than you can imagine. A *child*... How could they let it happen? Well, so it must be... There is a war coming, boy. The greatest war there ever was. Something like it happened before, and this time the right side must win... We've had nothing but lies and propaganda and cruelty and deceit for all the thousands of years of human history. It's time we started again, but properly this time..."

He stopped to take in several rattling breaths.

"The knife," he went on after a minute; "they never knew what they were making, those old philosophers. They invented a device that could split open the very smallest particles of matter, and they used it to steal candy. They had no idea that they'd made the

318

one weapon in all the universes that could defeat the tyrant. The Authority. God. The rebel angels fell because they didn't have anything like the knife; but now…"

"I didn't want it! I don't want it now!" Will cried. "If you want it, you can have it! I hate it and I hate what it does –"

"Too late. You haven't any choice: you're the bearer: it's picked you out. And what's more they know you've got it, and if you don't use it against them, they'll tear it from your hands and use it against the rest of us, for ever and ever."

"But why should I fight them? I've been fighting too much, I can't go on fighting, I want to –"

"Have you won your fights?"

Will was silent. Then he said, "Yes, I suppose."

"You fought for the knife?"

"Yes, but –"

"Then you're a warrior. That's what you are. Argue with anything else, but don't argue with your own nature."

Will knew that the man was speaking the truth. But it wasn't a welcome truth. It was heavy and painful. The man seemed to know that, because he let Will bow his head before he spoke again.

"There are two great powers," the man said, "and they've been fighting since time began. Every advance in human life, every scrap of knowledge and wisdom and decency we have has been torn by one side from the teeth of the other. Every little increase in human freedom has been fought over ferociously between those who want us to know more and be wiser and stronger, and those who want us to obey and be humble and submit.

"And now those two powers are lining up for battle. And each of them wants that knife of yours more than anything else. You have to choose, boy. We've been guided here, both of us: you with

319

the knife and me to tell you about it."

"No! You're wrong!" cried Will. "I wasn't looking for anything like that! That's not what I was looking for at all!"

"You might not think so, but that's what you've found," said the man in the darkness.

"But what must I do?"

And then Stanislaus Grumman, Jopari, John Parry hesitated. He was painfully aware of the oath he'd sworn to Lee Scoresby, and he hesitated before he broke it; but break it he did.

"You must go to Lord Asriel," he said, "and tell him that Stanislaus Grumman sent you, and that you have the one weapon he needs above all others. Like it or not, boy, you have a job to do. Ignore everything else, no matter how important it seems, and go and do this. Someone will appear to guide you: the night is full of angels. Your wound will heal now. Wait. Before you go, I want to look at you properly."

He felt for the pack he'd been carrying and took something out, unfolding layers of oilskin and then striking a match to light a little tin lantern. In its light, through the rain-dashed windy air, the two looked at each other.

Will saw blazing blue eyes in a haggard face with several days' growth of beard on the stubborn jaw, grey-haired, drawn with pain, a thin body hunched in a heavy cloak trimmed with feathers.

The shaman saw a boy even younger than he'd thought, his slim body shivering in a torn linen shirt and his expression exhausted and savage and wary, but alight with a wild curiosity, his eyes wide under the straight black brows, so like his mother's...

And there came just the first flicker of something else to both of them.

But in that same moment, as the lantern light flared over John Parry's face, something shot down from the turbid sky and he fell back dead before he could say a word, an arrow in his failing heart. The osprey-dæmon vanished in a moment.

Will could only sit stupefied.

A flicker crossed the corner of his vision, and his right hand darted up at once and he found he was clutching a robin, a dæmon, red-breasted, panicking.

"No! No!" cried the witch Juta Kamainen, and fell down after him, clutching at her own heart, crashing clumsily into the rocky ground and struggling up again.

But Will was there before she could find her feet, and the subtle knife was at her throat.

"Why did you do that?" he shouted. "Why did you kill him?"

"Because I loved him and he scorned me! I am a witch! I don't forgive!"

And because she was a witch she wouldn't have been afraid of a boy, normally. But she was afraid of Will. This young wounded figure held more force and danger than she'd ever met in a human before, and she quailed. She fell backwards, and he followed and gripped her hair with his left hand, feeling no pain, feeling only an immense and shattering despair.

"You don't know who he was," he cried. "He was my father!"

She shook her head and whispered, "No. No! That can't be true. Impossible!"

"You think things have to be *possible*? Things have to be *true*! He was my father, and neither of us knew it till the second you killed him! Witch, I wait all my life and come all this way and I find him at last, and you *kill* him…"

And he shook her head like a rag and threw her back against the ground, half-stunning her. Her astonishment was almost greater than her fear of him, which was real enough, and she pulled herself up dazed and seized his shirt in supplication. He knocked her hand away.

"What did he ever do that you needed to kill him?" he cried. "Tell me that, if you can!"

And she looked at the dead man. Then she looked back at Will and shook her head sadly.

"No, I can't explain," she said. "You're too young. It wouldn't make sense to you. I loved him. That's all. That's enough."

And before Will could stop her she fell softly sideways, her hand on the hilt of the knife she had just taken from her own belt and pushed between her ribs.

Will felt no horror, only desolation and bafflement.

He stood up slowly and looked down at the dead witch, at her rich black hair, her flushed cheeks, her smooth pale limbs wet with rain, her lips parted like a lover's.

"I don't understand," he said aloud. "It's too strange."

Will turned back to the dead man, his father.

A thousand things jostled at his throat, and only the dashing rain cooled the hotness in his eyes. The little lantern still flickered and flared as the draught through the ill-fitting window licked around the flame, and by its light Will knelt and put his hands on the man's body, touching his face, his shoulders, his chest, closing his eyes, pushing the wet grey hair off his forehead, pressing his hands to the rough cheeks, closing his father's mouth, squeezing his hands.

"Father," he said, "Dad, Daddy … Father … I don't understand why she did that. It's too strange for me. But whatever you wanted me to do, I promise, I swear I'll do it. I'll fight. I'll be a warrior, I will. This knife, I'll take it to Lord Asriel, wherever he is, and I'll help him fight that enemy. I'll do it. You can rest now. It's all right. You can sleep now."

Beside the dead man lay his deerskin pack with the oilskin and the lantern and the little horn box of bloodmoss ointment. Will picked them up, and then he noticed his father's feather-trimmed cloak trailing behind his body on the ground, heavy and sodden, but warm. His father had no more use for it, and Will was shaking with cold. He unfastened the bronze buckle at the dead man's throat and swung the canvas pack over his shoulder before wrapping the cloak around himself.

He blew out the lantern and looked back at the dim shapes of his father, of the witch, of his father again before turning to go down the mountain.

The stormy air was electric with whispers, and in the tearing of the wind Will could hear other sounds too: confused echoes of cries and chanting, the clash of metal on metal, pounding wingbeats that one moment sounded so close they might actually be inside his head, and the next so far away they might have been on another planet. The rocks underfoot were slippery and loose, and it was much harder going down than it had been climbing up; but he didn't falter.

And as he turned down the last little gully before they reached the place where Lyra was sleeping, he stopped suddenly. He could see two men simply standing there, in the dark, as if they were waiting. Will put his hand on the knife.

Then one of the men spoke.

"You're the boy with the knife?" he said, and his voice had the strange quality of those wingbeats. Whoever he was, he wasn't a human being.

"Who are you?" Will said. "Are you men, or –"

"Not men, no. We are Watchers. *Bene elim.* In your language, angels."

Will was silent. The speaker went on:

"Other angels have other functions, and other powers. Our task is simple: we need you. We have been following the shaman every inch of his way, hoping he would lead us to you, and so he

323

has. And now we have come to guide you in turn to Lord Asriel."

"You were with my father all the time?"

"Every moment."

"Did he know?"

"He had no idea."

"Why didn't you stop the witch, then? Why did you let her kill him?"

"We would have done, earlier. But his task was over once he'd led us to you."

Will said nothing. His head was ringing; this was no less difficult to understand than anything else.

"All right," he said finally, "I'll come with you. But first I must wake Lyra."

They stood aside to let him pass, and he felt a tingle in the air as he went close to them, but he ignored it and concentrated on getting down the slope towards the little shelter where Lyra was sleeping.

But something made him stop.

In the dimness, he could see the witches who had been guarding Lyra all sitting or standing still. They looked like statues, except that they were breathing, but they were scarcely alive. There were several black-silk-clad bodies on the ground, too, and as he gazed in horror from one to another of them, Will saw what must have happened: they had been attacked in mid-air by the Spectres, and had fallen to their deaths, indifferently.

But –

"Where's Lyra?" he cried aloud.

The hollow under the rock was empty. Lyra was gone.

There was something under the overhang where she'd been lying. It was Lyra's little canvas rucksack, and from the weight of it he knew without looking that the alethiometer was still inside it.

Will was shaking his head. It couldn't be true, but it was: Lyra was gone, Lyra was captured, Lyra was lost.

The two dark figures of the *bene elim* had not moved. But they spoke:

"You must come with us now. Lord Asriel needs you at once. The enemy's power is growing every minute. The shaman has told you what your task is. Follow us and help us win. Come with us. Come this way. Come now."

And Will looked from them to Lyra's rucksack and back again, and he didn't hear a word they said.

Appendix

Some papers in the hand of Dr Stanislaus Grumman, otherwise known as Colonel John Parry.

The provenance of these papers is obscure. It is possible that they came into the possession of Lord Asriel and were deposited with his own papers in Jordan College Library, but the absence of a library stamp makes that unlikely. It is known that Dr Grumman travelled widely in the Arctic and Siberia, and had numerous acquaintances among the witch-clans and the native people of the north as well as in the worlds of scholarship, politics, and science. Any of them might have acquired such things and inadvertently, or even deliberately, allowed them to slip out of one world and into another.

Items such as these papers are not uncommon. They turn up frequently in auctions, in book-dealers' catalogues, and the like. Usually their significance remains mysterious; it is only when they are seen in the context of a larger narrative that their meaning suddenly becomes apparent.

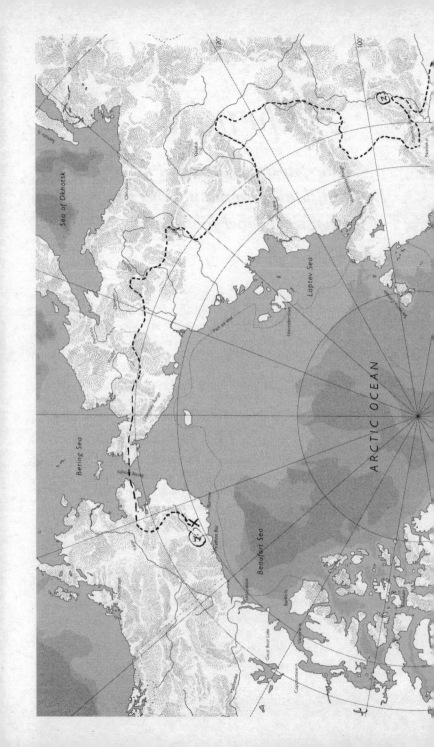

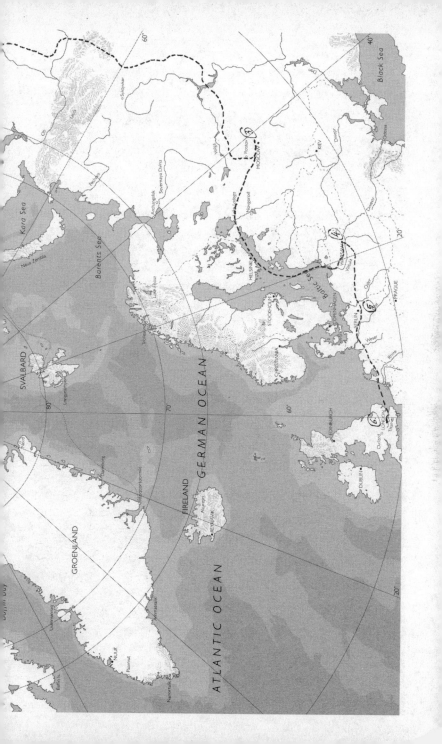

1. Here I walked through a window and out of my world into this one.

2. Here I met the Shaman Ivan Kasymovich Tyltchin, a great and good man who taught me everything I know about the spirit world. And here I met my Daemon

3. In Moscow I became a European again.

4. In Warsaw I began my scientific studies.

5. In Berlin I presented my thesis and was admitted to the Academy.

⑥ In London I realised how truly different this world was from mine. It was harder to live in the streets I thought I knew than in the wilds of Siberia. So I returned to the north, and later met Asriel, and everything else followed. —

The borders between the
Witch-clan lands are
definite but irregular,
and they vary from
season to season with
the flowering of plants
and the migration of animals
and birds.
Once I saw a dispute
between Tonja Lentara
and Tuta Kamainen,
peacefully resolved when
a cloud of midges drifted
east over the coat-moss
beds.

Ancient enmity between
Tkeshozero and Mickojärvi
clans. Reina Miti and
Katja Sirkka sworn to
kill each other on sight.
Ruta Skadi's consulat:
Novgorod: Semyon
Karlovich Mautins.

Asriel

I first encountered him near the mouth of the Lena. I was already a Shaman, but I was completing some solar observations for my Berlin thesis. I told him of the Alaska window through which I came into this world. He was aware of others, but he had never seen one. A remarkable man both proud and generous; you don't often see those qualities together. For a time he was the lover of Tanja Lentara. He had a daughter of whom he was very proud; he showed me her picture. Her mother was not a witch. If anyone could lead a rebellion against the church in this world or even further it would be Asriel.

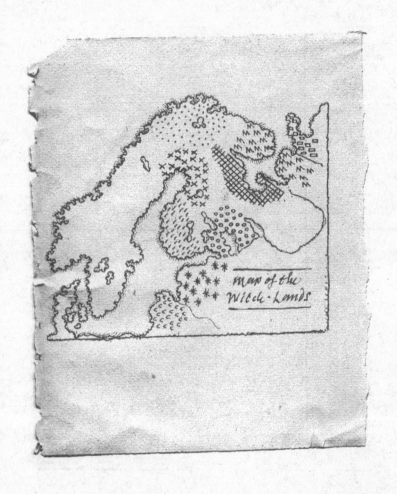

Map of the
Witch-Lands

⬚ (dotted)	Serafina Pekkala at Lake Enara
⬚ (c's)	Ruta Skadi at Lake Lubana
⬚ (diagonal lines)	Sara Leiro at Keitele
⬚ (small rectangles)	Juta Kamainen at Lake Visha
⬚ (7's)	Tanja Lentana at Lake Umolese
⬚ (crosshatch)	Reina Miti at Tiks hozero
⬚ (stars)	Julia Ojaland at Naria
⬚ (circles)	Paula Pyhäjärow at Lake Ladoga
⬚ (x's)	Katya Sirkka at Micokojärvi

Bloodmoss Ointment

This was taught to me by the
Shaman Turakhanek. Take
six handfuls of bloodmoss and
boil it with a thumb-sized piece
of harp-flower root. When
the root has turned black take
the pot off the fire and let it
cool. Press the bloodmass as
dry as you can and then steep
it for three days in just enough
grain-spirit to cover it.
Meanwhile prepare some goose-
-grease by boiling and chilling
alternately until it is clear
and white and sets hard. Take
the bloodmoss, squeeze it dry
and pound it in a mortar, and
then mix it with an equal
quantity of the goose-grease.
Seal it in a horn with
beeswax.

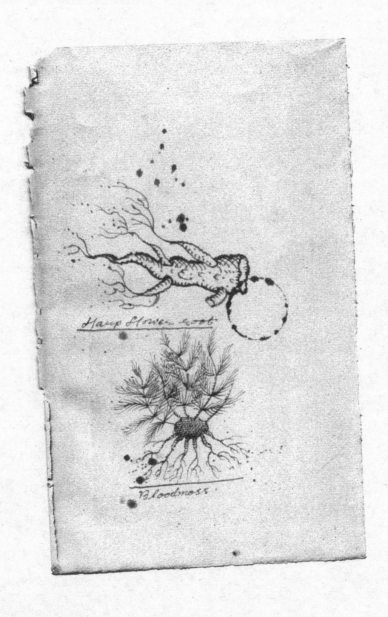

Harp flower root

Bloodmoss

The Knife

Giacomo Paradisi showed it to me in Baku on the Caspian. Because I cured a wound of his with the bloodmoss ointment, and because the burden of bearing the knife was becoming too great for him, and because I told him of the window I had come through, he trusted me with the knowledge!

This is the greatest discovery the human race has ever made; a million books would not begin to scratch the surface of what it means. And they use it to steal candy. Paradisi was a good man, but limited. I did not tell what else I knew, but at once saw that I should bring Asriel and the knife together.

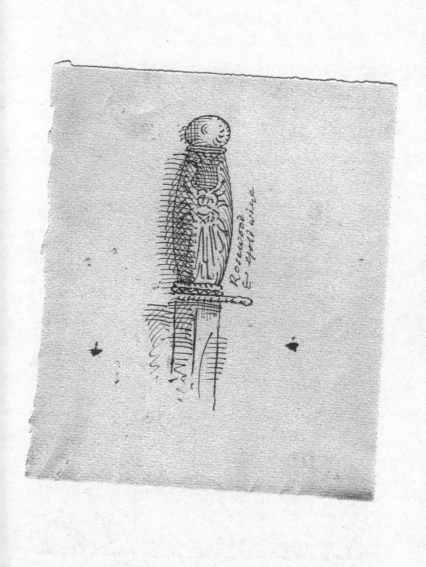

Rosewood
& split wire

Bear Rock

69° 02' 11" N 5 paces W of rock
157° 12' 19" W North of small creek

Sayou Kötter

NOW READ
the first chapter of the final book
in the *His Dark Materials* trilogy

THE AMBER
SPYGLASS

In a valley shaded with rhododendrons, close to the snow line, where a stream milky with melt-water splashed and where doves and linnets flew among the immense pines, lay a cave, half-hidden by the crag above and the stiff heavy leaves that clustered below.

The woods were full of sound: the stream between the rocks, the wind among the needles of the pine branches, the chitter of insects and the cries of small arboreal mammals, as well as the bird-song; and from time to time a stronger gust of wind would make one of the branches of a cedar or a fir move against another and groan like a cello.

It was a place of brilliant sunlight, never undappled; shafts of lemon-gold brilliance lanced down to the forest floor between bars and pools of brown-green shade; and the light was never still, never constant, because drifting mist would often float among the tree-tops, filtering all the sunlight to a pearly sheen and brushing every pine-cone with moisture that glistened when the mist lifted. Sometimes the wetness in the clouds condensed into tiny drops half-mist and half-rain, that floated downwards rather than fell, making a soft rustling patter among the millions of needles.

There was a narrow path beside the stream, which led from a village – little more than a cluster of herdsmen's dwellings – at the foot of the valley, to a half-ruined shrine near the glacier at its head, a place where faded silken flags streamed out in the perpetual winds from the high mountains, and offerings of barley-cakes and dried tea were placed by pious villagers. An odd effect of the light, and the ice, and the vapour enveloped the head of the valley in perpetual rainbows.

The cave lay some way above the path. Many years before, a holy man had lived there, meditating and fasting and praying, and the place was venerated for the sake of his memory. It was thirty feet or so deep, with a dry floor: an ideal den for a bear or a wolf, but the only creatures living in it for years had been birds and bats.

But the form that was crouching inside the entrance, his black eyes watching this way and that, his sharp ears pricked, was neither bird nor bat. The sunlight lay heavy and rich on his lustrous golden fur, and his monkey-hands turned a pine-cone this way and that, snapping off the scales with sharp fingers and scratching out the sweet nuts.

Behind him, just beyond the point where the sunlight reached, Mrs Coulter was heating some water in a small pan over a naphtha stove. Her dæmon uttered a warning murmur, and Mrs Coulter looked up.

Coming along the forest path was a young village girl. Mrs Coulter knew who she was: Ama had been bringing her food for some days now. Mrs Coulter had let it be known when she first arrived that she was a holy woman engaged in meditation and prayer, and under a vow never to speak to a man. Ama was the only person whose visits she accepted.

This time, though, the girl wasn't alone. Her father was with her, and while Ama climbed up to the cave, he waited a little way off.

Ama came to the cave entrance and bowed.

"My father sends me with prayers for your goodwill," she said.

"Greetings, child," said Mrs Coulter.

The girl was carrying a bundle wrapped in faded cotton, which she laid at Mrs Coulter's feet. Then she held out a little bunch of flowers, a dozen or so anemones bound with a cotton thread, and began to speak in a rapid, nervous voice. Mrs Coulter understood some of the language of these mountain people, but it would never do to let them know how much. So she smiled and motioned to the girl to close her lips, and to watch their two dæmons. The golden monkey was holding out his little black hand, and Ama's butterfly-dæmon was fluttering closer and closer until he settled on a horny forefinger.

The monkey brought him slowly to his ear, and Mrs Coulter felt a tiny stream of understanding flow into her mind, clarifying the girl's words. The villagers were happy for a holy woman, such as herself, to take refuge in the cave, but it was rumoured that she had a companion with her, who was in some way dangerous and powerful.

It was that which made the villagers afraid. Was this other being Mrs Coulter's master, or her servant? Did she mean harm? Why was she there in the first place? Were they going to stay long? Ama conveyed these questions with a thousand misgivings.

A novel answer occurred to Mrs Coulter as the dæmon's understanding filtered into hers. She could tell the truth. Not all of it, naturally, but some. She felt a little quiver of laughter at the idea, but kept it out of her voice as she explained:

"Yes, there is someone else with me. But there is nothing to be afraid of. She is my daughter, and she is under a spell that made her fall asleep. We have come here to hide from the enchanter who put the spell on her, while I try to cure her and keep her from harm. Come and see her, if you like."

Ama was half-soothed by Mrs Coulter's soft voice, and half-afraid still; and the talk of enchanters and spells added to the awe she felt. But the golden monkey was holding her dæmon so gently, and she was curious, besides, so she followed Mrs Coulter into the cave.

Her father on the path below took a step forward, and his crow-dæmon raised her wings once or twice, but he stayed where he was.

Mrs Coulter lit a candle, because the light was fading rapidly, and led Ama to the back of the cave. The little girl's eyes glittered widely in the gloom, and her hands were moving together in a repetitive gesture of finger on thumb, finger on thumb, to ward off danger by confusing the evil spirits.

"You see?" said Mrs Coulter. "She can do no harm. There's nothing to be afraid of."

Ama looked at the figure in the sleeping-bag. It was a girl older than she was, by three or four years, perhaps; and she had hair of a colour Ama had never seen before – a tawny fairness like a lion's. Her lips were pressed tightly together, and she was deeply asleep, there was no doubt about that, for her dæmon lay coiled and unconscious at her throat. He had the form of some creature like a mongoose, but red-gold in colour, and smaller. The golden monkey was tenderly smoothing the fur between the sleeping dæmon's ears, and as Ama looked, the mongoose-creature stirred uneasily and uttered a hoarse little mew. Ama's dæmon, mouse-formed, pressed himself close to Ama's neck and peered fearfully through her hair.

"So you can tell your father what you've seen," Mrs Coulter went on. "No evil spirit. Just my daughter, asleep under a spell, and in my care. But please, Ama, tell your father that this must be a secret. No one but you two must know Lyra is here. If the enchanter knew where she was, he would seek her out and destroy her, and me, and everything nearby. So hush! Tell your father, and no one else."

She knelt beside Lyra and smoothed the damp hair back from the sleeping face before bending low to kiss her daughter's cheek. Then she looked up with sad and loving eyes, and smiled at Ama with such brave compassion that the little girl felt tears fill her gaze.

Mrs Coulter took Ama's hand as they went back to the cave entrance, and saw the girl's father watching anxiously from below. The woman put her hands together and bowed to him, and he responded with relief as his daughter, having bowed both to Mrs Coulter and to the enchanted sleeper, turned and scampered down the slope in the twilight. Father and daughter bowed once more to the cave, and then set off, to vanish among the gloom of the heavy rhododendrons.

Mrs Coulter turned back to the water on her stove, which was nearly at the boil.

Crouching down, she crumbled some dried leaves into it, two pinches from this bag, one from that, and added three drops of a pale yellow oil. She stirred it briskly, counting in her head till five minutes had gone by. Then she took the pan off the stove, and sat down to wait for the liquid to cool.

Around her there lay some of the equipment from the camp by the blue lake where Sir Charles Latrom had died: a sleeping-bag, a rucksack with changes of clothes and washing equipment, and so on. There was also a case of canvas with a tough wooden frame, lined with kapok, containing various instruments; and there was a pistol in a holster.

The decoction cooled rapidly in the thin air, and as soon as it was at blood-heat she poured it carefully into a metal beaker and carried it to the rear of the cave. The monkey-dæmon dropped his pine-cone and came with her.

Mrs Coulter placed the beaker carefully on a low rock, and knelt beside the sleeping Lyra. The golden monkey crouched on her other side, ready to seize Pantalaimon if he woke up.

Lyra's hair was damp, and her eyes moved behind their closed lids. She was beginning to stir: Mrs Coulter had felt her eyelashes flutter when she'd kissed her, and knew she didn't have long before Lyra woke up altogether.

She slipped a hand under the girl's head, and with the other lifted the damp strands of hair off her forehead. Lyra's lips parted, and she moaned softly; Pantalaimon moved a little closer to her breast. The golden monkey's eyes never left Lyra's dæmon, and his little black fingers twitched at the edge of the sleeping-bag.

A look from Mrs Coulter, and he let go and moved back a hand's breadth. The woman gently lifted her daughter so that her shoulders were off the ground and her head lolled, and then Lyra caught her breath and her eyes half-opened, fluttering, heavy.

"Roger," she murmured. "Roger … where are you … I can't see…"

"Ssh," her mother whispered, "ssh, my darling, drink this."

Holding the beaker in Lyra's mouth, she tilted it to let a drop moisten the girl's lips. Lyra's tongue sensed it and moved to lick them, and then Mrs Coulter let a little more of the liquid trickle into her mouth, very carefully, letting her swallow each sip before allowing her more.

It took several minutes, but eventually the beaker was empty, and Mrs Coulter laid her daughter down again. As soon as Lyra's head lay on the ground, Pantalaimon moved back around her throat. His red-gold fur was as damp as her hair. They were deeply asleep again.

The golden monkey picked his way lightly to the mouth of the cave and sat once more watching the path. Mrs Coulter dipped a flannel in a basin of cold water and mopped Lyra's face, and then unfastened the sleeping-bag and washed her arms and neck and shoulders, because Lyra was hot. Then her mother took a comb and gently teased out the tangles in Lyra's hair, smoothing it back from her forehead, parting it neatly.

She left the sleeping-bag open so the girl could cool down, and unfolded the bundle that Ama had brought: some flat loaves of bread, a cake of compressed tea, some sticky rice wrapped in a large leaf. It was time to build the fire. The chill of the mountains was fierce at night. Working methodically, she shaved some dry tinder, set the fire and struck a match. That was something else to think of: the matches were running out, and so was the naphtha for the stove; she must keep the fire alight day and night from now on.

Her dæmon was discontented. He didn't like what she was doing here in the cave, and when he tried to express his concern she brushed him away. He turned his back, contempt in every line of his body as he flicked the scales from his pine-cone out into the dark. She took no notice, but worked steadily and skilfully to build up the fire and set the pan to heat some water for tea.

Nevertheless, his scepticism affected her, and as she crumbled the dark grey tea-brick into the water, she wondered what in the world she thought she was doing, and whether she had gone mad, and over and over again, what would happen when the church found out. The golden monkey was right. She wasn't only hiding Lyra: she was hiding her own eyes.